THE NOWHERE CITY

Alison Lurie is the author of eight novels, including *Foreign Affairs* (Pulitzer Prize 1985), *The Truth about Lorin Jones* (Prix Femina Etranger 1989) and, most recently, *The Last Resort*. She has received several awards for her work, including Guggenheim and Rockefeller Foundation grants and the American Academy of Arts and Sciences Award in Fiction. Alison Lurie is currently the Frederic J. Whiton Professor of American Literature at Cornell University, where she teaches courses in literature, folklore and writing. She is married to the writer Edward Hower and has three sons and three grandchildren. She currently divides her time between Ithaca, Key West and London.

ALSO BY ALISON LURIE

Fiction

Love and Friendship
Imaginary Friends
Real People
The War Between the Tates
Only Children
Foreign Affairs
The Truth About Lorin Jones
The Oxford Book of Modern Fairy Tales (editor)
Women and Ghosts
The Last Resort

Non-Fiction

The Language of Clothes
Don't Tell the Grown-ups

For Children

The Heavenly Zoo
Clever Gretchen and Other Forgotten Folktales
Fabulous Beasts

Alison Lurie

THE NOWHERE CITY

V

VINTAGE

Published by Vintage 1999

2 4 6 8 10 9 7 5 3 1

First published in Great Britain in 1965
by William Heinemann

Minerva Edition 1994

Vintage
Random House, 20 Vauxhall Bridge Road,
London SW1V 2SA

Random House Australia (Pty) Limited
20 Alfred Street, Milsons Point, Sydney
New South Wales 2061, Australia

Random House New Zealand Limited
18 Poland Road, Glenfield,
Auckland 10, New Zealand

Random House South Africa (Pty) Limited
Endulini, 5A Jubilee Road, Parktown 2193,
South Africa

Random House UK Limited Reg. No. 954009

A CIP catalogue record for this book
is available from the British Library

ISBN 0 7493 9784 5

Papers used by Random House UK Ltd are natural,
recyclable products made from wood grown in sustain-
able forests. The manufacturing processes conform to the
environmental regulations of the country of origin

Printed and bound in Great Britain by
Cox & Wyman Limited, Reading, Berkshire

For Harry and Bun

Part I: MAR VISTA

TO simulate the physical conditions of the first Thanksgiving, Miss Ling's B5 class went to the beach at Playa Del Rey recently. There, as the pilgrims of Plymouth Colony did, the children prepared the cornbread, succotash, and baked potatoes for their Thanksgiving feast, embellished with turkey prepared in the classroom.
—Monthly bulletin of the U.C.L.A. Elementary School

'It's so dark in here,' Paul Cattleman said. 'Don't you want me to open the window?'

'No, thanks,' said his wife. She turned and lay face down under the sheet, her head ground into the pillow. Katherine Cattleman had got off the Boston–Los Angeles plane three hours ago with a violent sinus attack which had been growing worse ever since.

Paul pulled one side of the venetian blind away from the bedroom window and stepped behind it. It was hot and bright outside. Eight-foot stalks of enormous bright green leaves ending in clusters of red and gold trumpet-shaped flowers (*Heliconia*) lined the small square of back yard.

'You ought to come and look at these fantastic lilies, or whatever they are, Katherine,' Paul said. 'They must be six inches across. And it's October!'

Katherine did not answer. He let the blind fall back against the window, noticing that each slat was coated with dust – possibly dust that had collected since he had moved in, possibly dust that the previous tenant had left for him. Whichever it was, Katherine would not like it.

With her face still buried in the pillow, she shifted restlessly, pushing the covers aside. Her loose night-gown had slipped up, and Paul observed a pleasing arrangement of pale round pinkish shapes, the important places marked with curly brown hair. Desire rose rapidly in him; he had been separated from his wife for six weeks. But if he were to propose to make love to her now she would feel hurt and misused; she would think him selfish, greedy, and inconsiderate. She would acquiesce, but she would not respond.

'How do you feel now?' he asked.

'Terrible.' Katherine smiled wanly. 'This is the worst attack I've had for months. I'm not having any of those shooting pains, but there's this horrible, horrible ache. It's as if an iron band were screwed around my head. No. It's more as if my whole head had been pressed into some kind of tight metal container.'

Over the past three years, Paul had developed the involuntary habit of picturing the images related to his wife's sinus attacks. As he looked at Katherine now, he saw her naked body topped by a tin can with a pink and white paper label—advertising canned apple juice, perhaps, or apple-sauce.

'I imagine—I think it might be the Los Angeles smog,' the tin can went on. 'It must be the smog, or something in the atmosphere here. I wonder if it will go on all the time. Affecting me this way, I mean.'

'Oh, I shouldn't think so,' Paul said. 'You'll adjust to it.'

Katherine half raised herself in bed on pretty pale arms. 'Sinuses don't "adjust",' she said in a sad whine. 'You know that. An allergic condition like mine doesn't ever adjust to irritants, it only becomes more and more sensitive to them.'

In other words, I won't adjust to Los Angeles, Paul heard her say. I hated the idea of our moving out here and I'm going to go on hating it, worse and worse. I'm going to be sick *all the time*. How could you have done this to me? He could think of nothing to reply. They stared at each other for a moment hopelessly; then Katherine sighed and fell face downwards on the sheet again.

'You get some sleep,' Paul said. 'You'll feel better.'

He went out of the bedroom into the living-room of the smallest house he had ever seen. However, Paul liked it: during the three years of their marriage he and Katherine had lived only in large, grey apartment buildings. This house was made of stucco, painted white outside and pink inside like a dolls' house. The west walls of the small living-room and smaller dining-room were almost completely filled by large picture-windows, increasing the resemblance to a dolls' house, one whole side of which usually stands open. Katherine's antique Victorian furniture had an air of being a little too large for the rooms, as sometimes happens with toy furniture.

All the houses on the street were made of stucco in ice-cream colours: vanilla, lemon, raspberry, and orange sherbet. Moulded in a variety of shapes and set down one next to the other along the block, behind plots of flowers much larger and brighter than life, they looked like a stage set for some lavish comic opera.

The southern California sun shone down on them with the impartial brilliance of stage lighting. And though it was late in the afternoon and late in the year, the temperature was that of a perfect windless June day, as it had been almost continually since Paul arrived.

But Katherine refused to be pleased. She wouldn't even open her eyes to see this warm, bright, extraordinary city. She behaved as if he had deliberately set out to make her unhappy by coming here—as if his professional career had nothing to do with it. Walking up and down and looking out of the picture-window, Paul reviewed his defence again. What was he supposed to do when, in April, his adviser and protector at Harvard had disappeared into Washington, taking with him, as it soon appeared, Paul's hopes of a teaching fellowship for the coming fall? What sort of a job did she think a young historian without a Ph.D. could find at that time of year? Paul had discovered the answer to that one: he could find a temporary instructorship at some remote college, with a twelve-hour teaching load.

He opened the front door and stepped out into the steady light —a tall young man of thirty, with dark hair cut short and an agreeable open face, dressed in the Harvard manner. He stood on his cement front walk and looked up into the sky: intense blue overhead, crossed by trails of jet vapour, dimming to a white haze at the horizon.

Then he looked along the block. A dozen architectural styles were represented in painted stucco: there were little Spanish haciendas with red tiled roofs; English country cottages, all beams and mullioned windows; a pink Swiss chalet; and even a tiny French château, the pointed towers of which seemed to be made of pistachio ice-cream.

The energy of all this invention both amused and delighted Paul. Back East, only the very rich dared to build with such variety: castles on the Hudson, Greek temples in the south. Everyone else had to live on streets of nearly identical brick or wooden boxes, like so many boxes of soap or sardines. Why shouldn't people build their houses in the shape of pagodas, their grocery stores in the shape of Turkish baths, and their restaurants like boats and hats, if they wanted to? Let them build, and tear down and build again; let them experiment. Anyone who can only see that some of the experiments are 'vulgar' should look into the derivations of that word.

He liked to think of this city as the last American frontier. Whoever has some little interest, even faith, in man, must ask what he might do if he were set free of a restrictive tradition, a hostile climate. Why condemn his first extravagances?

Paul even enjoyed the drive-in milk bar that they had passed near International Airport that afternoon, with a fifteen-foot plaster cow browsing among plaster or plastic daisies on the roof. But when he pointed it out to Katherine, smiling, she shuddered and turned her head away.

After all, Katherine had expected that he would take one of those shabby jobs back East. She had not listened, or not believed him, when he explained that this would be the most rapid form of professional suicide. Any other sort of work that he might have elected to do, even the humblest, could have been justified more easily. He might have, literally, dug ditches for a year with less prejudice to his career. There would have been many possible explanations of that, from Marx to Zen. But if he had accepted one of those cheap academic deals, he would have been typed forever as a failure, a second-rater—someone who has crawled off into the cold woods and covered himself with dead leaves, better forgotten.

It had been a wet, slow spring, and in spite of his natural optimism Paul had almost felt despair by the end of May, when he heard of this job in Los Angeles. The Nutting Research and Development Corporation, one of the largest electronic companies in southern California, was looking for someone with 'advanced training in history, and if possible some scientific background', to write a history and description of its operations.

Paul, with his degrees in history and literature, and his Navy radar training, was just what they wanted. The terms they named were amazing: his starting salary would be almost twice what any college had offered him. He would be sent at Nutting's expense to Los Angeles in September, and as soon as his security clearance came through, Katherine and his furniture would be delivered to him, also entirely at the expense of the company. He had to sign only a one-year contract, so he could return to teaching the following fall—with (he hoped) most, perhaps even all, of his thesis written.

'You're really going all the way out to Los Angeles?' some of his friends had exclaimed, men who spoke daily in familiar terms of ancient Mesopotamia or Transalpine Gaul. Paul had his answer to this. Historians looked backwards too exclusively, he said. Los Angeles obviously expressed everything towards which our civilization was now tending. As one went to Europe to see the living past, so one must visit southern California to observe the future. 'Why don't you come too?' he would finish by asking.

The air was still; the street empty except for the line of huge cars parked along the kerb, glittering and grinning with chrome and polish and enamel. They seemed larger, or at least on a larger scale, than the houses. They were designed for luxurious giants; the houses for international midgets. Paul had noticed already that in Los Angeles automobiles were a race apart, almost alive. The city was full of their hotels and beauty shops, their restaurants and nursing homes—immense, expensive structures where they could be parked or polished, fed or cured of their injuries. They spoke, and had pets—stuffed dogs and monkeys looked out of their rear windows, toys and good-luck charms hung above their dashboards, and fur tails waved from their aerials. Their horns sang in varied voices, and signs pasted to their bumpers announced: 'If You Can Read This, You're Too Damn Close' or 'Made In Pasadena By Little Old Ladies'. Among them Paul's 1954 Ford seemed an old, lifeless machine. It made a dark, dingy spot in the parade, although he had just had it washed. Maybe he should trade it in—he could afford that now—and (why not, after all?) buy himself one of these amusing monsters. If he wanted to find out how it felt to live in the future, wasn't that almost his duty?

'Paul, you always land on your feet,' other friends had said to him when they heard of this job, some of them adding enviously, 'Yes, you should go to Los Angeles. You'd do well there' or 'You're already a southern California type.' Criticism was implied in the laugh that followed this, but he was willing to take it as a compliment.

When Paul's acquaintances called him a southern California type, they were probably thinking of his love of the beach and other outdoor pleasures, and of the pleasure he took in movies, and even TV. No doubt they referred also to his occasional enthusiasm for such things as surf-casting, surrealist poetry, hypnotism, and the repair of his own household appliances — and his readiness for small adventures. They knew of enthusiasm mainly as an interesting phenomenon of eighteenth-century cultural history; not the characteristic of a serious historian—and yet, most of them would admit, Paul Cattleman was a serious historian. He was certainly not the standard graduate school product, though. He was too healthy and played games too well, for example, and he did not wear horn-rimmed spectacles. He did not wear spectacles at all; at large academic gatherings his brown eyes stood out oddly in a sea of glass goggles and refracting lenses, as if he were a man among Martians.

Paul walked up the narrow cement drive past his house to the back yard. Though the grass had begun to go brown in patches (he must water it again) flowers grew tall against the cinder-block walls, and there was a real peach tree, still hung with peaches.

Yes, he thought, leaning against the rough trunk of the tree, this city suited him: it suggested a kind of relaxed energy, the sense of infinite possibilities. Since his arrival, he had sometimes entertained himself by imagining that he saw parallels between Los Angeles and his 'own' period of English history, the late sixteenth century. Here was the same tremendous expansion of trade, building, and manufacture; the flowering of new art forms; the discovery of new worlds. And still the city remained a city of walled gardens like the imaginary gardens in late medieval romances, full of allegorical blooms—fruit and flowers ripe at the same time. Perhaps here, too, he might find other paraphernalia of courtly love: the impenetrable castles, the opening-night pageants and tournaments, the elaborate ceremonies of public praise, the worship from afar of the beloved movie starlet.

'You'll end up in bed with some starlet,' had been the jocose prediction of one of his friends. Paul had allowed himself to play with this fantasy a little. After all, there were plenty of starlets in Los Angeles, and some of them must get tired of the fat producers and vain, effeminate actors who surrounded them.

Of course he would never leave Katherine. He was in love with her; he had never seen a girl who moved him so deeply. On the other hand, in the three years since his marriage there had already been several episodes. It was Paul's belief, verified by experience, that among the people one meets every day there is an informal, unrecognized secret society—a confederacy of those who, though they may appear to sustain the conventional code in public, subvert it in private. These members of what he liked to call 'the underground' were able to recognize each other upon meeting by indefinable signs, rare in academic life: half a smile, a preference in fiction, a look of erotic aptitude and calculation.

Katherine was not, and would never be, a member of the underground. Cool, shy, affectionate but almost passive, she knew nothing of that side of life; love for her was an emotional, not a physical event. She was still very much the isolated country child, brought up in semi-rural New England by sickly parents whom it was impossible to imagine engaging in sexual relations. Maybe they had only tried it once, for Katherine was an only child. It seemed likely that their temperament had been hereditary.

As far as he could manage, Paul tried to be honest with himself; he was one of those fortunate people who, when they lift the lid of a dream or an *acte gratuit*, find mainly forgivable, if embarrassing, impulses. Besides, as an historian, he considered it his job to remember his own history. He therefore admitted now that it was just this shy, rural, even sylvan aspect which had first attracted him to Katherine. He had been moved to passion not only by her pale beauty, her white arms and long brown hair, but by something in her manner which recalled the unsophisticated, almost mute spirit of a tree or stream. She had the grace and tint of a Botticelli—and almost exactly the profile of the nymph who holds out a flowered robe to cover Venus as she rises from the sea. And she was all his; no one else had ever known her, in either sense.

Reaching up into the tree, Paul pulled down the largest, reddest peach he could see. After all, it had been stupid expecting Katherine to appreciate those plaster cows and artificial flowers. The thick stalks of the heliconia snapped readily, and soon he had a whole armload of them, brilliantly red and yellow and green.

Coming into the kitchen out of the sun, Paul could see nothing for a moment. Blinking, he opened cupboards, looking for a vase for the flowers, but could not find one, though he had unpacked the crates himself. Katherine would solve all that soon, but meanwhile— Impatiently he slammed the doors shut, took the mop out of the tin pail by the back door, and crammed the flowers into the pail (forgetting, in his hurry, to add any water).

Holding his offerings, he went into the bedroom. Here again he could not see at first; he had the blind sensation that comes when one enters a darkened movie theatre.

'Katherine?' His eyes adjusted; she lay looking at him, speechless and sleepless. 'Katherine, look what I brought you to eat: a peach off our own tree in the back yard.'

'No thank you, darling. I'm not hungry.'

'But look how beautiful it is. Don't you just want to taste it?'

Katherine shut her beautiful pale lips more firmly, and shook her head: the face of Persephone, he thought, offered food in hell.

'Katherine, darling.' Holding the pail, he sat down on the edge of the bed.

'You picked all those flowers,' Katherine said accusingly; she was by nature a conservationist.

'No I didn't; there's lots more. The yard's full of them. Besides, what good are they doing out there? I want them in here, where you can see them.' He laid his hand on her lank, silky hair, stroking it down.

'That was a nice thought,' Katherine said. She turned her head and looked at the pail of flowers, which Paul had put on the bedside table.

'I'm a nice guy,' he replied, stroking her hair.

'My head hurts so, so much.'

'I know.'

Katherine sighed, and stretched out; Paul continued to smooth down her hair, across her neck and shoulders.

'Oh, that's nice. So relaxing . . . Mm . . . I think I could go to sleep now,' she murmured presently. 'I'm very tired. Paul; you know, Paul, I couldn't sleep at all on the plane.'

Paul did not feel tired. 'Let me put you to sleep,' he said meaningfully. He felt Katherine's shoulders first stiffen, then go passive under his fingers. 'You know I haven't seen you for six months,' he added. 'I mean, six weeks. I guess it feels like six months,' he explained.

'I know.' Katherine smiled a faintly acquiescent little smile from under her arm. Paul began rapidly taking off his clothes.

'I love you so much, Katherine,' he apologized.

'Yes.' Katherine reached up and touched his arm. He put his hand on hers; their eyes met for a second. Then, burning, with one sock still on, he flung himself on top of her.

'Thank you,' he said after a while, and rolled over. It was darker in the room now. Night falls quickly in Los Angeles, as in the desert which it once was.

'That's all right,' Katherine replied in a small voice. 'I mean, you're welcome. Really.' She paused, and went on, 'But I'm sick. You know.' There was a silence. Paul did not admit that he knew.

'It was the altitude,' Katherine continued. 'When I decided to take the jet, I didn't realize that the difference in altitude would be so much greater. I think that's why I feel it so much, because of course jets fly so much higher than ordinary planes.'

'That doesn't make any difference; the cabin is always pressurized,' Paul said.

'Pressurized?'

'Mm.' He yawned, sleepy himself now. 'Well, see, the air in the cabin of a jet, or any big plane, is maintained at constant pressure after it leaves the ground. Has to be, or you couldn't breathe at all. The atmosphere is too thin up there.' He yawned again.

Katherine gave Paul a look which, even in the dim room, he recognized. 'You mean that I shouldn't be having a sinus attack now at all,' she said. 'It's all imaginary.'

'I didn't say that. I—' He sighed. Somehow whenever Katherine was sick she always managed to put him in the wrong, to make him feel guilty. It was Paul's belief that one of the causes of his wife's sinusitis was his wife's imagination, but he knew from experience that all hell broke loose when he expressed this view. 'I know it really hurts,' he said. 'You always get sick when you go on a plane.'

'I suppose in a way it's partly psychological,' Katherine said; she would sometimes admit this if she were not accused of it. 'I mean, even though I do have the kind of bone structure that predisposes me to get sinus infections—' (she ran her long, delicate forefinger down the bridge of her long, delicate, turned-up nose)—'still and all, I don't *always* have them. I mean, I do always have some postnasal drainage, but there usually isn't much pain. It gets worse when I'm overtired or upset about something, because of course my resistance is lowered when I'm tired, or frightened.'

'Frightened of planes?' Paul asked sleepily, looking up at his wife as she bent towards him in the darkening room. He deeply disliked being reminded that from behind that calm, lovely face, down into the round, lovely white throat, damp mucus was continually dripping.

'Of course not. Well, I suppose there is some natural anxiety. Travelling always makes me nervous. I don't like new places. Paul, you know, I don't like Los Angeles. It's going to be awful.' Katherine's voice rose higher.

'Kathy,' Paul said, reaching up and putting his arms around her. He pulled her down on to his chest. 'Don't worry so. It's only another city.'

'Not, it's not. It's more peculiar. Look at all those weird freak people we saw at the airport, those dressed-up little girls, and that old woman with the orange hair, and that man who had practically nothing on but bathing-trunks. And the houses. Everything's so exaggerated, so unnatural. I don't like lilies or whatever they are growing at this time of year, or peaches. I'd be afraid to eat one, really.' She laughed.

'Silly. You've only just come,' Paul protested. 'You've hardly seen anything of Los Angeles. Really, you mustn't be so prejudiced. You mustn't be put off by its reputation back East. This is a city like any other city. Thousands of people live here and work here at ordinary jobs.'

'Well, I'm afraid of them too,' she said, half seriously now. 'I think how I'll have to meet them and they'll all look at me and say, "Who's she? What's her excuse for existing?" It's all very well for you. You have a reason for being here; you have a job and an office and something to do. But I'm just nothing here. Nobody knows me or wants me around, and I'm really rather nervous.' Katherine laughed again, but not happily; it was too dark now for Paul to see her face.

'I want you.' As he said this, it occurred to Paul that he also did so in another sense.

'Yes. But that isn't it. . . . I don't want to depend on somebody else's emotions. I need—'

'Katherine,' Paul whispered. He rolled over on to his side,

pulling her with him, pulling at her nightgown. 'I've missed you so much, you know.'

'Mm.' Her arms lay slack around him; for some moments there was no further response. Then Katherine gave a faint moan, or croak, like something dying at the bottom of a well.

'Am I hurting you?' Paul said, pausing.

'A little. Never mind.'

At these words, and the tone in which they were said, Paul felt all desire leave him, to be replaced by something like despair. 'You should have told me,' he said, falling back on the bed away from Katherine.

'I didn't want to spoil your fun.'

'When you don't like it, it spoils it for me anyway,' he said flatly.

'Oh, Paul. I'm sorry.'

'I'm sorry,' Paul said simultaneously. He reflected that this had happened before with Katherine, many, many times, and felt: Oh, the hell with it. He swung his feet over the side of the bed and sat up.

'I guess I'm just out of practice,' Katherine added.

No reply. Paul continued to sit on the edge of the bed, his back to her. 'What time is it really?' she asked. 'It feels dreadfully late.' She held up her wrist, squinting at the luminous dots of the little gold watch which she never removed except to wash. 'My watch says—good heavens—ten-twenty.'

'Uh. That's Boston time. It's three hours earlier here.'

'That seems so strange. Seven-twenty, then.' In the dark, she adjusted the luminous dots.

'I'm hungry,' Paul said. 'Are you hungry yet?'

'I don't know. I suppose I should try to eat something.'

'Let's get up.'

Paul put on the light. The tiny room appeared around them: bare walls, bare floor, Katherine's outsize Victorian furniture. Here was the elaborate marble-topped chest of drawers and bedside stand her parents had used, and their massive mahogany bed, carved with wooden fruit. Beside the bed stood the mop pail, full of wilted leafage—leaves sagging, and scarlet and golden flowers wilting for lack of water; collapsed on their stems, or fallen on to the marble tabletop.

2

PAUL sat in the Publications Department of the Nutting Research and Development Corporation, surrounded by frosted glass. Actually only three sides of his office were frosted, but the view through his window, of smog-blurred roofs and smog-filled sky, gave much the same effect. The Nutting offices were on a hill a few miles from Paul's house, and his window looked east over the city. On very clear days they said you could see the mountains, but there had been no such day since Paul's arrival. It was half-past twelve, and he was hungry. He was waiting to go to lunch with his friend Fred Skinner, who occupied the adjoining office, but was now in conference with the head of the Publications Department, a man named Howard Leon.

For five weeks Paul had sat at his desk (of extreme modern design with an indestructible surface) in this office, with nothing to read except a few advertising brochures, personnel memos, and some more or less out-dated histories of California. His *Secret* clearance had not yet come through, and so hardly any Nutting publications had been available to Paul, nor had anyone been permitted to discuss Nutting matters with him. He read his books, and made notes on cards to the effect that the land on which the plant now stood was formerly part of a ranch owned by the Parducci family, or that forty-five per cent of the area of downtown Los Angeles was presently occupied by road surfaces. Sometimes he gazed out the window, or wrote letters. He described to his friends the speed and excitement of the city: the towers of apartments and oil-wells above swamps where the tyrannosaurus had leapt upon the brontosaurus in battles now petrified in rock for tourists; the tennis courts never muddied by rain; the pretty, tanned girls; the warm sea stroking the long, sandy beaches.

He also wrote to his parents in Columbus, Ohio. Los Angeles was amazing; you could almost imagine the city growing around you. Wherever you looked you could see the red and orange iron skeletons of tall buildings rising above the palms. The dust of

[13

excavation hung in the air, and the noises: the bang, bang, of construction and demolition, the groans of trucks hauling dirt up and down the hills. Even the faint shudders of earthquake or landslide, and the sonic boom as some aircraft broke the sound barrier, seemed to be part of it. The local and state political situation favoured this growth because—and Paul went on to explain why. His father was a real estate agent who also owned and managed business properties. He had done well, and was active in civic affairs, but he also found time to read current non-fiction and took an interest in the world situation. In a way you could say— that is, Paul's father could, and frequently did, say—that his hobby had become his son's profession. All the same, he was not a bad guy.

Paul's mother painted, and made pottery; she was in several local art groups, and an expert bridge player. For her he described the wonderful climate, the dry light, the white-walled houses with their orange and lemon trees, the Santa Monica mountains rising smoky green and brown against the north edge of the sky. Katherine's sinuses were bothering her, he wrote, but he had never felt better. His mother was interested in people's health. She had trouble with her own (indigestion, insomnia), which sometimes made her a little difficult. Still, she meant well.

Today, however, Paul's desk was covered with papers relating to Nutting and its works, and so was his bookcase. Last Friday his clearance had come through, and materials had been pouring in ever since. Piles of dusty, bulky manila folders; typed and mimeographed and printed drafts of Proposals in binders; statistical reports, financial reports, departmental and individual reports; carbon copies of letters, tables, graphs, estimates, diagrams, and memoranda. Apparently it was intended that he should read every piece of paper at Nutting.

Paul preferred this glut to the previous famine; he had the historian's love of primary source material, however untidy. He would mine the significant facts out of the mountain of processed wood pulp and erect them into an elegant and accurate record of the spectacular growth of a southern California corporation. He had in mind something which would both satisfy Nutting and (through a judicious use of irony and comparison) interest and entertain other historians. He had no instructions or outline to go by; the company had shown its confidence in Paul by giving him a remarkably free hand.

In front of him now was a large pile of memoranda marked *Confidential*, mostly dealing with office regulations. He leafed through them rapidly. *Confidential* was the lowest security classification; until recently Paul himself had been classified as *Confidential*. There was no lesser rank: just as the smallest bottle of soda one can buy now is the Large, so everyone admitted through the plant gate, and every memorandum, was designated at least as *Confidential*. Most people and documents were *Secret*, and some were *Top Secret*. Like the documents, every employee wore his classification in full view, in the form of a large round plastic badge bearing his name and photograph and the name of the company. Paul had worn this badge every working day for six weeks, and he still felt it to be embarrassing and ridiculous. The wearing of such a label, he thought, implies that one is continually among strangers or fools, like an exhibit in a museum.

Whenever he raised his eyes from his desk, Paul's attention was drawn to a large notice hanging opposite:

SECURITY MEANS YOU

Making Security Work Requires the Full Cooperation of Every Employee of This Corporation. REMEMBER: Any Danger to Our Security is Potential Danger to Our Country and Way of Life.

He heard Fred Skinner come back into his office next door, so he shoved the memos aside and went in.

'Ready to eat?'

Skinner did not answer, but continued to sit on the edge of his desk in an attitude of angry dejection. He was a small, spare, muscular man of about thirty-five, partially bald. The photograph on his badge showed him with his habitual monkey-like grin, in strong contrast to his present expression. The badge of Paul, who was now smiling, displayed the opposite contrast. When he had stood before the camera in the Personnel Office he had tried to look serious, and so his photograph had a solemn expression—like that of a depressed twin brother, whose portrait he had chosen to wear over his heart.

'How, Chief,' Paul said. During the last month Skinner had been promoted from Assistant Chief Technical Writer to Chief Technical Writer; this had resulted in some joking with American Indian references.

'Yeah, Cattleman?'

It was company policy for employees to call each other by their first names. Fred Skinner, as if in deliberate contravention of this policy, called his friends by their last names; they called him 'Skinner'.

'I'm hungry. Say.' He gestured at a disreputable object on Skinner's immaculate desk—a dirty, creased, half-charred piece of paper. 'Where'd you get that?'

'A guy in Systems found it on the road, outside the north fence.'

Paul looked closer. Most of the paper was burnt black or scorched brown, but he could make out:

```
learning period in which practice signals ar
adjustment of the outputs is accomplished si
improves in efficiency, that is, in freedom o
hence varies with each particular realization
```

Another legible area farther down the page was covered with equations. He frowned, puzzled.

'*Outside* the fence,' Skinner repeated, ' "constituting evidence of an unauthorized conveyance and/or removal of classified documents from the premises of N.R.D.C." ' Paul still looked puzzled. 'Not to tax your brain, it probably blew out of the incinerator.'

'Ah.' The security system for pieces of paper at Nutting extended from birth to death. Paul was allowed to use the wastebasket in his office only for envelopes, cigarette packages, newspapers, and so on. When he wished to dispose of any classified piece of paper he had to get up from his desk, walk down the hall, and place it in the special Classified Trash Container, located in full view of Howard Leon's office. Ordinary trash from the wastebaskets was collected by a city garbage truck; classified trash was ceremonially burnt once a week. It was Fred Skinner's job to supervise this process, which meant that he had to stand out by the incinerator every Friday afternoon and watch while two classified janitors reduced the documents to ash. 'So that's why it's burnt,' Paul said, and smiled.

'Wipe off that grin. This could mean the end of a damned important career. Mine.' Skinner did not grin himself; he grimaced. 'I think Leon's planning to get me for this.'

'To get you? But hell, he just promoted you.'

'Yeah, but he has to pin the blame somewhere. When there's a breach of security, you have to turn in your pals if you want to save your own skin. You'll find out.'

As usual, Paul could not be sure how serious Skinner was, or whether (behind his tough-ironic tone) he were serious at all. 'So what's going to happen now?' he asked.

'Whadayou think? Skinner is going to prepare-an-extensive-report-on-the-problem and make detailed recommendations. What's going to happen after that is the question.'

'Maybe nothing,' suggested Paul; even his brief experience at Nutting had led him to expect this outcome. 'If you make the report good and long.'

'Got any ideas?'

'Yeah; I think we should go to lunch.'

'Good idea. Let's eat civilian.' This meant, not in the plant cafeteria.

Skinner took down his old Marine raincoat from the hook behind the door, though it was not raining. It had not rained in Mar Vista for one year and three months, as a matter of fact; but this stained and worn coat, which did not match the *Esquire* polish of Skinner's other clothes, was one of his props.

Skinner and Paul passed the two obvious eating-places outside the N.R.D.C. gate, both much patronized by other employees, turned a corner, and entered the Aloha Coffee Shop, a small building set between two giant feather dusters on thirty-five-foot stems: fan palms.

Over sandwiches, they discussed what Skinner might say in his report on the burnt piece of paper. 'It has to be long. And we've got to dream up some completely new approach to the problem. Something that'll knock them flat.' Skinner pounded the flat of his hand on the table in demonstration.

'What the hell, I'll think of something,' he concluded in a worried tone.

'It's all crap anyhow,' he announced a little later. 'But hell, there's crap everywhere—everywhere you go you got to eat crap —only at Nutting we really get paid for it. In the academy you make the poor bastards eat crap for nothing.'

An early bond between Paul and Fred Skinner had been that Skinner was also a former (or as he put it, renegade) college professor. He had taught English for seven years at a local university without attaining tenure, and when he left abruptly he had been followed into industry by three of his graduate students, causing some consternation (or, as he put it, a fucking big blow-up) among his former colleagues. Skinner's resentment of 'the academy' was still considerable, and he liked to express it. Paul didn't mind that, but it irritated him when his friend insisted on personifying the enemy as 'you'.

I do not do so, Paul thought now, and he looked away from Skinner down the aisle between the booths, observing the back of their waitress as she walked away from them, balancing a loaded tray with professional skill. At the end of the room she pushed the swing door open with her hand, deftly catching it against her round arm and shoulder as she turned to steady the tray. Then she gave the door a neat shove with her foot and vanished into the kitchen, under an arch of crudely painted tropical fruits and flowers.

Paul enjoyed watching this waitress. She was young, and even pretty, with a chunky but good figure under her coarse starched green and white uniform. Moreover, there was a kind of charming proficiency and directed energy in everything she did which was lacking at Nutting. Some of the secretaries in the Publications Department were pretty and some were competent, but not both. Apparently girls who were both pretty and competent were not sent to Publications, but were routed instead to Systems or Administration. The secretary whom Paul and Skinner shared was neither pretty nor competent.

Paul kept his eyes on the kitchen door, and in a few moments his waitress reappeared. Again she flipped expertly round the door under the painted garlands, with a half-smile of concentration on her tanned, snub features. Not a drop spilled from the brimming glasses on the tray.

'Off in a hot dream world,' Skinner said loudly. Apparently

Paul had failed to answer some question; he had not really been listening for some minutes. 'Well, I'm going to get on back and get started on that report. Have fun.' He put a dollar down on the table, and went out.

Paul looked at his watch. Hardly half an hour had passed since he left the plant, so he sat on, finishing his sandwich.

'More coffee?'

'Oh yes, please.' One of the better things about Los Angeles, Paul thought, is that when you buy a cup of coffee you always get as many free refills as you want. He smiled gratefully at the waitress as she poured it. She smiled back, showing white but crooked teeth, and remarked:

'Hey, you forgot your book today.'

'That's right,' Paul agreed.

Until last week, he had found his lunch hours at Nutting embarrassing. Though he was always welcomed in a friendly way by the other Publications Department people in the cafeteria, as soon as he sat down with them their conversation faded into inanities, for they were afraid of inadvertently mentioning some Nutting secret in front of someone who was merely Confidential, and who might (they knew about Reds in Eastern universities, after all) turn out to be a bad security risk. All except Skinner were so obviously uncomfortable with him that Paul often chose to eat alone in the Aloha Coffee Shop with a book.

'Aw, too bad,' the waitress said, resting her coffee-pot on the table.

Paul made a conventional gesture of rueful resignation.

'Listen, I'll tell you what; I'll get you a book, soon as I finish with the coffee. I've got one out back . . . Nah, that's all right. no trouble.'

She was away before Paul could stop her; he was left to wonder what she would bring him, and then to speculate amusedly on a culture in which any book was the equivalent of any other. The incident was typically Los Angeles, he thought: in Boston or New York even a very stupid waitress would not imagine that he read the same books she read; nor would she step outside of her role to bring him anything not on the menu.

He must not and did not smile. In a way it was a challenge; an individual was trying to treat him as an individual, not as a mechanical task. He must rise to the occasion and behave in such a way as not to discourage such acts. There had been other hints of this attitude; for instance, the direct, curious gaze and speech of garage mechanics as he drove across the West. ('Where you from in Massachusetts? I got an uncle back there.') They seemed not to have classified him, other than as a person. How unlike New York, where every stranger is an object to observe or dodge on the street; or Cambridge, where one does sometimes speak to strangers, but only if they are obviously of one's own caste.

Well, he must behave like a native too. He had already resolved that while he was in Los Angeles he would do his best to follow the local mores; he wanted to create as little as possible of what sociologists call 'noise' or 'static'. Not only for the sake of better reception, but in order to preserve something which he was beginning to find agreeably unique.

The waitress had finished pouring coffee and gone back into the kitchen, and now Paul remembered reading in some sociological text that for the working classes the word 'book' means anything printed which is not a newspaper; every magazine is a 'book'. Maybe she would bring him a copy of Look or the Post rather than some popular love story.

Here she came. He composed his features into the beginnings of a friendly and grateful smile.

The waitress walked up to Paul's table, and laid down in front of him a new copy of Samuel Beckett's latest play.

With great difficulty, Paul prevented an expression of astonishment from appearing on his face. 'Well, thank you,' he uttered.

'Maybe you've already read this.'

'No, but I've been wanting to.' This was true. 'I—' But she had already whisked away to take an order at another table.

Paul opened the book, but could not concentrate; he kept looking up. Twice the waitress was simply waiting on a table, her back to him, and it passed through his mind that maybe the book had been left behind by some other literate customer. The third time he caught her standing by the kitchen door, balancing her tray and half smiling to herself in his direction. He realized that she probably knew what he had been thinking, and also what he was thinking now. He looked away; he tried to read, and could not; he tried to finish his sandwich. Finally, caught staring again, he signalled for the check.

'Like that book?' she said, scribbling on her pad.

'Very much. I wish I had more time to read it.'

She seemed to consider, adding the check—she added like any illiterate waitress, slowly, frowning and chewing on her pink tongue—then said: 'I can lend it to you, overnight, like, if you want.'

'Yes, I would. Thank you.'

'Only you get it back here tomorrow.' This was said in a tone of friendly threat; both smiled.

'All right. Do you read this kind of thing often?'

The waitress looked at him a moment, like Justice deciding whether the scale should rise or fall; she had large brown eyes, set wide. 'No,' she said finally. 'Mostly I read *True Screen Stories* and the *Saturday Evening Post*.' Paul laughed; she laughed too, softly. What a pretty girl she was.

'You're not really a waitress,' he said, and for the first time he spoke in the tone he would have used to an attractive girl at a party. But her reaction to this was unfavourable: her face became cold and blank, and she said in a voice like that of a waitress:

'I don't get you.'

'Well, really—' Paul smiled; no reaction. He laughed self-consciously. Then, determined not to give up, he said: 'Hey. What's your name?'

'Ceci. Can't you read?' CECI was embroidered in green on the pocket of her uniform. She shifted her hips and looked round the room, about to go. But Paul was stubborn; besides, her very rudeness, quite outside the conventional limits of rudeness for waitresses, gave him confidence.

'Just Ceci?'

'Cecile, then. If you must know, Cecile O'Connor.'

Paul had gone on staring at her, and when she finally glanced back to say this, they exchanged a look which unsettled him. It did not last long; Cecile O'Connor dropped his check on the table and walked off quickly towards the kitchen.

But who is she? Paul thought. As he left (late now), paying the check at the cashier's desk, he recalled that she hadn't bothered to ask *his* name. A wave of ridiculous depression passed over him because of this small incident, that a waitress had not wanted to know his name. Then he recalled that exactly who he was, and what he was (at least for the moment), was printed in capital letters on his chest: SECRET PAUL CATTLEMAN, NUTTING RESEARCH AND DEVELOPEMENT CORPORATION.

3

A BLACK Jaguar sports car was stopped on the west shoulder of the San Diego Freeway between Pico and National Boulevards, in full view of the southbound afternoon traffic, and two people sat in it quarrelling. They were Glory Green, a successful Hollywood starlet, and her husband Dr Isidore Einsam, a successful Beverly Hills psychiatrist.

'Okay, I get the idea. You're pissed off at me,' said Glory in her amazing voice, and she turned her amazing face away. She wore the conventional costume of a kooky starlet on vacation: high-heeled sandals; tight pink silk pants from Jax; long, baggy, bulky, dirt-coloured sweater; and a tall conical straw hat tied under the chin with a pink scarf. Her face, including the mouth, was painted chalky brown all over, as if with Kemtone; her heavy eye make-up was hidden by heavy dark glasses. She had the soft, throaty, resonant speech of the mature actress, but with a childish half-lisp which grew more pronounced in moments of stress, so that she actually described her husband now as 'pithed off'. But it did not really matter what Glory said, for first practice and then habit had brought her to the point where she could not even telephone for a plumber without sounding sexy.

'I'm not pissed off at you, pie-face,' Iz said. 'I just think it might be interesting to find out why you forgot your bathing-suit. I'm interested in your reasons for wanting to forget it.' Iz often cited Glory to his professional friends as proof that a stable personality need not be a conventional one; she was completely off-beat, completely and wonderfully original, without being neurotic.

'I didn't want to forget it, stupid. I wanted to pack it.'

'I don't think so,' Iz said, smiling a psychiatrist's knowing smile. Though he was only thirty-two, and had not been in private practice long, he did this smile most effectively. The psychiatrist's beard he had recently grown (small, dark, pointed) helped a lot. Like his wife, Iz wore huge black-rimmed sun-glasses; the rest of him was covered with inoffensively elegant sports clothes.

'Okay.' Glory sighed theatrically. 'Let's have your interpretation.'

Iz paused. For about a year after their marriage he had had a
sort of superstitious dread of disturbing this unique psychological
organization that was his wife by any sort of prying, but lately
he had begun to let what he thought of as professional curiosity
get the better of him.

'Well,' he said; 'there are a number of possibilities. Maybe you
really don't want to go to Mexico. Maybe you don't want to
expose your body to the Mexicans; or maybe that's just what you
do want. We know already that you prefer to swim nude. Or maybe simply you don't like any of your bathing-suits.' As every one
of these explanations was correct, and no secret to her, Glory
smiled and said nothing.

'Or maybe more than one of these reasons applies. Most of our
actions are after all multiply determined. I mean,' he translated,
since Glory had left school in the eighth grade, 'most people have
more than one reason for whatever they decide to do.' Glory did
not mind her husband's using technical language; she liked it,
even when she did not quite understand. The roar of long words
breaking over her head made her feel as if she too swam in deep
intellectual seas, washed about by great ideas. There was practically nothing she went for in a man as much as a really brilliant
mind. She had therefore been gazing affectionately at Iz; but
when he began explaining as if she were a feeble-minded kid, she
pouted. Both of these expressions were hidden from Iz by the
shadow of her hat and glasses; he continued. 'I think it might be
interesting if we were to ask sometime why you "forget" so
often.'

This was not a new or original idea, though it was new that Iz
should express it. Glory's headlong rush through her life had left
a trail of abandoned objects. She had forgotten handbags, suit-
cases, packages, contracts, and every imaginable and unimaginable piece of clothing, in every imaginable and unimaginable
place. She had also, at one time or another, misplaced a pregnant
police dog, a pink Edsel automobile, and two husbands. Some of
these things later turned up in unexpected places; others were
never recovered. Glory was already mildly famous for this, and
Maxie, her press agent, was doing his best to make her more so.

'Oh, I think you're right,' Glory said. 'We should do that some time. But right now, how about getting off your ass? I mean we aren't going anywhere here.' She gestured at Mar Vista laid out below the freeway: a random grid of service stations, two-storey apartment buildings, drive-ins, palms, and factories; and block after block of stucco cottages.

'So what're you going to do about your bathing-suit?' Iz persisted. Glory shrugged, raising both her shoulders and her celebrated breasts, but did not answer. Silence was her best weapon and also her best defence; nothing she could say was half so eloquent as her beauty. 'Goddammit. You try to go in without one somewhere along the coast, and we'll both end up in the jug. No thanks. I can see the headlines.' He stopped smiling. 'Or is that what you want? Maybe you're planning a publicity stunt?'

Here Iz did Glory an injustice; it had not occurred to her that she might be arrested for indecent exposure in Mexico. Maxie would shit poodles if she got herself into anything like that without clearing it with him first. For a couple of seconds she considered doing it just for that. But she decided not: after all, this was supposed to be a vacation.

'What *do* you want; you want to stop somewhere on the way down?' Glory shrugged again. 'Or do you want to try to buy a suit in Tijuana? So tell me.' Iz did not mention the possibility that he might turn around and drive back to their house in the hills above Hollywood, or else to the Beverly Hills shopping district, which was nearer. He abhorred all retrogressive movement. Also, he was determined to force Glory to ask him for what she wanted or, as he put it to himself, to assume responsibility for her own actions.

'Like where? In the desert I could pick something up, but not in Tijuana.'

'I see.' Iz smiled, and actually stroked his new beard. He contemplated her, and she eyed him, through their sunglasses; in the cars that sped past, drivers and passengers, mostly in sunglasses, continued to stare at them.

'Okay,' Glory said finally. 'I'll feed you the line. "Whadayou see?"'

'Let me ask you,' Iz said, holding his pose. 'What do *you* see?'

Glory did not answer. She continued to look at Iz almost

inquiringly, as if she had not heard the question. Had Iz been in his office he would have accepted this as the sign of total resistance to interpretation—so wait patiently a few sessions, at fifteen to thirty dollars an hour, then offer the interpretation again. But he was patient only in his office.

'You want to go to Palm Springs,' he said. 'You always wanted to go to Palm Springs.'

'That's a lot of crap,' Glory said.

'It should be,' Iz said. 'Because you know what would happen if we went to Palm Springs. As soon as you showed your face there you'd be surrounded by a crowd of voyeurs and parasites, massaging your ego, trying to participate vicariously in—'

'Talk talk talk talk,' Glory interrupted.

'All right. Ass-kissers and creeps, to you; sucking up to you, so they can get in on a good thing, just the way they are on Monday, Tuesday, Wednesday, Thursday, and Friday. And I don't think you need that any more. I don't think that's what you really want.'

'You know what I want, ass-head,' Glory said. 'I want to go away somewhere with you. I want to get out of this phoney no-where city and go somewhere where we can swim . . . and lie in the sun . . . and sleep.' Glory's voice deepened and slowed into a vibrating whisper of the kind that comes out of theatre amplifiers during close-ups.

'Right. That's what I thought you wanted,' Iz said in an appropriate voice. He leaned towards Glory, putting one hand under her pink silk thigh, another at her neck, pulling her up to him. Their large dark glasses stared into each other and the plastic rims grated together as they kissed passionately, much to the interest of the passing vehicles.

'I want to be warm,' Glory murmured, her mouth and tongue fluttering at the margin of his beard. 'We could go like somewhere out in the desert where nobody goes. Just get out there and keep driving until we hit some way out place. Mm?'

'Mm,' Iz replied.

Unwisely, Glory pushed her advantage. 'And then, well like tomorrow, I could just run into Palm Springs without anybody seeing me and pick up a bathing-suit.'

Iz drew his head back, and replaced Glory in her seat of the car.

'You really are a spoilt child, beautiful, aren't you?' he said. 'A beautiful, spoilt child.' Glory did not agree with him. 'You've got to have everything your way.' Glory opened her mouth, but he continued. 'Oh, I know it's not entirely your fault. Since you really were a child chronologically you've been flattered and indulged and taught to think that all Glory's little whims were very, very important. Because you weren't like other people. You were a child entertainer, a little third-rate goddess, so charming and so talented and so pretty. When you reached adolescence you got a big shock: nobody loved you any more. You had a tough time before you started making it again, and you should have learned something then. Maybe you did learn it, only I wonder if now you aren't forgetting. Maybe you're beginning to feel that all those years were just a bad dream. You know what I think is your problem now? You're starting to believe all that crap that Maxie grinds out about Glory Green, the beautiful, crazy, way out starlet. Ya, I think so. You're starting to believe your own publicity.'

During this speech Glory's mouth fell open wider and wider; then it shut as firm as a plastic flower.

'You've got a big explanation for everything, haven't you?' she said when he had stopped speaking. 'Oh yeth; you've got an interpretation. You know what's your problem? If you want to know, your head is swelled up with all those poor slobs lying on the couch in your office all day long, telling you how great you are, taking every word you say like the Bible. All those poor old bitches and hard-up homos throwing themselves around on the couch and bawling and telling you how hot in the pants they are for you, you really go for that. You think you can push everybody around like you push them around.'

'Oh, screw.' Iz swallowed, and got control of his temper and vocabulary. 'Your jealousy of my patients is understandable, sweetie,' he went on, 'but completely misplaced. And you really know that.'

Glory gave no sign of knowing it, but continued to stare stubbornly at him.

'Listen, sweetie. I've explained the transference relationship to you enough times. I told you already, the emotions my patients think they feel for me are only projections of emotions they feel,

[27

or used to feel, for somebody else. They're not really in love with *me*; they're in love with somebody they think I am, maybe their father or their mother. Their demonstrations of this emotion don't give me any personal satisfaction.'

'Pigshit,' Glory suggested.

Iz shrugged as if giving the whole thing up, and sat back. They looked at each other in an unfriendly way.

'Hey,' Glory said presently. 'If you don't mind, let's split. I'm sick of this scene.'

'But it's so interesting.' He smiled.

'Interesting?' Glory wrinkled her pug nose with disgust at Mar Vista, over which a smoggy pink sunset was now settling. 'That?'

'No. You. What you're really saying now, for instance, is that you want to split with me. You're sick of me.'

For a moment Glory said nothing. She turned to Iz and gave him a slow take, head to foot. 'Yeth,' she said. 'You're so goddamned right.' And, with the appropriate gesture, of cutting her own throat, 'I'm fed up to here.'

4

VISTA GARDENS: a long row of two-storey plaster apartment buildings backing on to the San Diego Freeway. There was no vista of course, and no gardens, Katherine thought. This whole city was plastered with lies: lies erected in letters five feet tall on the roofs; lies pasted to the walls, or burning all night in neon. Her head ached; her sinusitis was worse again.

She followed Paul down the cement walk, past dwarf palms illumined by a red spotlight, into a stucco building. She stood in a hallway while he rang the bell; she smiled nervously and without joy when the door was opened on a confused scene of strange people and cheap furniture. An unattractive man in a striped sport shirt put his arm around her, drew her into the room, saying something loud and facetious. She could not change her features into another expression; the little nervous smile was glued there, like a lie. 'Well, and how do you like Los Angeles?' 'Oh, very well, thank you.' Because she mustn't let Paul down. She was given a glass with faces painted outside, ice inside. People speaking, moving. Her head ached, ached.

'Katherine! Come on,' Paul was saying now. He had taken her by the arm, and was pulling her towards the door. Everyone was laughing and talking. 'All these buildings look alike to me, you know!' Paul exclaimed to them, laughing.

'Yes, they do look pretty much the same,' others agreed, smiling as if this were a delightful circumstance.

'What?' Katherine said. A grinning man took her glass out of her hand. Paul was still laughing as he pushed her outside and shut the door of the party behind them. He leaned back against the wall, in order to laugh better.

'What a joke!' he said. 'That wasn't the Skinners' place. We were at the wrong party!'

'Oh.' Katherine did not look up.

'Hey, what's the matter?' Katherine did not respond; she was leaning her forehead against the wall, her eyes were closed, her fists pressed against her anterior sinuses. 'Do you have a headache again?'

'Yes. It hurts terribly.'

'Isn't there anything you can do for it?'

'I already took all my medicines,' Katherine said through her fists; even talking hurt. 'The only thing else I could do is lie down and try to drain it. Maybe I'd just better go home; then you can come back and try to find the party.'

'Oh, I know where it is now. It's right in the next building. Would you really like me to take you home?'

'I don't care,' Katherine said through pains which were realer than the present scene; blurred wall crossed by blurred shadows, Paul's voice, the smell of cleaning-fluid. 'If you want to.'

Paul sighed. 'Of course I don't want to, silly,' he said. 'I want you to go to the party with me, if you can manage it.'

Katherine stood up, which made her head spin. 'I guess I can manage it,' she said.

'Come on, then. You'll feel better once you have a drink.'

Katherine followed Paul, her head bent. Steps, grass, steps, a door, another door, a room. It might have been the same apartment; there was the same tacky Danish modern furniture, brass bowls and blue denim; the same kind of people. Everyone seemed to be so large in Los Angeles, so tanned and athletic-looking. Though Katherine was only a little below average size, here she felt small, pale, and weak.

A brown, balding man crossed the room towards them, pushing before him a tall, blonde girl who looked like an illustration from a magazine. Her hair, bleached nearly white and with the texture of frayed silk, was bandaged round her head into a large structure resembling an Indian turban, and she had a tan so deep that her features were almost invisible. She wore sea-green velvet pants, a low-cut ruffled blouse, ropes of beads, and high-heeled satin pumps.

'Hiya, Cattleman! Meet the wife. Susy, honey, this is Paul and Katherine. What're you drinking?' He moved off to the bar with Paul.

'Oh, gee. How do you do! I'm so glad you could come,' Susy squeaked, or whispered—it was hard to say which. 'Gee, I've been wanting to meet you so much, Katherine. Won't you sit down?'

Katherine sat down on a simple, ugly sofa. Susy sat beside her, and asked whether she had any children. A moment later she was claiming that she had two herself. Where could they be, in this tiny apartment, and what on earth could they be like?

'Viola's in school all day now,' Susy confided, leaning towards Katherine, her eyes and teeth fluorescently sincere. 'And Mark has his Swim-and-Fun School in the mornings; and I know it's crazy, but honestly I miss them just terribly. We used to have such a real fun time together when they were little. The apartment seems so stupid and empty, with me all alone just pushing a dust-mop around. . . . Oh, I know it, I've got to get on the ball and do something. I ought to get out and take some courses and develop some of my potential. They have some wonderful courses, you know, up at the university.'

Susy bounced forward on the sofa. Under her blouse she had extremely high, full breasts, cone-shaped. But then so did all the other women in the room. For the first time in her life Katherine began to feel flat-chested, as well as undersized and pale.

'Oh, really,' she said, to say something.

'Oh yes, wonderful. Terribly stimulating. They have a marvellous course I want to take called World Tensions in the Space Era —Professor Bone's course—with audiovisual and everything, and he even has very well-known people come and explain the significance of the different world tensions to his class.'

Katherine's head ached terribly now with the smoke and the noise; she said nothing, but focused on Susy Skinner and nodded vaguely.

'Of course, it's too bad, the courses all started last month, in September, and they don't begin again until February; but maybe you could get into a discussion group. They have some awfully good discussion groups. They don't get the very best-known lecturers, but they usually have some very nice young instructor for the discussion leader. They meet in one of the members' homes once a week, and they serve coffee and refreshments afterwards. For instance, there's a New Book Discussion Group, with Mr Evert, that discusses all the new books. I mean if you're interested in keeping up with the new books.'

As sometimes happened during her sinus attacks, Katherine found it very difficult, even painful, to re-focus her eyes; she continued staring at the side of Mrs Skinner's face with a meaningless fixity which Susy no doubt took for deep interest. 'Well, I'd

[31

like to, but it's really a question of time for me—' she began slowly to say.

'Oh, I know it is. I mean moving and getting settled into a new house, it honestly is the complete end: you don't have to tell me. But when you have time you ought to look into it. Some of the discussion groups meet in lovely homes up in Bel Air and Brentwood. Fred used to lead a group on Major Trends in something, I forget what, Major Trends in— Anyway, it met at this absolutely gorgeous home in Laurel Canyon right above where Glory Green lives. You could see her swimming in her swimming-pool from their dining-room. It was at night, of course, but she has these spotlights built in underneath the water, so you could see her real well. American Realism. That was it. Major Trends in American Realism. Anyway, I'll lend you the catalogue, and Fred can tell you which are the best professors.'

Katherine returned Susy's hundred-watt smile with a weaker one. Her head was throbbing loudly. She was also confused by the innocent enthusiasm of this creature in what she would have unhesitatingly classified as the costume of a hard, successful chorus girl or, since this was Los Angeles, movie starlet. She rested her head on her hand, pressing the flesh along her cheekbones as if this might loosen the congestion. 'Thank you, it sounds very interesting,' she said. 'But I'm afraid I won't have much time for anything like that. I'm planning to find a job as soon as I can.'

'Oh, I see.'

Katherine put the other hand on the other side of her face. She felt dizzy and in considerable pain. Peering out at Susy above pale distorted cheeks and a mouth compressed into a grotesque pout, she said: 'I'm terribly sorry, but I'm afraid I'm not feeling very well. Do you suppose I could lie down somewhere for a little while?'

'Oh, gee. I'm awfully sorry. Would you like to lie down in the bedroom?'

'Yes, thank you.'

They went into a tiny room almost entirely filled by king-size furniture. Katherine lay down on the bed beside the coats of the guests and let Susy cover her with a green satin puff. She lay on her back because that seemed more normal, but as soon as Susy had shut the door she rolled over on to her face, crept across the chenille, and hung her head over the end of the bed at a forty-five-degree angle.

She lay there a long time, feeling neither happy nor well, listening to the blur of voices in the other room. How hot it was here, and dry; terribly dry. It was the dehydrated air of Los Angeles that she and her sinuses could not get used to; she imagined it full of minute grains of soot and sand. It wasn't her fault: she never wanted to come to Los Angeles. Why was she here, then? Well, because Paul had expected it of her, and so had everyone else. If she had refused to come there would have been questions, and talk, and opinions, and life cracked open in an ugly way. And besides, she had really not liked it very much in Cambridge either, or in Boston where she had gone to school. She had not liked it very much in Worcester where she had been brought up, the only child of a second-rate professor in a second-rate college; or anywhere in the East, or anywhere that she had ever lived or been, for that matter.

But Los Angeles was worst. She hung down farther off the bed; her long, silky hair fell over her face and brushed the straw matting, and her head throbbed as the blood ran into it. Paul must have noticed by now that she had left the party, and no doubt he was annoyed. Probably he too wished that she had never come to Los Angeles. Probably he wished she were dead.

No, that was unfair. Katherine knew that her husband's attitude of tolerant impatience concealed only impatient tolerance. He took life so easily, swimming through it as through a warm, shallow stream; he could not imagine what it meant to be rubbed raw by every ugly sight and sound. He had no idea of what it had cost her to come out here; of how nearly she hadn't come at all, of the weeks of anxiety while she had tried to make up her mind. In the end perhaps she had decided to follow Paul just because he didn't know and never would know what she went through—in the same blind hope that had encouraged her to love and marry him, the hope that somehow his good spirits and good luck would rub off on her.

Staring at the floor, Katherine thought these familiar thoughts. Meanwhile her position began to have its effect: drainage began on one side of her face. Being careful not to raise her head, she

[33

burrowed into her bag and took out a wad of Kleenex. She blew her nose.

'How are you feeling; are you feeling any better?' Susy said, coming into the bedroom suddenly. 'Oh, please don't get up.' Katherine subsided to a renewed view of matting flowered all about her head with used pink Kleenex like damp, crushed paper roses. 'Look, I brought you another drink. Or would you rather have some coffee or tea or something?'

'No, thank you, nothing. I'm draining my sinuses,' Katherine added, to explain the position in which she had been caught, as if she were either looking for dust under the bed, or planning to throw up. 'I have to lie this way to get drainage.'

'Gee, that's too bad.' Susy sat down on the far end of the bed. 'I know what it's like; my sister had sinus for years and years. Only hers went away after she moved to California.'

'Well, mine hasn't,' Katherine said. 'Ever since I moved to California it's been much, much worse.' She tried to gather up some of the Kleenex. 'Most of the time my passages are completely blocked.'

'But you've only been in L.A. a little while,' Susy objected. 'Just a few weeks. You have to get used to it. Why, I had a terrible skin condition when I came out here, and even though I went and lay on the beach practically every day it didn't get better for months. That's what you ought to do, go and—'

'When you came out here? I thought you were natives.'

'Oh, lordy, no. Nobody's a native in L.A. The whole city has practically been built from the ground up since the war. I'm from Muncie, Indiana, and Fred's from Tennessee. But of course we've been here, lemme see, eight and a half years. It was awful coming out here for the first time and feeling sick and sort of terribly lost; and I didn't know anybody and I hadn't a glimmer how I was going to live here. I mean I know just how you feel and I'd like to help.' Susy clasped her hands, red-nailed and loaded with gold and glass, around her knees. 'I mean it may seem funny me thinking I could help anybody,' she said in her soft squeak of a voice. 'Fred says I'm a bigger baby than my Markie is. But anyhow I could show you where to go to the beach, and which are the best places to shop, and you know, things like that.'

'Thank you,' Katherine said. She rolled over and sat up. Mrs

Skinner looked a most unlikely friend for her, but beggars cannot be choosers. 'That's very nice of you.' She drank from the glass Susy had brought, because it was the only liquid in sight.

'And maybe I could even help about finding a job. What kind of work do you do?'

'Well, usually secretarial.' Katherine had learned from experience that the phrase 'research assistant' conveyed nothing to most people. 'Back in Cambridge I used to work for some of the professors.'

'Gee; well then, that should be easy. I bet you could find something up at U.C.L.A. I'll ask Fred. You're lucky to have secretarial training.' Katherine had not had secretarial training—only an A.B. from Wellesley—but she did not contradict Susy. 'I wish I had sometimes, it's so easy to get typing to do when you want to make a little money for Christmas or something, but the only thing in the world I know how to do is teach nursery school.'

'Nursery school?' Katherine's voice rose in surprise. 'Gracious.' 'How do you mean?'

'Well, that is—' But Katherine could not think of an evasion. 'I'm surprised at your being a teacher. I suppose I thought you probably were an actress or a dancer or something like that,' she admitted with embarrassment.

'Golly, thanks. I'm awfully flattered: I adore the theatre. But honestly, I never had any talent that way. I couldn't even get into dramatic club in high school. Hey, you need another drink. Shall we go back in? I mean, how do you feel?'

Katherine felt better; there was a dim buzzing in her head, but it was painless. She looked at the tall glass in her hand, empty except for a cube of ice. I mustn't drink any more, she thought.

In the other room, the party was still going on, only louder. Nobody seemed to notice her return. 'Honey, Katherine needs another drink,' Susy said to her husband.

'Just plain water and ice, please. Lots of water: I'm very, very dehydrated.' Katherine giggled, and then bit her tongue. Oh dear, she thought. I must sit down and not say anything.

She sat on the sofa, stiffly upright, and pressed her knees together.

'Water and ice coming up, ma'am,' Fred Skinner announced, handing her the glass with a flourish which splattered her skirt.

'Sor-ry!' Lurching a little, he sat down beside her. 'Well, good to see you here.'

Katherine tried to think of a topic of conversation. 'How is your report coming?' she asked.

'Report?' He frowned like a cross ape.

'Yes, you know, your report on the secret materials that blew over the fence.'

'Who told you about that?' Skinner exploded, in irritation rather than inquiry, for the answer was obvious. 'I suppose your husband told you that story,' he answered himself, loud enough for Paul to hear him across the room and turn round. 'Hey, Cattleman, whatsa big idea, breaking our security in bed! Doncha read the regulations?'

'It's all right, Chief. I know I can count on her,' Paul replied. 'I just thought it was a good story, the way it showed up Leon.'

'Yeah? Never trust a broad is my motto,' Skinner said. By this time, most of those present were listening and laughing. 'Take it from me. And while we're on the subject, Cattleman—' (he lapsed back for a moment from tough into academic style)— 'I don't wanna hear any more of this disloyal talk about Howard Leon. He's a pretty committed guy.'

Paul smiled along with the rest, but Katherine could see that he was disconcerted. 'Wow! Now hear that,' he exclaimed. 'I get it. Gripe all you want in camp, but don't let on to the civilians.'

Skinner gave Paul his monkey-like grin. 'Yeah. Something like that.' The attention of the party remained fixed on him, and therefore on Katherine, but she refused to start another topic, or even to look at him. After a moment, he stood up and went away. Relieved, she lifted her glass and took two big swallows before she realized that he had deceived her—her 'ice water' was full of some kind of strong, colourless alcohol.

Katherine glared across the room at Fred Skinner; but when she caught his eye, he winked. She had a strong impulse to get up, walk across the rug, and slap his face. That'll make him wink, she thought, rising, dizzy, half out of her seat—and then subsiding in horror at the idea of the spectacle she had nearly created.

The party was in full swing now, with people laughing, shouting, and hugging each other. A few of them, like Fred Skinner, were dressed in conventional Eastern clothes; but most, like his wife, were disguised as Martians. A young woman with the face of a spinster school-teacher wore vivid purple velvet pants and sash and a yellow ruffled blouse printed with violets; a blond man about forty had on a Mexican shirt with blue embroidery and peculiar leather sandals—his behaviour, however, indicated that he could not possibly be a homosexual. Most of the guests, unlike Susy, looked all right from the neck up (these two even had horn-rimmed glasses), but somehow that made it worse.

Katherine had hoped no one would speak to her until she felt clearer in the head, but now a girl sat down next to her on the sofa. 'I'm Natalie Lenaghan,' she said pleasantly, 'and you must be Mrs Cattleman. How do you do?'

'How do you do,' Katherine said, since this was safe.

'We live in the next building but one,' Mrs Lenaghan went on. 'My husband's at U.C.L.A.; that's him over there.'

Katherine made no response. This was even safer. She observed Mr Lenaghan: he was all right from the waist up, but below that he wore red plaid shorts. Mrs Lenaghan, however, would have passed in Harvard Square.

'You've just come out here, haven't you?' Mrs Lenaghan said. 'How do you like Los Angeles? . . . Or don't you really know yet?'

'Oh, I know,' Katherine replied. She realized dimly that this was a wrong answer.

'Susy says you've found a nice house quite near here,' Mrs Lenaghan tried again after a pause. 'That's really wonderful luck. What's it like?'

'It looks like a gas station,' Katherine said. 'I mean, lots of these houses here look like gas stations, with those flat roofs, don't you think so? . . . They do, because they're white and made out of cement, and they have flat roofs.'

Mrs Lenaghan laughed. 'Well, but that's because it hardly ever rains in L.A. A sloping roof wouldn't be any use here. Still, I see what you mean. When you come to think of it,' she added, 'there are a lot of gas stations here that look like houses. There's one up in Brentwood that's exactly like a New England lighthouse.' She laughed again.

Katherine did not laugh. She wished that this agreeable and apparently intelligent woman would leave and come back some other time. I'm drunk, she thought of saying, so would you please go away now, before I make a fool of myself? But the utterance of this statement would be the action it was designed to prevent.

'Of course there are some ridiculous things here,' Mrs Lenaghan went on. 'But then think of the climate! That's what I always say to myself.'

'I don't like the climate,' Katherine said. 'I don't like the sun shining all the time in November, and the grass growing. It's un-natural, it's as if we were all shut up in some horrible big green-house away from the real world and the real seasons.' She raised her voice. 'I hate the oranges here as big as grapefruits and the grapefruits as big as, I don't know what, as big as advertisements for grapefruit, without any taste. Everything's advertisements here. Everything has a wrong name, I mean the name of every-thing, you see, it's always a lie, like an advertisement. For instance, this is Mar Vista, which is supposed to be Spanish for "view of the sea". That's because it has no view of the sea; it's all flat, it has no view of anything. Mar Vista!' she repeated scornfully. 'Spoil-the-View, I call it; Spoil-the-View, California.'

People were listening to Katherine again now, but she did not notice. 'I despise it here,' she went on to Mrs Lenaghan. 'You know what I saw the first day I got to Los Angeles, when Paul was driving me back from the airport, the first afternoon I was here? We were driving back from the airport, and we passed a dough-nut stand, and on top of it was this huge cement doughnut about twenty feet high, revolting around. I mean revolving. You know. It was going around and around.' Katherine waved her arm in demonstration. 'That was the first thing I saw, before I saw the stand. From a long, long way off, that big empty hole going around and around up in the air, with some name painted on it. Well I thought, that's what this city is! That's what it is, a great big advertisement for *nothing*.'

Katherine stopped speaking, or rather shouting. Silence fell over the Skinners' party, every member of which had been listen-ing to her.

5

It was the day before Thanksgiving, but in Mar Vista the perpetual summer continued. Babies rode barefoot in their strollers; front lawns were wet and green under the rotating sprinklers, or scorched brown by the heat, depending on the attentions of their owners, for water is expensive in Los Angeles. Only the angle of the sun through the palms, and the early dark, suggested that the winter equinox was approaching.

Paul still sat at his desk behind a growing heap of books and papers. He had finished the first section of his work on N.R.D.C., a brief historical description of Mar Vista from prehistoric times to the establishment of the Nutting plant in 1940. He had thrown in enough dinosaurs and *conquistadores* to keep the interest of the lay reader, while presenting sequentially the basic geographic and historical facts. Still, he was impatient to get on to the real subject. He tapped his foot on the synthetic floor, and his pencil on the desk top. Only now his impatience was more general; he just wanted to get through the next half-hour. Nutting was letting everyone off at three for the holiday, and he had an appointment.

He was going to have a cup of coffee with Ceci O'Connor. That was how he put it to himself; it sounded better than to say that he had an assignation with a waitress. Anyhow, she was not really a waitress: he was convinced of that. And it was not an assignation: they were going to have a cup of coffee, and talk about books, because there was no chance to talk at the Aloha Coffee Shop.

'Hey, Cattleman!' Fred Skinner put his chimpanzee's face round the frosted-glass partition. 'Wait till you hear this. All our problems are solved.' He sat on the corner of Paul's desk, knocking over a pile of books. 'Hell. Sorry. Look at this.' He spread out a glossy brochure.

UnDat

it read in multicolour, three-dimensional letters on a gold background.

Below, in the centre of a gold aureole, was portrayed a stream-lined green and silver machine, roughly the shape, and about twice the size (to judge by the pretty girl who stood with her arm about it, smiling erotically), of a large wringer washer.

'We've got it made,' Skinner said. 'No more incinerators, no more sifting ashes, no watching the janitors all afternoon.'

'You mean this machine is going to get rid of the classified trash for you?' Paul asked.

'For us, pal. You've got to start identifying with the corporate image. Our problems are your problems, Cattleman.'

'Yeah. How's it going to do that?'

'Well, like it says here.' Fred unfolded the brochure. ' "Materials placed in the hopper are first treated with a unique bleaching and dissolving agent which removes all traces of text, whether written—" Wait a moment. "Five distinct tearing and shred-ding arms then rapidly reduce the—" Here we are. "The UnDat is capable of completely processing all forms of paper, cardboard, and celluloid in a matter of minutes. For maximum efficiency of operation, large metal fasteners and rings should be removed be-fore insertion." Great, isn't it?'

'So you put all your, I mean we put all our classified trash into this machine; and what comes out?'

'It's a kind of green sludge. Looks like damp shredded wheat, sort of. I had a sample of it, but I had to leave it with Howard Leon. He's investigating the possibility that Bob Kinsman might be able to use some of it to pack components over in the plant.'

'We're really going to get one of these things?'

'It looks pretty definite,' Skinner said with satisfaction.

'Goddamn.' Paul laughed. 'Crazy.'

'What's so crazy about it? Listen, most of the big companies on government contract have already put in something like this—Sylvania, Ramo-Woolbridge—everybody.' Paul continued laugh-ing. 'Whoever thought this up had real genius. It fills a fucking felt need. I only wish I was going to collect one per cent of the net.'

'Is it expensive?'

'In the neighbourhood of nine or ten K.' Fred took out a new pack of cigarettes, and broke the Cellophane with his thumbnail. 'And of course it costs another K or so a year to operate.'

'But you won't be saving any money then,' Paul objected.

'Hell, no. Why should we save money?' Fred said, tapping his cigarette on the desk. 'Butt?'

'No thanks. Well, hell, I suppose so as to apply it somewhere else, to buy something you need, or save the Government some money, or raise our salaries—I mean, you read about how these automated machines are going to do all that.'

'Boy, have you got the wrong idea,' Fred said from between his hands as he crouched over the flame, for even in the windless air-conditioned climate of Nutting he behaved as if he were trying to light up on some stormy beach-head. 'You're all confused, boy,' he said. 'You can't apply your small-time civilian standards to this kind of operation. You're talking as if N.R.D.C. was your family budget, a few dollars saved on rent, a few dollars more to blow on whisky. It just doesn't work that way here. You don't have to get all shook up about a little matter of nine K. There's plenty more where that comes from.

'Think what we're buying with it,' he went on. 'Absolute security. Say, that's a good line: I can work that in. Another thing you've got to keep in mind. The bigger the yearly cost figures for the department, the bigger the yearly increment. I know it takes some getting used to after you've been up in that scruffy ivory tower. You don't have to tell me. Don't tell me, just ask me.' Fred grinned, and drew on his cigarette. 'Any time.'

'Thanks, Chief,' Paul said. 'Thanks for that generous offer.' He wished Skinner would go away, though, so that he could clean up his desk and be ready to leave at three.

'You've got to learn to ride with it,' Fred went on. 'Listen, when I was first here, soon as I began to see what the score was, I started requisitioning supplies. I put in for every fucking thing I could think of, every kind of paper and pencil and notebooks; even some furniture, a chair, and a couple of lamps, everything. I was testing, you know. Testing. I couldn't believe it. Well, it all came through. Not a bitch from anywhere. Jesus, when I think what us poor instructors used to go through trying to get a couple of red pencils out of Miss Rollins's supply cupboard.' He sucked in, then blew out smoke.

'What do you know?' Paul looked at Skinner's cigarette. Presumably Skinner would not leave until it was finished, and he always smoked them to a minimal stub. 'Guess I'll send in for some stuff tomorrow,' he said. He looked at the UnDat brochure again, comparing the model hugging the machine (unfavourably) to Cecile O'Connor. They were both dark blondes, though; not dissimilar in shape.

'That's the spirit,' Skinner said. 'Keep up the cost figures.'

The plant buzzer sounded, a metallic, penetrating hum. Paul stood up, and began to straighten his desk.

The Joy Superdupermarket covered nearly a whole block. It was brilliantly lit; noisy with piped music, with the screams of children and the jazz clang of twenty cash-registers; and packed from wall to wall with pre-Thanksgiving shoppers.

'This is really a great place,' Ceci said as the photoelectric doors swung open to coax them in, and they entered the maelstrom of consumption. 'It's got everything.' People surged up and down the aisles, buying not only food, but gin, shampoo, life-sized dolls, Capri pants, electric frying-pans, and photo-murals of Yellowstone National Park. 'All the cats come here.' Silently Paul imagined, among the men and women and children, a number of large cats of all colours, walking on their hind legs and dressed in beatnik clothes. 'Come on, here's a cart.'

Paul followed Ceci as closely as he could so as not to lose her in the crowd. She was difficult to follow—unobtrusively quick, as at her job in the coffee shop—rounding a corner suddenly, sliding her shopping cart between two others, reaching out as she passed to take something off a shelf: a kind of dance.

Luckily he was tall enough to see for some distance ahead, and Ceci was easy to spot: she was almost the only person here dressed entirely in black—tight black sleeveless jersey; full black cotton skirt. 'Now I know what you are!' he had exclaimed as she got into his car. 'You're a beatnik.' Ceci had made no reply, but when they were on their way to the market she had said, 'You have to have names for everything, don't you? First you tell me I'm not a waitress, and now you tell me I'm a beatnik.' 'Well, hell, you're dressed like a beatnik,' he had replied agreeably. 'And this a.m. I was dressed like a waitress.' Her voice was still flat. 'Yeah, but;

damn it—' Paul smiled, shrugged his shoulders and put out his hands in the gesture of a simple man bewildered. The car swerved to one side; but he caught it. They both laughed. 'I don't pick up on you yet,' Ceci said, smiling directly at him for the first time that day. 'It takes a while,' Paul replied. Suddenly he felt better, even euphoric. The depression that had come over him during the brief, disappointing cultural discussion they had just had in a noisy restaurant—a shouting of conflicting reading lists, really—had lifted.

He was standing still, and Ceci had disappeared again. People pushed against him and bumped him as they passed with their loaded shopping carts; being without a cart himself, he was particularly vulnerable. He started walking down the aisle past shelves of pet food, ranks of brilliant cans and boxes in front of which stood pet lovers selecting from among the full-colour portraits of eager, affectionate dogs and sensuously cute kittens.

He rounded the corner. There was Ceci over there, beside a pyramid of canned fruit. She saw him and waved. God, she was pretty enough to make one dizzy. But more than that; her manner towards him, at certain moments, seemed to promise a rather immediate intimacy. She looked at him right now, as she had in the car, as if she wanted and expected to get into bed.

'It's really great of you to bring me here,' she exclaimed as he came up. 'Shopping without a car is such a drag. I only wish I had the bread today; I'd clean out the whole store.'

'Don't overdo it,' Paul said, smiling. 'I'll take you shopping again.'

'You will? Big.' Ceci put her hand on Paul's wrist and looked up at him with eyes circled in black like a kitten's. 'You really are a good guy, aren't you?' she said.

'I hope so,' Paul replied, covering his sudden sexual excitement. 'I don't know.'

'I'm nearly through. I only want to grab some melon for our dessert. Come on.'

Our dessert? Does she think I'm coming to dinner? But I can't do that: I have to go home. Or has she got someone living with her?

Ceci let go of his wrist. Released, but still caught, he followed her down another aisle and out into the fruit and vegetable department. Paper turkeys and pumpkins hung from the ceiling, in celebration of Thanksgiving; but the counters below were heaped with summer fruit: apricots, damp red plums, and melons cut apart and sweating lusciously under Cellophane—canteloupe, honeydew, watermelon. The time of year gave them a special glow, as of forbidden fruit, out of season. He looked directly at Ceci, and she looked back. Yes: it was going to happen.

Paul had never thought of himself as slow; in fact he prided himself on his ability to seduce, or let's say persuade. But he was used to girls who, however much they might like it later, had at first to be convinced. Katherine, for instance—Ah, shit; that was it—Ceci didn't know about Katherine. She had no idea that he was married.

All right, what could he do? He could decide not to tell her, eat the forbidden fruit, and let her find out later, or maybe never, that he was married. Or he could be honest, and if so the sooner the better. He was really a good guy, wasn't he?

'What d'you dig the most? Watermelon or canteloupe?' Ceci asked. She looked very young with her hair down, much younger than he had thought—not over twenty-five.

'I don't know,' he mumbled. 'The watermelon looks good.' And then, deliberately. 'I mean, my wife likes canteloupe, but I guess I really prefer watermelon.'

'Okay.' Ceci lifted up a section of it, heavy, red, dripping juice.

'You didn't hear me,' Paul said.

'Yeah, I heard you.' Holding the melon, Ceci looked at Paul, but did not smile. 'You're married. O.K. So am I, if you want to know.'

'Oh,' Paul said, while she lowered the melon into her cart. So it was for the husband, not for him. He felt stupid. But if she didn't mean anything, she had no right to look at him that way.

'There's just one more thing I've got to have for this dinner,' Ceci said. 'Wild rice. I think it's over here.' Paul followed the tail of gold hair, brooding. Wild rice as a sop to her husband and her conscience, maybe; but he was going to have her first, whatever she thought. Still, wasn't it rather— 'Jesus Christ, one seventy-nine for that measly little box! Oh no, uh-uh. Hey, Paul.' Using his name for the first time, Ceci also moved a step nearer to him, so that their bodies were touching.

'Put it in your pocket,' she said in a low voice. 'Come on, you've got lots of room.' Leaning up against him as they stood side by side in front of the shelves, Ceci began shoving the box of wild rice down into Paul's jacket pocket.

'What're you doing? For God's sake.' Paul pulled the rice out of his pocket. 'You want me to go to jail?'

'Aw, don't be chicken. Nobody's going to see you.' Both Paul and Ceci continued to hold the box of rice. It had a picture of an ugly Indian in a canoe on it. 'I thought you were a good guy,' she went on. 'What's the matter: haven't you ever lifted anything before?'

'No, I haven't,' Paul said. 'And I'm not going to start now.' He put the box back on the shelf. Not only is she married, he thought —she's a kleptomaniac. How did I ever get into this? Her kitten face, soft mouth and snub nose answered him.

'Listen, you shouldn't steal from stores,' he said. 'You'll get into trouble.'

'You run your own life, pal.' Ceci took the box off the shelf. 'Don't look if it scares you,' she added, pressing more closely up against him, and began to pull her black jersey out from the wide leather belt.

'There.' Holding her sweater up, Ceci shoved the box of wild rice down between her skirt and the soft, white skin of her stomach. 'Okay.' Paul dared to look along the aisle; no one seemed to have noticed anything.

Letting the jersey down over the skirt, Ceci stepped aside. 'Does it show?' Paul shook his head. 'Great.' She put her hand on the shopping cart again. 'Anybody looks at me, they'll think I'm pregnant. With a real square baby.' She grinned, and Paul could not help smiling.

'You're crazy,' he said.

He was pleased with this explanation, and repeated it to himself several times as he and Ceci passed slowly through the checkout stand, left the Joy Superdupermarket, and loaded her groceries into his car. She was crazy. It formed an important part of the legal defence he was composing in his head in the expectation of being picked up at any moment for shoplifting. When they turned out of the parking lot on to National Boulevard, he let out a sigh.

Ceci turned in the seat to look at him. 'That really bugged you, didn't it?' she asked.

'You're goddamned right it did.' Half-consciously, he was trying to use her language. 'I was waiting for them to grab us the whole time. Listen, you'd better not try anything like that again.'

'Oh? Will you shop me?' Ceci smiled at him, but rather coolly. Paul did not answer. 'Will you turn me in if I do?' Aware that he was being mocked, Paul looked away and continued driving. He began to feel that he had not been on an exciting assignation with a beautiful, crazy beatnik girl, but instead that he had been coldly used as a taxi by a married kleptomaniac waitress.

Following Ceci's directions, Paul pulled up in front of a two-storey shack on an alley in the beach slum of Venice. He got out of the car and began unloading her bags of groceries on to the sidewalk. One. Two. Three.

'There you are,' he said flatly.

'It's upstairs.' Hardly glancing at Paul, Ceci picked up a carton of beer and began climbing a rickety stairway at the side of the building. Paul stood and looked at the three bags sitting on the dirty, cracked sidewalk, each printed in large letters with the name of the Superdupermarket: JOY, JOY, JOY. Then, furious, but a gentleman to the last, he picked them up and followed her.

The door at the top of the stairs opened directly on to a kitchen, shabby and dim. There was a big bowl of fruit and vegetables on the table, dishes stacked in the sink; the walls were covered with paintings and drawings and photographs. There was no sign of her husband. He set the bags on a table.

'Hey, you brought them all. Great. Thank you.' In Paul's suspicious mood, it sounded like a dismissal.

'You're welcome,' he said. 'Well; see you next week, probably.'

'What d'you mean?'

'Oh, you know. At the restaurant.'

'Aren't you staying for dinner?'

'Was I supposed to stay for dinner?'

Ceci released the groceries she was holding, two cans of soup and a head of lettuce. They fell on to the table. 'Don't put me down, man,' she said. 'Don't do that. I know you're bugged because I scammed off with that rice. All right, but you don't have to walk out on me.'

'I'm not walking out on you,' Paul protested, confused again. 'I didn't know you expected me to come to dinner. Honestly. Anyhow, I can't come to dinner. I have to go home.'

'For Christ's sake. What'd you think I got all this stuff for?'

'I don't know. For you and your husband to eat, I suppose.'

'Christ. I wouldn't buy crab meat and stuff like that for him. We're separated. I mean he doesn't live here any more.' She laughed shortly, then widened her eyes and looked at Paul warmly. 'So come on. Stay.'

'I'd love to. But I can't, really. I have to go home.'

Now Ceci narrowed her eyes: sexy kitten into watchful cat. 'I get it,' she said finally. 'You have to go back and have dinner with your wife. Great.'

'I'm sorry,' Paul said.

'So we blew the whole afternoon dragging around in that market, and now you have to go home. Or maybe you want to go home?' She spoke steadily, but Paul saw the slope of her shoulders, the way her mouth remained open at the end of the question, and knew that she was as tense and disappointed as he.

'God, no.' He extended his arms; immediately, or so it seemed, Ceci was pressed up against him, kissing him lightly all over the face; he was kissing her.

'Wow,' she said. 'Ow. Wait a minute.' She stepped back, lifted her jersey, and pulled the box of wild rice out of her skirt. She laughed: 'I forgot about this; I thought for a second it was some crazy thing you had on.' She leaned against Paul and began kissing him again, rubbing up against him very gently with her arms, breasts, legs, and belly. The blood ran into Paul's head and private parts. He clutched at Ceci and bit her on the shoulder, getting a mouthful of cotton jersey. She put her feet on his feet, stood on tiptoe, and looked into his eyes.

'Hey.'

'Hey yourself,' Paul remarked inanely.

'Listen.' Very gently, Ceci brushed her breasts across his shirt. She had no bra on; he could feel the nipples lifted to hard points. 'Do you have to go home to dinner now or not?'

'I have to go home to dinner eventually,' Paul murmured, stroking her bottom, 'but now—'

'Okay. Cut out, then.' She stepped back, and put her hands

behind her head, where the hair was beginning to come loose.

'No, I was going to say I could be half an hour late.' Automatically, Paul looked at his watch: he was half an hour late already.

'Uh-uh. I don't go for that, man. I need a lot of time the first time. Or like it won't really swing. You know.'

'But I want you.' Paul grasped Ceci again; she pulled back, half-resisting.

'Okay, okay. When do you want me?' She smiled.

'Now. I can stay about an hour.' What would he tell Katherine? It was after five already, he saw.

Ceci shook her head. 'Yeah, with your eye on the clock,' she said. 'Make it some other time, huh?'

'Whenever you say. Tomorrow?' With the remaining fraction of his brain, Paul began to think how he might possibly explain being absent on Thanksgiving.

'No good. I'm on all day. How about Friday? I don't have to be at the place till four. You dig lunch on Friday?'

The image came to Paul of himself digging lunch, in the form of a great hole in Venice Beach, in which Ceci was half-buried, naked. 'Yes,' he said. 'About when?'

'Let's make it noon.'

'Good.' He began to construct his excuses for Friday.

'Okay.' Disengaging herself from Paul, Ceci walked over and opened the door for him, with a succinctness that he found disconcerting. Surely there should be more conversation, more hesitation over a thing like this.

'You're right near the beach here, aren't you?' he said, moving slowly in the direction of the door. 'Maybe if it's still warm we could go for a swim; what do you think? Shall I bring my suit?'

'We won't have the time, man.' Ceci gave him a cat's half-smile.

Paul paused in the doorway. 'Well,' he said. He bent to kiss her good-bye; the door was between them, and only their mouths met; warm, wet. Now, he thought, and started to go round the door; but Ceci leaned against it and pushed, hard. Thrown off balance, he staggered back and outside, on to the porch.

'Ceci—'

'Later,' she said, and shut the door on him.

In a state of mild shock, Paul went down the stairs, got into his car, and began to drive home. It was because things were happening too fast, he thought, too soon, that he felt this way. He was used to having to force his way through a lengthy routine of flirtation and discussion, first base and second base; used to beating down a series of defences with all the sensual, emotional, and intellectual energy he had. This lack of resistance threw him off balance. From an ugly, desperate girl he might have expected such directness, but not from Ceci O'Connor. Maybe she was a nymphomaniac.

What to tell Katherine? Well, he could say something like about a special project at N.R.D.C. A rush job, so he had to go in on Friday. She would believe it, because she had no idea of the real situation. In fact, no one at Nutting ever asked him to do anything. Executives from the top offices came by sometimes with visitors and he was introduced as a Harvard historian who was writing the history of the company. Even that wasn't true yet. He was trying to write it, but the trouble was he still couldn't find the data he needed in all those piles of paper on his desk: the basic facts and figures like the names of the original stockholders and the size of their investments. And nobody seemed to have the time to help him. They didn't care about the past: they were only interested in the present and the immediate future.

'So why worry?' Fred Skinner had said. 'You're pulling down your salary.' Katherine would have understood why he worried, but since Katherine already despised Nutting, he hadn't told her. Which as it now turned out was just as well.

Only he would be crazy to get mixed up with a girl like Ceci. She was unbalanced; must be. A nymphomaniac, a kleptomaniac; a psychopathic personality. She was very pretty; beautiful. Her hair, breasts. Probably she slept with everybody she knew. She might even have something catching. It would be crazy to go back there on Friday.

Paul started down the other side of the hill into Mar Vista, and the sun set behind him; the rosy flush on the stucco dimmed, the smog among the palm trees in the middle distance turned from blue to grey. On his street, the outlines of the houses were beginning to blur, and the colours of the flowers shone softly: great white roses, yellow chrysanthemums, and many more that he could not name, fantastic in shape and colour.

He had suggested to Katherine that she might find out something about these flowers. She had always liked that sort of thing: when they visited in the country in New England, she would come in from a solitary walk on the coldest, wettest day with a handful of damp leaves or twigs in bud, crying out their name with joy. Why shouldn't she take an interest in the local vegetation? There must be hundreds of new plants here. So he had thought and said, but to no use.

Their lawn was as green now as the neighbours', Paul thought as he pulled into the driveway. Green, lush, long—in fact, it needed to be mowed again. And it was getting into the flower-beds, he noticed as he crossed the yard. Long runners of grass had leapt the trench between lawn and garden and were spreading spiderlike towards the house. What was more, as if in reprisal the flowers were getting into the grass: white flecks of allyssum spotted the lawn, and some heliconia had sprouted near the front door, breaking the ground like moles. He should cut and weed at once; it was too late tonight, but he would have plenty of time over the weekend, if he didn't go to Venice.

The house was dark. 'Katherine?' he called, and walked through to the kitchen, turning on lights as he went. Katherine's kitchen was as clean and tidy as an office, unadorned except for an engagement calendar and a shelf of herbs. The pots and pans that should have held his supper hung on the wall, their copper bottoms shining.

Paul went into the bedroom. The blinds were drawn down, and his wife was lying in bed in the dark.

'Hello!' he said.

His wife groaned, or sighed.

'It's late. Don't you want to get up?'

Katherine heaved herself up in bed, a white shape lit vaguely from the hall. She was wearing a cotton flannel nightgown with flannel ruffles. Paul raised the venetian blind. It clattered up over a view of Los Angeles evening: a smoky dark blue mist decorated with blurred lights—red, white, green. The branches and leaves of the peach tree outside the window were close and black. Above, hazy blades of searchlights crossed and recrossed the sky. It was spectacularly fine, Paul thought, and was going to say so, when Katherine remarked flatly:

'Hell. That's what it looks like: hell.' She sat up, the sheets twisted round her shoulders. Paul looked at her, and found her not attractive. Maybe his standards of comparison had changed—the good-looking girls here were all deeply sun-tanned, outdoor types, glowing with light and life. Or maybe she had changed. But anyhow, it was as if the pale flame that had burned so steadily in the grey, damp New England air had become invisible—extinguished in a blaze of sun.

'I suppose you want something to eat,' Katherine added.

'Well, I was thinking of it,' Paul said. 'Aren't you hungry?'

'No.'

'Do you have sinus again?'

'Yes.'

A moment of nothing to say followed. Paul looked at Katherine; Katherine looked at the floor.

'I'm sorry, I simply don't feel up to cooking,' she said finally.

'That's all right. I'll find something in the icebox.'

'There isn't anything in the icebox, really. I meant to go to the store today, but I didn't feel up to it. . . . Why don't you go out and get something, and I'll try to sleep. I've been trying for hours, and I'd just dropped off when you woke me up. It really wasn't very considerate of you.'

'Well, it wasn't very considerate of you not to get anything for supper,' Paul said, in what he intended for a humorous tone.

'If you had any idea of how I feel,' Katherine said, not humorously, 'you wouldn't ask me to get up and cook. I'm so dizzy, and I have pains shooting through my head like long needles. All through my head. Or maybe you would ask me, I don't know,' she concluded in a dull shrewish voice.

'I'm sorry,' Paul said flatly. Katherine might have managed to buy him a pound of hamburger, considering that she had practically nothing to do all day. Which was probably part of her trouble.

'Oh, by the way,' he said. 'Did you call up U.C.L.A. yet? Skinner asked me about it, you know.'

'I know.' Katherine raised her eyes briefly. She was suspicious of Fred Skinner: she would not believe that he had thought she had been 'really great' at his party; she was convinced that he had deliberately tried to make her drunk out of boorish malice. Suspecting some similar trick, perhaps, she kept putting off investigating an apparently good job he had heard about at U.C.L.A.

'Susy called today. She wants us to go to the beach with them and some friends on Friday. I said I didn't know. I really don't want to go, but I thought you might.'

It occurred to Paul that going to the beach with the Skinners would prevent him from being crazy enough to see Ceci O'Connor again, so perhaps it was a good idea. Besides, he had been trying for weeks to show Katherine the sea, the sun—'We ought to go,' he said. 'It's insulting to keep turning down invitations all the time. Fred and Susy will think you don't want to see them.'

'I don't want to see him, and I don't want to go to the beach.' Katherine lay down again, pulling the sheet with her. She tugged it into position with weak gestures. 'I don't mind seeing her, but I can do that any time.'

'You should go. Maybe you'll be feeling all right by then. You haven't been to the beach at all yet.'

'If I feel all right, I'll have better things to do than go and sit in the dirty sand with a crowd of vulgar people.' Katherine half sat up, twitched the blanket over herself, and fell back. 'Would you mind putting the blind down again?' Paul looked at her; then he looked for the cord of the venetian blind, and let it down. 'Thank you. Why don't you go by yourself if you want to?' she added.

'I can't,' Paul said. 'I have to go back to the office on Friday. I have to finish a special project.'

6

ALONG the Pacific Coast Highway, in an unsteady stream of cars, moved the pink station wagon in which Katherine Cattleman, Susy Skinner, and Susy's two children were going to visit the G. J. Putty mansion, art museum, garden, and private zoo. Katherine and Susy were in front; Mark, aged three, lay on his stomach in the cargo area, digging up the rubber matting with a toy bulldozer, and Viola, aged six, sat primly in front of him holding a plastic purse in white nylon gloves.

The Putty estate is not open to the general public, but it may be visited on certain days by those who have made previous arrangements, and Fred Skinner had made such an arrangement through someone he knew in the U.C.L.A. Art Department. Katherine admitted to herself that it was thoughtful of him to have done so. She had no interest in the mansion, the garden, or the zoo, but the collection included paintings by Rubens, Renoir, Matisse, etc. which few people had ever seen, and she felt (or rather knew she ought to feel) gratitude to Fred for this opportunity. In the same way, she owed him gratitude for the job she had just accepted at U.C.L.A. which would start next week. It had turned out not to be a trick at all, but a bona fide position: research assistant on a project two professors in the Department of Social Sciences were starting under a grant from the National Institute of Mental Health. Yes, she owed gratitude to Fred Skinner, but it irritated her to pay him; she preferred to deliver it to his wife.

'What awful, awful traffic!' Susy said. They had got to a break in the Santa Monica cliffs where the canyon opens out on to the beach. On both roads, cars stood jammed together in the hot sun. The sidewalks were crowded with muscular people in bathing-suits and sun-glasses and beach robes, most of them burnt to the colour of furniture. They crossed the highway in front of the stopped cars, carrying canvas umbrellas, surf-boards, portable radios, towels, and bottles of Coke, under a banner of red and green spangled letters two feet high: MERRY CHRISTMAS. The lunch counter on the corner repeated this theme: two nearly naked boys stood eating popsicles behind a window painted with white, metallic snow and ice. In the window of the bar next door the snow was solid Styrofoam, strong enough to support a cardboard sleigh and plastic reindeer. The glittering sun made Katherine's sinuses hurt, and she squinted her eyes.

'Want to go to the beach, Mommy,' Mark said.

'Some other day, honey. Today we're going to the zoo, and see all the animals.'

'Honestly,' Susy added, as the lights changed and then changed back without their having moved more than a few feet. 'You'd think everybody in L.A. was trying to get to the beach today.' She started forward as the lights changed, then put on the brakes sharply and blew the horn at a bunch of high-school kids who had begun to cross in front of her. Honk! One of the boys turned and made a face at her over the hood, putting his thumbs in his ears, waggling his fingers vulgarly, and sticking out his tongue. In the rear-view mirror, Katherine was surprised to see Viola imitating him, white gloves and all.

'The way some people bring up their children,' Susy said, glancing round as if with some sixth sense; but Viola had returned her hands to her lap.

'When are we going to get to the zoo, Mommy?'

'We're nearly there, love.'

Again on their right the cliffs rose up sheer, a high wall of pale dried mud, eaten by the wind into uneven patterns like giant ants' nests. Presently Susy pulled off the highway and stopped in front of an iron gate which was wedged into a break in the cliff. She got out of the car, rang a bell, and spoke into a box. A buzzer sounded, the gate opened, and they drove in. As soon as the tail of the station wagon was through, the gate swung shut behind them with a loud iron clang.

'They're locking us in, Mommy,' Viola exclaimed. 'They're locking us into the zoo!'

'It's all right, lovey. They're not locking us in. They're just shutting the gate again, in case some bad men wanted to get in and steal something.'

They started uphill on a narrow road crowded by dark trees, crowded in turn by the steep sides of the canyon. High above, shreds of bright blue sky appeared and disappeared. From somewhere not too far off came the sound of a machine or carnivorous animal roaring and grinding its teeth.

'What's that, Mommy?' Mark asked. 'What's that noise?'

'I think I want to go home, Mommy,' Viola announced.

Round a last bend the gully opened out into a shallow landscaped basin: a circular sweep of drive, massed trees and flowers, and a long stone villa. 'Here we are, kids!' Susy said.

At first sight the effect was European—Sussex or the Île de France; but the trees were too tall and of strange shapes, Katherine thought; the flowers were too large, and the hills behind the house were much too near: they looked dry and flat, like the canvas backdrop of a stage.

Susy parked the car, and they got out next to an orchard: rows of pruned trees, the ground beneath them littered with huge, heavy yellow oranges— Why no, they must be grapefruit; hundreds of grapefruit lay here, ripe and over-ripe, rotting in conspicuous waste.

They walked towards the house. About two hundred flower bushes were growing beside the drive, and both the bushes and the earth beneath were covered with burning scarlet and crimson blossoms. 'Camellias—those are all camellias!' Katherine exclaimed; the camellias she knew always came in groups of one or two from florists' shops.

'Golly, yeah. And look over there on the lawn,' Susy said 'Peacocks. See the peacocks, Markie, the pretty birds . . . No, honey, we'll go over that way later. Come on, now.'

Katherine walked up the drive behind Susy, Mark, and Viola, outlandish figures in their identical tight pants and rubber sandals and butter-coloured hair. The flowers seemed to grow larger, their odour thicker, as they approached the house, and she thought with pity of the paintings locked up inside, shut away here at the world's end among monstrous flora and fauna.

Of course these Los Angeles clothes did not mean what they appeared to mean. At first she had thought Susy's style of dress a personal aberration, a freak. But when she went to visit her, she saw that most of Susy's neighbours at Vista Gardens dressed the same way. She began to realize that all the tarts and starlets (in her mind interchangeable terms) whom she had seen in the streets and supermarkets of Mar Vista might be only housewives.

'Golly, will you look at those flowers!' Susy said. 'They have so many they're even throwing some of them away.'

'Where?'

'Right over there.' She pointed to a freshly-dug plot at the side of the house. A trash can stood by it, stuffed indiscriminately with roots, branches, leaves, and flowers: pink, scarlet, white.

'Oh, lord,' Katherine sighed. 'The waste of it!' That's what's so terrible. And all those grapefruit, just spoiling down there.'

'Well, I guess Mr Putty can afford it,' Susy said. 'I guess he's practically the richest man in America.'

'The waste of it!' Katherine repeated. 'Those flowers are just going to die.' She began rummaging in the trash can. 'I'm going to take them home.'

'Do you think you ought? Maybe they wouldn't like it,' Susy said, looking around for 'they'.

'I don't care. It isn't right.' Katherine stood up, her arms full of exotic plants. 'I'm going to put them into the car.'

She ran down the drive, trailing roots and leaves, shut the strange flowers safely into the station wagon, and walked back.

'Let's go see the pictures,' she said. Her sinuses ached more and more. She held her breath, as it were, until they entered the museum; then she looked only at the floor. She shut her eyes to the view through the windows of the hall, waiting for the sane views, miraculously preserved for hundreds of years and greedily transplanted here, that awaited her inside. When they were admitted to the principal gallery she hurried into the room, turned her back to the Skinners, and raised her eyes.

Her first impression was one of behinds. Rose-pink behinds by Boucher; white behinds by Ingres; misty Impressionist behinds and full, fleshy Rubens behinds. Nearly all the paintings in the room were of nudes. They lay spread out on sofas—they lolled half-erect, embracing people or urns; they cast their eyes down provocatively, or looked boldly over their rounded shoulders out of thick, sticky gold frames. At intervals along the walls below them stood antique sofas with the legs of beasts, covered in rose and gold brocades, as if awaiting the convenience of this crowd of whores. Even the few landscapes and still-lifes seemed to ooze a vulgar sensuality: the baskets of ripe, dewy fruit and the sunlit hills repeated the same forms.

Katherine stood in the centre of the room and clenched her hands. Meanwhile Susy circumambulated the gallery as if she were in any museum, standing for an equal interval in front of each canvas, seeing nothing, making polite comments, watching the children as they ran about.

'I want to go now. I want to see the animals,' Mark said.

'What's that lady doing, Mommy?' Viola asked loudly. 'Why is she holding that big bird in her lap?' She pointed at a large, darkly varnished Baroque canvas. Varnish-coloured female arms and legs were confused with brown clouds and the wings, neck, head, and beak of a whitish bird.

'Well, I don't know, darling,' Susy replied. 'I guess she's petting him.' She cast Katherine a look of adult conspiracy and suppressed laughter; Katherine did not cast it back.

'I want to go. I want to see the animals!'

'All *right*, Markie. I'll take them outside and let them run around for a while, Katherine. Don't hurry.'

Katherine walked down the gallery. It occurred to her what a very typical Los Angeles phenomenon it was, one which could be described in letters to acquaintances back East. They would hardly believe her, though; they would think that she was exaggerating. Also, just now there was no acquaintance to whom Katherine owed a letter; they all owed her letters. When she and Paul had been in Europe two summers ago they had got lots of mail, but not now, even in the same country with the same postal system.

'Quite a collection, isn't it?' a voice said immediately behind Katherine. She jumped. No one was there except the museum guard, the usual grey man in a grey uniform. He was looking at her, so he must have spoken.

'Oh, yes,' she replied.

'You should see the upstairs, too.' The guard swayed towards her like a pendulum, from the feet. 'Take a look at the bedrooms; see the Amours of the Gods tapestry.'

'Oh yes, well, some other time,' Katherine said. She began walking away backwards, smiling nervously, and did not stop until she had left the building.

Susy was watching the children in the courtyard. They returned to the car and drove on up the canyon to where the animals were kept. Here a more respectable aspect of Mr Putty was displayed, insofar as it is respectable to keep wild animals in one's back yard. The bear, the deer, the Rocky Mountain goats, the bobcat; all were housed in large outdoor pens; they did not appear especially unhealthy or ill cared-for, but they seemed discouraged and bored. They stood under the eucalyptus trees or lay about on the ground with the air of creatures who have been forcibly torn from their natural habitat, and wish and hope only to return to it. They did not have the hysterical stared-at gaze of animals in public zoos, but they looked at Katherine, she felt, as if they blamed her, along with all humans, for their being there—not realizing that she was their fellow.

'That's everything,' Susy said. 'Except the buffaloes. Do you want to see the buffaloes before we go?' Viola and Mark shouted that they did. 'All right. But it's a long walk. Let's go in the car.'

She turned up a dirt road marked TO THE BUFFALO. 'It won't take long,' she told Katherine. 'There's not much to see, they keep them in a big field and last time they were way over at the other side of it.'

The eucalyptus ended; they were now in an orchard of young citrus trees, five to six feet high, set out in rows. The road grew dustier and more irregular, and then came to a dead end in front of a high cyclone fence. 'Caution,' read a metal sign. 'Do Not Feed or Annoy the Buffalo.'

As Susy had said, there was nothing much to see: a few large dark-brown shapes could be made out, motionless in the dry grass, about a hundred feet farther up the hill. Mark was disappointed, and banged on the fence, while Viola shouted: 'Buffaloes! Nice buffaloes! Come here!'

The sun was falling, and it seemed pointless to stay. They all got back into the car. Susy started the engine and began to back down the narrow road, scraping the fenders against first one and then the other of its banks.

'Ouch! I'll scratch the car all up this way; Fred'll kill me.'

She drove forward again to the fence. 'I'm going to turn round here in the orchard. Hold tight.' Susy pulled the wheel to the left. The station wagon leaped up off the road on to the soft dirt. 'There. Now.' She put it into reverse, and stepped on the gas.

The engine roared, but nothing else happened; the station

wagon remained stationary. 'Oh, golly,' Susy said. She pumped the gas harder, and manipulated the wheel.

'Oh, golly,' she repeated finally, and got out to look.

'What's the matter, Mommy?'

'Stay in the car, children.' Viola and Mark did not obey her.

'Are we stuck, Mommy? Mommy, are we stuck?'

'No, darling. Get back in the car.'

They did not, so Katherine got out too. She walked back and joined the Skinners in the contemplation of a rear wheel half-buried in loose, sandy earth.

'Stand back, kids. Mommy's going to start the car now. Stay with Mrs Cattleman. Maybe it'll go now, without all of you in it.'

Susy got back behind the wheel and started the engine. Nothing happened, except that the rear wheels spun violently.

'I want to go home,' Mark cried.

'Why don't you try to rock it out?' Katherine called from where she stood with the children. 'Put it into forward, and then right back into reverse.' Susy nodded. 'And give it plenty of gas.'

'Okay.' With a shudder, the car leapt forward, but only a couple of feet, and stopped with a crunch, its nose buried in one of the young orange trees, which now stuck out ahead of the hood at an angle.

'We hit the tree,' Susy said, in a voice that was beginning to show hysteria. 'Do you think we killed it?'

'Mommy, let's go back!'

'It's only bent,' Katherine said. 'It'll be all right. All you have to do is back up a little.'

'I want to go home, Mommy.'

'I'll try that. Shush up, children, for heaven's sake. We *are* going home, as fast as we can. Stay with Katherine.'

Pulling the shift lever back into reverse, Susy gunned the car: the hood shook, and the engine roared; it also gave out strange pounding and snorting noises. No. That wasn't coming from the engine; it was something alive—

'Aooh! Aooh!' Mark saw it first, and began to scream; something rushing towards them down the hill, a charging mass of something dark and horrible. It was the buffalo: heads down, feet beating on the ground, like a huge mass of hairy carpet pads charging towards them.

Mark and Viola, screaming, flung themselves into the car; Katherine stood paralysed. The buffalo rushed towards her and towards the fence—but of course, there *was* a fence, Katherine remembered with a gasp, seeing it—then they wheeled round without even touching it and stood, pawing the ground.

'You see, it's all right. They can't get through the fence!' Katherine shouted, catching her breath. Mark and Viola continued screaming.

'They can't get out, lovey. Don't be frightened. There, there, Markie.' Susy gathered a child in each arm. 'Lord!' she said to Katherine. 'I was terrified, weren't you? I forgot all about the fence. I honestly thought they were going to attack us. There, there.' She opened the door with which she had shut her children away from the buffalo, and shut Katherine out to be trampled to death. Maternal instinct, Katherine thought.

Behind the cyclone fence, the five buffalo shifted restlessly about, glaring at Katherine. She could see them very well now. They had black, bulging eyes like wet rubber, and satanic horns; their shoulders were hunched and their legs knotted, ending in hooves. In front they were covered with masses of dirty, matted dark brown hair, but their hind-quarters were bare, like those of monstrous poodles. They snorted, and wheeled about, and jostled each other angrily.

'I don't like those buffaloes, Mommy!' Viola sobbed. 'I want to go home right now.'

'All right, darling.' As if she had not tried it before, Susy started the car, shifted into reverse, and stepped on the gas. Awhoor, whoor! Viola, Mark, the engine, and the buffalo roared.

'I can't get it out.' Susy's voice trembled. 'I just can't do it!' She burst into sobs, and the children followed her example. 'Oh, what'll we do now?'

'Don't cry. I'll walk back to the house and get somebody,' Katherine said. 'They must have a truck, or something. You stay there.'

'No, don't! Please, stop!' Katherine stopped, a few steps from the car. 'Don't do that. They'll be so angry at us. And then Fred'll have to find out, and he'll be furious!'

Her voice rose to a high wail. The buffalo, excited, stamped the ground and butted against the cyclone fence, making a clashing wiry sound. Viola and Mark continued to cry steadily.

'For heaven's sake,' Katherine said. She looked at the three Skinners as they sat howling hopelessly in their pink station wagon.

'All right,' she called over the noise of them and the buffalo. 'You can't go back, so you'll have to go forward. At least it's downhill.'

'But I'll knock the tree over.'

'You'll have to knock it over. Unless you want me to go and look for a truck. Just drive straight ahead, and you'll come out on to the road down there.'

'But—'

'Go on. I'll hold those other trees out of the way.'

'Okay.'

Susy started the car again, and let out the brake. The station wagon crashed suddenly forward over the tree, on past Katherine, and back on to the road. Katherine ran after it, scrambling over crushed leaves and white, broken wood, the buffalo roaring behind her.

'We made it!' Susy cried happily as she came up. The children had stopped howling, and were talking excitedly.

'We smashed the tree!'

'We're all right now! We're all right now!'

'Get in,' Susy said, flinging open the door. 'Before they catch us.' She giggled. 'Golly, I thought we'd never get out of that.'

They drove downhill away from the house, the Skinners still congratulating themselves. When they arrived at the gate, an electric eye opened it automatically to expel them.

'Golly Christ, am I glad to get away from there,' Susy said as she sat waiting for a break in the traffic. 'What an adventure!' She laughed. 'Gee, Katherine, you know you were wonderful! You really saved us. You know, children, if it hadn't been for Katherine we just probably wouldn't have got out of there at all. Honestly, you were so cool and collected.'

She turned on to the highway, back towards home. 'Oh, my goodness,' she added. 'You've ripped your skirt.'

Katherine looked down. Her narrow cotton dress was torn roughly up the side to the thigh.

'Gee, I'm sorry,' Susy said. 'That's the trouble with wearing skirts: something like this always happens. I hope you can fix it.'

'I can't fix it,' Katherine said. 'It's just ruined.'

'I'm sorry. I'll get you another one. It's all my fault. I'll tell you what, I'll get you some Capris. You ought to wear Capris on trips like this, anyway.'

'It's not important,' Katherine said in an odd voice.

Susy looked at her. 'Why, Katherine, what's the matter?' she asked. 'Why are you shaking all over like that now?'

Part II: VENICE

7

PAUL lay on his back, looking up into a fantastic jungle. Strange trees spread their marbled, many-coloured leaves; exotic flowers and vines twined round them, and creatures never seen on land or sea sat on the branches. There was a man with a bird's head, some winged lizards, and a dog that had an electric toaster for a body. Irregular white patches showed among the foliage, where the plaster had fallen from Ceci's bedroom ceiling.

Most of the painting was on the ceiling, though the trees rose from trunks sketched on the walls and gnarled roots descending into the moulding. One, perhaps the inspiration of the whole composition, began as a peeling hot-water pipe. The illusion was increased by the absence of any furniture in the room except for the mattress on which they lay.

Ceci was asleep, sprawled beside Paul where she had fallen after a last long climax, her legs still spread wide, her hair damp over her face. Her arms were flung out, the hands relaxed now next to the marks they had made in cloth and flesh: the sheet crumpled into folds; white scars, fast fading, on his arm.

He was very happy. With Ceci everything was so simple, so easy. She asked no questions about his life or his feelings; she said nothing about her own. She had no psychic or somatic complaints that had to be got through first; she did not make any declarations or demand any promises, only pulled off her clothes and gave herself to him. Was it always like this for her? He wanted her to wake up and answer this question; he wanted to hear that for her, too, it had been a unique experience.

'Ceci.'

No answer. It was strange to watch her lying there so close, naked, sleeping. Her head was tilted back, her mouth a little open, loose. Most of the girls he had known preferred to do it in the dark, or at least in the dusk. And they always pulled their skirt down or the sheet up afterwards, however boldly they might have shown themselves earlier. As if they were ashamed, or didn't trust him.

'Ceci.' He said it louder this time, impatient to establish communication. 'Hey, Ceci.' He turned on to his side, shifting her warm body with his.

'Mmm.' She moved her legs towards him, her mouth against his shoulder. 'Wha?'

'Hey. You were out cold, weren't you?'

Ceci opened her eyes, light brown today, almost yellow; she did not speak. They stared at each other for about four seconds.

'You,' Paul said, pulling her towards him. They kissed long and deeply. 'Is it always like this with you?'

Ceci had shut her eyes; now she opened them again: wide, golden. 'No,' she said. 'Sometimes.' She raised her head slowly, sleepily, supporting it on one hand, yawned, smiled. 'But I knew it was going to be like this for us.'

'How could you know that?'

'Easy. Because I wanted you the first time I looked at you.'

'Did you. Well, so did I.' Paul laughed. 'Love at first sight?' He felt embarrassed at having used the word 'love', so he laughed again, less easily. 'Do you really believe in that?'

Ceci lay back, pushing her hair out of her face. It fell on the sheet, streaked light and dark like frayed hemp. It wasn't dyed, though; there was a great tangle of the same colours between her legs. 'You know what I mean,' she said. 'Somebody you want right away; they're the only ones you can ever really make it with. . . . I mean you can try, with the others, but it won't swing. Like somebody you don't dig much at first, but maybe later on you get to talking to them and they turn out to be pretty intelligent and hip. So you get to know them, and finally you think, oh well, he's kind of attractive, I guess. When you try to make it with somebody like that, it's always a bust. It's just pretty sad, because probably by that time you're friends, so you keep telling each other that it's all right; sure, it's great. Uh-uh. If you don't want somebody right off, they've got nothing for you. I mean physically.'

'You're right,' Paul said. 'Yeah, I think you're right.' He sat up and kissed one of Ceci's breasts lightly, pulling up the large brown-pink nipple. Then he kissed the other one. But something bothered him. 'The trouble is,' he said, 'sometimes you want somebody very much and it still doesn't work out too well when you

[65

get them.' He realized that he was talking about Katherine. Whom had Ceci been talking about?

'Sure, that's true. Like with us, last time wasn't so great. I'm never much good the first time; I'm too charged up. Anyhow, your body's got to get used to somebody else's body. The better they know each other the better it gets.'

That wasn't true of him and Katherine, Paul thought. The longer they knew each other, the worse it seemed to get, at least for her. But he didn't want to discuss Katherine, or even think about her now. Instead he bent over and kissed Ceci again, this time under the breast where her tan ended. The line was so clear that she looked like a brown girl wearing a pink two-piece bathing-suit.

'I like it the way you have the mattress right on the floor,' he said presently. 'It makes me feel safe.'

'Mm?' Ceci spoke indistinctly against his arm, which she was licking dreamily.

'When I was a little kid, I used to be frightened all the time that there was a wolf under my bed at night. It was a story I read, the Sheep in Wolf's Clothing. I mean the Wolf in Sheep's Clothing. I used to hate to go to bed. I had to turn out the light by the door, and then I would take a running jump into my bed, so the wolf couldn't grab hold of my feet. Sometimes he stayed there under the bed all night long.'

'Bad.' She moved up towards his shoulder. 'Is he still there?'

'Oh no. Anyway, he's certainly not here.'

'Maybe he's squashed flat under the mattress,' Ceci suggested. She lifted her head. 'Hey. How about some lunch?'

'Lunch?' With surprise, Paul realized that it was daytime, probably still morning, of some definite day. 'Is it time for lunch?'

'Lunch for you, breakfast for me. I have to be at the gig at two.' Ceci stood up. 'How about if I blow us some eggs, and you can call it an omelette?'

Saturday. It was Saturday morning. 'Fine,' Paul said. He continued to lie on the bed, gazing at the ceiling. How fine everything was here, how easy. First you make love, then you eat. Everything you wanted and no strings attached. No regrets, no voices wailing about involvement and guilt and jealousy. It was so simple, so restful.

Cooking sounds came from the kitchen, mixed with jazz. Paul felt hungry. He sat up, gathered his clothes from where they had fallen, and began to dress. Saturday morning. Katherine was at home cleaning the house again, or maybe she had finished that by now and was out shopping. She would never schedule love before lunch. It was all right for him when the light was on, she had once said: he only saw her or the bedclothes usually; but she couldn't help seeing the furniture and the curtains and whether there were any cobwebs on the ceiling, and it distracted her. What would she think of Ceci's ceiling?

Katherine would dislike Ceci even if she never saw the painting on the ceiling and had no idea that Paul knew her. She thought beatniks affected; nobody would act that way, she thought, unless they *were* acting.

If she knew— But he didn't want to imagine that, and she didn't know. She wouldn't suspect; she had other things to think about. She had started working at U.C.L.A., and she was fixing up the house, if you could call it that. When he came home yesterday afternoon, he found her trying to move the sofa outside. It was a hell of a job, because the front door was so narrow. They finally managed to get it out, and into the garage, where Katherine covered it with a sheet. She said that Los Angeles was too dirty and gritty; if she didn't put her good things away they would simply be ruined.

Though she disliked their house, Katherine was also worried about their being thrown out of it. She had discovered that some of their neighbours across the street had got notices from the Highway Department to vacate by March first. Everyone on that block had received eviction notices, it turned out; the city was clearing the land for a new freeway. Katherine became hysterical, then, and made Paul call up their landlady.

Oh, there was nothing to get excited about, the landlady told him. She had inside information from her brother in the real estate business that construction wasn't going to start over there for a long time—two or three years, at least.

'You see, there's nothing to get excited about,' Paul had explained after he hung up. 'She's lying,' Katherine said, holding on to a chair in the middle distance. 'Wait and see. I suppose she's known about it all along, but she didn't say anything so she could get you to rent her house. Probably nobody else would have taken it. Probably everyone knew they were going to build a freeway here, right across the street, except us. You should have asked somebody before you signed the lease.'

And since then, Paul thought, Katherine had looked in the mailbox daily as if she wanted to find an eviction notice there whatever inconvenience it might cause her; it would prove the landlady a liar and her husband a fool. She hadn't said anything more about it, but he knew her well. Too well: maybe that was the trouble.

And Ceci? Not well enough: nearly all she said or did was like a collection of road signs in a strange language. He could remember coming upon such incomprehensible signs when they were driving through Europe. Screams of warning, perhaps—or directions to the heavenly city?

Massi caduti!
Gravillons Roulants 30

('Let's go back,' Katherine had kept asking; even then.)

Even more puzzling than Ceci's statements were her silences. She was the only girl he had known who did not say anything in bed. She asked no questions, made no requests, expressed no pain or pleasure; even when the room seemed to shake around them she did not cry out, only held him harder. At the end she gave a long, breathy laugh, the laugh of a creature that does not know any words. What did it mean? Was she happy, or was she amused? Was she laughing at him?

Fully clothed, Paul walked into the next room. It was roughly whitewashed and littered with junk—crates and plaster and broken furniture and cans of paint and heaps of newspapers. And a lot of drawings and canvases: crated, stacked against the walls. even piled on the floor. There was no easel, but propped up on an old trunk was a work in progress, a large painting in which black shapes of flames and rocks and tangled string were starting to rush across an empty white canvas. He stood and looked at this for some time. A lot of time and expensive oil paint had been used here. Ceci was an artist; that was what she really was. Not for the first time, he wished he knew more about contemporary art.

He went back through the bedroom into the kitchen. The record was still playing.

'Hi.' Ceci turned. She was wearing a man's old work-shirt, with the sleeves rolled up, open all the way down the front. Otherwise she was wearing nothing.

'Hungry? It's ready.' She pulled the pan off the stove, slid eggs on to a plate, added sliced tomatoes, green pepper, and onion, wiped her hands on her shirt-tail, pushed her hair back, and sat down. 'You can sit there.'

Paul walked round the kitchen table, past the kitchen chair full of Ceci, and sat. *Déjeuner sur l'herbe*, he thought. He might at least have left off his jacket and tie.

'This is great,' he said, referring to everything.

'Thanks.' Ceci smiled. 'You're sort of great yourself,' she added.

'So are you.'

They ate.

'What's so great about me?' Paul asked.

'I d'know. I guess what I like is, you've got a lot of go but you're not hung up on anything. And I think you're kind of happy with yourself, so you don't have to put anyone down.'

They smiled at each other. Ceci put her hand out across the table; Paul took it. He continued to eat with his left hand.

'You really trust me, don't you?' he asked. 'The way you went to sleep in my arms like that. You trust me like that and you hardly know me. How come?'

'You have to trust people. That's the way it is.' She shrugged. 'Sure, they might shuck you; but if you don't trust anybody you shuck yourself worse.'

This answer pleased Paul, but not completely; he would have liked it to include some testimonial to himself. Whom else had she trusted? He relaxed his hold on Ceci's hand; she took it back, and began to butter toast.

He tried another subject. 'I really like the way you paint. That big picture you're working on now. That's really interesting.'

'Which one?'

He described it.

'Aw, that's finished. I finished it last month; it's only still up there because I haven't done anything big since. I only blow a picture sometimes; you know, when I really feel like it. Here.' Ceci stretched across the table to put a piece of toast on Paul's plate, skimming the butter with her right breast.

'Thanks.'

She sat down again, but the breast did not make it back under her shirt; it remained outside, the full lower curve shiny with butter, the nipple pointed towards him.

'But what I dig most,' (he used her idiom rather self-consciously) 'is the painting in the bedroom. On the ceiling. That's great.'

Ceci put down her coffee cup. 'I didn't paint that,' she said. 'My husband made it.'

'Oh.' Paul had forgotten about the husband. 'It's good, anyhow,' he said. 'Is he a painter too?'

'He could be. He's everything. Only he's nothing. He's a shit. Let's not talk about him.' Ceci became visibly disturbed as she spoke. Unconsciously, she pulled her shirt together in front; the breast disappeared.

Paul made an effort, and began to talk about something else: Ceci's painting. He told Ceci that painting was very important and that she was very important. Meanwhile he kept thinking about the husband. Who was he; where was he? She ought to paint more and take it more seriously, he said. Then maybe she could have a show.

'What for?' Ceci sat back. 'So they can take my pictures away and put them in somebody's store, and then in somebody's house, like some rich square? Uh-uh.' She grinned, and put her elbows on the table. 'I feel like keeping my pictures.'

Paul grinned back. A good moment. She was a beautiful, a really original girl. But he kept thinking about her husband.

'What's his name?'

Ceci did not pretend to be puzzled. 'Walter.' She put her cup on to her plate, beginning to clear the table.

'Walter O'Connor.'

'Christ, no. O'Connor's my name. Walter Wong.'

'Wong?'

'Yes. He's half Chinese.' Ceci was standing up now, gathering plates. She looked at Paul hard, to see how he took this. He did not know how he took it himself, but he felt uneasy. What was he supposed to say?—Some of my best friends are Chinese—?

'My wife's called Katherine,' he volunteered, thinking he might at least reciprocate. 'She's really a nice girl, but she's very unhappy in Los Angeles.' These remarks sounded stupid. 'She misses the East.' Ceci, continuing to stare at him, gave no help. 'And she's sick, most of the time.'

'That's tough. I'm sorry. What's the matter with her?'

'Sinus trouble. She gets terrible headaches.'

'For Christ's sake.' Ceci put a pile of plates down loudly in the sink. 'Headaches! I thought you meant like she had cancer or something.' She wrung out a dish-rag. 'So you could still be making it with her, only you don't feel like it,' she said indistinctly, wiping the wooden table. Paul heard concern in her voice, and insecurity. She really cared. Maybe it was this that made him lie by implication.

'She doesn't feel like it either.'

'Only you still live with her. Like in the same house.'

'Well, yes. Only—' Paul paused.

His marriage had, up to now, kept him safe through the stormiest encounters: it was like an invisible aluminium armour against which the most passionate blows, either from within or from without, would always beat in vain. He had never deceived anyone—he always made it plain at the start that he was deeply committed to his marriage. As it happened, no woman had ever turned him down for this reason. Some of them broke out at once in a gale of sobs and protestations, subsiding eventually to sad looks and sighs. Others replied that that was just fine with them: they, too, did not wish to 'get involved'—but sooner or later there would be sulks and arguments, an odour as of something smouldering, rising sometimes to a sudden blaze in which fists beat on cushions and objects of apparel or household use were thrown. Paul was always strongly moved when he saw women in tears or in a rage. It roused both his affections and his passions; his warm heart leapt to meet theirs—but it, too, fell back, checked by the invisible armour.

He should have explained himself to Ceci already, but this time everything had happened too fast. Still, the sooner the better; he told her now. He said that he loved his wife and that she loved him, in her own way; he announced—what he knew to be true—that she needed him very much and that he could not leave her.

Ceci made no comment whatsoever. She shook detergent over the dishes in the sink, and turned the tap. A thin twist of brownish water came out of the tap. 'Damn it.' She turned both taps back and forth. 'Shit.'

'What's the matter?'

'The water pressure's gone off again. It's always doing that; sometimes we have practically no water in the building for days. I might as well leave the dishes and get dressed.'

Paul followed her into the bedroom. Why hadn't he left it alone? 'You didn't say anything,' he finally burst out.

'Say anything?'

'About what I told you just now.'

'What's there to say? I heard you.' Ceci pulled up the sheet and blanket, her back to him. Then, as if relenting, she turned to Paul and smiled, a half smile. He felt immeasurably relieved, reprieved.

Ceci took off her shirt and put on a black cotton jersey and a striped skirt. 'Don't you ever wear any underwear?' he asked.

'Don't have any.' Ceci smiled. 'It saves money.'

Paul laughed. But it also disturbed him. He thought of Ceci walking around Los Angeles, her secret parts exposed to the air and smog beneath her loose skirt. 'Don't you get cold in the winter?'

'What winter?'

'I keep forgetting.' Paul smiled. 'This *is* winter, here.'

Or waiting on tables in the Aloha Coffee Shop, he thought, with her full pink naked breasts rubbing against the sleazy starched uniform. It made him feel nervous, almost jealous. If he were married to her he wouldn't like it at all.

'What if you were caught in an accident?'

'Big bang for the cops.' Ceci grinned, looking up from fastening her sandals.

Paul saw a car smashed and smoking by the side of a freeway. Ceci was lying beside it, her eyes closed, her striped skirt wrenched up, her streaky gold hair loose at both ends, surrounded by gaping, leering policemen.

'Let's see,' she went on. 'Today is Saturday, tomorrow must be Sunday. Next week I'm on from eight to two every day. What're you doing Monday afternoon? Can you get off early?'

'Sure, I can get away for an hour or so. But I have to be back by four; there's a meeting. Why don't we meet for coffee, about two-thirty?'

'Uh-uh. That's no good. You know we can't make it here and back in an hour and a half.' She stood up. 'Two-thirty Tuesday?'

'All right.' Paul was bothered by her tone of passionate practicality. If they weren't going to make love, didn't she even want to see him?

Ceci opened the door. On the outside was printed in black crayon:

O'CONNOR

WONG

TOMASO

Paul looked at this as he went past. 'Who's Tomaso?' he asked. Cecil did not seem to hear him. They began going downstairs. Paul decided that he really wanted to know. 'Who's Tomaso?' he said again.

'This used to be his pad.' Ceci did not look at Paul. 'Damn, I forgot the garbage.'

She ran back up the steps; Paul continued to descend them slowly. O'Connor, Wong, Tomaso. What had he got himself into?

An odd aching feeling had begun in his stomach, and his hands felt tense and nervous. What was the matter with him? He was both excited and worried. What the hell was it? The feeling wasn't exactly physical; he remembered it from before, years before. But it had something to do with Ceci.

He stood still on the second step from the bottom. Yes. Now he recognized it: it was intense physical jealousy.

'Okay!' Ceci called out, hurrying down the stairs.

'Okay,' Paul called back, in an even more casual tone. After all, the whole thing was casual, uncomplicated. What he had always wanted. He stepped out on to the sidewalk and waited, smiling. As Ceci reached him, she looked up briefly out of her round, deeply fringed brown eyes.

No. It was no use pretending. Somehow, when and where he had least expected it, he had been caught.

8

ONE a.m. on Ambrosia Drive, high in the dry hills above the Strip. Glory Green went through her house turning out the lights. She should have been in bed hours ago—she had to be at the studio at eight—but she was too restless and depressed to sleep.

She stood in the archway of the long sunken living-room, her hand on the switch. The ten-foot artificial Christmas tree, pale pinkish blonde (it just matched her hair) had been put up and trimmed that morning by a professional interior decorator. Maxie had conned him into doing it gratis, for the plug. The tree was loaded with pink and silver balls and trinkets and candy. Three dozen little pink electric candles kept bubbling and winking off and on, and a music-box concealed in the stand tinkled 'Silent Night', over and over again.

Glory didn't go for it. In the first place, it was three weeks to Christmas, and by that time the whole set-up would be dirty and everyone would be sick of it. Besides, the silver angels'-hair that Maxie's gay-boy had spread all over everything in a last burst of inspiration, leaping from ladder to chair in his suède shoes, was too spooky. It reminded her of the scene in that old English movie —what was its name?—where the crazy old lady burns up in her room. Because long ago her boy friend stood her up on her wedding day, and she flipped, so ever since she's been holed up in this same room waiting for him to come back to her, in her ratty old-fashioned wedding dress, and spiders' webs over everything, especially this great big wedding cake. It was with Jean Simmons.

Glory had been photographed under the tree that afternoon, in a silver *négligé*. If Maxie was lucky, she would come out in one of the Sunday papers the day before Christmas: 'Miss Glory Green, opening some of the hundreds of gifts she has received this year from friends and fans around the world.' (The fag had brought the prop presents too, all done up in pink and silver.) 'The two lovable puppies, Castor and Pollux, are a special gift to Glory from the Suharaja of Banipur. They are Manx Spaniels, one of the rarest and most expensive breeds of dogs in the world.'

The Suharaja had wanted very much to be in the picture too, but Maxie wouldn't let him. It wasn't only because she was married now; the straight dope was that the Suharaja sounded a lot better than he looked. He was a dim little brown man with gold neckties who didn't speak English too good. It was just like the Suharaja of Banipur to give a girl something stupid for Christmas like two rare expensive dogs that weren't even house-broken.

He didn't have all that fabulously much loot either, ever since Banipur didn't need him any more. He wasn't really Suharaja of anything now. The way Glory understood it, he went and let his country have an election, and they didn't pick up his option, and now Banipur belonged to some people called the Christian Marxists. So he was out of a job. He was always hanging around Hollywood; Glory had dated him a couple of times before she met Iz, and now he was back again. Probably eventually some girl who wasn't making out too well professionally would marry him. If he was lucky it would be some decent kid that would really like him and give him a good time. But you couldn't count on the Suharaja's being lucky. More likely he would pick up a real little bitch.

Glory looked round the room, and sighed. She turned off the tree; 'Silent Night' and the candles stopped. Then she turned off the other lights. The room became a long cave of dark, soft shapes —spooky really. It was kind of scary living up here in the hills all alone.

She walked down the hall and through to her bathroom, turn-ing out lights as she went. She had already taken off her make-up and put five different kinds of skin conditioner on different parts of her face and body. Roger, the make-up man at the studio, would have been proud of her. He was always yakking at her about something she ought to use regularly every night, and mostly she never paid any attention. All that stuff interfered with a girl's private life.

She took a roll of toilet paper out of the cupboard and began wrapping it round and round her head to protect the pink-blonde bouffant hair-do that had taken three hours in Mr Gene's place that morning. Round and round, until she had used up half the roll and constructed a bulging paper turban. She pasted the edges of it to her face and neck with Scotch tape. Now, if she slept carefully, it would keep till tomorrow.

She glanced at herself briefly in the bathroom mirror, quite without vanity. For Glory, beauty was a dress she could put on whenever she wished to, and after twenty years she was tired of it. Since kindergarten she had worn it, walking through the city like a child wearing a golden coat, and people had grabbed at her as she passed, greedily, but only because she was stuck inside the coat. Now it was her working clothes, her uniform, and when she was at home she took it off, quite deliberately. In the mirror shiny patches of pink, greased face alternated with dry patches of white and blue medicated lotion, so that she looked like a freakish clown.

Iz should have been in the photo. Maxie had wanted her to call him up and ask him over, if you can imagine, but she wouldn't. So Maxie phoned Iz himself. He couldn't reach Iz at the apartment he'd taken over in Westwood, or at the University, where he was working on some research thing, so he called the office in Beverly Hills.—Did Glory tell you to call me? Iz asked. (She was listening in on the extension.)—Uh-uh, Maxie said, it was my idea.—I thought so, Iz said. It's the kind of thing I would expect from you. You really believe that I would come back just to pose for a picture so you can prove to everybody, the newspapers, that Glory and I are still living together.—There's been a lot of unfavourable comment, Maxie said. It's been now a month; people are speculating.—Well, screw them, Iz said. Tell them to hedge their bets. —You want to ruin this girl's career? Maxie asked. Is that what you want to do? All right, don't answer me now; think it over. Only why don't you have some consideration for her? It's a little thing, it's a nothing to you, a few minutes of your time. So why be a louse? —I have a patient waiting, Iz said. I can't discuss it with you now. Is Glory there? I'd like to speak to her. Glory shook her head violently. —Glory's not here, Maxie answered. —All right. Let me give you some professional advice, Maxie, Iz said. I'll give you this advice gratis, absolutely free. Go fuck yourself. He hung up.

Glory extinguished the bathroom and went on into her all-white bedroom. Her bare feet sank into thick white carpeting and white fur rugs; the opaque glass lamps threw soft fans of light

76]

along the white walls. She had always gone for this room. Iz dug it too; he had helped her shop for all the kooky white or near-white plants that stood along the sliding glass doors to the patio.

Iz had never liked Maxie in the first place. Before he met him he already didn't like him, because of Maxie's profession. Maxie had a more open mind; he liked Iz fine until he met him. And you couldn't blame Maxie, the way Iz treated him, like he was some kind of bug. When he heard they were getting married he kept shaking his head. —What are the fans going to think: a psychiatrist? he said. 'Whatsa matter, is she sick? Or maybe she's becoming an intellectual.' —What's wrong with that? Glory had protested. Jill St. John is an intellectual, I read all the time. Monroe married a writer. —Yeah, Maxie said, and look what it did for her. Anyhow, for you I don't see it.

Glory took off her white silk bathrobe. Her spectacular body was a very pale, glowing pink—she avoided sun-tan, because it photographed badly and dried out your skin. (The hair between her legs also matched the Christmas tree. Like her girl-friend Mona said, you have to keep up the property: never know when you'll have guests.) With her weirdly painted face and paper fez, she looked like one of those Egyptian gods who wear the heads of beasts.

Naked, she crossed the carpet, got into the huge bed, and turned out the light. Now the room seemed even larger than it was; funny-shaped shadows moved on the curtains, advanced and re-treated across the walls. Glory got up again, went over to the closet, and after some searching found and put on a pair of pyjamas which had never been worn except in publicity stills. It was dumb, of course, because if anything bad wanted to come and get her tonight a pair of white silk pyjamas wasn't going to stop them. She lay down in bed again, on her stomach, her paper turban disposed to one side.

Ever since Iz walked out on her, Maxie had been giving her trouble. —What am I supposed to do, he kept asking. What do you want me to say to the papers? Have a little consideration for my problem. Make up your mind: it's over; it's not over. —Why don't you ask Iz? Glory finally shouted. Because I don't know! As far as I'm concerned, we're still married! I'm merely simply waiting for him to come home. —Aw, now, Maxie said. Don't

[77

give me that. You threw him out, you got to ask him back. A man has his pride. —Listen, Glory said. He knew perfectly well I was putting him on when I said to split. I have some pride too. Any time he feels like it he can—

What was that? Glory raised her head. From outside came a noise like someone walking up the gravel drive. Wait. No: everything was quiet now. She lowered her head carefully again, turned on her side, and crossed her arms over her breasts.

Where was Iz now? What was he doing? Glory stared into the dark. She felt ugly and rejected. Like a goddess betrayed by a god, it made absolutely no difference to her that temples still stood all over the land in which her image was worshipped nightly by multitudes, that praises and petitions arrived daily from the faithful.

Two a.m. She wasn't going to sleep; she would look a mess tomorrow. And it was too late to take a pill; if she did that she would be dopey and stupid at the studio next morning. It was too late to phone up anyone, and if she did, what would she— There it was again. Somebody or something was out there, around the corner of the house near the living-room.

Hell, probably it was just some dog. But Glory knew that she would never sleep until she was sure. Without turning on any lights, she got out of bed and walked down the hall. Now that her eyes were used to the dark she could see the shapes of the furniture, the dim reflections from pictures and mirrors, the tall spiderweb silhouette of the Christmas tree against the window, the— Oh God. There *was* somebody out there: a man, standing near the glass doors.

In panic, Glory pressed the light switches in the hall. The rooms sprang up bright around her, the Christmas tree began to sparkle and play 'Silent Night'. She was exposed as if on stage.

She reached, fumbling, trembling, along the wall to turn on the patio lights, the pool lights, all the outside lights. For a split second as they went up she thought the intruder was Iz, because he had a beard. But Iz's beard was short and neatly trimmed—this man's was long and scraggy, and he had a pale, flat sort of Oriental face, like a villain out of the grade-B spy thrillers of her childhood. But the worst thing was the way he stared at her—totally without admiration or desire, rather with an expression of inscrutable disgust. For twenty years no man had looked at her that way.

He stepped forward and put his hand on the glass door. Glory could see and hear the inside handle turn. She opened her mouth to scream, as the beautiful victims had screamed in all those thrillers; as she herself had screamed on cue before the cameras. Only nothing came out; her throat had turned to cardboard.

But the latch held; the door remained closed. The man slipped off to one side. Wait. Wasn't that him around at the window, trying to open the window! But it was locked too. Was everything locked?

Now a nightmare chase began; Glory ran from room to room of her house checking the locks of the doors and windows, panting across her thick carpets, stopping to listen, afraid every time she pulled back a curtain that she would come face to face with that look of repulsion. He must be a pervert or something. Bathroom, bedrooms, dining-room, kitchen.

Finished, she leaned against the wall by the front door, breathing hard, and listened. Every sound to her now was the enemy walk-round her house, in every direction, rattling the doors. She ran back and forth aimlessly: a few steps one way, a few steps another. Down the hall in the living-room the Christmas tree went on twinkling and playing.

The telephone! She could telephone the cops! She grabbed the receiver off the wall and dialled O. 'Therth a man!' she lisped. 'A man here, trying to get in. I want the cops.' Her voice began as a hoarse whisper, but it came back to her as she spoke.

Ten minutes, they assured her. They would be there in ten minutes. But in ten minutes he could still smash a window, force his way in, and rob and rape and murder her. If only she had kept those dumb dogs; they might at least have barked. She was going to keep them in the first place so as not to hurt the Suharaja's feelings, but then one of them made a mess on the rug, and she screamed at Maxie to get them out of here.

Glory was still holding on to the phone, though now it was connected to nothing. Everything was quiet; she took a breath. She still didn't feel as if she could scream: 'There's a man here.' The way the girls shrieked in the films was all wrong. It was much scarier this way. She must remember how she had said that, if she got out of this: 'There's a man, trying to get in.'

[79

She hung up the phone, walked down the hall, and looked out. A dark shape was hurrying away along the edge of the illuminated pool, which glowed green in the dark. He dodged round the chairs and tables, and then stopped for a moment in front of a fat rubber sea monster, a pool toy that Maxie had given them. Was he flippy enough to be afraid of that? No. He picked it up, and put it under one arm. Then he ran into the bushes, out of the light, and disappeared down the side of the hill. Thank God he didn't turn round; she didn't want to see that look again.

In a few minutes the cops would be here. Her pyjamas were all right, but she probably ought to put on a bathrobe too. Suppose there was a photographer with them. Oh hell, she'd better call Maxie. His wife would flip, three a.m., but still—Glory began to rush up and down the hall again, this way and that, without reaching any objective. Maybe no bathrobe. It didn't look frightened enough. And turn off the damned Christmas tree. That was better.

As she stood dialling Maxie's number, she suddenly caught sight of herself in a gold-framed mirror on the opposite wall: her face a patchwork of dried cosmetic mud, her hair wrapped in a turban of toilet paper. Christ! No wonder he had stared at her like that! She began to giggle out loud with hysterical relief. Why, she looked like something out of a Dracula film.

And the cops would be here any minute. Frantically, as the phone started ringing in Maxie's house, she began to pull at her headdress and rub her face with her free hand. Shreds of paper fell all round her, but more clung fast, and the paint wouldn't come off.

Outside, a police siren sounded down the hill. Glory slammed the phone back and raced for the bathroom, shedding lengths of toilet paper. She made it in time. When the officers knocked on the door she was standing before the mirror, smearing green eye shadow on with her fingers.

9

'OH, hell,' came a voice from the kitchen.

It was late in the morning. Paul was just getting out of bed, for the second time; and the second bed. He had got into the habit of going to Nutting, working at his desk for an hour or so, and then leaving for Ceci's. She would usually be asleep when he arrived; but he had a key now and could let himself in. She slept deeply. Sometimes he managed to take off his clothes and slide into the warm bed before she woke up. He would get back to Nutting about two hours later.

He did this practically every day. He quieted his conscience by pointing out to it that nobody was doing any work in Howard Leon's department anyhow; they were always having coffee and telling stories; he got there earlier than anyone else and worked harder while he was there, etc. Anyhow, he was in no danger of getting fired. No one kept track of his comings and goings—if he wasn't in his office he might be on another floor, or doing research up at U.C.L.A. The history of the company still wasn't moving along very fast, but he had done a couple of popular-science-type articles that had gone over big. Leon had practically said that he could stay on another year if he wanted to. There would be a lot of advantages to that: for one thing, it would give him more time to finish the thesis. There would probably be a raise, too.

'Oh, hell!'

'What's the matter?' Paul called. 'Is the water gone again?'

'No, I am. I forgot to get coffee. I know what let's do—let's go over to the Tylers. Josie will give us some breakfast.'

'Okay.' Paul was pleased that finally Ceci was going to show him some of her friends. 'Who're the Tylers?'

'He's a writer. Really way out. They have five kids and a big pad over on Beach Street.'

'Five children? How can he support five children, if he's a writer?'

'Oh, he drives a cab for bread. Hey. What'd I do with my clothes?' Dressed only in the old shirt that she used as a bathrobe, Ceci knelt down and began rummaging in her closet. 'Here they are. Jesus, look at that hole. I've got to go over to the Goodwill again.'

Paul laughed. 'Is that where you get your clothes?'

'Mostly.' Ceci pulled the jersey over her head; there was a long rip under the arm, through which the curve of a breast showed. 'Sometimes I go to the Salvation— Wow. Do that again.'

'I've made the hole bigger,' Paul said a moment later. 'You can't go out on the street like that.'

'I can too. I'll hold my arm down, this way. Everybody will think, the poor chick, she has a gimpy arm. Besides, it's all I've got that's clean.'

'You're crazy,' Paul said fondly. He began to put on his shirt. 'How do you know these people, the Tylers?'

Ceci answered, but not immediately. 'They're friends of Walter's.'

Within his shirt, Paul made a face. Instinct told him to drop it, but reason, or what he chose to call reason, urged him on. 'You never mention him, do you?' he asked. 'It's funny, he's your husband, and I don't know the first thing about him.'

'What would you like to know?' Dressed, Ceci was brushing out her hair.

'I don't know,' Paul lied. 'Well, for instance; what does he do?'

Ceci glanced up at him. 'I can tell you,' she said. 'But it won't mean anything.' He went on looking at her, not letting her out of it. 'Okay. When I first met him he was washing dishes in the same place where I worked and taking courses at City College. Then he went into the Merchant Marine for a while. . . . Last year he was mostly reading for exams up at U.C.L.A., and he had a gig with a pool man.' She explained: 'Like he went round in a truck with this guy and cleaned out people's swimming pools. Right now he's pushing Fuller brushes.'

Paul clutched at the item that fitted into his frame of reference. 'Exams? Exams in what?'

'Philosophy. Master's exams in philosophy.'

They were both dressed by now; Paul moved over to Ceci and put his arm round her as if to take the chill off their conversation. 'Did he pass them?' he asked.

'Uh-huh.'

'Then he has an M.A. in philosophy. And he's a Fuller brush man? I don't get it. Couldn't he find a job teaching anywhere?' Paul remembered what he had heard from Fred Skinner about local discrimination against Orientals.

'He thinks teaching's a drag,' Ceci said. 'He only took the exams because he digs taking exams. It's like a kind of game for him.' She leaned gently against Paul, then stood aside. 'Let's go, huh?'

'Okay.' But Paul frowned. He wanted to understand Walter Wong in order to understand Ceci O'Connor—Ceci Wong she must be legally. Only the more he heard the less he understood either of them. He tried again. 'Does he like selling Fuller brushes?' he asked, trying to keep his tone light.

'Dunno.' Ceci smiled, taken in. 'He said it might not be so bad, only they screwed him on his territory. They sent him over to Hollywood, where nobody thinks about cleaning their place up, and they're not home all day anyhow. But he was telling me, Sunday, he's started going round at night now, and he's running into a lot of weird scenes.' She laughed, and was about to go on, but Paul interrupted her; again he had heard only one thing.

'You saw him this Sunday?'

Ceci stopped laughing, and stared at him coolly. 'Yeah,' she said. 'He was here to supper.' With difficulty, Paul made no comment. 'He makes it over here for supper every week, mostly, if you want to know.'

'I guess I want to know,' Paul said. He controlled his voice. 'I don't mean to get all excited about it,' he said. 'I know you're not involved with him any more or anything.' Did he really know this? 'Hell, I mean I have supper with my wife all the time. We don't communicate; we don't even talk much, but anyway, we sit at the same table and eat.' Now he was beginning to lie; he did talk to Katherine at supper. He grew ashamed. Ceci continued to look at him, waiting. 'Oh, hell!' he said, flinging out his arms in desperation. 'What's the matter with me? I don't want to act like this all the time.'

Ceci smiled; her eyes grew warm. 'You don't act like that all the time,' she said, moving over and rubbing against him a little, like a cat. 'Just sometimes.' She laughed; he turned and kissed her closely, wrapping his arms so far round that each hand held the curve of a breast. He still felt a little ashamed, so he kissed her

[83

harder, biting the inner curve of her lip. God, how warm she was, how great it was here; he would be crazy to ruin it.

'Y'know what I want?' Ceci whispered.

'No. What?'

'Breakfast.'

It was cool but bright outside. A white sun glared down out of a white sky on to the slums of Venice. All the scars and stains of the one- and two-storey frame buildings were exposed in miserable detail: the broken steps, the split shingles, the scabs of rust and paint on the bent iron railings. The narrow, deserted streets were pock-marked with holes and congealed lumps of tar and asphalt.

Paul and Ceci walked along cracked sidewalks with rough pebbly bites taken out of the kerbs; they passed abandoned storefronts, with windows painted over black, or soaped white. Some of these stores were deserted, but in others people seemed to be living. It was garbage collection day, and trash cans loaded with empty bottles, sticky smudged papers, rags, and half-eaten hotdog rolls stood at intervals along the sidewalk, lit as if on a great stage.

In this decay, only one thing was whole: the automobiles. Not all of them—there were many rusted old machines. But among them, and even more gorgeous by contrast, were cars of equal or greater age that gleamed with polished chrome and glass and chalk-white tyres — hot rods. Most were models of the early 1930s that had been more or less radically altered: their running-boards cut down, their metalwork rolled under at the bottom; one or two sported superchargers. They were freshly painted in all the colours of the TV screen: red, electric blue, neon green. Many were decorated with symbolic designs—lightning or red flames spurted out of the radiator and across the hood, or the whole front end of the car became a grinning monster with headlamps for eyes. They were impressive even asleep in the full light of day; roaring down the throughways at night they must be magnificent. Paul was glad he had left his car parked over by Ceci's place. It was no fun driving around in that old heap, but if he had one of those hot rods—

Well, and why shouldn't he have one? They couldn't cost too much. He wouldn't want to drive around in a car like that back in Cambridge, but nobody would care out here. He turned to Ceci and asked her.

'You want to buy one of these crazy shorts?' She began to laugh, pleased. Sure, she said, he could probably pick one up. There was always somebody around trying to unload a car. Steve Tyler might know of something.

They had come out of the maze of back streets now, into the main square of Venice. The ruins of its earlier glory—for at the turn of the century it had been a fashionable seaside resort—still stood: the long arcades, the graceful balconies, arches, and pilasters of coloured stucco. But it was all in the last stages of desecration. The cobbled streets were crusted with dried mud and trash, and dirty paper blinds sagged in the dirty windows. The open shops under the arcades sold gimcrack souvenirs, over-ripe fruit, and girlie magazines.

There were more people about here, but all of them, like the buildings, seemed damaged and soiled. Bums leaned and spat in the arcade in front of a dark, smelly bar; shapeless women in shabby clothes were out marketing, every wrinkle and scar on their faces revealed by the glaring sun. A beggar with no legs sat on the sidewalk; the newsdealer had dark glasses and only one arm. Bums and cripples and criminals, the dregs of the city (even of the continent) washed up on Venice Beach as if by a land-locked tide. This was a dangerous place, too; Ceci ought not to be living here in these back streets, alone at night in that rickety old building. Why, anything could happen to her. As they crossed the square, Paul tightened his arm round Ceci; she looked at him, and smiled.

'Like it? Crazy, huh?'

Paul was not sure what she meant; he compromised. 'I like you. Where's this place we're going?'

'Right over there.' She pointed up an alley to a one-storey build-ing of dirty cream-coloured brick. It must have once been a grocery store: faded red letters across the top spelled out GOOD-MAN'S PRODUCE MARKET. The shop windows had been painted over in irregular rectangles of red, blue, green, and white up to about a foot from the top. Ceci knocked at the door, which had a hole in it where the handle should have been, and called, 'Josie?'

There was no answer. Instead of knocking again, she went over to a garbage can that stood against the building, lifted the lid, rummaged about inside, and took out an old doorknob. She fitted it into the hole in the door, and turned it.

Paul went up two steps into a long, dim cave of a room. Here, as at Ceci's, practically everything was on the floor: plants, shelves of books, lamps, dusty pillows, and several mattresses with faded spreads. No wonder they called these places 'pads'. The only chairs were a couple of wicker and iron contraptions like the ones Katherine had brought to replace her own furniture, which she was gradually moving into the garage.

The upper three-quarters of the room were completely empty, with bare whitewashed walls against which drawings, newspaper clippings, poems, and photographs had been nailed or pasted. Painted directly on the wall, right up by the ceiling, surrounded by strange leaves and flowers like those in Ceci's bedroom, was the slogan DONALD DUCK IS A COMMUNIST.

In the centre of the room was a playpen, mostly occupied by a large inflated rubber beach toy in the shape of a green sea monster with red spots. It also contained a plump blonde baby about a year and a half old.

'Hello, Psyche,' Ceci said. 'Where'd you get your friend?' Psyche did not reply. 'Josie? Steve?' She pulled aside a curtain. 'Hi!'

'Hi,' replied a man's voice from beyond the curtain. 'Come on in.'

Paul approached and looked over Ceci's shoulder into a bed-room. Clothes hung from pegs on the walls, and there was a mattress raised about a foot off the floor on blocks. The blankets had been pushed into a heap on one side, and a man about Paul's age was lying under the sheet, with his head propped on one hand. He had a round, pleasantly ordinary face, and long, thinning fair hair.

'Hey, this is Paul. Steve. I mean, like, Paul Cattleman, meet Steve Tyler.'

'How do you do,' Paul said, helping to continue the joke, if it was a joke.

'Hi,' Steve said lazily. He looked Paul over, lowering his eye-lids and smiling just slightly. His blunt features took on a look of peasant irony and cunning, like Clever Hans in the folk tales. Paul felt that Ceci's friend might be waiting for him to do something which he could later ridicule or disparage.

'Hey, Josie.' Steve addressed the heap of blankets. There was no response. 'We had a big night last night,' he said. 'Didn't break up till about three, four o'clock. You should have been here. Where were you, anyhow? Wow, am I beat.' He blinked his eyes.

'You want us to cut out?'

'No, stick around. I've got to get up anyhow. Hey, Josie. Company.'

A sound came from the heap of bedclothes. 'Tellem t'go 'way.'

'It's Ceci.'

'Ceci.' The blankets moved. A thin, pretty blonde girl with nothing on sat up in bed, rubbing her eyes. On seeing Paul, she pulled the end of the sheet up over herself, but without haste or any exclamation of surprise. 'Hi.'

'Hey, Josie, this is Paul.'

'Oh, hi!' Josie did not inspect Paul as her husband had done. Her face opened; she smiled warmly. Paul felt that he would like her.

'I'm sorry we disturbed you,' he said.

'Aw, no. That's all right. Got to get up sometime and feed the kids. You want some coffee, or lunch or something?'

'Anything you've got,' Ceci said, smiling. 'We haven't had breakfast.' Paul wondered if she was telling Josie that they had just been in bed together. But Josie didn't seem to react. Maybe it was just her way; but more likely the Tylers already knew that Ceci was having an affair with him and all about him, whereas he hadn't even heard of the Tylers' existence before this morning.

'I'll make the coffee,' Steve offered. He swung his legs over the far side of the mattress and sat up. Paul realized that he too was naked. Turning his long, brown back to them, Steve pulled on a pair of blue jeans. Josie continued to sit in bed holding the edge of the sheet loosely against her breasts. Paul felt that if she knew him just a little better she would have got out of bed to dress. It was all innocent and natural. But he wasn't used to so much nature yet. He turned back into the other room; Ceci and Steve followed him.

'Where's all the kids?' Ceci asked.

'Oh, they're around somewhere.' Steve began to clean out a

huge coffee-pot. 'I guess maybe Starry took them down to the beach.'

'How old are your kids?' Paul asked.

Steve smiled, as if this question pleased him. 'Lemme see. Well, Psyche, that's her there, she's about nineteen months. Nathaniel's four, and Ezra's six. So Freya must be seven, no, eight now; and Astarte's ten and a half.' He held the coffee-pot under the water tap of the sink. As at Ceci's pad, a mere trickle of brown liquid came out. 'Hey, siddown, why don't you?'

Ceci sat, and so did Paul, on one of the long wooden benches at the kitchen table. He began to feel easier; he decided he liked this place.

Ten and a half. Either Steve and Josie were a lot older than they looked, or they must have been married pretty young. 'Unusual names,' he said.

'Nathaniel's for Hawthorne. Ezra's Pound, of course. The girls are all called after goddesses. That was her idea,' he added, grinning at Josie, who had just come into the room. She was wearing old blue jeans like her husband's, with the addition of a white T-shirt which clung to her small, pointed breasts.

'Hey, I hear you had a party last night,' Ceci said to her.

'Yeah.' Josie began to take food out of a dilapidated refrigerator with COOL, MAN painted in large letters across its door. 'It was kind of a great scene. You should have been here. Angus came over with some new sides, and Becky; and John was here with his guitar; and we had some beer, and everybody was singing like crazy. And then later, must have been about two, Walter fell in. How's about pancakes?'

'Walter,' Ceci said. It was not a question.

'Mm. Matter of fact, he might still be here. He passed out last night, and he wasn't up yet when I blew the kids breakfast. Let's see.' Josie walked towards the front part of the room. 'Yeah! Here he is.'

Paul looked where she pointed. On the floor, in a dark corner behind the hi-fi speaker, was what he had dismissed as a heap of blankets and coats. Now he identified a man lying face down among them, with most of his head covered.

'Hey, Walter,' Josie said gently. 'Do you dig some pancakes?' Paul tensed himself for the encounter.

But the man on the floor did not move. 'Leave him sleep it off,' Steve advised. 'Hey, I'll play you the new Adderly side Angus brought over last night. Cool.'

He put the record on. A medley of jazz sounds in a lazy, complicated rhythm began to issue from the speaker. Ceci and Steve sat down on one of the mattresses to listen to it. Paul sat down too, in a position where he could see if Walter Wong were waking up, by turning his head just slightly. Every time he did this, he became more uncomfortable. He didn't want Wong to catch him staring. On the other hand, he didn't want Wong staring at him.

He tried to concentrate. His enthusiasm for and knowledge of jazz had stopped about 1952; he found it difficult to follow this music. Anyhow, the etiquette of listening to jazz was something he hadn't caught on to yet. It was going all the time at Ceci's; sometimes she would stop everything and listen, but sometimes she wouldn't. Sure, it made a good background. There were a couple of records, for instance, that Ceci liked to make love to. One called 'Walkin'' especially. Sometimes, if she were already up when Paul came, she would put it on the player before she got back into bed. It had a slow, uneven beat that she said really sent her physically. By now, it had the same effect on Paul.

He had lost track of what was playing again. Ceci and Steve were still following closely; now and then they would exchange a smile, or Steve would say to them, 'Get this.' The baby sat in her playpen sucking her thumb and listening docilely. Back in the kitchen part of the room Josie was mixing up pancake batter and frying bacon. It was a pleasant domestic scene; except that there on the floor in the corner, not moving, out cold, lay Walter Wong.

They sat down to eat. Josie had made a big stack of hot pancakes, and there was syrup, jam, honey, and cheese. Another record was playing, or maybe it was the same one, but now nobody seemed to be paying much attention. They talked about music, about the different kinds of great pancakes they had ever had all over the United States and in Mexico and Europe, and about the poetry readings at the Gashouse. They discussed the troubles they were having with the local cops. The Gashouse might be closed down; one friend's studio had been condemned as unsanitary; another friend had been picked up for questioning because he was walking on the beach at five a.m. He had been taken to the station house, shoved down half a flight of stairs as if by accident, and released covered with bruises.

Paul would have liked to join in, to ask questions; but the silent presence of Walter Wong made him uneasy. They spoke of cars; Ceci told the Tylers that Paul was thinking of maybe buying one. Yes, he said, he thought he would. The car he had now was a 'drag', he said, testing their language; what he wanted was something more alive. He was going to go on, but he looked over his shoulder as he reached for the syrup, and fell silent. Nobody pushed him; maybe they knew what was bothering him, he thought.

'Hey, where'd you get the sea serpent?' Ceci asked between mouthfuls.

'Walter brought it over last night for the kids' Christmas present,' Josie said. 'I guess he lifted it somewhere.'

'Aw, come on,' Steve objected. 'You couldn't lift a thing like that. It's too big. Even Walter couldn't get away with that.'

'Walter can get away with anything.' Ceci poured syrup. 'You know how he got that hat Becky wanted so much out of Jax.' Everyone smiled.

'He gets all his clothes that way,' Josie explained. 'That's how come he looks so Ivy League.' Paul glanced again at the mass of crumpled material on the floor. 'Yeah, he goes up to Saks or Bullocks or somewhere and he takes like a new tweed jacket and puts it on and then he hangs his old jacket back on the hanger and just walks out. If anybody stops him he just makes like the absent-minded philosopher. Maybe he's got some heavy book with him and he's reading it all the time, you know. Okay, baby. Here you are.' She spooned pancake and jam into Psyche, who was sitting on her lap, her mouth open, like a plump, pink bird. 'I tried that a couple of times, only it's a lot harder for a woman on account of womens' clothes aren't all the same. When you go in with a blue dress on and come out with a red one the salesgirl is liable to tumble.' She grinned at Paul. He could not help smiling back at this friendly, ingenuous criminality.

'Walter's the most,' Steve said. 'How about how he lifted all the dishes and stuff for John's pad!' He looked at his wife and Ceci for confirmation, but he also looked at Paul, as if to say, Are you as much as Walter. 'John was staying here for a while,' he explained, 'but then he found this great new pad. He wanted to give a big house-warming party, Alice was cooking a ham and all, only they didn't have any dishes. So they all went over to the More Store, and John picked out some great Japanese stuff, all black and white. Then Walter got into the cupboard under the counter and found a big carton with Japanese writing on it, and began loading the stuff in. He was practically finished when this salesgirl chick came over and asked what was he doing. Walter looked at her completely blank, like he didn't understand one word, very Oriental, and went on packing. That stopped her for a bit, but pretty soon she began to say, like, Stop that, or I'll call the manager. So then Walter began to talk to her very fast, in Chinese and English all mixed up, like, Dishee no good, all no good for white peoples, makee velly sick, poison. And all the time he was shutting up the box and walking towards the back door. The chick just stood there, stunned; but then she started looking for the boss, but John and Alice came up and sort of surrounded her and began asking a whole lot of dumb questions about the stuff on the counters, and Walter walked out the back door looking like a delivery boy and nobody stopped him.'

Steve glanced at Paul. All right, he seemed to be asking, have you ever done anything that can stack up to that? Thank Christ, no, Paul wanted to say. But Josie and Ceci were watching too, laughing and waiting for him to laugh. So he laughed, and said, 'Where was all this, right around here?'

'Oh hell, no,' Steve exclaimed. 'It was at the More Store, over in Mar Vista.'

'Walter wouldn't boost anything from around here,' Josie explained. 'I mean like down here he knows everybody. He wouldn't shuck them here.'

'Hi, Mommy! Hi, Daddy! Hi, Ceci! We went wading. Starry said we could.' The door banged open, there was a rush of children into the room. Two, four, five, six—they couldn't all be the Tylers'; in fact, Paul noticed, one of them was coloured. Some ran round in circles, others flung themselves on Steve and Josie. 'I'm hungry!' they cried. 'Who's that man? Can we have some pancakes too?'

'Sure,' Josie said. 'Just let me up. Wow, you're all wet! Take off your wet clothes, everybody. Starry, help Ezra get his jeans off.

This is Paul, kids. He's a friend of Ceci's.' She stood up from under a heap of children. 'Okay, beat it out of the kitchen.'

'And cool it, everybody,' Steve said. 'Turn down the volume.'

Surprisingly, considering how casually their parents had spoken, the children stopped shouting and clamouring. They poured back into the front part of the room and began to take off their clothes. Then, as Steve, Ceci, and Paul left the table, they crowded up to it and took their places, quite unconcernedly naked or half-naked. But then, everybody in the room except Paul was partly naked: Steven with his bare brown chest and back, Josie in her skimpy shirt, Ceci who no longer troubled to conceal the gaping hole in her jersey. But it wasn't exhibitionistic: it was just natural and careless. What was this thing he was wearing anyway, Paul thought, this anachronism called a 'suit', with its flaps and pads and buttons that did not button? Why was he all wrapped up in these layers of cloth? There was nothing wrong with his body. No wonder Steve looked at him suspiciously. It's because I have to go back to work, he wanted to explain to them.

'We better split,' Ceci said to Josie. 'Thanks for breakfast.'

'Yeah, it was great,' Paul said. 'You're all great,' he suddenly added, and thought, at once, What a dumb thing to say. But Josie broke into a delighted smile, and even Steve looked more friendly.

'Make it over again soon,' Josie said. 'I'm sorry Walter never woke up. You should meet him.' They all looked over at the corner. The heap of clothes still lay there on the floor. Maybe he's dead, Paul thought. But no, it moved faintly, regularly.

'That's all right,' Ceci said. 'We can wait.'

10

IT was noon on New Year's Day. Katherine was getting ready to go to the beach with Paul. She did not want to go to the beach very much, or really at all. In the first place, it was the middle of the winter. Back East people were putting on their boots and shovelling snow, but Los Angeles was suddenly having a heat wave. Though it was hot out, and the sun was shining hard, the water would certainly be freezing. Paul wanted her to see what it was like, he kept saying. He had seemed very surprised when she agreed to go today, but she had decided she might as well get it over with. Once she had gone to the beach, Paul would stop talking about it. And the disagreeable man she was working for up at U.C.L.A. would stop teasing and persecuting her about how she had been living in Los Angeles for three months and never gone in the Pacific Ocean.

This man was one of the most annoying people Katherine had ever met. Luckily, the two other professors working on the grant with him were quite pleasant. They were reasonable, predictable, and considerate of her. Dr Smith was a large, rather stout professor of experimental psychology from Illinois; Dr Haraki was a small, rather plump professor of sociology from Berkeley. They came to work on time, read their fair share of the relevant previously published material, and dictated sensible reports on it to Katherine. They paid serious attention to planning the project: A Preliminary Study of Some Relationships Between Perception and Delinquency was its official title.

Katherine preferred working in the humanities, but unfortunately that wasn't where the grants usually were. She had had employers she liked better; still, Dr Smith and Dr Haraki were all right. Only Dr Einsam was impossible.

In the first place, he wasn't even a professor at U.C.L.A.; he just had some sort of temporary research appointment. He was really a psychiatrist, with an office over in Beverly Hills. Although Katherine had never met a psychiatrist before, either socially or as a patient, Dr Einsam exemplified her prejudices against the profession. He was lazy, untrustworthy, and opinionated. He came late to meetings, having read different articles and prepared different outlines from those he had promised to read and prepare, or none at all; and in discussions he kept introducing topics that had little or no connection with the project. He thought he knew everything. He ridiculed and contradicted his colleagues to their faces, and they did not object, out of good nature, or out of fear. And he ridiculed Katherine. He asked her personal questions, or made personal remarks, in front of everyone. Last week he told her that he liked the shoes she had on better than the ones she was wearing to work before, because they were more feminine; didn't Bert and Charlie agree that these shoes were more feminine? So then they all looked at Katherine's feet. Dr Smith said that he had never noticed the other shoes; Dr Haraki, who was really very sweet, said that he had never thought any of Mrs Cattleman's shoes were masculine. No, not masculine, Dr Einsam said. Neuter.

Besides, he dictated too fast.

Oh well, it was only for six more months. Katherine put on her bathing-suit, and packed a canvas bag with towels, sun-glasses, suntan lotion, a white rubber bathing-cap, and a white sweater. Over her bathing-suit she put on a pair of brown slacks and a brown and white flowered shirt which Susy Skinner had persuaded her to buy last week at the More Store. Then she tucked under her arm those parts of the Sunday edition of the *New York Times* which she had not yet read. (It takes four days for the *Times* to reach Los Angeles, so this was last Sunday's *Times*. Paul and Katherine bought it when it arrived on Thursday and saved it to read on Sunday morning.) She went outdoors into the glaring sunlight, and got into the car, where Paul was already waiting.

Paul was careful to take the most scenic route to Venice Beach, along Centinela Boulevard and then up and down over the hills of Ocean Park. But Katherine watched the streets wheel by without interest. Los Angeles all looked the same to her—flat, crowded, vulgar. When she rode up to U.C.L.A. on the bus the houses grew a little larger and cleaner, and the grass greener. Now they became smaller and dirtier, and the yards grew brown. That was all.

'Look!' Paul said, as they came to the top of the last hill. Ahead, at the bottom of the sky and extending as far as she could see in either direction, was a band of bright grey material, glittering so that it hurt her eyes. 'There's the ocean!' Paul cried. Katherine said nothing; they plunged downhill again among the dirty houses.

Deliberately (he had scouted the area beforehand) Paul stopped the car on one of the better streets in Venice. His effort was futile. Standing on the sidewalk, Katherine glanced round with distaste at the unpainted houses, the dusty gardens planted with pots of cactus and bird-of-paradise (the coarse blue and orange plastic-looking exotic flower that is Los Angeles' official emblem), and the designs in shells and coloured gravel. Nothing else was in bloom here now: the rose bushes that Paul had seen a week ago had been pruned back almost to the ground and now looked like large insects half-buried in the sandy soil.

At the end of the street, nearer now, was a glittering grey rectangle, which grew longer and brighter as they approached and finally opened out into a great blank panorama of air and water. Now they were on the Promenade, a long, paved walk open to the beach on one side, on the other lined with tawdry shops and houses, many boarded up for the winter season. Wooden and concrete benches had been placed along the edge of the sand at regular intervals, facing the ocean. On these benches, which stretched as far as Katherine could see, old people were sitting, waiting to die. They were dressed in their good clothes: the men in worn, shiny suits, the women in print dresses and coats and stockings and dark shoes. Almost all of them wore hats. A few were reading newspapers, or talking to themselves or a neighbour; but most simply sat, staring ahead, the hot noon sun shining down upon their clothes and their shoes and their dry, knobby hands. The wind blew into their faces across four thousand miles of empty ocean.

Katherine turned her head away, feeling self-conscious, as she and Paul walked along the beach past bench after bench. Paul apparently had some particular spot in mind, lord knows why—as far as she could see it was all the same. For miles in each direction the thick, bright grey sea sloshed against the pale brown sand. The beach was relatively empty—a few swimmers sat on mats; here and there drunks lay against the low wall by the walk, sleeping off last night's debauch in the sun. Farther down towards the water, where the slope of the beach changed, seaweed was drying in disordered heaps, investigated by gulls and sand-flies.

Now Paul stopped, in the middle of nowhere near a trash can, and dropped his towel on to the sand. 'I'm going in,' he announced. 'Coming?'

'Maybe later,' Katherine temporized. 'I want to sit down first.' She knelt, and began unpacking the beach bag.

'Okay.' Paul started across the beach towards the Pacific Ocean, first walking and then breaking into a half-run. He looked silly, Katherine thought, bouncing over the sand that way and waving his arms around. She watched as he jogged across the wet shingle and into the water, which sent up a heavy grey-green wave, edged with suds, to stop him; then she turned away. She spread the towels out side by side, weighing down the corners with shoes. Then she took off her new slacks and shirt. 'Those'll make your husband sit up and take notice!' Susy had predicted; but they hadn't. Paul noticed nothing about her any more. They hardly had any real talks lately at all, except a few times about history or sociology. He was always busy. It was probably all the fault of this horrible place and the horrible job he had.

Opening the bottle of suntan lotion, she greased her white arms, legs, shoulders, and back; she put on her sun-glasses; then she lay down on her stomach, facing away from the water, and began the *New York Times Magazine Section*.

It wasn't unpleasant here, she thought, as she turned the pages. And her sinuses hardly hurt at all today. But it was scarcely worth going to all this trouble just to lie in the sun and read the paper. To do that, she need only go out into their own back yard, where there was no sand to get into her clothes or wind to blow the pages around. Of course she never did go out into the back yard; it was simpler to look at the paper indoors, sitting up. Lying down to read, like this, always made her feel sleepy. Katherine yawned, and slowly lowered her forehead on to the first page of an article titled 'Education in a Changing World'. In the intense sunlight the type shimmered, blurred into illegibility. She shut her eyes.

She was aroused by the sounds of voices and a portable radio playing jazz. Squinting out from under her arm, she observed the approach of a group of young natives, all extremely tanned and freakishly dressed. She assumed and hoped that they would pass on. But they did not. Although there was plenty of room on the beach, they spread out a straw mat and sat down not fifteen feet from Katherine.

Katherine turned her head, and observed the natives with displeasure over her shoulder. There were three of them. They must be some sort of actors or beatniks, because both the men had beards. One, who was large and blond, had a blond beard, tightly curled; the other, who was small and wiry, had a straggly brown one. They wore the barest pretence at bathing-suits, brightly-coloured briefs that clung indecently tight, while the girl was spilling out of her bikini in every direction. Really it was pretty disgusting, on a public beach.

Katherine started again on the *Times*. But the wind, blowing off the ocean, blew the music towards her, a frantic, insistent hum. She sat up and looked round again, crossly. And now she became aware that the natives were staring at her, all three of them quite shamelessly, out of their dark glasses. Since they were lying farther down the beach towards the water, they could look without turning their heads.

Katherine's bathing-suit, which covered her more than adequately, began to feel too small, especially in back. She recalled that she had not shaved her legs for several days. But she certainly wasn't going to be forced to move. After all, she was here first. She lay down again, on her back, and put her white sweater over her face, completely covering it. For some reason this reminded her of the classic college anecdote, about the girl who was on her way to her room from the showers, with nothing on but a small towel, when suddenly she saw the janitor coming down the hall. Quick as a flash, she whipped the towel off her body and wrapped it round her head, preserving her anonymity forever.

Dots of sun shone through the wool and into Katherine's eyes. She lifted the sweater and looked down the beach. The girl in the bikini had her head down now, her long, bleached hair spread over her face; but the two men were still staring in Katherine's direction. Really, how *rude*. Where was Paul? There, down by the water. He had progressed no farther into the Pacific Ocean, but still stood waist deep, waving his arms, rebuffed by wave after wave.

With irritation, Katherine sat up and began piling her things on to one of the towels. Then she stood, took hold of one end, and dragged her possessions away along the sand until she was about thirty feet from the intruders.

It was at this moment that Paul decided to come out of the water. He walked up the beach, not towards Katherine, but towards the natives. For a moment she feared that he was going to say something rude to them on her behalf and start a fight, so she beckoned nervously to him. He waved back, but went on, though more slowly. The men sat up as Paul approached, the girl in the bikini raised her head. Now he had come up and was shaking hands with them, one after the other. What in heavens' name was going on? Paul pointed down the beach towards Katherine, and waved at her to come over. Then, as she did not move, he ran towards her.

'Come on,' he called as he came near. 'These people want to meet you. One of them is the guy that has the car I'm thinking of buying. He's going to show it to me today.' He stood beside her now, still panting from his exercise, dripping salt water. He picked up one of the towels, shook it out, and began to rub his hair.

'Oh, I see. I wondered how you knew them.' Though relieved, Katherine did not sit up. 'I had to move all our things away because they had their radio on so loud,' she said. 'I don't want to meet them. What should I meet them for?' She laughed a little. 'I just couldn't believe it when I saw you talking to them: how could you ever know people like that, I thought. Did you ever see such dreadfully vulgar bathing-suits?'

Paul hung the wet towel around his shoulders. He grinned briefly at Katherine, but made no answer. 'He wants to show me the car now; it's parked near here.'

'All right, go and look at it.' Katherine lay down again. It was no concern of hers what car Paul bought, or from whom. All cars looked the same to her.

'Aren't you going in? The water's great.'
'I don't know. Maybe I will later.'

Neither Paul nor Walter Wong spoke as they walked up the beach, casting occasional covert looks at each other. Paul was feeling very uncomfortable; he had not expected Walter to be here today. He had come to meet a friend of the Tylers named

Kelly who was going to Mexico and wanted to unload his car. It sounded pretty good—a 1932 Ford with a '45 Ford flathead V-8 engine. It was a 'street drag' (the term 'hot rod', he had learned, was obsolete) equipped and tuned for riding around town in, rather than a 'competition drag' intended for racing.

But Kelly had already left for Mexico, it turned out, and had asked Walter Wong to sell the car for him. Paul did not want to derive anything more from Wong, or have any further dealings with him. He was going to go through the formalities of looking at the car, because that was socially easier than refusing to see it, but he wasn't going to buy anything.

It was a long way to where the dragster was parked, and his feet slipped in the hot sand. He was tired from his struggle with the Pacific Ocean, and had difficulty keeping up with Walter, who moved rapidly ahead up the beach, spraying back sand with his thin, knobby feet. How the hell did Ceci ever get mixed up with this skinny little creep? Will you look at that scraggy beard, like Fu Manchu or something. And he sells Fuller brushes for a living.

'That's her.' In an alley off the ocean front Walter and Paul stood before a beautifully preserved Ford coupé, shiny jet-black with dark green trim. Paul wanted it at once, in spite of his resolution. He walked round, looking it over.

'What kind of brakes has it got?' he asked.

'1956 Mercury brakes and wheels in front, '46 Lincoln brakes in back.'

'Hm,' Paul said, impressed. A technical discussion followed. Walter Wong opened the hood, pointed out what he said were two Stromberg 97 carburettors on the engine or 'mill', and started the motor. Gradually Paul became less exclusively conscious of their conflicting relation to Ceci, and more aware of Walter's patience, automotive knowledgability, and even a kind of wry charm. The more he saw and heard of the Ford the better he liked it. After all, he began to say to himself, it's not Wong's car. But for bargaining purposes, as well as to discourage his own covetousness, he continued to denigrate it mildly ('I was hoping to pick up something with fuel injection').

'Why don't you take it over yourself?' he asked presently. 'You could use it for your sales work; it ought to make a big impression on the customers.'

Walter shook his head. 'I've got a car. Anyhow, I've quit the brushes.'

'Yeah?'

'Had to.' He leaned back against the Ford, under the open hood. 'You have to hustle too much on these commission deals. Like you've got to have the salesman's mentality.' He smiled. 'You know: the Protestant ethic. I was running into some real swinging scenes, but I wasn't making any bread. I've got a new gig now.'

'Oh? What're you doing?'

'I'm an exterminator.' Walter pantomimed squirting with a can of Flit. 'Universal Insect and Rodent Control. Like ants, roaches, spiders, silverfish, mice, rats—all that.'

Paul laughed, though a little nervously. Looking at Walter Wong, with his strange thin beard, his hard brown arms and legs, his brief bathing-suit patterned in black and yellow, he thought that he could not have chosen a more suitable profession. But was he the Pied Piper or the leader of the Insects and Rodents?

'Rats?' he said. 'Do you really have rats in Los Angeles?'

'Do we have rats? The place is crawling with them. All kinds. The worst are the big ones up in the palm trees.'

'Oh, come on,' Paul said. He looked up. Not far away, the dry, brittle fronds and rough trunk of a palm broke the pale expanse of sky. 'Rats in the palm trees?'

'Man, I'm telling you,' Walter said. 'We don't take care of them —it's too much for us. The city has to do it. That's why you see those big yellow trucks going around all the time stripping the trunks, like so the rats can't climb up there. You watch them some time when you see one of those trucks. It's some fun. When they start on an old tree, wow, you'll see those bastards jumping off it and running to beat hell in every direction. Crazy!' He grinned.

Paul did not believe this. He decided that Walter was trying to make fun of him. Well, he would show that he wasn't taken in. 'Yeah,' he said dryly. 'It must be almost as much fun as when they chased the Japs out of town.' As soon as the words were sounded he remembered that Walter Wong was half-Chinese.

Immediately, Walter's whole face changed. His amused smile was wiped off as if with a sponge; his expression became impassive —Orientally impassive. Paul knew he ought to apologize, but before he could arrange the words, Walter began to speak in a flat, slow, anonymous voice, a completely new voice, making some complicated remarks about the car and what sounded like 'Iskenderian cams'. Paul did not try to understand him.

'Uh-huh,' he said as soon as Walter had stopped speaking. 'Listen, I'm sorry about that crack. I guess I just wasn't thinking.'

'Yeah,' Walter said, leaning against the car and staring into space. His voice altered slightly in the direction of humanity. 'It's like we minority groups have got to stick together.'

'I guess so,' Paul agreed heartily, unsure of what was meant.

'That's the way it is. What minority group do you represent?' Walter turned his head and looked at Paul.

'Well, I,' Paul said. 'I guess none.' He realized that he was making it worse. But Christ, he couldn't do more than apologize.

'Oh no,' Walter said slowly. 'Can't be. You've got to belong to some underpriviledged order, or Ceci wouldn't be interested. That's her kick, see. I thought maybe you were a Jew. But hell, of course she's already had a Jew. Funny.' He stared impassively but insolently at Paul, who thought, well, I insulted him, now I suppose he has to insult me.

Leaning against the shiny fender of the car, Walter eased a cigarette and a folder of matches out of his trunks, and lit up without offering Paul anything. 'How're you making it with Ceci these days?' he said suddenly, in a friendly voice.

Paul flinched. 'All right.'

'She's a real cool chick,' Walter continued, in a tone almost of self-parody. 'She really is.' Paul thought he recognized a move towards establishing masculine solidarity, but he didn't want to get together with Walter over this topic. He said nothing. Walter looked at him; then he went on, 'She's always on some new kick. You met that Tomaso yet, that crazy Mexican runner?' Paul shook his head stiffly. 'A long-distance runner, man. He's big in the track world. Like he's broken all kinds of records for endurance.' He gave Paul a malicious smile.

'Never heard of him,' Paul lied briefly. (O'Connor, Wong, Tomaso.) 'Hey,' he said. 'How's the muffler?'

Walter stared at Paul, his face impassive again. 'It's the best, man,' he said. 'Dual straight-throughs with scavenger tail-pipes.'

'I think I'll take a look at it,' announced Paul.

'Yeah,' Walter said. 'Why don't you do that?'

Paul lay down in the dust and gravel of the parking lot, and awkwardly eased his head and shoulders under the side of the Ford. As he looked up at the underside of the car, he heard the door open, and metal grate against metal. Suddenly he had the conviction that Walter was going to release the brake so that the car would run over him—he would say afterwards that it had been an accident. In a panic, as fast as he could, he scrambled out from underneath.

He got up. Walter was standing on the opposite side of the car, leaning against the open door. His face was expressionless, but he raised his eyebrows as he saw Paul. 'Wow,' he said. 'What happened to you down there?'

Paul became conscious of a stinging pain in his right shoulder and arm; he saw that he had scraped it raw against the gravel and cinders, while the rest of his body was blotched with dust and grit. He tried to brush himself off, thinking that it was even possible that Walter had just been trying to frighten him. He said nothing.

Watching Paul, Walter began to smile. 'Hey!' he said. 'I get it now. I know what group you represent. You're a square.' He laughed. 'That's it, man.'

Paul felt that he had never disliked anyone in his life as much as he now disliked Walter Wong. If he hadn't really wanted the Ford he would have walked round it and hit him. 'Oh, fuck it,' he said. 'You want me to buy this heap, you better knock off that kind of talk.'

For a moment they faced each other across the open engine, with the expressions of enemies. Then Walter put on an innocent Oriental houseboy air, and turned his hands out, palms up. 'What you want, man?' he asked. 'I talk to you the way I feel. You want me to give you some used-car-lot pitch, "oh, you're such a hot guy, boss, such a great cat, I love you so much I want you to have this fine car, this colossal deal"?' He shut the door of the Ford: blam! Then he walked forward and shut down the hood with a crash so sharp that Paul, already in fantasy its owner, feared he would hurt the finish.

'All right,' Paul said. 'How much does he want for it?'

Walter turned and looked at him, his hands still resting on the hood of the car. Then, very slowly, he smiled. 'What's it worth to you?' he asked.

After sitting on her towel for a little while longer, Katherine got up and walked towards the ocean—partly to escape the continuing stares of the large bearded man and the girl in the bikini, partly to have an answer for disagreeable Dr Einsam, who would be sure to say to her: 'Did you go into the water?'

She picked her way through the heaps of rubbery wet seaweed, and down a slope of coarse brown sand. In front of her the ocean flung itself again and again on to the beach, lifting a solid heap of dark green salt water which broke into foam against the sand, then another. A shallow sheet of cool water came up and licked her feet after each attempt. Reassured, Katherine took a few steps forward. As the water went out, each time, it left a crust of pebbles and bubbles on the shore, and sucked grains of sand down the slope and over Katherine's feet. The rhythm was restful. She forgot for the moment that she was Mrs Katherine Cattleman, thirty years old, a native of Worcester, Massachusetts, an employee of the University of California, a sufferer from chronic sinusitis. She looked out to sea; her eyes rested on the long peaceful horizontal line where air and water seemed to meet. Nearer in she could see the waves rising and advancing towards her, growing larger.

She walked forward; her knees were wet now, and now her thighs; she felt spray on her face. Suddenly the sea came up and pulled at her. Katherine tried to step back, but the ground was uneven, and the undertow had already buried her feet in sand. With a great effort she freed herself and, almost falling, struggled back out of the ocean.

A DAMP night. Fog blew in from the sea steadily, smothering the beach towns; the neon lights along Venice and Washington Boulevards smouldered, sending out plumes of coloured smoke. Ceci clung to Paul's arm, but it was he who had to be guided as they made their way through the black alleys behind the beach.

'Here.'

She stopped before a shabby store-front, so dimly lit that Paul would have passed it by without a second look. The windows were heavily misted; here and there drops had gathered and run down, leaving a crack through which yellow light seeped.

They entered. A long, very dark room, a jumble of wooden tables and chairs, walls scrawled from floor to ceiling with draw- ings and writings, all obscure in the gloom. On every table a squat candle, the kind lit in churches, burned in a glass container—each soft flame flickering in a pool of coloured wax.

'We're early,' Ceci said, looking round at the empty tables, on some of which games of chess were set up ready for play.

'It's ten-thirty.'

'Mm. This place doesn't really heat up till around midnight. Well.' She slid on to a bench by the wall.

Paul sat beside her and looked about. In the rear corner two men in shirts and sweaters were playing chess. A small dark girl, with curly black hair that hung over her face like a poodle's, sat with them. Otherwise the room was empty. Paul removed his raincoat. He had dressed for the occasion: the chino pants spat- tered with house paint were his own, but the oil-paint-stained sweat-shirt had been borrowed from Ceci. She had even dug up a pair of sandals for him; a little too small, but not much. As a final gesture, he had decided not to shave that morning. It was wonderful how much difference it made to get out of the tight case of fabric he usually wore. In these old clothes he felt as if he could really move, swing his arms, jump, run.

'Hiya, Dinny,' Ceci greeted the girl with the poodle haircut, who had come over to him. 'This is Paul.' Dinny smiled prettily at him, but said nothing. As nearly as you could tell in the gloom, she was wearing only a pair of orangish tights and a baggy grey sweater. 'Who's winning tonight?' Ceci asked. 'Is Leo beating again?' Dinny shook her head. 'Cool. Expresso, I guess. What d'you want, Paul? . . . Two Expressos. You want something to eat?'

'Sure, I'm starving. What've you got?'

Dinny, though addressed directly, still said nothing. 'How about some of that pastry?' Ceci asked. 'Dinny blows great pastry. Have you got any of that way out cake tonight, you know, with all the different-coloured layers?' Dinny nodded. 'Great. Bring us two of those.'

'Hey. Why doesn't she ever say anything?' Paul asked in a whisper, as soon as Dinny had disappeared behind the curtain at the back. 'Can't she talk, or something?'

'Uhuh.' Ceci did not whisper. 'She can if she wants to. Only Dinny just doesn't dig words. Like she doesn't relate verbally.'

The two men studying the chess-board gave no sign of having heard this, though they must have done so. Well, maybe we all talk too much. Paul fell silent himself, just looking around and enjoying being there. Then Dinny brought coffee and cake, the Expresso steaming black and hot, the cake cold and thick with whipped cream. What a great place. Why hadn't he been here before? Because he never saw Ceci at night, when Venice came alive; that was why.

'I like it here,' he said. 'Look at those plaster flowers along the moulding; I wonder what this place used to be. You know, Venice was an elegant resort town about fifty or sixty years ago. Named after the real Venice. I've been looking up the records: lots of these streets were canals then. There were about fifteen miles of canals, all of them built out of concrete by a retired manufacturer from the Middle West named Kinney, who wanted to make this a big cultural centre. He put up all those arcades and imitation palazzos in the square, and he got gondolas with singing Italian gondoliers to take the tourists from the railroad station to their hotels. I've seen pictures; the men in straw hats and knickerbockers, and the women all got up in white, like Gibson girls, with parasols. He brought Sarah Bernhardt to play *Camille* in an auditorium he built on the end of the pier, over the waves.'

Ceci did not seem to be listening very hard; she looked at the candle flickering on the table dreamily. 'Right around here, right up the main street, only it was a canal then, there was an out-door restaurant with hanging gardens called l'Esperanza. . . . What are you smiling at?'

'You,' Ceci said. 'You're funny. How come you're all hung up on the past like that?'

'Well, hell,' Paul said. 'After all, I'm a historian.'

A diversion was created now by the entrance of a group of extremely beat-looking people: men in turtle-neck sweaters and dark glasses, girls tightly wrapped in black, high-heeled, and dangling with coloured beads. 'Who're they?' he asked eagerly.

'Never saw them before.' Ceci studied the newcomers as they took their places at a table by the door, then turned her head away. 'Tourists,' she pronounced scornfully. 'Yeah. They're all tourists. Ever since that piece came out in the paper some of them always make it down here on week-ends to see the beatniks. Maybe try to buy some pot or pick up a free lay. . . . Look at their clothes. That's supposed to be like beatnik costume. You could tell them a block off.' Again Ceci spoke in a normally loud voice. But the tourists were talking among themselves, and did not hear her.

But I am disguised in beatnik costume, Paul thought. Does she mean I am a tourist? No, of course not. I come down here all the time, this is where my real life is. If I could, I'd live here. He began to run over a vague fantasy: suppose Katherine should be hit by a car, or let's just say she can't bear L.A., like she keeps saying, so she leaves Paul, goes back East. He stays at N.R.D.C.; next year he gets a raise to let's say twelve K. He could move to Westwood or Brentwood or Pacific Palisades on that; but instead he goes to Venice. He lives just like all his friends, a simple pad, maybe with a view of the ocean. He uses the extra dough to build up a really fantastic book and record collection, with which he is extremely generous. Maybe he buys some pictures from local artists. He gives some money to the Tylers so Steve can stop driving the cab and finish his novel. After a while, he leaves Nutting to work on his thesis. He also writes articles, perhaps a book. He establishes a reputation as a historian and essayist. Ceci has already quit her job, of course. Now he marries her. And they have kids, like the Tylers; only maybe not so many.

'Ceci!' he said, but in a joking tone, putting his arm round her. 'Hey, let's get married.'

Ceci turned and looked at him, holding her Expresso cup half-way to her mouth. 'Sorry,' she said through the steam. 'Can't do it. I'm never going to be married again.'

'Really?' Paul asked. 'Why not?' He forgot that he was joking; his voice became serious.

'Because it's a shuck. When you get married, pretty soon you're doing it with somebody you don't love, because the law says you have to. Or just because they're around, maybe. Anyhow, that's how it is with me.' She drank, and put the cup down. 'Besides, I couldn't marry you. You have too much bread.' She spoke as if of a simple but insuperable fact; as if Paul were living in a room piled to the ceiling with pound loaves wrapped in waxed paper.

Before he could answer, they were interrupted. Many more people were coming in now out of the fog: some neighbours of the Tylers named Tony and Jeanne took the table next to theirs, and then Steve turned up himself; with him was John, the fellow who had been at the beach on New Year's Day. John had brought a guitar. Suddenly all the tables seemed to be full. The room was thick with smoke and noise, people calling for Dinny, who rushed back and forth through the crowd carrying cups of Expresso, looking strained. Seeing this, Ceci excused herself and got up to help wait on the customers.

Watching, Paul was reminded of how he had admired Ceci before he knew her, back when he first used to go to the Aloha Coffee Shop for lunch. But now, with her hair streaming down and dressed in a black jersey and pants, Ceci looked more like a dancer than a waitress. She moved with speed and grace, working the taps of the big Expresso machine or swinging her way among the crowded tables, sending him a quick, special smile as she passed. God, she was so great. What fantastic luck that he had met her. Thank Christ he had decided to come to Los Angeles, where people were really alive and things happened right now as well as in the past.

And maybe she was right. They couldn't love each other more than they did, so why get married? It was only a convention. He felt good again. What a hip place, and here he was in the thick of it. He hoped that a lot would happen tonight—that people would play the piano, fight, recite poems. . . .

'You going to buy Kelly's car?' Steve Tyler asked him.

'I think so.' Paul had finally called Walter Wong up at Universal Insect and Rodent Control (he had no home phone number—Ceci said he was probably sleeping with some girl or in his car), and offered him $725 for the dragster, $75 less than Kelly was supposed to be asking.

Tony, who had been observing Paul casually for some time, now asked: 'You a painter?'

'Uh-uh.' Paul shook his head. 'Just kind of a house painter. Not like John, an amateur. I was painting the kitchen over in my place,' he explained. This was true, but of two weeks ago.

'Yeah.' Tony and his wife smiled, and Paul felt he liked them.

'He works for Nutting Research and Development,' Steve Tyler informed them. Paul imagined that the expressions of Tony and his wife changed subtly, as if they were thinking: Oh, an outsider, a square. Maybe they weren't; but there was no mistaking the look of cool dislike on Steve's face.

'What's so bad about that?' Paul said, in as open a tone as he could manage. You drive a cab, he thought, John's a part-time painter and carpenter, Tony (he had just learned this) is an actor who supports himself by working for a bookie joint, and your friend Walter Wong is an exterminator, for Christ's sake—what's so bad about N.R.D.C.? But Steve leaned forward, smiling, as if he had been waiting for this question a long time.

'Like it's shit, man,' he said. 'What do you think that place is making over there in Mar Vista? It's just making death. You got to have some bread, all right, there's other ways to get it.'

Everyone nodded. Paul felt out of breath, as if he had received a blow under his ribs. He knew what Fred Skinner would have said: that Nutting was not making death, but labouring desperately to stave it off—that only through a relentless effort to produce the means of destruction could we deter the enemy from destroying us. Therefore we must keep on, keep on, etc.

But Paul did not say this; for one thing, he was not sure he believed it. Also, he knew that the argument would irrevocably mark him as an outsider.

'You've got it wrong,' he objected lightly. 'Nutting's just a research outfit. The only stuff they're really producing in quantity, right now anyway, is television components.' Unsympathetic looks greeted this; Paul remembered that in Ceci's opinion TV was not a low-brow nuisance, but a carnivorous brain-washing monster.

An uneasy sensation had started in his stomach, too—probably it came from eating cream cake at midnight. He felt in his pocket for the envelope of digestive tablets that he sometimes carried.

'You mean you don't have any government contracts?' Steve said.

'Hell, yes, of course we—they have contracts.' Paul worked one of the tablets out of the envelope. 'But you're over-simplifying.' He swallowed it unobtrusively, with a bitter chaser of tepid Expresso. 'We're just working on—well, I can't tell you what they're working on, it's against regulations, but it's not really military. Anyhow,' (he laughed, trying to get them back on his side) 'from what I've seen, you don't have to worry about Nutting developing anything dangerous. They're spending enough money and time to build a mountain, but all they've made out of it lately is some pretty sick-looking mole-hills.' He laughed a bit more; Tony, Jeanne, and John joined him, but Steve did not.

Paul tried to ignore Steve; he went on. 'Like I'll give you an example. This isn't breaking security—it happened years ago. They got a contract at Nutting to do a job on the repair and servicing of radar stations. You know there's radar equipment set up all along the coasts to look out for enemy aircraft, and they have to revolve constantly to cover the whole sky. But they had to be checked and oiled from time to time, and sometimes a part would have to be replaced. So the problem Nutting had was, how much would the radar have to be slowed down for a mechanic to repair it without getting too dizzy, and still lose as little sky coverage as possible. They had mathematicians working on the problem, of course, and physicists, and engineers, and communications specialists, and electronics men, and even psychologists. There were all kinds of angles, like, for instance, maybe the equipment could be redesigned a little, or different kinds of repair work could be done at different speeds, and maybe the physical make-up and personality type of the mechanic would be significant. They built a mock-up of a radar station in the plant and had a lot of volunteers revolving on it. Anyhow, so this went on for a whole goddamned year, and at the end of the year they got out a report in several volumes presenting all the data and tables and drawings and formulae they'd worked out, and making a whole lot of very complex recommendations.

'But meanwhile, all this time, another company somewhere else was working on perfecting radar equipment. Naturally. And so, just about the time the N.R.D.C. report was finished, these other guys came up with a new type of radar that didn't ever need to be oiled or repaired.'

This time even Steve laughed. 'Jesus, that must have finished them!' Tony said.

'That's what I thought too,' Paul agreed. 'But it wasn't true. Nobody gave a damn, apparently; they just filed the report away and started on the next project. I was talking about it to a mathematician who was here from Boston; he has a theory about the whole thing. His idea is, it's supposed to turn out like that. He calls it Watson's Law; that's his name. Watson's Law says that the purpose of this whole economy is to expend as much time, money, and material as possible without creating anything useful. Otherwise, see, the productive capacity of the country would get out of hand. You notice it most in organizations like Nutting. Wherever they're working on a government contract, they can't afford to produce anything that might compete with private enterprise. But the process is going on everywhere.'

'Only not here,' Jeanne put in. 'We're all out of it. I mean, it's like Steve once said—what was it?—we don't any of us here hustle for death or deception.' She looked at Steve; he nodded.

'All right,' Paul said. 'I mean, no. You can't opt out of your society like that.' He was facing Steve, not Jeanne. 'The same people I work for at the plant, you're driving them around town in your cab, and John's painting their houses and your friend Walter's killing their bugs. If you want to keep your hands really clean, you can't stay here, you've got to go be a hermit in the mountains somewhere. And even then you wouldn't be clear, you'd be depending on the Government to keep the area safe from gangs of bandits and forest fires. And what'd happen if everybody started acting like you?' Paul became aware that he had finally been forced into the position of The Other, but went on, still trying to speak casually. 'There'd be terrible unemployment, depression, maybe a war. What're you going to do about that?'

'Christ, I don't know,' Steve said. 'That's not my business. You got us into this mess; you get us out.'

Paul glared at Steve, infuriated by his cool tone and his use of the second person singular; he was about to accuse him of being solipsistic and irresponsible. But now John, who had been listening silently, took his guitar out of its case and played two chords; then two more, in a loose blues rhythm, humming under his breath. Someone across the room began beating softly on the table in accompaniment.

Gradually the place grew quieter; some of the people at the tables stopped to listen; some went on talking, but in lower voices. Ceci slid back into her seat beside Paul and took his hand under the table. He clasped hers hard.

As John continued to play, Paul's anger and the pain in his stomach moderated. He thought that he was right, but that whether or not he was right, he would never convince Steve, who for some reason was permanently down on him—maybe out of loyalty to his pal Walter Wong. Still, you couldn't expect to please everybody—the rest of Ceci's friends liked him. He began to feel better, to be ready for the next thing to happen, whatever it might be. Maybe someone would sing now, or recite beat poetry.

In fact, a man with a bunch of papers in his hand had just come up to the table, and was speaking to John, when something did happen. The front door was shoved open with a loud crash, and two large policemen entered the coffee house. John broke off the middle of a phrase. Within thirty seconds everyone in the room had stopped talking.

There was a scuffle in back by the Expresso machine. Two more cops appeared through the burlap curtain, pushing ahead of them a customer who had been in the washroom. Paul had noticed before how the Los Angeles police, because of their uniforms (tight gaiters, leather windbreaker, ammunition belt, black leather gloves) resemble stormtroopers or juvenile delinquents more than they do the cops back East. These four were no exception. He was not frightened of them, but he found it necessary to remind himself that he had not done anything illegal lately, had he?

'Okay, who owns the joint?' one of the cops said loudly.

One of the men who had been playing chess in the corner stood up. Thin and slight in his grey sweater, at least a foot shorter than any of the policemen, he looked like a member of another species. Apparently in response to some command, he began to take things out of his pockets and place them on the table.

'What's going on?' Paul whispered to Ceci.

'They're looking for drugs.'

Paul took a breath. Safe. But anyhow he had not done anything. He began looking round the room, wondering which of the other customers would turn out to be addicts. Some of them did look pretty odd. Two of the cops were going along the tables, search-ing the crowd, while the others stood guard at the front and back exits. They looked through the handbags of the women and made the men turn out their pockets. Not a very thorough search, com-pared to those in detective movies; they probably wouldn't find anything (and he felt a twinge of disappointment). Maybe they don't expect to, just trying to make things hard for the beats again.

At the table next to theirs a cop sniffed suspiciously at a pack of Camels, then emptied them out on to the table, and broke one apart to smell the tobacco. 'Hey!' the owner protested. 'Those are my last cigarettes.' The cop said nothing, but he began to tear up the rest of the pack, smelling the cigarettes only perfunctorily. Leaving the table covered with shredded paper and tobacco, he passed on to Paul and Ceci.

'Lessee your bag,' he ordered. Ceci set the bag in front of her, and Paul watched with some indignation as the cop pawed through it: comb, wallet, keys, an orange, a paperback book (a play by Genet with a lurid cover, at which he squinted sus-piciously).

'Okay.' He passed on to Paul, who began to empty his pockets, first the right side: keys, wallet, change—he took his time, begin-ning to appreciate if not to enjoy the experience, and thinking that this deliberate delay was the least he could do to show how he felt. Then the left: handkerchief, nail file, comb— 'That there! What's that you got?'

'Oh, that's nothing,' Paul said, 'just some pills for upset stomach.' He reached out, but the cop was ahead of him, slam-ming his paw on to the table.

'Oh, yeah.' Heavy irony; he held up the plain white envelope and peered into it.

'Listen, that's just medicine. They're called Alkogel or something; you can get them anywhere, without a prescription.' The cop paid no attention to Paul, although everyone else in the room was listening to him; he spoke out of the side of his mouth to his partner.

'Okay. You come with us,' he added in a tough voice. 'Stand up,' he said, as Paul, astonished, did not move.

Paul stood up. 'Listen, officer. You're making a mistake,' he said, and was aware that he had uttered a stock line from TV drama. 'I mean this isn't dope or anything.'

'Move.' But before Paul had a chance to move, the policeman pushed him heavily, so that he staggered and nearly fell on to the next table, where Steve and John were sitting.

'Hey, why doncha leave him alone?' Steve said.

The cop turned and glared at Steve. Then he glared at Paul. 'This a friend of yours?'

'Uh-uh,' Paul answered automatically, shaking his head. Why had he said that? Because Steve was not his friend. And besides he was in enough trouble already; he wasn't going to admit knowing somebody who probably had a record around here for shoplifting or God knows what.

'C'mon.'

While the entire roomful of people watched, the four policemen escorted, or rather shoved Paul out of the coffee house.

Twenty minutes later. Paul sat alone in a small room which, although it had no bars, he presumed to be a cell. It contained two chairs, a table, and a battered standing ashtray bolted to the floor. The walls were painted a disagreeable shade of green and there was no window, only a ceiling ventilator grille. High up on the door was a small glass panel, presumably so that the cop on duty could look at Paul if he felt like it.

Paul had never seen the inside of a police station before. He felt angry, worried, nervous; even claustrophobic. His feet hurt, because these sandals (whose sandals? Probably Walter Wong's, he realized) were too small. His stomach was still unsettled, very unsettled, but they had taken away his envelope of digestive tablets. Of course they would let him out as soon as they discovered that it wasn't heroin, or codein, or whatever they thought it was. He hoped. Everybody knew that the cops in Venice hated the beats. They wanted them to move out, and were following a policy of deliberate harassment and bullying to effect this purpose; and he had fallen into the jaws of that policy. He remembered tales and rumours now that he had heard from Ceci and her friends, about things the cops (or as they called them, 'the fuzz') had done. Scenes from TV plays, stories of police brutality. But of course they wouldn't dare (why not?). As soon as they found out that it wasn't.

It was stupidly ironic that he should be arrested for taking dope, something he had never done, but always wanted to try—at least he would have liked to try smoking marijuana. He knew that Ceci's friends had often done so, but they, and she, always grew silent whenever he mentioned it.

He wanted to be out of this windowless room, badly. But what could he do? The head cop, or sergeant (desk sergeant maybe: he was sitting at a desk out there) had said he could make one telephone call. But he couldn't think whom to call: Ceci knew already, and God forbid that Katherine should ever hear of this. (They wouldn't call her anyway, would they? They had the address.) In movies people always called their lawyer, but he didn't know any lawyer in Los Angeles. He might call Fred Skinner, but that would involve telling him what had happened and showing him Paul in the Venice jail dressed up in beatnik clothes, goddamn these clothes. At the very best he would laugh to himself, and anyhow it would be better if nobody from Nutting ever heard of this; and they needn't, because as soon as the cops discovered, etc. This was a false arrest; he was completely innocent, but the security people at Nutting didn't like it if you even got near to anything irregular. Even adultery made you a security risk, because you might be blackmailed. Unless you were screwing a girl with clearance, Fred said once, referring to a rumour about the secretaries in Personnel and Security. Booked on suspicion of possessing drugs, how would that look? He could even be fired.

An eye appeared in the window of the door; then the door was opened.

'Your wife's here,' the policeman informed Paul.

'Here?'

'Out front.' He gave a jerk of his head to indicate the direction.

'Oh, God.'

An expression of sympathy came over the section of large red face which was visible through the door. 'You don't hafta see her if you don't wanna,' the cop said.

'In a little while. I'll see her in a little while,' Paul promised. The cop nodded, and shut the door. Paul slumped back in his chair. What in Christ's name would he tell Katherine, who believed that he had gone to a late movie in the opposite direction, over in Hollywood. If he didn't appear soon she would probably conclude that he was drunk, he realized. She must be in a complete state anyhow, got out of bed after midnight by a telephone call from the police. Well, he would have to say that he went to the movie, and that he met some people there, and they suggested, etc. All right, let's get it over with. He stood up.

But the policeman had gone, and Paul was locked in; he looked out through the square of glass at an empty corridor. He knocked on the inside of the door. No one came. He knocked again, louder. Waiting, he walked back and forth, pacing the room; as prisoners are supposed to do, he thought. He sat down again, in the other chair this time. Goddamn the cops, and the coffee house, and Venice, and everyone in it! Had he really been thinking of coming to live here just a couple of hours ago? Goddamn it all.

He got up again, and knocked on the door, and called out 'Hey!' as loud as he could: 'Hey, hey! Let me out!' He heard an edge of panic in his own voice.

'Whassa trouble?' the cop said, unfriendly now. He did not open Paul's door, but looked in through the window.

'You can let me out now,' Paul called. 'I'll see my wife.'

'Let yourself out,' the cop said, grinning. 'The door's not locked.'

Paul turned the handle. It was quite true. Feeling foolish on top of everything else, he followed the policeman up the corridor, a broad back covered in serge. And what he was wearing himself —how would he explain that? Well, he would just have to say—

'Paul!' Ceci cried, jumping up from a bench as he walked into the room. 'Are you okay?'

Paul looked nervously around him. Four cops, a clock reading 2.15, but Katherine was not there. Understanding what had happened, he let Ceci put her arms about him, and even reciprocated, though with a sense of policemen watching. 'Sure, I'm okay. Are they going to let me out?'

Ceci shook her head. 'I don't know. I don't think so.'

Holding on to Ceci by one arm, Paul advanced towards the nearest cop and asked the same question. Nah, the cop said. They couldn't let him go, see, until they found out what was the stuff he had on him. There wasn't anybody around now to analyse it, and there wouldn't be until nine next morning. So he would have to spend the night, wasn't much left of that anyway. 'But I can't do that!' Paul protested. The cop shrugged, indifferent. It was likely, he implied, that Paul would turn out to be a drug addict, but he would not be very interested either way.

'I can't stay here,' Paul said. 'I've got to get out before eight tomorrow morning; I've got to be at work.'

'Yeah? Where?' The cop looked at him: dirty clothes, sandals, beard now almost two days old.

Paul hesitated; then he decided to plunge. 'Nutting Research and Development,' he said. 'And listen, I've already been investigated and cleared by their security department. You know Nutting wouldn't have cleared me if I took dope. They would have found that out. Now why don't you let me go on home? I can come back here tomorrow in my lunch hour if you want.'

'You work for Nutting?' Paul nodded. 'Lessee your badge.'

For Reasons of Security this Badge Should Be Carried upon the Person AT ALL TIMES was printed upon the back of Paul's badge. It had been pinned to his jacket, but his jacket was at Ceci's. Had he remembered to take it off? Paul searched through his pockets. No, no, no. The policeman and Ceci were watching. Wait a moment. Hadn't he pinned it to his shirt? Yes! There it was, underneath Ceci's dirty sweater. He fumbled to unfasten it and get it out.

'Huh.' The cop looked at Paul's badge as it lay in his hand, Secret Paul Cattleman staring solemnly at the ceiling of the police station, in his real clothes. Then he handed it to the cop nearest him. Both then went to the far end of the room and entered into consultation with the head cop. Paul's image was passed from hand to hand.

Paul and Ceci stood waiting. They exchanged a glance, and she squeezed his arm, but he did not feel that any message or information actually passed.

Finally the policemen turned towards him.

'Okay,' the one at the desk called out. 'You can go.' He held out Paul's badge. 'Lemme give you some advice, mister,' he added as Paul went over to take it. 'Don't come down here again. Stay out of joints like that one, and you'll stay out of trouble.'

'Thank you,' Paul replied mechanically. He put the badge into his pocket.

The heavy golden-oak door, barred with iron, swung shut behind them, and Paul took a big breath of air. 'Jesus!' he said, balancing on the step. 'I feel like I'd been in there for years.'

'Come on,' Ceci urged him. 'Around the corner.' She pulled him along the street and into an alley. In the shadow there a car was parked, or more accurately, a hearse—complete with black curtains at the windows. Paul had a moment of absolute panic, as if he had fallen from one bad dream into another. 'Hi!' Ceci called.

'Wow, you made it,' Steve Tyler said, opening the door of the hearse. 'What happened?'

'It was way out,' Ceci said, climbing in beside him. 'C'mon. He pulled it on them how he worked for the Government, like he was investigated by the F.B.I. already. He really laid it on.' She laughed.

'Cool.' Steve turned the car out of the alley and drove south, while the events in the police station were described to him. Soon they drew up in front of the coffee house.

'Say,' Paul asked. 'Could you drive me over to Ceci's place? I left my car there.'

'Aw, make the scene for a minute,' Steve said. 'All the cats want to see you.'

'Okay,' Paul said, not very enthusiastically, thinking that it must be almost three a.m.

The coffee house did not look like a place that had recently been raided. It was just as before: candles burning softly, dim figures sitting before them. But this time, as they entered, a wave of recognition, and then almost a cheer, ran round the room. Before the door had shut behind him Paul was surrounded. People were slapping him on the back, congratulating and thanking him, while Steve and Ceci told the story, now expanding into a saga of cunning and heroism, of his release. Dinny, the waitress, clung to his hand, smiling silently like a delighted child.

'Sit down, have some coffee on the house,' her husband urged. 'Have something to eat. Hey, Dinny! Bring him something good.' Paul allowed himself to be propelled into a chair.

'You practically saved my life,' John told him. 'Man, was I happy when they busted you! I was shaking, waiting for them to make me open up the guitar case.'

'*You* were shaking,' said someone else. 'Listen, man, I had my shirt *pocket* full of gage. Like you could smell it a mile off.'

More Expresso and another, double-sized slice of cake were placed on the table. To Paul they signified insomnia and indigestion. But he knew he had to make a gesture of ritual consumption. Without trying, he had become a hero. And after all, why not enjoy it?

'Hey, you know you were great,' Steve told him. The crowd around them had dispersed; most people had gone home. Ceci had vanished too, probably to the washroom. 'It was so cool, the way you made like you didn't know me. That was really thinking fast. I guess you saved me a night in slam.' He looked down, rotating his coffee mug on the table. 'I was all wrong about you before,' he apologized. 'I'm sorry I tried to put you down all the time and all like that.'

'That's okay,' Paul said.

'Josie was right,' Steve went on. 'She always thought you were a good cat from the start.'

'That's all right.' Paul felt acutely that he was in a false position with Steve, who had taken his instinctive revulsion for loyal strategy. He opened his mouth to explain, but could not manage it. 'I mean, no reason you should have liked me,' he said instead. 'After all, I'm mixed up with your best friend's wife.'

'Aw shit, no,' Steve protested. 'That wouldn't make any difference. I mean, that's between them. No, it was just the way you came on looking so square. And you were working for Nutting, and that really bugged me. I mean most of these cats don't dig what a place like that is about, but I used to have a gig with one of them. Yeah,' he answered Paul's look of inquiry. 'I was a physicist.' He turned round in his chair to face Paul. 'I know how it is; it took me a while to catch on too. Sure, you're just in the P. R. department, maybe you're telling yourself the lies they're putting out are harmless, or anyway what *you're* doing is harmless. Yeah, only it's not.'

'Well,' Paul said. He definitely didn't want to defend Nutting or public relations on principle. 'All right.' On the other hand, it was Steve and his friends that had got him into the Venice jail, and Nutting that had got him out.

'So, you got to quit.'

'Oh, come on,' Paul tried to assume a buoyant tone. 'Somebody has to work for them.'

'Why? There's plenty of gigs.'

The argument was back to where it had started earlier in the evening; but Paul was spared having to continue it by the return of Ceci, with Dinny and Dinny's husband. Almost everyone else had left now; again the tables were empty. The candles burned low, and a few chessmen stood on each board in final attitudes of victory and defeat.

'Hey!' Ceci announced. 'Larry's got some pot. Enough for everybody.'

'Cool,' Steve said.

'I'll throw in a stick,' John offered. 'That's all I've got, but it's the best. Real green.'

Paul looked from face to face. Were they crazy? John was searching in the lining of his guitar case; Larry begin laying out cigarette papers on the table, opening a little box of what looked like chopped grass. Dinny sat smiling beside him, a red-striped dishtowel thrown over her shoulder.

'You're going to smoke marijuana here now?' he asked. 'Are you crazy?'

'This is the best time,' Steve said. 'They won't hit this place again for weeks.'

'For Christ's sake,' Paul said. 'At least let's go to somebody's pad.'

'Aw, come on,' Ceci said. 'Don't be chicken.'

'No thanks,' Paul replied. 'It's too late for me anyhow. I've got to get on back.'

Part III: WESTWOOD

HURT by Love? Madame Anni, psychic reader, can help you.

TALL, handsome man, 29, seeks employment as companion, etc., to female. Steady or occasional. Eves after 7.

LEARN Massage. Seeing and Doing. $5 per Lesson.

Los Angeles Mirror News

12

KATHERINE was sitting in a temporary office building at U.C.L.A., in the small, stuffy office which belonged to the Project on Perception and Delinquency, waiting for the bi-weekly conference to take place. It was not quite two o'clock. In the office with Katherine were some chairs, a table, a filing cabinet, and a desk. There was one odd piece of furniture: a long varnished wooden box set up on end, about the size and shape of a penny weighing-machine. Seen from the front, it was simply a narrow panel in which were two pushbuttons, with a red light above each one, and the mouth of a chute at the right-hand side. If you got up and looked around the back, you could see a mass of coloured wires and relays inside, all feeding into a seismograph-type of recording device.

This object was the Fraudulent Response Perceptor, or Cheating Machine, which Dr Einsam and two graduate students had built for the project. By the use of electrical tape, the two red lights could be illuminated in any desired planned or random series and at any desired speed. The task of the subject (or S) being tested was to guess which one of the red lights would come on next, and to register his guess by pressing the button under the light he chose. If he were right, as soon as the light came on a marble would drop out of the chute.

It was possible to cheat at this game, because if you did not make your guess at once, but delayed until the light had just come on before you pressed the button, the marble would still drop out of the chute. Meanwhile, however, the unseen recording device would make note of your wilful delay.

This was the general principle of the Cheating Machine; but many variations of the procedure were possible. For instance, the preliminary instructions could be altered; an element of competition against other Ss might be introduced; or of praise and blame (the experimenter, or E, coming in during the rest period to remark, as if casually, 'Say, you're catching on pretty well!'

or 'I don't think you're really trying today, are you?'). Or the marbles might be exchanged at the end of the session for pennies, nickels, or dimes.

At this time, a final experimental form had still to be worked out. But test runs on the machine with a varied group of Ss had revealed that, as Dr Smith put it, 'Almost everyone will cheat like crazy if they think they can get away with it, though some will cheat more than others.' This finding did not surprise Katherine, who had a pessimistic view of human nature in general and of southern Californians in particular. Neither was she surprised at the deception practised by the experimenters. She had worked for social scientists before; she knew that almost all psychological tests were rigged somehow, and thought anyone who volunteered to take them, even for money, a fool. Whenever her eye fell upon the Cheating Machine, she made a mental note to be on her guard. At any moment her employers might try to turn her into an S or worse. As when, a few weeks ago, Dr Einsam (of course it would be him) said, 'So let's see, we've already tried two kinds of reinforcement, money and approval. What else should we cover; let's think. Definitely we ought to work in physical gratification. Maybe we could plug in Mrs Cattleman somehow; say we have her sit next to the subject during the experiment, in a tight sweater, to encourage him: what do you think? Or maybe we should just give a bottle of gin to the ones who make the highest score.' Everyone laughed, but Katherine sat stiffly. It especially infuriated her to be equated with a bottle of gin.

The door opened, and Dr Haraki came in, just on time for the conference. He was always on time, as Dr Einsam was always late. For about two months Dr Smith had also been on time, but finally he had got tired of having to wait for Dr Einsam, and now he too was always late.

'Hi. Nobody else here?' Dr Haraki said, smiling cheerfully. 'I wonder if I could dictate a couple more letters then, while we wait?'

Katherine got out her book. Her salary was paid by the National Institute of Mental Health, but in practice only part of her time was spent on the project. This morning she had been working for Dr Haraki, writing letters to field interviewers; but now she recorded a letter recommending a student for graduate school and one gently complaining to the Pacific Telephone Company of an overcharge, before Dr Smith arrived.

'Iz not here yet?' Dr Smith asked, looking round as if Dr Einsam might be hidden behind the Cheating Machine. 'How are you today?' He made his voice especially cordial to cover the lack of a name.

Dr Smith knew her name, of course; but at the conference last week Dr Einsam had suggested that henceforth the three investigators should address Mrs Cattleman as 'Katherine', while she should call them 'Bert', 'Charlie', and 'Iz'.

The idea did not please her. It was simply another sign of Dr Einsam's insolence and of the meaningless, vulgar informality of Los Angeles. These people were not her friends, and they would never become her friends. Katherine suspected that Dr Smith, who had some sense (he was not a native Californian, but came from Chicago), was as much embarrassed by the idea as she was. But he refrained from calling her 'Mrs' now, and sometimes managed 'Katherine', which came more easily to Dr Haraki. The truth was they were both afraid of Dr Einsam. Probably because he was a psychiatrist: everybody seemed to be terrified of psychiatrists, especially out here. It was particularly spineless of Dr Haraki to let Dr Einsam push him around like that, because after all he was the Principal Investigator for the project and older than Dr Einsam and an associate professor. He was too good-natured; that was the trouble. But what could Katherine do about it? She could hardly object; she retaliated, though, by addressing Dr Smith and Dr Haraki sometimes by their first names; and Dr Einsam, invariably, as 'Dr Einsam', or 'You'.

Katherine typed; 'Bert' and 'Charlie' recommenced their favourite conversation: the comparison of mechanical and electrical devices. Both of them, and also Dr Einsam, were amazingly knowledgable about all sorts of project equipment, from typewriters to high-speed computers. They followed the new models in calculators with the enthusiasm and detailed technical interest of sports-car buffs. They also followed the new models in sports cars; in cameras, boats, and hi-fi components—and, what's more, in refrigerators, electric blenders, and washing-machines. Last year Dr Einsam had become so interested in a de luxe Norge washer-dryer that he did a little study of its effects on the attitudes and perception psychology of the user. Dr Smith was deeply loyal to his red Porsche, Dr Haraki to his TR-3 and Dr Einsam to his black Jaguar XK-E.

'Good afternoon; I'm late,' Dr Einsam announced, as if this were a surprise, sliding in the door. 'Sorry, sorry. Katherine, how are you?' Katherine, who had a sinus headache, said she was fine. 'What's new? How's the space race?'

Dr Einsam was not referring to international science, but to a purely local if equally intense competition for office and laboratory space in the new Social Sciences building now being erected on campus. The four sub-departments of Social Sciences (Clinical and Experimental Psychology, Anthropology, and Sociology) each wanted a large share of the available area, and so did every faculty member. The problem was, of course, in the hands of a committee, which had already drawn up a series of conflicting floor plans. The question for the Project on Perception and Delinquency was what sub-department to line up with—whether Soc. or Experimental Psych. was more powerful and would give them more and better space in return for the prestige and graduate fellowships that went with any large project. But in playing off the committee members against each other they might end up with no space at all.

'I talked to Jekyll today,' Dr Smith said. 'He was a little withdrawn, but I think he'd like to have us up on the third floor with the other Psych. labs, on the south side.'

'Jekyll is a good guy,' Dr Haraki remarked. 'He projects hostility sometimes, but basically he's a good guy.'

'The way I brought it up was,' Dr Smith continued, 'I dropped in after lunch, just casually . . .' Katherine had heard the story before, and stopped listening, but Dr Einsam sat silent, attentive. He looked lean and dark and foreign and secretive. Unlike Dr Smith and Dr Haraki, who were always telling each other about their wives and children, he never said anything about his private life. According to the girls in the Social Sciences office, he was actually married to, though separated from, a beautiful Hollywood starlet.

Obviously he thought very well of his own appearance, too, sitting there in his very English tweed jacket and those ridiculous horn-rimmed glasses, smiling and stroking his pointed beard as if it were a pet dog. Really, Dr Smith and Dr Haraki had much more pleasant faces. The trouble with them was that they were both overweight: Dr Smith bulkily fleshy, and Dr Haraki round and soft, like a Japanese boy doll. As Dr Einsam occasionally told them, they ate too much.

'Okay,' he said finally, as if *he* had been waiting for *them*. 'Let's get to work.'

Katherine brought her sharpened pencil into juxtaposition with a clean page of her stenographic pad, and the meeting began.

The hands of the clock had moved round to four by the time it was over. Dr Smith and Dr Haraki had left the project office, and Dr Einsam sat reading a summary of several articles on juvenile delinquency among immigrant groups which he had dictated to Katherine two days before. He frowned as he tossed the pages over, and pinched his dark beard, as if the dog had misbehaved.

'Look, Katherine. You've got this all wrong. It should be "Nisei" here. Not "Isei". And this word here is "Sansei", not "Sansi". He flapped the report at Katherine, beckoning her to come and see.

Katherine moved her chair a minimum distance. 'I can change it,' she said, uncomfortably aware of being at fault. These unprofessional errors were the result of her aversion to Dr Einsam. Had she been typing the report for anyone else, she would have taken the trouble to ask them about any word she didn't understand, or looked it up in the dictionary. 'I'm sorry, Dr Einsam,' she added stiffly.

'Iz.'

She did not repeat either name. 'The trouble is, those terms are rather confusing.'

'No, it's easy. Look.' Dr Einsam turned the paper over and wrote on the back in his spiky European scrawl: *Issei, Nisei, Sansei.* 'Now. The Issei are those Japanese-Americans who were born abroad, and emigrated to this country. Like me. I would be an Issei if I were Japanese. Nisei: those are their children; second-generation Americans. Charlie Haraki is a Nisei; his parents both came here from Japan before he was born. The Sansei are the third generation; for example Bert. His parents were born here, but his parents' parents came from Europe. Now you understand.' He turned his head to look at Katherine, so near that she could see the separate shaved hairs growing out at the edge of his beard.

'I think so, yes,' she said, moving her chair slightly away along the floor.

'Good. Okay, which would you be?'

'None of them. I mean, I'm afraid I don't qualify,' Katherine said, rather superciliously. 'My parents and grandparents were all born in America. My great-grandparents too. Our family's been here quite a long time.'

'Is that so? A real Daughter of the American Revolution.' A current of hostility passed between the two citizens of the United States.

'Come back here,' Dr Einsam ordered. 'Let's go over this.' He waited for Katherine to move her chair towards the desk. She did not do so, but merely sat on the extreme edge of it and leaned forward. 'You can't see from there.'

'I can see perfectly well, thank you,' Katherine replied chillily.

'Come on,' he insisted. 'Don't be so defensive. I'm not going to rape you.' Bending towards Katherine, he took hold of the near leg of her chair and dragged it across the floor towards him. 'There. Now, look here. "The Isei group . . ."' Katherine followed his pen along the page; afraid to cause a further scene by moving her chair again, but insulted and furious.

'So okay,' Dr Einsam said finally. He shoved the pages along the table towards Katherine. 'Can you type that up now?'

Katherine hesitated before she answered. Five pages, and since Dr Einsam had written on all of them with his ballpoint pen, she would have to do the whole thing over. 'I suppose so,' she said, resting her headache on her hand.

'If you can't do it, say so. I'd like to have this before tomorrow, but it actually doesn't matter.' Tomorrow was Saturday; he had no reason to want anything then. 'There's nothing at stake.' Katherine looked at Dr Einsam; she did not agree. She did not like being in the wrong, and badly wanted to put him back there where he belonged.

'Oh, I can do it,' she said. 'I can take a later bus home.'

'I tell you what. You type this for me, and I'll drive you home. That way you won't have to worry about the bus.'

'But I don't live anywhere near the campus. I have to go to Mar Vista.'

'So? You type it. Okay?'

'All right.'

The descending sun had just reached the tops of the trees; in the speckled golden light the little coloured stucco houses looked more unreal than ever.

'Here you are.' Dr Einsam pulled up sharply in front of Katherine's walk. 'Not bad.' She did not know whether he meant the house or their breakneck drive to it in his open car; in either case, she disagreed. She took her hands down from her head, where she had been futilely clutching her hair against the whipping wind, and tried to catch her breath. Dr Einsam was the most dangerous motor-vehicle operator she had ever ridden with. She had managed, just barely, not to protest or cry out at the perilous way he drove, several times endangering both himself and others.

'You know,' he added; 'I'd like to meet your husband, if he's around. When does he get home?'

'About five-thirty,' Katherine answered. 'I don't think he's here yet.' She fumbled along the smooth leather side of the car looking for the door handle, though her impulse was to stand up on the seat and jump out. But Dr Einsam got there first and held the door open for her.

'Ten after five.' He consulted his watch. 'Maybe I'll wait for him. I haven't got anything else to do. If you don't mind, that is.'

'No; that's all right,' Katherine replied. What else could she say?

'Good.' Dr Einsam followed her into the house, which had never looked smaller, pinker, or more impossibly Los Angeles. At least it was neat. She put her bag on the shelf, turned on some lights, hung her coat in the closet, washed her hands, and then she had to go back and face Dr Einsam, who was sitting on one of her new wicker chairs stroking his pointed beard and appearing to read the *American Historical Review*.

'Would you like a cup of coffee while you wait, or something?'

'No, thanks. You sit down over here.' Katherine had been about to sit down, but now she did not do so. It was intolerable, being ordered about not only at work, but now in her own house. She stood, and Dr Einsam looked at her, through his horn-rimmed spectacles.

'You don't like me, do you?' he suddenly asked.

Katherine looked back at him, at the end of her patience. 'No.' She heard herself speaking. 'I don't like you, if you must know.' How could she have said that?—not that it wasn't true. Well, at least now he would go.

Instead, Iz sat back. His face broke into a smile, as if Katherine had given him a big present. 'Good,' he said. 'And why not?'

Katherine was flabbergasted. She could think of a dozen reasons, but she paused. 'Come on,' he urged.

'Well,' she said unwillingly. 'You're inconsiderate.'

'How am I inconsiderate?' Iz was still smiling, almost laughing at her; Katherine grew more enraged.

'You ask rude questions, like why does someone dislike you. Why shouldn't someone dislike you, if they want to? Who do you think you are, anyhow?'

Iz nodded his head once, and kept it lowered. Katherine felt that she had won round one, though with some loss of poise. 'All right,' he said. He looked up, not as subdued as she had expected, but somewhat so. 'Now will you sit down? How about that chair there?' This time he pointed to a modern one in the shape of a large brown wicker fish. 'You didn't get that back in Boston, I'll bet.'

'No, I bought it here, at the Akron,' Katherine said. Obviously he wasn't going to go until Paul came home, so she sat down on the edge of the fish. 'All this furniture is new. Of course it's just cheap stuff; I won't take it when we go back East.' Iz nodded, but made no comment. She went on, pleased to have put the conversation back on a conventional basis so soon. 'Paul's company moved our own furniture out to Los Angeles for us, but it just didn't look right here. This house is really much too small for it.'

'So you sold all your old furniture?' Iz asked.

'Oh no. It's in the garage. I wouldn't *sell* it; it belonged to my parents. Some of the pieces have been in the family for generations. They're really too good to use.'

Iz seemed to ponder this, stroking his beard. 'Your parents also don't use this furniture,' he remarked. 'Or maybe they have more at home?'

'No. My parents aren't living now,' Katherine answered.

'Ah.' Iz held his chin; he did not offer the usual condolences.

'Too good to use,' he said. 'What kind of furniture is that? It is like clothes that are too pretty to wear, food so delicious you can't eat it. Some sort of art object.'

'Well, some of the pieces really *are* art objects,' Katherine explained. 'There's a Hitchcock chair that's like one in the Worcester Art Museum. And the Empire clock—that's really very valuable.'

'I'd like to see this unusual furniture,' Iz said. 'Could I see it?'

'If you want to,' Katherine said, rather surprised; she would never have suspected Dr Einsam of an interest in antiques.

They went out through the kitchen door. The sun was behind the trees now, and golden motes swam in almost horizontal layers across the little back yard. The heliconia, still blooming now in February (but did it ever stop?) was intensely red and yellow against the wall. Katherine opened the garage doors.

Gradually, over the past few months, the garage had filled up with ghosts: white-sheeted objects stood awkwardly about on the stained cement like a collection of ill-trained modern dancers. Katherine raised the shroud first from an early Victorian loveseat, tightly upholstered in velvet and encrusted with mahogany roses. The marble-topped pedestal table with bird's claws, the tall chests, the chairs, the lamps, and the Empire clock supported by two gilded deities—all were displayed, explained, and recovered one by one. Iz, now apparently harmless, stood and listened to what she said.

'Interesting,' he remarked. 'Very interesting. And is it comfortable?' He sat down on the sheet which again covered her father's wing chair. 'Uhh,' he groaned, and got up again. 'I see what you mean now: too good to use. Yah, I think this furniture is much better off here in the museum.'

In spite of herself, Katherine laughed too.

'I'll tell you something else,' Iz added, leaning over the back of the chair now. 'Maybe you don't know it, but I think you're happy to have the excuse to get it all out of the house.'

'Of course not,' Katherine told him, but not with irritation. 'You don't understand.'

'Oh yes,' Iz said. 'I understand exactly. I know this type of fetishism. We have more in common than you think. When my parents left Germany—they had the foresight to get out early, in 1933—they took all their most dear possessions with them. To Brussels, to London, and then to Montreal, and then to New York, all those trunks and crates, and barrels of Meissen china, too good to eat off of, all went with us. And the heavy drapes, most of the furniture, the Biedermeier, you know what that is? Very beautiful, very valuable, very uncomfortable.'

'And where is it now?' Katherine asked.

'In their apartment in New York. A very small apartment, much smaller than the one we had in Berlin, but all the things are there. In the apartment now are so many things there is almost no space for my parents. Each time I get married, my mother says, Take, Izzy, take some of the furniture. Of course there is ambivalence: Yah, I think, why not? But I always manage to refuse. Sell it, I tell them, sell it so you have some room to breathe, so at least you can see New York City out of your windows.'

'You could take a piece or two,' Katherine suggested. Iz shook his head.

'No, I couldn't. Not in my apartment.'

'Of course, if you have modern things already,' Katherine said, 'I see what you mean. Because I did have some old pieces inside for a while, along with the new furniture, and it looked all wrong.' She twitched the dust-sheet straight over the bow legs of a table, then, followed by Iz, she left the garage.

'I can't imagine where Paul can be,' she said. 'He's usually home by this time.' That wasn't true, she thought; lately he was delayed more often than not. She shut and locked the garage doors and they walked down the driveway to the street. The sun was just setting; the smog-blurred sky had begun to turn from smoky blue to pale red; lights were on in the houses next door, but across the street everything was dark.

'Looks as if nobody's living over there,' Iz said. 'All the houses look empty.'

'Oh, that's where they're building the new freeway,' Katherine explained. 'The city's bought all that property now, and they're going to move the houses away, or tear them down. They'll probably take this block too, eventually.'

'Is that so.' Iz stared across the street.

The houses across the way had been vacant for three to six

weeks. Uncut, the grass around them had continued to grow; in some places now it was half a foot high. The sample Spanish villa, English cottage, and French château looked like toys forgotten on the lawn by some child who had been playing with them until, at sunset, he was called in to supper.

Stepping off the kerb, Iz crossed the street; Katherine followed him.

Seen close to, it was even more apparent that the houses were deserted, though venetian blinds still hung in many of the windows. Flowers had bloomed and fallen on to the front walks, and here and there an avocado or a bitter orange tree held its branches out over a litter of bruised fruit. Cars continued to pass at both ends of the block, but their street was empty and very quiet.

'It's nice here,' Iz said, wading into one of the overgrown lawns.

'Um,' Katherine agreed. 'A little weird, though.' Dr Einsam wasn't as bad as she had thought, she decided. He was crude, of course, and had absolutely no tact—imagine such a person trying to be a psychiatrist! But he wanted to be friendly, and once you knew how, it was easy to manage him. 'Look at those rose bushes,' she added. 'Imagine just abandoning them like that; I don't understand people. All these beautiful flowers just going to waste. I come over here sometimes, and pick them.'

'Is this where you get those roses you've been bringing to the office?' Katherine nodded. Iz laughed. 'What do you know.'

'Well, why shouldn't I?' she said. 'Nobody else seems to want them.'

'I'm not criticizing you,' Iz said. 'Don't get hostile.' Katherine took a few steps away, feeling irritated. 'Listen, Katherine,' he went on, following her. 'Do you know what you said that struck me a while back? About your parents. You said: "They aren't living now." What comes to mind is the idea that they have chosen to be in a state of suspended animation. But they might be back at any time, so they could see what you'd done with their furniture and whether you were stealing flowers from other people's gardens.' Both of them glanced at the roses, which glowed white and velvety dark in the twilight. 'Only your parents aren't living now; and they weren't living yesterday, and they won't be living tomorrow. Do you understand what I mean?'

Katherine looked at Iz without speaking, stunned at this intrusion into the privacy of her feelings: she was actually trembling. She ought to snub him directly, but she doubted that she could do so calmly, and she was determined not to lose her temper again. Besides, wouldn't that be stooping to his own level?

'I don't know where Paul can have got to,' she said in a high rapid voice, turning aside towards the street. 'But I really ought to start supper. It's—' She looked at her watch, but it had become too dark to read the tiny gold dial. 'It must be getting late,' she concluded, and began to cross the street.

Iz ignored this. 'Don't repress what I've just said,' he ordered, coming after Katherine and blocking her way, so that they faced each other in the middle of the street. 'Even if you think I'm wrong, say something.'

'I don't have to say anything.' For the second time that day— how awful—Katherine found herself losing control. 'Don't tell me what to think,' she said. 'I'm not one of your patients: I'm your secretary! I didn't ask you to explain my childhood.' She clenched her fists and got hold of herself, and walked around Iz towards the kerb in front of her house.

'Oh, hell,' Iz exclaimed, following her. 'All right. I'm sorry.' He did not sound very sorry. 'That's what my wife kept telling me,' he added to Katherine's averted profile. 'She said I always tell people more than they want to hear, and I ask them too many questions.' This was the first time Katherine had ever heard him mention his wife; she turned her head slightly back. 'I'm going,' Iz went on, moving towards his car. 'I know it's late. . . . So what else can I say?' He turned and held out both hands in a gesture of charming European helplessness. Katherine did not advise him. She frowned, and put her fingers to her head; the small nagging sinus headache that she had had all day was growing worse, as it usually did in the evening. 'Aren't you going to speak to me at all?'

'I'm sorry,' she said. 'It's just my sinusitis.'

'That's too bad.' Iz's immediate sympathy had a professionally warm resonance. 'Do you have it often?'

'Most of the time, since we moved out here. I think it must be the smog, or something in the atmosphere, because I never got it this much back East.' She shouldn't have said that; now, of course, he would tell her that it was psychosomatic, due to repression or something.

'It could be,' Iz said. 'That's a shame. Have you seen a doctor about it?'

'Not yet.'

'You ought to. Maybe a doctor could clear it up for you very easily, who knows? Take a day off next week and go to a specialist.'

'Thank you,' Katherine said. 'Maybe I will.'

'You sound surprised. Did you think I was the kind of boss that never gives anyone time off?'

'No,' Katherine said, though she had thought this. 'I suppose I expected you to say my sinus was all a delusion, and explain it away by some psychological reason.'

'No one can "explain away" a physical symptom,' Iz said. 'What a stupid idea. Pain is a real event, and real events have real causes.'

'Mm,' Katherine murmured, committing these words to memory as well as she could for use against Paul later. Iz walked round his car to the other side and stepped into the driver's seat over the side.

'So long,' he said. 'Tell your husband I'm sorry I didn't get to meet him.'

'I will. But listen, don't you think emotions have anything to do with it at all?' she added, wanting to make sure. 'Is that the new view?'

'How do you mean?' Iz paused with his hands on the wheel.

'Well, bad emotions. Anger or unhappiness or something; you don't think they might make someone sick, just by themselves?'

'Possibly,' Iz said. 'If they weren't properly expressed.' He turned the ignition key, and started the engine, making a loud uneven noise in the quiet street. 'But there would still have to be some physical basis.' He looked at her through the growing twilight. 'I like the way you get angry,' he went on, almost shouting over the roar. 'Don't try to suppress it. It's promising. So; see you next week.' Gunning the motor, he sped off.

13

THOUGH it was mid-morning, all the blinds in Paul and Katherine Cattleman's house were drawn. The sun poured against the walls and then flowed back, leaving a cube of pale shadow inside. In the bedroom the sheets and blankets had been pulled off on to the floor at the foot of the bed, a heap of darker shadows. Ceci O'Connor Wong lay on the striped mattress, naked, while Paul stroked her breasts.

'So good.' She gave a murmur of pleasure.

'What's so good?'

'I like the way you still like me afterwards. You know some men are great beforehand: they love to lie around and kiss and make out; but as soon as it's over they don't even want to touch you. They get up right away and wipe themselves off like they'd been to the bathroom. I figure they really hate women.'

Paul made an indistinct noise in reply. He felt uneasy here, though he was almost certain that Katherine would not come home. (But suppose she suddenly got sick at work?) Maybe they should have gone to a motel and asked for a room (at nine a.m.?). But he didn't like the idea of love in a motel; and here was a whole house standing empty, after all.

Things had been in this state for a week, ever since Ceci's friend Tomaso and Tomaso's girl friend Carmen had arrived. Under other circumstances Paul might have liked Tomaso, a short, powerfully-built young man with black hair and an intelligent, good-natured manner. He would have had nothing against Carmen, a plump, pretty Mexican girl who spoke hardly any English. But what the hell were they doing in Ceci's apartment? Tomaso was supposed to be looking for a place to live and a job teaching Spanish, but he wasn't looking very hard. He lay around on the floor reading Spanish and French poetry and playing Mariachi records at top volume. The bathroom was full of Carmen's intimate black lace laundry and the kitchen of stacks of tortillas and strings of hot sausage. How long were they going to stay, for Christ's sake?

As far as Ceci was concerned, there was no reason for Paul to stop coming over and climbing into her bed just because Tomaso and Carmen were there. After all, she argued, Tomaso knew that they were making out; *he* didn't mind. Which implied that Tomaso had a prior claim—that was what Walter Wong had implied, wasn't it? Tomaso had lived there before; his name was painted on the door. But maybe Wong had still been there then.

Paul moved his hand down a few inches on to Ceci's softly rounded belly, shield-shaped within the pelvic hills, and divided heraldically into brown above and pink below by the sun. He wanted to settle, once for all, whether it had ever belonged to Tomaso, and now, while she lay yawning with gentle pleasure under his hand, would be a good time to ask. How should he put it? He thought back to her last remark, and said:

'Have you known many men like that?'

'Like what?' Ceci asked drowsily. 'Oh. No. One or two, maybe.'

'How many men have you been with?' he asked in an assumed sleepy tone, lying back.

'Gee. I d'know.'

'You mean you don't want to tell me.' Paul imitated playfulness.

'No; I don't know. I never counted them.' Paul heaved himself up on his elbow again and looked into Ceci's face to see if she were lying; she returned his gaze directly. 'Why should I?'

'I should think you'd want to know.'

'What for?' Now Ceci was quite awake; she opened her eyes fully and put her hand on Paul's to stop a caress that had become somewhat automatic. 'Do *you* keep score? Do you add them up, so you can go around counting to yourself, like "twelve, thirteen, fourteen, and little Ceci in Venice makes fifteen"?'

'Hell, no,' Paul said. But he could not help thinking, first that Ceci had over-estimated his score, and second that her own total must be among the figures she had just named.

'This place makes me uncomfortable,' he said. 'I keep thinking somebody'll walk in. Let's get up, huh?'

'Okay.' Ceci stretched and sat. 'Hey, we can have a shower! Let's have a shower.'

'You take one.' Paul smiled. 'It's not such a big treat for me.'

While Ceci splashed and sang in the bathroom, Paul pulled on

his clothes and hurriedly made up the bed again. Katherine's bed
—Katherine's parents' bed, really, with its tall headboard and
suspended wooden garlands—no wonder he felt constraint here,
he thought, even with Ceci. And no wonder Katherine lay so still,
or moved so mechanically, under that frieze of dark, petrified
fruit.

His wife had been in Los Angeles six months now, Paul thought,
and she still existed here as a sad, angry exile, whining for the
past. The variety and excitement of the city, the warm, easy
climate, hadn't had the good effects he had once hoped for. Of
course Katherine had never been a very happy or lively person.
But now it was as if southern California, where poinsettias were
six feet tall and roses grew to the size of cabbages, had increased
both his elation and her depression. She seemed to bear a perpetual grudge. It discouraged him to think about it, so he did not
think about it often.

He pulled the cord of the blind, and light poured in through a
lattice of red and green leaves. Maybe he shouldn't have brought
Ceci here, but there was a lot to be said for getting her out of
Venice. After all, there was a whole great city here—why should
they limit their lives to a few run-down shacks and a strip of
dirty sand?

The shabby decay and disorder of Venice no longer seemed
attractive to Paul; he was surprised that he had ever found it so.
There was nothing intrinsically great about taking your bath in
a cracked laundry tub (listen to Ceci now). Or those rusty black
second-hand clothes she always wore—what was the point of
them? Los Angeles was an economy of abundance, for Christ's
sake.

And Ceci's friends' sloppy, pointless defiance of authority was
beginning to get on his nerves. It wasn't that they didn't like him,
now. For a while after the night of the police raid he had been a
kind of culture hero in Venice; he was still included in the crazy
schemes they talked of for getting back at the cops. Childish—
but what were they all anyhow but a bunch of disobedient
children: abusing the grown-ups, shouting 'I won't!' behind their
backs, refusing to wash their faces or comb their hair or tidy their
rooms, and smoking illegal cigarettes down in their club-house.

Take Ceci's painting. She had some new canvases that were

first-rate, really beautiful and original. She ought to have a show, and get some recognition, so she wouldn't always have to work as a waitress. But according to her and her pals, that would be selling out. Maybe, but look at it from the other side: you could almost call it selfishness to hide these pictures away from the world in a shack in Venice. Of course, he would have been thought incredibly square if he were to say anything to Ceci and her friends about the artist's responsibility to society. Right away they would start sounding off, with examples, on the shitty way society treats artists. It was one of their favourite subjects; part of their creed.

Everything was a war between Us and Them, who were imagined as all narrow, hostile Philistines. Which was another reason for Ceci to leave Venice, and meet some of the other intelligent people in the world.

Holding a towel around her, Cecil came out of the bathroom. 'Hey,' she said, grinning. 'That was big.' She walked past Paul into the centre of the darkened living-room and turned slowly round, looking at everything. 'Pretty nice place.'

'It's too small.'

'Well, yeah, maybe. You couldn't have much of a blow-out here. But it sure is neat. Everything's so new and spiffy and clean. I bet you don't even have bugs. It looks like nobody moved in yet; like one of those store window displays. . . . Cool chair.' She sat down in a dish-shaped wicker chair, clasping her arms round her bare legs like a child. 'Yeah, I really dig this chair.'

'You want one? I'll buy you one like it,' Paul offered.

'Aw, no, don't do that. I don't need it. Hey lookit, my hair got all wet.' Ceci began to take down her hair, which she had pinned up roughly for the shower.

'I'd like to buy you something.'

'Uh-uh. I don't want it. I don't like to have stuff around I don't use. It bugs me. I guess I'm afraid my pad'll get to look like my mother's place.'

'Oh? What's that like?' He knew of Ceci's background only that her father, a pretty square advertising salesman, had deserted her mother, a completely square bookkeeper, when Ceci was in kindergarten in Long Beach.

'Awful. It's just full of crap. Like, you know. Painted wall plaques and plastic flower arrangements and magazine racks and smocked satin pillows. There's all these things that you're supposed to do something with them, open coke bottles or light cigarettes or hang up your coat, only they're made to look like something else; puppy dogs maybe, or babies or funny Indians. For instance, on top of the TV she's got this cute ceramic rabbit about three feet high with an aerial growing out of his ears. After you've been there ten, fifteen minutes, you feel like you're being smothered.' Ceci unwound the towel from herself and began to rub her hair dry. Though the blinds were closed, it made Paul uneasy to see her sitting completely naked in Katherine's chair. It was something Katherine had never done and would never do: she didn't like to go around without clothes on.

He shouldn't have brought Ceci here; it was a messy thing, mixing up one part of his life with another. He had never made that mistake before; he had always been careful to keep his affairs separate from the very different kind of relationship that he had with Katherine.

'And it's the same outside,' Ceci went on. 'All those houses down there are the same. Their yards are all crapped up with stuff, rock gardens and bird-baths and iron flamingoes plugged into the grass. Uh-uh. I can't take it more than once or twice a year.'

'Is that all you see your mother, a couple of times a year?' Ceci nodded. 'Doesn't she mind?'

'Nah. She never dug me much, anyhow. I moved out of the house when I was fourteen; I didn't like the man she was married to then and he didn't like me, so I went to live with a girl-friend, and I just never went back. And of course *now* she thinks I'm completely flippy. I only go down there when it gets to be Christmas or something and she wants to put on an act like she's got a family.'

Paul looked at Ceci, naked and vulnerable under her long damp parti-coloured hair, and felt a surge of pity. He would have liked to make it all up to her: to give her, say, a house in Pacific Palisades with a view of the ocean, all the showers she wanted, clothes, furniture, a studio. And perhaps he would, one day.

'Well, maybe you're lucky,' he said meanwhile. 'If *my* parents lived in Long Beach I'd have to go there for dinner every week.'

'Oh yeah?' Cecil said, rubbing her hair. 'Why?'

'Well, because they'd expect it. I mean, they'd want to see me, and I'd really want to see them, sort of. You know how it is.' But of course she didn't.

Making the towel into a white turban, Ceci got up and began to survey the room again. She flipped through the magazines so neatly laid out on the polished coffee table, and leaned across the sofa to look at the facsimile of a page from a medieval manuscript which hung above it. Paul could see the wicker pattern of the chair imprinted in red and white on her behind.

'All boxed in,' she remarked, not turning her head. 'There's a wall around the garden, and a wall around the castle, and a border of thorns around the whole picture, and another border outside of that; and then the frame. Say, that girl is really in a bad way.'

Paul frowned, but said nothing. As far as possible, he had always avoided discussing Katherine with anyone he got involved with, or with anyone at all. Such matters were private; he despised the kind of man who explains to girls exactly how his wife does not understand him.

'*The Dream of Success; The Maturity of Dickens*—' Now Ceci was reading the backs of the books aloud. Paul refused to react; he stared at the carpeting, which was pinkish grey, with a thick nap. They should never have come here today; it was as if Katherine, and not Ceci, stood exposed in the centre of the house.

They ought to leave. He looked up; where was Ceci, anyhow? He turned round, and saw her in the kitchen, standing full in the sunlight by the sink reading Katherine's Phillips Brooks engagement calendar.

'Hey,' he exclaimed. 'Come out of there! Somebody'll see you.'

'In a sec. Listen, it's so sad. Nothing ever happens to her. "Tuesday, 10 a.m., Dr Dituri, get prescription. Wednesday—" '

'Come on out of there.' Paul gesticulated from the shadow of the doorway; he was unwilling to join Ceci in the natural picture frame provided by the uncurtained kitchen window.

'What for? "Wednesday, 5.15, haircut and set, Lotta. Thursday p.m., change shoes, Bullocks." Only on Friday and Saturday, there's nothing to do. See, she never goes anywhere. She gets her hair done and buys new shoes and then she never goes out. It's just so bad. Don't you ever take her any place?'

'You stand there, somebody'll see you.'

'Aw, nobody's looking.' She turned the page. 'Next week—'

Paul glanced past her through the kitchen window. Across the street all the houses were empty, and looked it now: dust and trash had blown on to the porches, soot streaked the windows, flowering plants hung withered on their stalks. The long grass, unwatered, had mostly turned a pale dirty brown. But on this side of the street he could see two children riding tricycles next door and a woman clipping green grass further down the block. 'Ceci! Will you please come out of there?'

Ceci looked over her naked shoulder, grinned provokingly, and shook her head. 'Uhuh.'

Paul set his jaw, took two steps into the kitchen, seized her by both arms, and pulled. She resisted strongly at first. Then suddenly she relaxed, so that he stumbled backwards. They both fell on to the living-room rug, Ceci roaring with laughter.

'You idiot!' he exclaimed. Ceci lay beside him and laughed; he could feel her bare flesh shake. In a flood of exasperation and desire he put one hand over her mouth, the other arm across the warm landscape of her breasts.

'Mmm,' she murmured, and bit the side of his hand. In a moment they were thrashing about on the carpet in a forest of chair and table legs.

'Ceci, Ceci, you crazy fool,' Paul whispered.

'Let's, let's,' she replied. 'Let's do it again;' and she wrapped her arms, legs, and long hair round him; and this time he managed to forget almost everything.

14

'WHY is Dr Einsam always late to our meetings?' said Bert Smith to Charlie Haraki, leaning back in the chair and setting his feet upon the edge of Katherine's desk. 'What's your interpretation of this?' Dr Haraki held out his hands, palms up, and shook his round head with comic rapidity, meaning I don't know. 'Does it express a rejection of us as individuals, perhaps?'

Dr Einsam, who had just come in forty-five minutes late, went on hanging up his coat in the corner and affected not to hear.

'But he's also late to departmental meetings, we've got to remember,' Dr Haraki remarked. 'And often to dinner parties.' He played with his pencil, drawing small circles on the pad.

'Maybe we have to deal here with a more global pattern,' Dr Smith suggested. 'A diffuse unwillingness to meet all his responsibilities. For instance.'

Iz took off his glasses and polished them.

'Still, I happen to know he's always on time for his patients,' Dr Haraki said.

'That's true. He *is* always on time for his patients. What do we make of that?'

Iz took a group of papers out of his briefcase. He pulled up a chair and sat down to read them, still paying absolutely no attention to his colleagues' baiting. He looked tense, though, Katherine thought, and nervous. Or perhaps she only thought so, because she was tense and nervous herself, and sick: in the grip of the worst sinus attack she had had since the day she arrived in Los Angeles. Her nasal passages were completely stopped up, her head ached fearfully, her throat was sore, and her left ear reverberated with a whuffling, buzzing noise as if an insect had flown into it and got stuck there. She should have stayed home today, really. But the truth was that since last night she couldn't abide her own house, after what she had discovered there, or thought she had discovered there.

Soon, perhaps tonight, there would have to be a painful scene in that house. But she wasn't going to think about it now; she had a job to do. She propped one inflamed cheek on her hand, and tried to attend to the conversation. Dr Smith and Dr Haraki, with some assistance from Dr Einsam, were talking now about the trouble a colleague called Dr Jekyll was having with his dicta-phone — a cheap new model which he had purchased out of foolish economy and against their advice. This soon led into a continuation of last meeting's argument about which tape record-er they should buy for field interviewing. Charlie Haraki favoured the Moscowitz, which was sturdy, long-playing, and reliable. Bert Smith thought the Moscowitz was too bulky for field work. He wanted to try a new Japanese-made machine, the Kitano, which weighed only half as much and could be concealed in a coat pocket or handbag. However, it cost more, and had a record-ing capacity of only forty minutes. (This cultural reversal was not a freak, but typical. Dr Smith's cliffside apartment in Pacific Palisades was full of Japanese screens, silk pillows, and Oriental crockery; while Dr Haraki lived in a split-level ranch house in Culver City with modern walnut furniture and a barbecue pit.) Katherine's head hurt; her throat hurt.

'What do you think, Katherine?' Dr Haraki asked suddenly. 'Which would be easier for you to transcribe from?'

She blinked. 'What? I'm sorry, I'm afraid I wasn't listening.'

'Katherine doesn't look well today,' Dr Einsam said, observ-ing her for the first time.

'That's true,' Dr Haraki agreed. 'She looks pale. How do you feel, Katherine?'

'I'm all right. I have a sinus headache, that's all.' Dr Haraki had heard of Katharine's sinus; he made a sympathetic face. 'A rather bad one.' She smiled deprecatingly.

'For God's sake,' Dr Einsam said impatiently. 'We don't want you to come in when you're sick. Go home and go to bed. What do you think we are here, white slavers?'

'I don't want to go home,' Katherine said. 'I'm not really sick. I mean I don't have a fever or anything. I know I'm not con-tagious.'

Dr Einsam looked as if he were going to object, but then seemed to change his mind. 'Okay,' he said, and re-arranged the papers in his hand.

'You shouldn't have sinus infections now,' Dr Haraki suggested mildly. 'It's spring.' He gestured out the window, where some green-leaved shrubs that had been there all along were speckled by the same smoggy sunlight.

'No it isn't,' she said. 'Not really.'

'Oh? Why not?'

'Well, it's just not the same. You can't have spring when you haven't had winter. It's — well, you'd understand if you'd ever lived in the East.'

'You don't like Los Angeles, do you?' Dr Einsam said.

'No,' she admitted, cornered.

'Really? What don't you like about it?' Dr Haraki asked. Katherine looked at him defensively—she hated being the centre of group attention. But he smiled back with such polite, friendly interest, so different from Dr Smith's formality or Dr Einsam's ironic over-familiarity, that she tried to answer him.

'I think it's partly that kind of thing. There being no seasons. Because everything runs together out here; you never know where you are, when there isn't any winter or any bad weather, ever.'

'Most people would consider that an advantage,' Dr Smith said.

'Well, I don't,' Katherine replied. 'This way the months don't mean anything.' She addressed herself to Dr Smith; he came from the Middle West and ought to understand. 'And the days of the week don't mean anything: the stores stay open on Sundays and people keep coming to work here. I know it's mostly because of the rats and the other animal experiments that are going on, but all the same. It's so confusing. Then there's not really any day or night here either. You go to a restaurant for dinner and you see people sitting at the next table eating breakfast. Everything's all mixed up and *wrong*.'

Dr Smith regarded her with a professional stare. 'Lack of expected cues,' he announced to the group. 'It's like those experiments of Skinner's, where he had the dogs on a very elaborate schedule for food and sleep, and then when he took the apparatus away the ones who'd been on the schedule longest went into a kind of neurotic daze. They began rushing back and forth in the cage, and showing diffuse anxiety and really highly unstructured behaviour. But there was some emotional exhilaration too.'

'I heard about that,' Dr Haraki said. 'One of my students was telling me. It was that pretty girl, Mrs Dodge: do you know her?'

What Katherine wanted to know was, what had happened to the dogs after the experiment? Did they ever get right again? But already the conversation had turned to other subjects.

The meeting was brief that day: Dr Haraki had a special seminar on delinquency with some social workers, and Dr Smith went off to the animal labs to look at the twenty rats in whom he was trying to induce alcoholism by manipulation of their liquid intake. Dr Einsam remained; he told Katherine that he wanted to dictate a letter. She opened her notebook again and poised her pencil.

'Hm.' Iz tilted his chair back and looked at the ceiling. Katherine waited. Two minutes passed.

'What time is it?' he said suddenly.

Katherine consulted her little gold watch. 'Five past three.'

'Would you like some ice cream? I'll drive you down to the Village.'

Nothing, Katherine had promised herself, would ever make her get into a car with Dr Einsam again.

'No thank you,' she said. 'I don't really feel like it.'

'Sure you do. It'll be good for you.'

'But I'm not hungry.' Katherine's voice, ringing through the aching and buzz inside her head, sounded shrill, even to her.

'Okay; you can take notes while I eat.'

The distance from U.C.L.A. to Westwood Village is short, and though there was a close call with a green Buick coming out of Bullock's parking lot, they arrived without incident. The ice-cream parlour was a small, awkwardly-shaped room, dimly lit by imitation gas lights and furnished with red-and-white striped wallpaper, flimsy wire chairs and tables, and innumerable mirrors and fringes and flounces. There were jars of hard candy, coy signs in Victorian Gothic ('Our Own Scrumptious Strawberry Shake, 65 cents'), and stuffed animals.

Dr Einsam made his way through this little cave of childish indulgence without appearing to notice how out-of-place he looked there, like a humorous collage in which the black-and-white photograph of a bearded European gentleman has been cut out and pasted on to a coloured advertisement.

'Let's go into the courtyard,' he suggested. 'It's warm today.'

[145

It was not warm in the courtyard, which except for themselves was empty. A fresh, chilly breeze blew through the stucco arches, among deserted tables and chairs; it ruffled the foliage and flowers in the concrete pots. Katherine drew her thin raincoat around her shoulders. For the first time she was aware of wind and weather — of the city as more than a great stale room, walled with mountains and roofed with smog.

'You're cold, aren't you?' Dr Einsam said. 'We'd better go back inside.'

As always, his bossy dogmatism angered her. 'No; I'm all right. Let's stay here.' She took her shorthand pad out of her bag and put it on the table so that Dr Einsam could see her staying here and ready to take dictation.

Dr Einsam looked at the shorthand pad, and then into the air, and then at Katherine. 'So. What'd you think of the meeting?' he said vaguely.

'Oh, I don't know,' she answered, surprised. But as a matter of fact there was a question she wanted to ask. 'Tell me something, though. What happened to the dogs in that experiment?'

'What happened to what dogs?'

'In that experiment, the one Dr Smith was talking about that got the dogs so mixed up. What happened to them afterwards?'

'Don't know.' Iz shrugged. 'The same as happens to most experimental animals, I would guess.'

'And what's that?'

'Send them over to the nearest med. school labs.' He observed Katherine's expression. 'You see, once animals have been through one psychological experiment, you can't use them in another, because they wouldn't be normal subjects any longer.'

Katherine set her mouth. 'I think that's terrible,' she said. 'Those poor dogs. First you put them through all that misery and confusion, for months and months, and then you send them off to be tortured by medical students. I'm not an anti-vivisectionist or anything,' she added. 'I realize they have to use animals for research, I mean to test new medicines and so forth. But what does that experiment prove? Just that if all the order of life is taken away it's depressing and terrible. Everybody already knows that.'

Iz looked at Katherine intently throughout this speech. When she finished he cleared his throat, as if he were about to speak, but apparently thought better of it.

'The professor that did that experiment, he must be a sadist or something,' she added, looking at him for confirmation.

'I don't know him. Maybe he is, who knows? They have that motive, occasionally, these guys who go into experimental psych. But most likely, it was pure scientific curiosity. He really wanted to see what would happen. Or he had an idea what would happen, and he wanted to prove it.'

A waitress appeared in the courtyard, shivering in a teased hair-do and a pink uniform. 'Did you want something?' she asked in an affected, unfriendly voice. 'We aren't serving out here yet.'

Katherine started to get up, but Iz motioned her back. 'Please,' he said. 'I'd like some ice cream. Tell me,' he went on, looking at her persuasively. 'This flavour-of-the-month you have this month, this Ginger Fluff. Is it any good?'

The waitress looked down. 'Well,' she said distantly. 'You might like it. I don't care for it myself.'

'Ah. Why not?' Iz gave her a direct, solemn glance, appropriate to the most weighty question or respondent—as if he were professionally engaged. Katherine had never been inside a psychiatrist's office, and never intended to be, but she recognized it, perhaps from movies.

'Well, I d'know. I guess I don't like ginger much. And then the Fluff part, that's marshmallows.'

'And you don't like marshmallows,' Iz interjected.

The girl giggled. 'Nah, I don't mind marshmallows.' Her voice had completely changed; it was now cheerful, nasal, unrefined.

'You don't mind marshmallows, but you don't like them with ginger.'

'That's right.' Now she gave him an open, confident smile, like a patient pleased and surprised by a diagnosis. 'Yeah, that's what it is.'

'Well,' Iz said. 'I don't mind ginger but I don't like it with marshmallows. So I'll have orange sherbet. Two dishes of orange sherbet?'

'I'm not hungry,' Katherine insisted.

'One dish of orange sherbet.'

Though the waitress had gone, Katherine said nothing. She

[147

glanced round at the empty tables and chairs, the stained cement, the lush plants in their containers. Looking more closely at the pot nearest them, she realized that the foliage was half real, half artificial: the living shrubs and vines, winter-faded, had been eked out with shiny plastic ones.

'This matter of the lack of cues,' Iz said. 'It doesn't have to create a panic. Look at it this way. Man is not a dog: he is a rational animal. If there is no schedule, then you are free to work out your own schedule. A place like this, Los Angeles, actually it's a great opportunity. Consider me, for instance. When I first got here I was still beating out my brain trying to be at work every day at nine a.m. I don't do that any more. I get up when I feel like it, at twelve or one, I don't see any patients before two, so I'm still fresh for evening hours. So, I get home about eleven and have supper and I'm still completely awake at midnight. And between then and four a.m. is the best time in Los Angeles, Katherine. The city's beautiful then: no heat, no smog, no crowds. Almost quiet.'

'I'd like to see that,' she said, a little sceptically.

'You should.' Iz pulled at his beard. 'There's only one thing wrong with my schedule: Glory wouldn't play. She never wanted to stay up with me, because she always had to be at the god-damned studio at eight a.m. the next day.' He frowned above his heavy horn-rimmed glasses. 'Sometimes I think that's what really broke us up. Ah, good,' he added, as a tall dish of orange ice was placed in front of him.

'Can I get you anything else?' the waitress asked. 'We just made some new coffee.'

'No thanks. This is fine.'

Katherine watched the girl hover a moment, and depart. 'She wanted to talk to you some more,' she remarked. She wasn't trying to change the subject—she was interested and flattered that Dr Einsam should confide in her. For the first time she felt sorry for him: he was an employer and a psychiatrist, with a high-bracket income, yet something he wanted had been taken away from him. At the same time, why had he wanted to marry a person like that, a movie starlet? She simply could not think what comment to make.

Iz shrugged. 'I'm talking to you now.' He attacked the mound

148]

of sherbet. 'For an example, last night,' he went on. 'It wasn't so late, only about one-thirty. I was up in Malibu at the Positano —we used to go there often. There was a new singer I wanted Glory to hear. I really thought she would be interested. So I got on the phone and called her. She wouldn't come up. All she could talk about was how I had woken her up and how tired she was. She didn't even listen to me.' He chopped at the cone of ice-cream with the side of his spoon. 'Well, that's the problem. Well, it's one of the problems, at least. So what would you do in that situation?'

'Me?' Katherine jumped nervously. 'I don't know,' she said through her headache. How simple Dr Einsam's problems were, compared to hers, was what she thought. Imagine breaking up a marriage over something so trivial. It reminded her of those news items in the Los Angeles paper in which someone was suing for divorce because their husband snored, or their wife ate crackers in bed. 'I don't know; maybe your wife could take a nap in the evening, before you get home. You have to compromise. After all, you can't really expect her to stay up until four a.m., when she has to go to work the next morning.'

'You think I should adjust my schedule to her needs,' Iz said, frowning aggressively.

Though Katherine realized that Dr Einsam's bitterness was directed through her rather than at her, she quailed before it. 'Really,' she said. '*I* don't know anything about it.' She pulled her coat closer, somewhat ineffectually, and rested her forehead on the back of one hand.

Iz looked at her. 'You have a headache,' he recalled. 'How is your headache?'

'It's rather bad.'

'I'm sorry. Where does it hurt exactly?' he added, with a note, though a rather forced one, of professional sympathy.

'It hurts everywhere today. Here and here and here and here. All around my eyes. The worst pain is right here under my eyebrows—it's as if my forehead was being hammered in a vise.' Katherine laughed a little, uncomfortably. 'In my lower sinuses, under the eyes, it's mostly only a tingling, burning sort of feeling.'

'All around your eyes,' Iz repeated, smoothing his sherbet gently with the back of his spoon. 'That's really too bad. It sounds to me as if you wanted to cry.'

[149

'I don't,' Katherine contradicted. 'I never cry. Why, I haven't now since I can't remember how long, years and years. No matter how terrible the pain is, I just,' she shrugged, 'can't cry.'

'You can't cry.' Iz repeated her words softly. 'That's very interesting. Why not?'

'I don't know,' Katherine said; she was aware of being handled, but it was so agreeable to find someone who was interested in her complaint, and Dr Einsam himself had just spoken about much more personal matters. 'Maybe it all goes into my sinus.'

'You mean that when something occurs that would naturally produce tears, the reaction is turned inwards, and creates instead a sinus condition. You *are* crying all the time, only inside.'

This was not quite what Katherine had meant, or rather, she had meant it only facetiously. What Iz said struck her like a sudden, glancing blow, or the flash of a light on a cloudy day. Maybe she had meant that. Certainly, today— She caught her breath, and parried the attack (if it was an attack: Iz was sitting eating ice-cream so casually, not even looking up) with another joke. 'Well, maybe,' she said. 'Anyhow, if that's so, I ought to be grateful. At least it keeps me from making a public fool of myself.' She laughed slightly, or rather simultaneously hummed and blew air through her stopped-up nose so as to create the impression.

'That's an unusual attitude,' Iz said, slowly stirring the remains of his orange sherbet round with his spoon. 'It's also non-utilitarian.'

'Non-utilitarian?'

'Yah. Because weeping doesn't cause you as much pain, or last as long as a sinus attack, does it? It is after all the natural re-action, under many circumstances.' Now Iz raised his head and looked at her. He had bright grey eyes behind his glasses. 'Why shouldn't you cry sometimes?' he asked. 'Maybe you have a good reason.'

At these words, all Katherine's despair and mortification, pent-up for nearly twenty-four hours now, seemed to flow throbbing into her eyes and nose. Suddenly she felt as if she were going to burst out sobbing right there.

'You've got to let it out,' Iz went on. 'It's important. I know this from my own experience. The danger is, if you inhibit yourself completely from expressing one kind of emotion, eventually you get so you can't express any kind of emotion. You feel depressed, so go ahead: cry.'

'I—' Katherine began, and swallowed. 'Of course, I—' This time the word rose from her throat in the form of a wail. 'As a matter of fact, I am rather depressed today,' she managed to say, but then she was caught up in a series of dry, creaking shudders.

'Come on,' Iz said. 'You can let go now.'

Katherine recognized the professional phrases, the standard sympathetic tone, but could not stop herself from being affected by them. Covering her face awkwardly with spread hands, she began to sob: a loud, uneven, tearing noise.

Iz watched her; his face showed sympathy. He reached out to touch or hold her arm, which, in a pale violet sweater, was not far from him. But a half-inch away he hesitated, as if remembering some precept, and finally withdrew his hand.

'What is it?' he asked quietly, after allowing a minute's interval. 'Tell me.'

'It's. Uhh. It's Paul, I suppose,' Katherine sobbed. The realization came over her that she was about to tell Dr Einsam everything. She wanted to get up and run away; but she was so sick, so cold, so confused, she simply didn't have the energy. 'It's just that he's deceiving me. And I found out last night. I'll get over it.'

'Ahh. How did you find out?'

'Well, when I came home from work.' Katherine swallowed. 'When I walked into the house I knew, really. I mean I knew he must have been there with somebody, because everything was all wrong. The towels for instance: they were hung up the wrong way in the bathroom.' Her voice trembled. 'I always fold them into thirds, and Paul just kind of throws them over the pole; but last night they were folded in half, and the wash-cloth was next to them, instead of over the tub. And the bed was made up all wrong, with the quilt—' She groaned, despairing of explaining what was wrong with the quilt; she thought how hysterical and silly she must sound to Iz. But he did not smile; he continued to look at her with serious concern. 'And on the carpet in the living-room,' she went on. 'You know that fluffy pale nylon carpeting we have? Well, there was this big kind of bruise where it was all flattened down. As if animals had been rolling on it. And hair.'

Katherine choked down a final sob. Iz had not changed his expression, did not look shocked. Perhaps he didn't believe her. She looked at this floor, grey stained cement marked into tiles. 'It really was.'

'Ya,' Iz murmured. He pulled at his beard, thinking. 'And what did your husband say about this?'

'He didn't say anything; he had a late meeting, so— Maybe it wasn't a meeting. I don't know. Anyhow, I was asleep when he got in, and he was asleep when I left this morning. So nobody said anything.'

'Ah.' Iz took off his glasses, and began to polish them with the paper napkin, which had a scalloped border. Was he going to have no reaction?'

'In my own house,' she said in a tight voice. 'I suppose that's the worst thing. Right in my own house.'

'That makes you feel worse about it,' Iz said in a very sympathetic, yet somehow neutral tone. 'You mean, you wouldn't mind so much,' he added slowly; 'if it weren't for that?'

'Well, I . . . It wouldn't be so awful. So *disgusting*.'

Again Iz paused. 'Maybe you already knew about it?'

'Oh no. I didn't know anything— I— He's always—' Katherine looked down. 'There've been things before,' she admitted. 'I mean, back East, not out here. Well, I have wondered here, once or twice, but I didn't say anything. I think it's better not to say anything, if you really don't know, then you don't *have* to know. I mean—' Her voice, either out of pain, or as if realizing what it was saying, trailed off, and Katherine sat staring into the middle distance, at a mess of tropical vines swarming out of a plaster pot. 'How can I be talking to you like this?' she said, letting her forearms fall on to the table. 'It's just terrible.'

'It's not so terrible.' Iz slid his hand out again towards hers, and again drew back; he blinked as if in irritation with himself. 'You need to talk to somebody: why not me?'

'Well, it's very kind of you,' Katherine said, sitting back. 'You must spend so much time listening to people tell you their troubles. Professionally, I mean. And of course, they pay you for it.'

'Ah, cut it out,' Iz said. 'Tell you what,' he added clumsily, as the look on her face did not alter. 'I'll pay you when I talk, and you can pay me back when you talk, so today we're even. Okay, Katherine?'

Katherine smiled an uneven smile. She realized that Iz was also embarrassed; that he was really asking for her confidence. 'Okay, Iz,' she said. 'But it's really not fair; you must have so many people you can talk to already here.'

'What makes you think that? Sure, for my work I have many good friends, colleagues. But they don't want to hear my personal problems. They would be embarrassed.' He frowned, as if aware of how unlikely this sounded. 'Anyhow, a lot of them think it was unbalanced of me to marry Glory; I told you so, they would say. Because they don't know her, they are prejudiced. Sure, she has an unpromising background, and she has learned from it some very bad values; but basically she is a very warm, spontaneous person. She has more ego strength than most psychologists I know.'

Simultaneously, Katherine had several reactions: she was deeply pleased that Iz seemed to like her, but apprehensive about having told him so much. She hadn't confided in anyone like this since college, when after all she had had nothing much to tell. But like many people who have the habit of reticence, once she had started she couldn't seem to stop. Also, she was confused by Iz's style (part colloquial Californian, part European psychologist), curious about and jealous of his wife, and ashamed of the way she had spoken of her husband.

'Paul isn't really so awful,' she said. 'I don't want you to think that. I mean, I suppose he has an excuse, in a way.'

'Oh? How is that?'

'Well.' Katherine looked down and sideways. 'Because, you know. Marriage is rather hard on men.'

'No,' Iz said. 'I don't know. How is marriage hard on men?'

Katherine glanced up; his expression was serious, not ironic; all the same she resented being made to say it out.

'Well, because they have greater needs than women do. And I suppose Paul has more than the average man. . . . And I . . .' Her voice, which had been growing fainter, died out entirely.

'Ah, nonsense.'

'You don't think that's true?'

'Not in my experience. If you're speaking in terms of basic

erotic drive. Naturally there is the problem of blockage, but that's just superficial. And no doubt you have, occasionally, the effects of chronic disease, low vitality, faulty hormone balance. But this applies to both sexes, and it would be obvious that the person was physically ill.'

Katherine wondered if it were obvious to Iz that she was ill. Of course she did have a chronic sinus condition; even today——
She suddenly realized that her terrible headache had almost disappeared, while she wasn't watching it. Almost completely disappeared! She had to frown, now, to feel it at all.

'I suppose it comes to the same thing,' she said, frowning.

Iz looked at her as if he were deciding which of several things to say. He pulled at his beard several times.

'Let me ask you,' he began finally. 'I get the impression that you and your husband have had, let us say, a silent agreement: You will allow him to be unfaithful, and he will keep his affairs to himself.'

'No,' Katherine exclaimed. 'He's never said anything like that. Neither one of us *ever* mentioned——'

'I said, a silent agreement. . . . Let me make another guess. In my observation, people are never found out unless they want to be found out. It occurs to me that perhaps your husband arranges to leave these clues. I don't mean consciously, deliberately. He just gets careless; I have done this myself. Maybe he wants to have a scene, to prove that you love him. Or he would like this affair to end now, but he doesn't know how to arrange it. He wants to be able to say to his friend: "We have to stop seeing each other; my wife is getting suspicious." I don't ask you to accept this now,' he added, observing Katherine's expression. 'But try a little experiment. Don't say anything to him this time. If this clue isn't picked up, I bet there'll be others. Wait and see.'

'All right,' Katherine said. She didn't know what good Iz's plan was, but at least it would postpone a very unpleasant scene. And it did make her feel, for the first time since yesterday, or much longer, that she was in control. Or was she only pretending to be? A cool wind blew through the courtyard; the shadows seemed greyer. Katherine looked at her watch. 'Oh, lord. It's almost five.'

'Okay. Let's go.' Iz stood up, and placed on the table a tip greater than the price of the ice-cream. They made their way back through the shop to the street.

'Would you like a ride home?' he asked.

'No, thank you. I have to go to Bullock's to pick up some shoes.' But also she wanted to get away from Iz, in order to think over what he had said.

'Okay. I'll drop you off on the way to my place.'

Here on the street, in the car, Katherine did not want to go on discussing the personal matters which crowded her mind. She felt the need of some conventional conversation, to re-establish balance.

'You live quite near Bullock's, don't you?'

'Um, up the other side of the campus.' Iz turned the corner between the yellow and red lights, with a screech. 'On Gayley.'

She knew this, of course. 'Is your apartment nice?'

'Great. I've got a superb view in three directions. North, south, and east. At night it's out of this world. Ah, you psychotic bastard!' He braked with a jolt, inches behind another car. 'Why didn't you keep going?'

'I'd—' Katherine clutched at the seat, and avoided falling forward. 'I'd uh like to see it.'

Waiting for the light, Iz turned round and looked at her through his dark glasses, with what seemed unnecessary intentness.

'I'd like to show it to you,' he said. 'But I have a problem.' He gunned the engine nervously. 'I only let women into my apartment when it's understood that I'm going to sleep with them.'

Katherine flushed, and looked into her lap. 'Oh, I see,' she uttered.

'It avoids misunderstanding. Here you are.' He drew up with a squeal of the brakes at the back door of Bullock's.

'Well, thank you very much,' Katherine said. This time she did not bother trying to work the handle; she stood up in the car, and before Iz could come round to open the door for her she climbed out over the window-sill, so fast that she tripped and nearly fell on to the sidewalk.

15

In his office at the Nutting Research and Development Corporation, Paul sat with his head on his hands in front of disordered layers of paper—the notes and material for his history of the company. All colours: pink, yellow, white, beige—all sizes: they were like flakes of paint fallen on to his desk from some high, invisible ceiling—broken, meaningless messages.

He had just returned from an interview with Howard Leon, the head of the Publications Department, concerning his history. Nearly two months ago he had handed in the first draft. It really wasn't a bad job, either. He had gone to a lot of trouble to get the data together: looking up old city records, asking questions all over the building, searching in the backs of filing cabinets. As he had pieced it together, the growth of N.R.D.C. made an interesting and impressive story.

But since January he had had no word on it. Apparently the manuscript had just vanished into the interstices of the Nutting bureaucracy. All he could ever get out of Howard Leon was that 'they were looking it over' in the central office.

Now, just as last summer, Paul sat at his desk with nothing to do. When he complained of this, he would be handed a pile of other people's reports, press releases, and technical descriptions, and asked to go over them for style—'Take out the grammatical errors—you know, give it the Harvard touch.' So he would work his way through reports on things called 'scintillation detectors' or 'interlock resistor mechanisms' in which there were, of course, no grammatical errors. Sometimes he would sit for minutes at a time, though, staring at a sentence like 'In the presence of radiation peaks, the speaker of the peak squeaker emits squeaks'.

Or he would write letters. Or he would look out of the window. Or he would go to Ceci's, which was fine until Tomaso and Carmen moved in.

What had happened to the history? He had got tired of wondering; this morning he had decided he was going to solve (or as they said here 'stabilize') the problem—he would go in and confront Leon.

The Department Head's office was spacious, well and indirectly lit. It faced west, and should have had a view of the sea. But, just as in Paul's cubicle, the architect had placed the window so far up the wall that when you were sitting down all you could see was the dusty tops of a few palms and the pale, empty sky. Leon sat in a complex steel swivel chair behind a large L-shaped desk: he was a rather small man with the battered face and inscrutable expression of the wise old rancher in TV Westerns.

'Sit down, Paul. What's on your mind?'

Paul did not sit down; he remained standing, looking at some fragments of blue ocean between the dusty palms. His manuscript was on his mind, he said. What was the story? He was beginning to wonder, he said in a joking tone, if N.R.D.C. really wanted its history written. What was going on in the administrative offices, anyhow?

'Who knows?' I don't know, so don't ask me, Leon's shrug and tired, sympathetic smile seemed to imply. But Paul did not believe him: office gossip, as well as the whole appearance and manner of Howard Leon, suggested that he knew everything there was to know, and then some.

'They're still looking it over, I suppose,' Paul said, trying to speak in low, unexcited tones like those of the Department Head.

'Well, no,' Leon said; swivelling himself slightly from side to side in his chair. 'I don't believe it's actually under consideration now. The policy now seems to be to shelve this project temporarily.'

'Oh. Temporarily? How temporarily? You mean maybe for ever?'

'Who knows?' The shrug.

'That's great,' Paul said in a kind of joking tone, waving his arm. He had noticed before that in contrast to Leon, who hardly moved during these conversations, his own gestures tended to become large, vague, and violent. 'I wrote it, and now they don't want it. . . . What'd they hire me for, then? For a tax loss?'

Again, very gently and with infinite cynicism, Leon shrugged. As Paul looked at him, what had been only an angry wisecrack, a puff of steam, began to harden into reality.

Now, back in his own office, he laid the arguments for this reality out invisibly in front of him, over the littered desk. The original lack of specific directives as to what kind of history he was supposed to write, and what aspects he should stress, which he had taken for their flattering confidence in him. The way Fred Skinner kept telling him to relax: 'Take it easy, boy, don't drive yourself so hard over all those details.' The fact that although now and for the last two months he had had nothing to do, his job was not in danger. ('Then are they going to let me go?' he had asked Howard Leon. 'Why, no,' Leon had replied, his voice rising almost to the normal number of decibels with surprise. 'Don't worry about *that*. You have a contract, don't you?')

Of course, he needn't have been deliberately hired to produce a tax loss. Not conscious financial calculation of waste, but mismanagement of a larger, more unconscious sort, might be the explanation of what had happened. Nutting's hiring him was another example of Watson's Law: it was the expensive public manufacture of nothing; the vaguely deliberate consumption of time, energy, intelligence, knowledge, and money, with no result —no product.

But there was a product: his history. It was a good job, a goddamned serious, careful piece of work. At least, that was what Paul had thought when he handed it in. He would have liked to recheck this opinion, but at present all three copies of the history had disappeared into the administrative offices; nothing remained but these scattered notes and scraps. Angry, he brushed his hand across the desk, and flakes of paper fell to the floor on all sides, some dropping directly, some drifting and gliding downwards like withering leaves.

He looked up, and his eyes registered the picture of the Universal Data Processer, or UnDat, which in a more light-hearted mood he had affixed to his wall. The large green and silver machine, with its wide chrome mouth into which unwanted classified materials could be inserted for speedy and complete destruction, seemed to be smiling at him greedily. Fred Skinner's recommendation had been adopted, and the twin of this machine was now installed at N.R.D.C., down by the air-conditioning plant. Had it already eaten his history?

Or perhaps it was smiling at the pretty girl who stood leaning sexily against its shiny bulk, one arm about its shoulders. She was an attractive piece, no doubt about that. Now that he came to notice it, she somewhat resembled Ceci, with her dark yellow hair, snub nose, and Irish kitten's face. But, in that case, who was her companion? For a moment he saw himself as another kind of UnDat: another 9K investment of the Nutting Research and Development Corporation whose function was to process unwanted and obsolete materials, embraced by an anonymous California blonde.

Twisting and tilting, Beverly Glen Boulevard rose into the hills above Westwood. Paul's Ford climbed the curves under protest; he kept having to shift back into second and even into first.

'Damn this heap,' he exclaimed to Ceci. 'I'm going to sell it and get a decent car. An MG maybe . . . or maybe a Jag,' he added, as one behind them, growing impatient, swerved out into the other lane and passed the whole crawling line of cars, accelerating uphill with a scornful roar.

The canyon was very narrow: though it was barely past three o'clock, it was half in deep shadow. The houses clung close to either side of the road, crowding together under the tattered trees. Slopes of rock, scrub bushes, and ground creepers rose up steeply behind them.

Paul was taking Ceci out into the country. Because, after all, where else were they going to go? He was determined not to use his own house again, and her pad was still overrun with Mexicans —more so, even, for now Tomaso's cousin, an owlish, talkative Latin named Roberto Nuovomo, had arrived.

Earlier this week, Ceci—finally giving in to what she called Paul's hang-up on hiding things—had sent the whole lot of Mexicans down to the beach one morning, so they could have her place to themselves. At first it had been just as good as before. But afterwards, lying beside Ceci while she slept, Paul kept staring up at that mural on the bedroom ceiling. Once he had thought it exotically romantic; now he began to imagine that Ceci's husband had painted it there on purpose to make people uncomfortable. Walter Wong was up there somehow, watching everything they did, in the shape of a scarlet lizard, or the dog with the body of a toaster—it looked sort of Chinese, with its scraggy Airedale's beard. Or maybe he was the bird-man—who, Paul noticed for the first time, had a tremendous erection. Anyhow, he was there; and all the others were his friends or familiars. Paul began to wish Ceci would put out the lights like his other girls.

But it wasn't only that: he wanted to go to the country for its own sake. For him love had begun out of doors; he had many warm distant memories of summer fields and hedgerows in the outer suburbs of Columbus; then later, during college, of wooded glens in Belmont where the sunlight was sprinkled in patterns through the trees, and the grassy banks of remote streams in Concord and Lincoln. How he had liked to take off his clothes and feel part of the landscape! He wanted to get back to that state of innocent delinquency. And whom that he had ever known would be a better companion there than Ceci, who so loved to take off her clothes?

Besides, he was concerned about the state of their affair. At first, and for a long time, it had become more and more passionate and engrossing; maybe finally too engrossing. But now Paul felt that the tide was ebbing. It had receded almost too far, and he wanted to hold it back. A year of his life had been turned into nothing by N.R.D.C.—but his coming to Los Angeles was not wholly a loss, because he had found Ceci there. The scene this morning with Howard Leon had made him feel used, and unreal; now he wanted to fling himself on to the real Ceci, on to grass, on to earth.

It made no difference, in a way, that she hadn't been able to comprehend what had happened to him that morning. From her point of view any gig was a drag: the less you had to sweat, the better deal it was. It was pretty obvious, she said, that Paul could get away with murder; like today, saying he was going up to U.C.L.A. to do some research, and then just walking out. And look at the bread he was making! Of course if they had really fired him that would have been a put-down, but they hadn't, so what was his hang-up? Ceci said she didn't see what he was griping about. She was in an off mood today, touchy: but once they got out into the country, that would change.

'I thought you were going to take over Kelly's dragster from Walter,' Ceci remarked.

With difficulty, Paul came back to the conversation. 'Oh,' he replied. 'Oh, that. I guess not.' He wondered again whether he should tell Ceci what Steve Tyler had said to him—with reluctance, for after all Wong was his friend— 'Hey, better stay away from Kelly's car. Walter's been cannibalizing it.' The term was unfamiliar; in the moment before he understood it, Paul saw Walter Wong sitting on the front fender of Kelly's dragster, eating pieces of the engine.

Why shouldn't he let Ceci know that her husband was trying to cheat him, taking out the vital parts of the Ford and, he supposed, exchanging them for broken-down parts of other automobiles? But he decided to let it pass. It might make her mood worse. Besides, now that he had given up the fantasy of living in Venice, all those dragsters looked like teen-age jokes. He was too old for such a car; he didn't want Ceci to try to find him another one.

Around the next curve the houses stopped. The bare, steep banks of the road, unwatered, were suddenly dry instead of green. The waste ground was bright with real estate signs: *Glen-View Estates to be Erected Here. Level Exclusive Homesites! For Information Regarding This Desirable Property Call. . . .*

Now they were at the top of the range of hills. Ahead of them, blurred by smog, was the San Fernando Valley. Paul turned off on to Mulholland Drive; this was a narrow road along the crest of the mountains, badly paved, twisting and turning around heaps of earth and rock, skirting sheer cliffs of mud. The long dry grass and sparse greyish weeds which grew beside the road erupted at intervals into tufts of wild flowers: yellow, white, even brilliant red.

Paul's spirits rose. 'Well, how d'you like this?' he asked.

'Yeah, it's nice.'

'Look at those flowers! We're really getting into the country now.'

He began to drive more slowly, searching for an uninhabited side road. They passed houses that had been recently completed, houses under construction, and more real estate signs. Paul began to be aware that they were losing a lot of time.

Well, here; maybe this would do. He turned uphill to the right. The springs of the Ford squeaked angrily as it jolted over the dust and stones, around a sharp corner. Now there was a view: below, to their left, the mountain was being sliced into like a loaf cake, for "development". The flowers and brush on the slopes had been bulldozed away, and flat rectangular lots, dirty brown, were aligned one above another along a curve of roadbed, marked out with sticks and string and red rags.

His first thought was that they should turn back and look for another place. But it was getting late. The construction site was empty, anyhow: the tractors and graders and dump trucks stood motionless down the hill; the workmen had gone home. And the other side of their road was undisturbed. The chaparral grew high there, and in the ditch by the car were star-shaped white flowers. He turned off the engine.

'Hey! Let's get out and walk.'

'Okay.' Ceci's reply, though not as enthusiastic as his suggestion, was fairly agreeable.

Together, they started uphill along the dirt road, now only a track. After all, this landscape had its own kind of beauty, Paul thought. The smoky green and indigo of the hill behind the construction site, the intense blue sky, were exotic and interesting. The barren ground and the greyed foliage made the flowers seem much more miraculous than those back East — it was as if a swarm of fragile, bright butterflies had suddenly settled on a dead bush.

But round the next bend, with the trucks and bulldozers still in sight, the road ended in a trash pile: a heap of smashed bottles, cans, and dead sticks and leaves.

'Goddamn it,' Paul said. 'Well, I guess we'll just have to strike out across country.' Digging his feet into the sides of the bank, he climbed up it, releasing a small landslide of dirt and stones.

'You're crazy,' Ceci said. But rather fondly.

'Yep. Come on.' He held out his hand; she took it, and he pulled her up the bank and into his arms. For the first time that day they really kissed. Her lips and tongue fluttered against his face. He would have liked to lay her down right here, but it was too close to the road.

'Hey.'

'What?' Ceci mumbled, kissing him under the chin.

'Come on.'

Crossing the waste ground was not easy. The sage put out stalks of brittle, whitish leaves to scratch them; and the sumac held them back with its woolly, awkward stems, and slapped their faces with clusters of faded red leaves. The larger scrub trees had thorns. The ground was dry, uneven, and stony; and each plant, bush, or tree was surrounded by an area of barren earth.

'Hey,' Ceci said. 'Where're we going to?'

Paul stopped. 'Nowhere.' He turned and caught hold of her by her brown, bare arms, now marked with white scratches.

They kissed. 'Oh hell,' Ceci whispered, rubbing herself against him. 'I'm still so hot for you. Ah, goddamn it.'

'Let's sit down,' Paul gasped. Crouching, he tried to clear a patch of ground; he broke off twigs and threw stones to one side. 'Ceci. Come on.' He ran his hand up her warm, scratched brown leg.

'You want to do it *here*?'

'Yes.'

Ceci was bending down towards him; her breasts were heavy under the tight cotton jersey. Paul took hold and pulled her over, on to him.

'Ow! Paul, you're flippy. We can't make it here, right out in the open. I mean, anybody came along, they could see us.' She giggled.

It was true that though the field seemed to be grown over with an almost impassable network of coarse bushes, the foliage was so sparse that there was hardly cover enough for a dog. But Paul's body was quivering with excitement; even the prospect of having to overcome Ceci's reluctance, so rare for her, excited him. And if not here out in the country, where?

'Who cares?' Holding Ceci down, Paul began deliberately to do all the things that he knew aroused her most: he bit her neck, and forced his leg between her legs, dragging up her skirt, and rubbing against her curly mound of hair with his knee, so that she began to pant and cry out.

'Ah. Oh! . . . Ah! All right; all right.'

He lifted her aside and as rapidly as he could began to pull off most of his clothes, kneeling in the dust. Ceci did the same. Paul spread their things hurriedly over the dirt and stones to make a kind of patchwork bed. He could not help, meanwhile, glancing over his shoulder to see if anyone were coming up the road. Cars going to the dump, construction workers, hikers, or whoever owned this property. Because at the very least they were trespassing; there was probably a city ordinance against what they

were about to do. Somehow they had got out of *Walden* into
'The Waste Land', from private pastoral to public lust.

'Come on, huh?' As usual, Ceci, who wore many fewer clothes,
was ready first.

'Just a moment.' Paul took off his shorts, and then, rather self-
consciously, pulled a piece of gold wire off one finger. It was his
wedding ring, the result of an elaborate ceremony nearly four
years ago. Sentimentally, or superstitiously, he always took it off
before he did anything he had promised then not to do. He put
the ring into a pocket of his jacket. Then, shutting his eyes, he
fell upon Ceci.

'This bed's pretty hard,' Ceci said presently, breaking the silence
that follows climax. 'Wow, my back.'

'My knees,' Paul replied, echoing her joking tone, and thus
tacitly accepting this excuse for what had been as intense, but
not exactly as protracted as it might have been. It was true that
his knees were sore; one of them, he noticed, was even bleeding
a little. This made him feel better, because it proved how much
he had been able to forget himself in nature; but worse in that it
proved how hostile this particular nature was.

The hazy white spot of the sun was dropping towards the tops
of the scrub thorn-trees. 'Well.' He stood up, glanced around the
field again (still no one in sight) and began to put on his clothes,
which wasn't easy here with nothing to lean on or sit on except
sharp branches. His undershorts, his shirt, his pants, his socks, his
shoes; everything was wrinkled and smudged with dust.

'Look at that,' he complained to Ceci, holding up the dust-
streaked jacket of his olive-green dacron suit.

'Yeah, me too.' Ceci grinned, showing her skirt. 'Looks like
we've been rolling on the ground or something,' she said, leaning affectionately against him.

'Your clothes aren't so bad.' Paul brushed and slapped at his
jacket. Why hadn't they brought a blanket from the car, or even
some newspapers? He shook the jacket angrily in the air. Then
he remembered something, and put his hand unobtrusively into
the inside pocket. His wedding ring was not there. He felt all
round the pocket; then he felt around the other pockets of the
jacket. Then he looked down at the ground.

'What're you looking for?' Ceci asked.

'Uh. My ring,' he muttered unwillingly. 'I put it in my jacket, but it must have fallen out.' He felt through his pockets again. 'It must be here somewhere.'

Ceci said nothing. She stood waiting, making no effort to help, while Paul bent and then knelt on the stony ground, turning over gravel and disturbing leaves and twigs in a widening circle.

'Can't you find it?' she said presently.

'I've got to find it.' Paul shuffled a heap of dead vegetation. He searched in his shirt pockets, and partly lifted a decaying branch.

'Is it that important?'

'Well, in a way.' Paul's first impulse when he felt attacked was to compromise, but he corrected himself. 'Yes, it's important.' Ceci was looking at him; he went on. 'I don't mean it's valuable. It just means something.' He stooped again to the dust and brittle leaves. After a moment, Ceci bent down too, but only to read his watch.

'Hey; it's quarter to five,' she said. 'I'll be late. Come on.' Paul shook his head. 'You can get yourself another one.'

'I cannot,' he replied crossly.

'C'mon,' Ceci coaxed, leaning against his shoulder and impeding his movements. 'Forget it. It doesn't mean all that much. It's just a thing, and anyhow, you're not even making it with her.'

'How do you know that?' Paul asked, looking up. His face was hot and marked with dust, and he spoke without thinking.

'Why, you told me so,' Ceci sounded surprised. 'Didn't you?'

Too late, Paul realized what he was getting into. But he was too irritated, as well as too straightforward, for deliberate deception.

'No.'

'Sure you did, too. Right at the beginning.'

'You must have misunderstood me. I never said anything like that.' Ceci's eyes began to dilate, her mouth opened, and she took half a step back. 'Maybe you assumed it,' he said more gently.

Paul started to stand up, but before he could rise very far Ceci hit him in the head with her handbag. 'Ow!' he exclaimed, and toppled over sideways into a coarse, prickly bush. She hit him again, less accurately now because there were branches in the way. 'For Christ's sake!'

[165

'You shit!' Ceci shouted. 'You cheap, lying, two-timing shit!'
She burst into angry tears.

Paul picked himself out of the bush. The sharp twigs clung to
his clothes; he stood up, trailing shreds of dacron suiting. He
moved cautiously towards Ceci, one arm advanced to put round
her shoulders, the other to ward off further blows.

'I'm sorry,' he said.

Ceci did not raise her bag again; it hung limply to the ground.
But she jerked aside from his touch.

'All this time!' she gasped. 'Mother of God, all this time you've
been shucking me. What a bringdown!'

'You don't understand.' Paul did not attempt to hold Ceci
again, but sort of swayed towards her. 'What's between me and
Katherine has nothing to do with us. It's a completely different
kind of thing; it's not really physical. We don't really make love
very often. And anyhow, that side of it isn't very important. I
mean, well. I don't enjoy it very intensely physically.'

If it were possible to make the situation worse, he had done so.

'Christ almighty!' Ceci shouted, brushing aside the tears and
strands of hair with which her face was streaked. Her small hands
were clenched into fists: Paul thought she was going to hit him
again, and took a step backwards. But she only glared, and drew
her breath in like a cat hissing. 'You think that's an *excuse*, that
you don't like doing it with her? Man, what a hypocritical, fucked-
up square you really are, underneath!'

'I don't get it,' Paul said. He felt shell-shocked. 'What do you
want me to do? Hell, what do you want me to say?'

'Ah, shit.' Ceci's voice was thick with tears. She controlled herself, and went on, 'If you really liked it—say if you really dug
making it with your wife, whenever she felt well enough to
want to, I could pick up on that. I wouldn't like it, but I'd have
to relate. . . . You thought you had to make up a cheap story
for me.' She focused on Paul's face, his expression of blank confusion. 'Man, you really are dumb,' she said. 'Walter was right.
You're just nowhere.'

'Listen,' she added. 'I've got to get to the restaurant. Stella will
be flipping trying to cover for me. I oughta be there now.' She
turned and began to pick her way back across the field.

The mention of Walter Wong reminded Paul that he, too, had a grudge. Maybe if he named it they could compromise and this could still turn into an ordinary fight. 'Ah come on,' he said to the back of her jersey, her disordered streaky gold hair, her bare scratched arms. 'You've been involved with other people too, a lot of people. Wong, and that guy you went to San Francisco with that you told me about, and Tomaso, and maybe even John and Steve.' To extend his list, Paul included what he had only sometimes suspected, and even an improbable guess.

'I have not!' Ceci turned to face him on the bank above the road, crying again. 'I mean, hell, so what if I have, that's all the *past*. I didn't even know you then.'

At these revelations, a feeling like a paring-knife turned in Paul's intestines. But he tried to pay no attention to it. It was more important not to lose Ceci. Making an effort, he saw it from her point of view; admitted that he had, at least, let her deceive herself. But if he had known how seriously she took it—

'Ceci! Listen.' He spoke with emphasis; held out his arms to embrace her, and bounded forward. But at the same moment Ceci jumped off the edge of the bank on to the road.

Paul clasped empty space; he lost his balance, shouted 'Ahh! Help!' and waved his arms wildly to avoid falling head first. His feet slid out from under him and he skidded down the bank on his back in a landslide of stones and dust.

'Oof!' He came to rest on his rear in the ditch, considerably shaken and bruised. He looked up. Ceci stood on the crest of the road watching him. For the first time that day she was laughing.

'Wow, uh, oh God!' she laughed. 'Ha ha ha ha!' Her mouth was stretched wide, and the small white teeth showed in a kitten's grin. 'Wow, do you look *dumb*. . . . Well, get up,' she added. Don't just lie there. Climb into your Jag and drive me to the restaurant.'

```
ju        lu
lu        mu
nu        tu
```

Katherine typed, with an I.B.M. electric typewriter, on to a white index card. She rolled the card out of the carriage, inserted another, and typed:

```
mu        fu
lu        fu
pu        wu
```

She was copying a set of 1,008 flash cards for an experiment on the psychology of learning. Each card consisted of six out of a possible ten nonsense syllables selected and arranged at random.

It was now ten-thirty; Katherine had been working on this project for an hour and a half, and had completed 185 cards. And it wasn't even her job. She was supposed to be working for Iz that day, but he had lent her to Professor Jekyll. So she was sitting in Dr Jekyll's office, and Iz was probably still asleep in bed, unless he was lying on the beach somewhere. It was a pleasant warm day, outside.

```
fu        mu
su        pu
nu        fu
```

This job was not only an insult to Katherine's intelligence and education, but a waste of university funds, because she earned $2.71 an hour, much more than an ordinary typist. Since there was no meeting, and Iz was not coming in, she would be doing it from now until five o'clock.

Usually, the days that she worked for Iz were the best ones: partly because his projects were apt to be more interesting, but mostly because of the conversations that went with them.

Now that they were friends, when Iz came in he would sit down on the edge of Katherine's desk and say, 'Well, Katherine. What's new?' And she would tell him, or he would tell her, before they started work. Later, in the middle of dictating a report or a case history, he would exclaim, 'Hey. I haven't eaten anything since last night. I'm starving. Come on.' And they would climb into Iz's car and skid downhill to the Village Delicatessen for thick pastrami sandwiches, or to the English teashop on Westwood Boulevard which had scones with eight kinds of marmalade and jam. Once they went all the way out to Santa Monica because it was the only place for real strawberry cheesecake outside of Hollywood. At first Katherine wouldn't order anything, but her refusals made so much trouble ('You have some problem about accepting food, don't you? What is it?') that presently she gave in. She had to resign herself to letting him pay, too. ('I'm rich, comparatively; you're poor. When you make twenty dollars an hour, I'll let you take me; okay?')

Katherine had learned, in these last two weeks, a good deal about Iz. She knew something about his childhood, which had been spent in ten different cities in six different countries; she knew something about his marriages, and something about his politics. 'Do you know what Jackie in the office told me the other day?' she had asked him. 'She told me to watch out for you, you were a Communist.' Iz groaned. 'Oh no, no,' he said. 'Here we go again. Listen, I'm less of a Communist than you are. Or Jackie is. I'm an *anarchist*. And anarchist is the *opposite* of a Communist.' Katherine's face did not show immediate comprehension. 'Of course some of the early anarchists were also Communists, they thought, but that was their mistake. See, a Communist believes always in more order. An anarchist believes in *less* order: less government, less rules, less system.' But—' Katherine began; he continued. 'Now you admit all organizations are terrible, inhuman; the larger they are the more they are terrible, okay?'

Did she admit this? Katherine was not sure; she had never thought about it. She smiled uncertainly. Iz took this for agreement, and went on to talk about placing random messages on the telegraph wires, confusing policemen by disobedience of unwritten laws, and giving deliberately absurd answers to questionnaires. 'Every day you should create a little disorganization somewhere, that's the idea.' 'Like Boy Scouts,' Katherine could not help saying; but Iz did not get irritated. 'That's right,' he said, smiling. 'A good deed every day. You're starting to understand. Only the anarchist is unkind, unthrifty, irreverent, disloyal, etcetera.' 'All

I ever heard about anarchists was that they threw bombs at things,' Katherine remarked, half giggling. 'What's that song? "In an anarchistic garret so meagre and so mean, You can smell the pungent odour of nitroglycerine. They're busy making fuses and filling cans with nails—"' 'Ah, not any more,' Iz had said, laughing so that it was impossible to know whether he were serious. 'That was in the early days, when our methods were more crude.'

And as she found out about Iz, she told him about herself. It was true, for instance, that she really thought makeup was vulgar and nasty—she daubed on lipstick and powder every morning simply because, after all, it was the rule. 'Whose rule?' Iz had inquired. 'If you don't like grease on your face, so leave it off. Who cares?' And after all nobody seemed to; at least they didn't say anything about it. Of course out here everyone was so weird, it didn't matter what you did. It would have been different back East.

They had a joke between them about Katherine's being one of Dr Einsam's patients. If I were your patient, she would ask sometimes, what would you advise me about this? And he would give sometimes an outlandish, sometimes a reasonable answer. 'Basically,' he had said last time, seriously, 'you can't do anything until you decide what you actually want from your husband. Why don't you think about that?'

So Katherine was thinking about it. Meanwhile, following the advice Iz had given her that first day in the ice-cream shop, she had begun what he called 'Paul-watching'. It was amazing how, with Iz's assistance and interest, what in the past had hurt so much had become almost a game. As he had predicted, signs of Paul's infidelity continued to appear, increasing in obviousness. Finally last week he had come home to supper looking as if he'd been in a fight, all bruised and scratched and covered with dust. How puzzled he had seemed when she didn't ask any questions! Katherine had to smile when she recalled it — and the way he had taken off his filthy suit and laid it out on a chair for her to see, instead of putting it into the laundry hamper as usual. 'He's trying to tell you something,' Iz had said. 'I had a German Shepherd like that once.'

nu	tu
pu	mu
wu	pu

Dr Jekyll's office, like most in the Department of Social Sciences, was dark, airless, and hot; it looked upon a yellow brick wall, with three aluminium ventilator hoods approaching along the top. No wonder everyone wanted to move. Katherine had come to the end of the pack of index cards; she swivelled her chair round and reached for more in the bottom drawer. As she did so, she noticed part of a floor plan sticking out from some papers on Dr Jekyll's desk. Taking care not to displace anything else, she eased it out.

Almost at once she realized that this must be the final plan for the allocation of space in the new Social Sciences building; and that the Project on Perception and Delinquency was allotted nothing. From the attached memorandum she learned that this plan was being sent to all the full professors as a last step before it was put into effect. 'Any objections or proposed changes must be sent to the Chairman of the Space Committee *on or before March 30*,' it ended ominously.

March 30. That was today. What was going to happen, then? The shack in which the Project was now located would be torn down in June, and Perception and Delinquency would have no place to go. Dr Jekyll must have forgotten that he had promised to take care of them. Or they had forgotten to remind him, or they didn't know that today was the deadline in the 'space race'. What ought she to do? Oh, why wasn't Iz here? She couldn't speak to Dr Jekyll herself, but someone ought to speak to him, right away. A feeling of anxious excitement began to expand inside Katherine.

This was a crisis. She must get in touch with Iz, as soon as possible. It was past eleven — Dr Jekyll had classes, he had said he wouldn't be back until one. There was time, if she went now, if she hurried, to get to Iz, show him the plan, and bring it, and him, back. Then he could speak to Dr Jekyll, and Dr Jekyll could speak to the Committee, and the space race could be won after all; all due to a fortunate accident, and to Katherine Cattleman.

Without stopping to think any more, Katherine stood up, shoved the floor plan into her bag, and left the office, locking the door behind her. As fast as she could go without actually running, she went along the hall, down two flights of stairs, and out of the building.

As usual, it was glaringly bright outside. The sun on the cement walks and brick walls hurt her eyes. To Katherine's right was an orange steel skeleton for the plans she had in her bag, the rooms marked out as cubes of empty space. In imagination, she saw herself and the rest of the Project sitting triumphant up there, suspended in the air around an invisible desk. In the distance, across Westwood Boulevard, she could see the trees and pale roofs of apartment houses; somewhere among them was Dr Einsam's apartment.

She started towards it, at first along the path. But soon, becoming impatient, she veered off straight down-hill past another excavation, picking her way around construction equipment and piles of cinder-blocks. Another immense modernistic building, six floors of poured concrete and steel, was rising here. According to a sign, it was to be called Parking Structure F. Dust covered her shoes, the ones Iz approved of.

Was she acting crazily? She had never done anything like this at her other jobs. But there had been no need to: back in Massachusetts there was a tradition of administrative calm — changes came so slowly, in such an orderly way, that they were hardly felt. Whereas here everything was always in flux, growing, shifting.

Westwood Boulevard, at the bottom of the hill, was crowded with shiny cars. The eucalyptus trees raised long bare arms like white wooden snakes above the traffic. Katherine crossed over, and started down the path by the tennis courts. Balls flew at her through the air as she went, and rebounded from the wire netting a few feet away — involuntarily she flinched and ducked, and hurried on faster. On the other side of the path, enclosed by an even denser grid of fence topped with barbed wire, the university's experimental citrus trees were in flower and fruit; the air was sticky with orange blossom scent.

She came out on Gayley Street, and ran across between the cars. Dr Einsam's apartment building was almost immediately opposite — a large white object, poured over the hillside like a plaster-of-Paris pueblo. An outside stairway followed it uphill through purple bougainvillaea and palms, with open galleries at each landing.

Katherine stopped at the top of the steps, panting and hot. Her pulse was loud, and her knees weak from climbing so fast. She leaned against the wall and looked at her watch. Fifteen minutes were already gone; there was no more time to lose. She pulled the plans out of her bag, turned to the first door along the gallery, and knocked next to the nameplate: *I. Einsam.*

There was a pause. Katherine didn't want to stand staring at Iz's door, so she turned and looked down at the descending steps, the palms and creepers, the glitter of the sun on the cars below. Suppose he weren't home, what then?

'Well,' Iz said. 'You surprise me.' She turned; Dr Einsam stood on the threshold wearing a red plaid bathrobe.

'I didn't mean to disturb—I mean, I'm sorry I had to disturb you,' she began, still breathing hard. 'But it's really important: I found the floor plans—here—for the new building. They were on Dr Jekyll's desk, and the Project isn't on them *anywhere.*' Iz continued to watch Katherine without changing his small smile of curious interest; she felt that she must be explaining herself badly. 'You see, this is the deadline, *today,* for any changes. The letter says. So I didn't know what to do—I thought, if you could talk to Dr Jekyll in time—he'll be back from class at one—and so I just rushed over to find you. Here.' She held the plans further out towards Iz, but he still did not take them.

'I'm glad you came,' he said. 'Come on in.' He pulled the door open, and Katherine followed him into a long low room, with trees and sky spread across one wall. Large exotic plants grew out of containers on the floor. 'I was just having my breakfast,' Iz said. 'Would you like to join me?'

'No, no thank you.' Katherine was really hungry, or should have been, as it was lunch time, but she was starting to feel uncomfortable. Iz's very unconcerned manner gave her a sense of having done something serious and possibly wrong—as if soon he would turn on her and rebuke her for having stolen papers off Dr Jekyll's desk, or something worse. She looked at the floor and saw dark red carpeting and Iz's bare feet. His legs, below the bathrobe, were bare too, and covered with dark hairs.

'Well, Katherine, if you don't mind, I'll finish my coffee. Here, sit down.' He gathered some newspapers off a low couch.

Katherine sat on the edge of the couch, about six inches from the floor, bending her knees sideways awkwardly. Through an open door at the other side of the room she could see Iz's bedroom, with an unmade bed and a chest of drawers. On top of the chest, leaning up against the wall, was a racing bicycle. She held out the floor plans again, as if they were her passport. This time Iz took them. He turned the pages quickly while he stood above Katherine, drinking his coffee.

'Uh huh,' he said finally. He looked down at her, and then glanced out of the long window at the view of palms and roofs and distant hills.

'The deadline is today,' Katherine told him again. 'It's right there in the covering letter. It says—' she jumped up and pointed it out on the page he was holding— ' "Any objections or proposed changes must be sent to the Chairman of the Space Committee on or before March 30," you see, that's *today*.'

'Ya,' Iz said. 'I see. Katherine. Look at the city out there. How do you like it?'

Katherine stood up, and went over to the window. Something was very, very wrong; but what? 'Oh yes, it's beautiful,' she said nervously. 'You really do have a wonderful view. The university looks so pretty from here, with the sun on it. Or is that Bullock's over there?'

'There's no difference,' Iz said. 'It's like a friend of mine says, "I work in the big store at the bottom of the hill." Well.' He put his coffee cup down carefully on a table, dropped the plans to the floor, walked up behind Katherine, and ran both hands down her arms.

'Eh!' she cried out, and jumped as if she had touched an un-insulated wire.

Iz paid no attention; he took a step forward, pushing Katherine up against the cold glass of the window, air and trees, and kissed the back of her neck; she felt his body forced against hers, the coarse hair of his beard, his mouth.

'Oh no; I don't want—' Katherine twisted round, and tried to pull away. 'No!'

Iz stepped back, releasing her from the weight of his body, but he kept one hand against the window on each side, so that she could not move away. 'What's the matter with you today?' she said shakily.

'I want to sleep with you,' Iz said. 'That's what you came here for, isn't it?'

'No. Of course not!'

'Ah, come on. I told you what my rules are. You knew I wasn't joking.' Though he was not touching her, Iz was standing so close that Katherine could feel his breath and see the hairs growing out of his face into his beard. His arms, too, were covered with wiry black hair; it was on the backs of his hands, and on his legs, and matted on his chest. She felt she had been cornered by a dangerous, irrational animal.

'I didn't even think about that!' she said, terrified. 'I found the plans; and I knew they were important, and I had to get them to you; that's all.'

'Ah, don't kid me. You didn't have to bring them all the way over here. You could have called me on the phone.' It was true; why hadn't she thought of that? 'Now couldn't you have?' Iz smiled. Katherine recalled how she had run across Westwood, and wanted to run right back.

'I didn't think of the telephone,' she said in an embarrassed voice. 'I just rushed over. I'm sorry. Of course you're right. That wasn't necessary.'

'Depends what you need.' Iz leaned back, and let his arms fall. Though he continued to look at Katherine, she felt that the threat had diminished. 'And why did it have to be me?' he went on. 'How was it you didn't try to get in touch with Charlie or Bert up at school?'

This idea, too, had simply not occurred to Katherine. 'Well, but it's you I usually . . .' she began feebly, but could not think how to end the sentence, and let her voice trail away.

'Another thing,' Iz continued, really grinning now. 'Why did you jump at the conclusion that the plans you found are going into effect? How are you sure that our project hasn't already been taken care of?

'I don't know,' she said. 'Has it already been taken care of?'

Iz nodded. 'Uh huh. Charlie and I saw Jekyll Saturday. He's talked to Dr Braun and it's all set: we're going to have two lab. rooms and an office on the third floor.'

'Oh, that's good.' But Katherine's pleasure was extremely dim compared to her nervous embarrassment. 'I'm sorry,' she repeated. 'I was stupid. I don't know why I didn't think of all that.'

'You really wanted to come over here,' Iz told her. 'You don't have to feel sorry about it. I'm flattered. It's a great thing, the unconscious mind.' He smiled, and stepped back.

'But I didn't think—' Katherine began, and stopped. 'I mean, it never occurred to me that you—I suppose I thought I was safe,' (she attempted a joke) 'because I know psychiatrists don't sleep with their patients.'

'Yah, they don't,' Iz said. 'They sleep with their secretaries.' He laughed. 'But I'll let you off this time,' he conceded. 'You can go—' He broke off, looked at her, and said in an offhand way, 'No; I don't want to be rude. I'll give you five—no, ten minutes. You can stay ten minutes and talk to me, before you have to leave. . . . I think I'll have another cup of coffee.' He walked across the room towards a wall kitchen. 'Would you like some coffee?'

Should she go now? But everything had become so casual and ordinary that Katherine could hardly believe what had just taken place. Maybe it had all been a joke. 'That's very kind of you,' she said.

'Cream? Sugar?'

'Just cream, please.'

Iz handed Katherine her cup and sat down at a round table not unlike the tables at the ice-cream shop.

'Thank you,' Katherine said, and sat down opposite. He must have been kidding her. Still, she felt something had to be said to make sure, and fit the scene together; it couldn't just disappear; that would be too weird, and really rather awful.

'Well, at least I did get to see your apartment,' she remarked. 'It *is* pleasant. That long window, and all the plants, like a jungle.' Iz smiled, but made no other contribution. 'Wouldn't you really ever have invited me here? Even if I brought my husband. Wouldn't that have been safe?'

'Of course. But he isn't here, is he?' In pantomine, Iz leaned down and peered under the table, and then behind a low book-case by the wall. The implication was that Paul was an insignificant object, small enough to be overlooked. Actually, of course, he was five or six inches taller than Iz. But Iz was somehow more concentrated, denser.

'How is Paul, incidentally?' Iz felt his face to see whether he had shaved the outlines of his black beard properly.

'Oh, he's all right.' Though she felt much easier, Katherine could not quite manage to continue her confidences to Dr Einsam. 'How's Glory?'

'I don't know. I haven't spoken to her for almost two weeks. She's keeping busy, I suppose.' Iz's voice was so dry and sour that Katherine felt a wave of sympathy.

'I'm sorry.'

Iz looked up. 'You really are, aren't you?' he said without irony. 'You're about the only one. Do you want to know what Dr Robinson said to me yesterday?' She nodded. 'He had the stupidity to come up and congratulate me on my separation.'

'What, really? How could he do that?'

'For him it was easy. You don't know that department, Katherine. You should have been around here two years ago, when Jekyll first put me up for a teaching appointment. It was quite incredible. Academically I looked great, but they had also to take into consideration my character. They are all of course self-appointed clinical diagnosticians. They concluded I was immature, and my personal life was unstable. Because I had been married and divorced, and now they heard the rumour I was going around with an undergraduate. I told Jekyll, "I am not 'going around with an undergraduate'. I am living with a very attractive and intelligent girl who happens at the moment to be taking some courses in the Department of Social Sciences." Only from their point of view it was as if I had deliberately selected some abstraction called *an undergraduate* to sleep with, exactly because it was against their rules. . . . Jekyll's a good guy; he tried to see it my way, but he just wasn't flexible enough. If she had only been a graduate student, he kept saying, even a first-year graduate student, that would have been better. But, I pointed out to him, none of the first-year graduate students were as good-looking as Nancy. They were really a sad lot that year.' Iz looked quietly at his watch.

'That's awful,' Katherine said. She was fascinated, though really shocked by the behaviour of both sides. 'I mean trying to interfere with people's personal lives like that.'

'That's not the end of it. Jekyll and Charlie Haraki brought me up again last year. By that time I wasn't living with Nancy any longer, but I was engaged to Glory; they liked that even less. Two

[177

unsuccessful relationships, they said to Jekyll, and now he wants to marry a movie star. Isn't there something rather unhealthy about that? I was furious. Unhealthy, to want to marry Glory! I said to Jekyll, what about them? What about Mrs Braun: don't you think anyone who would stay married to her for twenty years is pretty unhealthy? What about Robinson? He's never been married at all; I bet he couldn't even get it up for Glory; isn't that pretty unhealthy?'

Iz looked at his watch again. A smile slowly appeared on his face. He drained his coffee cup and put it down. 'Well, Mrs Cattleman,' he said. 'Look what time it is.'

'Oh, that's right.' Katherine checked her own watch. 'I'll go now.' She stood up and started towards the door.

'No,' Iz said, getting up. 'You've missed your chance. You see, you wanted to stay.' He spoke casually, and began casually to walk towards her.

'I'm sorry; I forgot to look at my watch,' Katherine explained, a little nervously. 'I was too interested in what you were saying, I guess.' She picked up her pocket-book, and turned towards the exit. 'I'll see you tomorrow, then.'

'Uh-uh.' Iz put his hand over Katherine's on the doorknob, so that she could not turn it.

'Now come on, Iz,' she exclaimed. 'I'm leaving now. Don't be difficult.' She twisted and pulled to get her hand free, and open the door, but unsuccessfully—Iz only tightened his grip. The muscle of his arm pressed against hers. 'Oh, really, don't be so silly again,' she continued, putting on a primly humorous tone. 'I only stayed a moment longer than you said I could. You're not going to make anything of that, surely!'

'I'm sorry,' Iz said in a not-sorry voice. 'But I've never let any woman make a fool of me twice.' With his free hand he took hold of Katherine's hair at the back of her neck, and turned her face forcibly towards his. 'I'll tell you what I'm going to do.' He spoke in a friendly, reasonable tone, almost as if he were dictating a report. 'I'm going to give you what you came here for. Don't play coy with me. If you won't take your clothes off, I'll tear them off. If you won't lie down, I'll knock you down. If you won't make love with me, I'll rape you.'

He smiled, but behind his dark-rimmed glasses his pale grey

eyes were serious, looking into hers. Katherine began to tremble violently.

'No,' she said. 'Please, no.' Iz put his arms round her.

'Ah, Katherine,' he said, holding her. 'You don't have to be frightened. You'll see. It will be a good experience.'

Part IV: HOLLYWOOD

17

THE empty sound stage was like the inside of an immense dark cardboard box; a vast cube of obscure space. Against the distant walls hung painted drop clothes representing in meticulous detail the landscape and architecture of the imaginary planet Nemo, setting of Glory's current picture, a science-fiction musical comedy. Assemblages of platforms and steps rose here and there in the darkness like hillocks on a plain, among herds of folding chairs. On the dusty ground, black electrical cables and wires of all sizes were coiled and crossed, in some places resembling a nest of enormous snakes. Steel and aluminum skeletons supported the spotlights and floods, and the immense cameras on their travelling booms. More hanging lights, microphones, ropes, flats, and cables disappeared into the shadows far above.

All these lights were dark now; the only illumination came from the long strip of hot sunshine slanting in from the open doorway, fading as it fanned aross the cement; and from the electric bulbs around the make-up mirror in Glory's trailer dressing-room.

It was hot everywhere today; densely hot and smoggy outdoors; only a little less so where Glory and her agent Maxie Weiss were sitting in front of her trailer on two wooden chairs. Glory's make-up was caked with sweat, for she had been working for three hours, rehearsing dance numbers; or standing about waiting in the excruciating boredom of film-making while other members of the cast rehearsed, or while the choreographer conferred endlessly with the director, the assistant director, the musical director, the dance coach, the man in charge of the extras, and his and their assistants. The tower of pink-blonde hair, though skewered to her head with innumerable pins, had begun to fray at the edges; her rehearsal clothes (black tights and loose sleeveless white top) were wrinkled and damp.

She sat in the naturally graceful pose of a dancer, one leg tucked under her, the other pointed out along the floor, drinking from a Thermos bottle a health-food drink called Frozen Tiger's Milk.

Maxie was eating two pastrami sandwiches which had been wrapped in waxed paper; he looked hot, fat, and worried. He would have been lunching at Scandia, an air-conditioned restaurant near his air-conditioned office on Sunset Strip, and Glory would have been at the studio lunch-room, if they had not had to confer about a crisis.

The trouble had all started yesterday. It had been a bad day for Glory, an unlucky day. While she was eating breakfast, her girl friend, a starlet named Ramona Moon, had called up to warn her that Pluto was square with Neptune in her tenth house and she ought not to engage in any new or important professional ventures. Also she should avoid all occasions that might lead to serious emotional conflict; in fact about the best thing she could do would be to get right back into bed and stay there. Glory was not, like Mona, a follower of astrology; all the same, it would have been better if she had listened to her.

The first thing that happened was that she broke off one of her finger-nails starting the T-Bird. The traffic on the way to the studio was hell, and when she got there Roger, the best make-up man, was out sick. Then, while they were waiting around between takes, Petey Thorsley, a little dancer who was playing one of the other natives of Nemo, came over. He leaned on the back of a chair, in his green rubber costume with pink polka-dots and webbed hands like a duck, and remarked to Glory that Dr Einsam had been seen eating cheesecake in Zucky's out in Santa Monica with a brunette, and what was the story? 'You tell me, don't ask me,' Glory said, thinking that Mona had been right. 'Gee, that's all I know,' Petey said, his wire antennae quivering. 'Listen, don't let it get you down. My friend said she was nothing anyhow, kind of an intellectual type. . . . Aw hell, Glory, I'm sorry.'

'That's okay, Petey, it doesn't bother me,' she had replied, manufacturing her smile.

Her real mistake had been to think that the stars were through with her after that one. She grew careless when nothing more went wrong on set the rest of the day; when she even got off early and beat some of the traffic driving home. She forgot about astrology; she had a big evening ahead.

There was a première that night of a picture called *Dancing*

[183

Cowboy, starring Rory Gunn. Rory was also the star of the musical that Glory was making now, and in which she had for the first time what might be called a second female lead, even if she did have to play it with antennae and green hands. As it was, naturally, top priority that Rory Gunn should be well disposed towards Glory, ever since the picture started Maxie had been putting out stories about how much she thought of him as an actor, and what a tremendous thrill it was for her to have the chance to play with him. For that evening he had arranged that after the showing, when Rory was on his way out of the theatre, Glory would rush up to him and kiss him in a spontaneous demonstration of her admiration; kind of kooky, but lovable, and really *sincere*. He had cleared this with the studio and with Rory's agent, and alerted the local papers and also two wire services. Glory had a new dress for the occasion, short white bouffant satin printed with pink roses, and she had borrowed a white mink stole from the studio. So it was all set.

Rory Gunn came out of the theatre first, right on schedule, taking it slow and giving the crowd behind the ropes a good look at his profile. Glory was close behind him, but at the door of the lobby she held back a couple of seconds, waiting for a good clear space to open up between her and the photographers. Then she stepped out, saw Rory, did a big take—excitement, adoration—and began to run.

She had waited a moment too long. As she approached Rory, a girl in the crowd, one of his fans, broke through the police line and also started racing towards him. They got to the star about the same time, and Glory stepped in front of the kid, but before she could open her mouth to speak this juvenile delinquent put her hand in Glory's face and gave her a violent push. Glory staggered back on her three-inch pink satin heels; tripped, screamed, and fell on her ass on the sidewalk, with a noise of ripping cloth. From this position she saw the girl fling her arms around Rory Gunn and kiss him passionately, while he just stood there looking dumb. Without stopping to think, boiling with fury, Glory scrambled up in the ruins of her dress, one shoe off, limped forward, and slammed the kid in the jaw. Even as the blow went home she knew she had made a terrible mistake; she heard a louder howl rise from the crowd and the flash bulbs popping, like all Mona's unlucky stars machine-gunning her down together.

Maxie had done what he could to mop up the mess. First he got the girl back into the lobby and started talking to her; come on, after all, he told her, Glory is a fan of Rory Gunn's same as you are; you ought to appreciate what she felt like when you shoved yourself in like that; beside you ruined her new two-hundred-dollar dress for her. It went over pretty well: at least the kid stopped crying, and Maxie got a taxi around to the stage door and sent her home before the newspaper guys could get to her again. In the morning he ordered two lots of flowers delivered to the kid's house: some daffodils and a whole lot of other spring stuff from Glory, and three dozen red roses from Rory Gunn. Of course Maxie couldn't kill the story—but he spoke to the guys, giving them pretty much the same line: that Glory was so stuck on Rory Gunn and his marvellous performance in *Dancing Cowboy* that she just saw red when anybody got in her way. This story had appeared in the morning papers which lay about on the floor at Maxie's and Glory's feet. As he said now, it could have been a lot worse, even the photos.

'Uh-huh,' Glory uttered. 'Listen, thanks for everything, Maxie,' she added in a dull, throaty voice, and drank some Tiger's Milk. 'You're a doll.'

'That's okay. At least you appreciate.' Maxie wiped his face and began stripping the crusts off half a sandwich. 'I wonder should I check up on that kid again this afternoon, how she's feeling, is she okay?'

'No,' Glory said. 'Let's drop it.'

'Maybe you're right. I sent flowers already; we don't want to start a correspondence.'

'Yeah. Besides, she hit me first,' Glory pointed out, not for the first time.

'She's a fan,' Maxie said. 'It doesn't make any difference what she did. You can't sock a fan. Also she's only fourteen years old. A kid.'

'Yeah, well, shit: how was I supposed to know that? You tell her next time she wants to push somebody in the face bring her birth certificate.'

Maxie winced. It always bothered him when Glory's language

became too vulgar; he was trying to put her across as basically a sweet kid. He shifted around and sat sideways in his chair, facing her. 'Something else I got in my mind,' he said. 'I want to suggest a new image. We got to black out this picture you don't like fans. I thought of a gimmick this morning we could use, maybe. I want to put out a release—how does this sound?—Glory Green, now working in Superb's big new musical, etcetera, has a very *personal* relationship to her growing number of fans all over the world. Glory reads every day all the letters she receives, and she says she picks up lots of acting tips and good advice about her career from the girls and boys who follow her pictures: how does that sound?'

'Okay,' Glory said listlessly.

'Swell. Also I thought I'd call up Camilla at *Screen Scoops*, offer we could give her an exclusive. Maybe she can send somebody over this week-end and get some pictures. Like an example, I see you sitting at your antique writing-desk, nice outfit, serious expression, big piles of mail, dictating to your secretary. I like that.'

'Okay,' Glory repeated. 'My secretary? You think I should have a secretary? Don't you think that looks kind of too snooty?'

'Oh, nah. Everybody has a secretary. Liz Taylor has a secretary. Look at it this way: it shows how you're real serious about your responsibilities; it's like your business, these fan letters. I want to build up a nice picture. Anyhow, you got to get a secretary to answer the mail.'

Glory put the Thermos down and, turning her head slowly, looked at her agent through her fog of depression. 'Aw, Maxie,' she said. 'Do we really have to play this scene? I don't think I can make it.'

'Don't aggravate yourself. It'll be no trouble.' Maxie registered Glory's expression, and sought its probable cause. 'Hey, you had a conversation with Iz this morning?' he asked. 'Maybe he called you.'

Glory shook her head. 'Why should he call me? He's got nothing to talk to me about,' she said in a strained voice. 'He doesn't give a shit what happens to me.'

'Aw, Glory, baby. He's calling you all the time already. This last month he's phoned you eight, ten times.'

'Theven times,' she corrected him. 'Exactly theven times.'

'That's what I mean. He's obviously carrying the torch. And look at you: six months, and you're still very involved emotionally. I don't understand. Next time he phones, why don't you be a little nice to him?'

'That's how you thee it,' Glory said. She opened her mouth to relate Iz's latest betrayal, but could not bring herself to do so, and remained silent, staring into the dark spaces of the sound stage.

'Incidentally,' Maxie said, following his own train of thought. 'I spoke to Bo Habenicht this a.m.' Bo was Rory Gunn's agent. Maxie waited for Glory to ask 'Yeah?' As she did not, he continued. 'Rory's happy as a kid about the statement you gave. You know it's all gravy for him, that scene. Also he really appreciates your compliments. He wants to take you out some time this week, maybe tonight if you can make it.'

'You mean you and Bo want Gunn to take me out,' Glory said as flatly as was possible for her. This 'commercial socializing', as he called it, was one of the things Iz picked on most about her profession. 'What's the matter with him, doesn't he know I'm married yet?'

'Aw, come on now.' Maxie laid his sandwich down on its waxed paper. What with the trouble last night and his nervous stomach (he had something inside there that was probably planning to be an ulcer) he had got practically no sleep. But this was his job; he gathered his forces. 'What's the difference to you? All I'm asking is you should sit at a table with Rory an hour or so in a couple of night spots. I'm not suggesting to spend a weekend with him.'

'With that fag? You better not. That guy's so minty he gives me the creeps.'

'Baby, you got to think of the publicity angle. If you show around town with Rory a couple times, all this trouble could blow over; it even could be to your advantage. Also, the studio would like it. How do you think it's going to look to them, you turn down a date with Rory Gunn? You should be flattered.'

Glory paid no attention to this hard sell, but continued with her own thoughts. 'I'll bet that's the first time in that fruit's life he ever had two women really fighting over him. No wonder he was stunned.' She gave a short laugh.

With a grating noise, the sliding door to the building slid open behind them. The strip of smog and sunlight widened across the floor, and a party of five or six new starlets entered the sound stage, accompanied by a minor studio executive named Baby Petersen, who was showing them over the lot.

'Glory, baby!' he called out. 'Hey, c'mon over here, girls! I want you to meet a kid who's really making it.'

Squeaking and tripping over the electric cables, the starlets crossed the floor towards Glory. They were all very young, more or less beautiful, and immensely got up, with laquered hair, nylon eyelashes, and layers of petticoats—exquisite dolls, dressed for a party by some little girl too old to play with dolls. One by one they held out their pink, sharp, manicured hands to Glory while Baby told her their brand-new studio names.

Glory responded politely. Four years ago she had been a kid like these; she had been through all it had taken to get them here and all they were about to be put through. They were the usual assortment—a couple of brunettes, one sultry and the other the ladylike type; a redhead who moved like a dancer; and some blondes of varying shades, at whom Glory looked hardest because there was a remote chance that one of them might be competition some day.

'And this is Maxie Weiss, one of the best agents in the business, or should I say the best, baby?' Petersen gave Glory a quite meaningless wink. It was unknown whether he was called 'Baby' because of his predilection for this epithet, or whether it was a nickname retained from his childhood, an era now some distance away. Detractors claimed that Baby was really over sixty; he admitted variously to fifty and forty-five, but dressed and deported himself like an extremely young man or boy. He had a deep tan and very white teeth, and wore a seersucker suit, perforated shoes, and some well-made artificial hair.

'And how're you, Glory; how're you doing today?' he asked noisily, meanwhile putting his arm round one of the blondes and pinching her haunch in a friendly way. 'Is the sun smiling on you?' It had sometimes been suggested that Baby had his dialogue written for him cheap by hack writers that had been dropped by the studio.

'Just fine, Baby.' Of course it was impossible that Baby had not seen the papers this morning. He would not speak about the brawl in front of these kids, but the look he gave her was greedily searching under the smile and the tan. Glory certainly pulled a boo-boo last night, it said. Is she cracking up, maybe? Is she already on the way out? 'How're you feeling yourself?' she counter-attacked, turning a sexy smile on and then fading it off, like an electronic door opening and closing in a supermarket.

'Ah, I'm in great condition. I was working out in the gym two hours this morning.' To demonstrate his vigour, Baby grabbed another one of the starlets, this time the redhead, with his spare arm, and squeezed her with some difficulty to his chest. 'I'm ready for anything!' This time he winked at Maxie.

'Isn't he a great guy, huh!' the blonde said, rubbing against Baby. He pinched her again, in gratitude.

'Well, got to get back to work,' he added in a heavily kidding voice. 'It was really fine to see you, baby. All right, girls.'

Squeaking, they trooped out.

'That guy makes me sick,' Glory said as they disappeared. 'He's a creep, that's what he is.'

'Aw, he's not so bad.' Maxie had returned to his sandwich. 'He's got good intentions.'

'He has my ass. Do you know he was blowing off to Petey Thorsley last week how he's screwed with two hundred and thirteen girls, or some number like that.'

'Yeah? Whew.' Maxie sighed, as when one hears of an exhausting athletic feat.

'The little blonde in pink wasn't bad-looking,' Glory went on, testing for reassurance.

'I liked the redhead better. She had a good walk.'

It was not exactly the right answer; what Maxie should have said was that none of the bunch would ever rate a look if she was around, or to that effect.

'Yeah, but did you get a look at her expression when Baby grabbed her like that. She really didn't like it.'

'Oh, she'll learn to play along.'

'Maybe,' Glory said, drinking from the Thermos.

'If she can't, there's plenty others where she came from.' Maxie's tone was quite neutral; still, it implied that the clients of a successful press agent, too, were not irreplaceable. He had the tact not to point his moral, but allowed a minute of silence for it.

[189

'How about half a pastrami sandwich?' he asked then. 'I eat any more a day like this, I'll get acid indigestion.'

'Uh-uh. . . . You want some Tiger's Milk? It's good for your stomach.'

'Uh, no thanks.' Maxie could not control a tone of distaste for this drink, which he knew to be made of orange juice, powdered skim milk, brewer's yeast, vitamins, minerals, and raw egg. He shifted around and sat sideways on his chair again, facing Glory directly, but not looking at her.

'What I don't like to picture,' he said, beginning to fold the waxed paper around what was left of his sandwich. 'It's how Rory is going to feel when he hears you turned him down. Naturally, he's going to be hurt.' He finished wrapping the sandwich and put it into the paper bag. 'Aw yeah, he's going to think, all these nice statements she put out, she won't even have supper with me. She can't stand to talk to me for a couple hours with food. Actually she must hate me, probably.'

'Ah, Maxie, you know it's not like that,' Glory protested throatily. 'I mean, considering he's a complete lunk-head and a screaming queer, Gunn's a pretty straight guy. And he's a real dancer. He's got a style that won't quit.'

With the shrewdness born of hard experience, Maxie did not speak; he only looked at his client with a sad expression, waiting.

'You really figure he'll be all broken up if I don't go out with him?' Glory asked, in a tone half ironic, half serious.

Maxie shrugged. 'A guy like that, naturally he's sensitive. Already he's got the idea he can't make it with girls, not even as a friend. . . . An incident like this comes along and proves it, there's still less chance he's ever going to be able to relate normally.'

'Gee, you sound like my husband,' Glory said. She frowned, gazing up into the darkness above them. Maxie said nothing.

18

THE sun shone down hard on Wilshire Boulevard, and everything under it glittered. Spots of light rebounded off chrome and glass and painted metal, and a thousand blinding sparks leapt up from the grains of sand in the sidewalks. Katherine squeezed her eyes almost shut, painfully.

It was Friday afternoon, and she had come to Beverly Hills for the first time, looking for something to wear to a beach party the Skinners were planning. Susy Skinner had gone through Katherine's closets and said that nothing there would really do; and Iz had suggested that she try the stores in Beverly Hills. He had given her part of the afternoon off. By three o'clock she was supposed to have finished shopping, and report to his office on Bedford Drive.

How could everyone else on the street endure the glare? Because, she suddenly realized, they all had on dark glasses. That was what she needed, right away. Squinting, she plunged across the street towards a drug-store.

There was a tall rack of sunglasses inside the door, octagonal, and spinning round on its pole at the least touch, so that a hundred pairs of green and black eyes quickly looked at her; at wicked, impossible Katherine, the sex criminal, the adulteress. But, of course, there was nothing behind all those eyes but cardboard. Nobody was watching her; she was in Los Angeles, she reminded herself again, where nobody saw or cared what she did. And at this thought, as always recently, came a little burst of giddy euphoria, like a gas balloon exploding far up in the sky on a bright day: It didn't *matter*, nothing mattered here!

Rapidly, like a movie run through a projector at high speed, scenes passed through Katherine's mind. That first day, trembling or shivering as Iz pulled her into his bedroom. The green plants, the smooth sheets, the shades drawn down against the sun. Her hands were wet, cold. 'What's the matter?' 'I'm afraid of you'; a nervous, hysterical whisper. The hair on his body was black, curly, dense and fine, as if a design had been drawn all over him in India ink. And when she was feeling most cold, clumsy, and despairing (but she hadn't said anything, only made an ambiguous noise that might even have been a sigh of passion), 'Ah, Katherine. Don't try so hard. There's nothing at stake.' And later, lying back with the pillow folded under his head, 'I'm sorry. Next time we'll take it much more slowly.'

'Can I help you with something?' A salesclerk had appeared.

'No thank you; I'm just trying some sunglasses.' To prove it Katherine took a pair off the rack at random and put them on. Immediately the whole store, and the retreating clerk, turned dark green.

And the next time, taking it slowly. The long silence in Iz's apartment, deepened by the murmur of cars below, an occasional horn. The murmur of his voice: 'It's a long time since I just lay in someone's arms. I needed that.' Her feet growing warmer against his feet. 'Look! We're on television.' Katherine opened her eyes; dimly reflected on the pale tube beside the bed, grey bodies and limbs glistened on a grey sheet, intertwined. Like scenes from the faded print of a French art film, anonymous shadowed faces: *L'Homme Barbu et La Femme*. 'Mmm,' she murmured, shutting her eyes again. 'That was so good.' 'But you didn't come.' 'Yes I did,' she whispered defensively. 'I mean, that's how it always is for me. I don't come very hard.' 'Don't worry,' Iz said aloud. 'You will. It's in you.'

Katherine took off the sunglasses and tried on another pair. These had white rims, and the lenses were paler, purplish blue. Instantly the racks of shampoos and vitamins and paperback books were tinged mauve and azure; the neon tubes above glowed with a blue light. It was pretty; better than the reality.

Two days ago. The television set had been turned away, the covers thrown on to the floor; it was very hot outside. 'Trust me,' Iz was whispering. 'Do you hear what I'm saying? You don't have to prove anything. Just trust me.' Hands slowly joined by sweat, and then bodies. And then an amazing thing happened: a well of desire opened inside her, as if a huge washing machine had been turned on, with steaming water and suds foaming, splashing, thrashing, faster and faster. 'What will he think of me?' she wondered, but could not hold on to that or any thought. She shut her eyes and flung herself into it.

The salesclerk was hovering again. Katherine changed the blue sunglasses for some brown harlequin ones. The store flashed out in a coarse confusion of real colours for a moment, and then became deeply suntanned. In the slice of mirror at the top of the rack her face was reflected, brown with great dark slanted eyes. Very aware now that the clerk was watching officiously, she tried on several pairs of glasses in rapid succession. Different strange faces appeared in the mirror: green, blue, and ochre faces with eyes round, square, and oblong, some edged with glittering stones. Why didn't the man go away? Did he think she was going to break something, or steal from the store? She glared at him coldly.

'Yes?' The tone was pushingly familiar.

'I'll take these.' She held out the brown sunglasses.

'Yeah; they look fine on you. But you have to pay at the check-out stand, over there.' Katherine began to walk away. 'Say,' he added. 'I haven't seen you in here before. You just moved out here?'

Embarrassed by this inquisitiveness, Katherine shook her head, smiled very slightly at the clerk, and made a polite negative noise as she continued towards the front of the store.

'Aw, don't run off like that,' he said. 'Stay and talk to me.'

Katherine turned her head and focussed on the sales clerk for the first time. She saw him to be a well-constructed young man with rather long shiny hair and a knowing expression. Then the conventional response clicked into place—she gave him a routine cold stare, and walked away.

'Well!' he called after her. 'Don't trip, Lady Jane.'

What a strange city this was, Katherine thought as she walked along the suntanned sidewalk, and how oddly people here behaved. Men had tried to pick her up back East, but not very often, and never so boldly—certainly no one working in a store would have ventured to do so. But everything was strange here. Look at the women on the street: instead of the summer suits people wore when they went shopping in Boston or New York, most of them had on costumes out of a chorus line or a comic book. They wore high-heeled sandals, tight pants in metallic colours or fluorescent pastels, and brief tops which often left a strip of skin bare around the waist. Their hair was teased and puffed like heaps of cotton candy, or slicked up into varnished cones.

At the corner of Wilshire and Beverly Boulevards, a billboard stood on top of a row of shops. It portrayed a glowing and steaming cup of coffee twenty feet across. A cardboard figure of a woman, about life size, was climbing up to the brim of the cup on a cardboard ladder, smiling. A brand name was written below; above, in huge red letters, appeared the simple message, 'Indulge Yourself'.

The shop Iz had recommended was odd-looking, even for Los Angeles: situated on a wedge-shaped corner, it was also wedge-shaped and painted dead black. The interior was even odder: an immensely high irregular room, centred about a huge rectangular white pillar, indirectly lit and hung with long mirror and grey plush curtains two stories high, it resembled a stage-set by Gordon Craig. This was where Glory bought most of her clothes.

According to Susy Skinner, what Katherine needed for the Nutting barbecue was a 'Capri set'—fancy slacks and a matching top. She went through a rack of clothes of strange materials and cut, taking out a few things. Then she looked round for a sales-woman and a place to try on. But nobody came forward—the room was empty except for two girls in black stretch pants and sandals sitting talking in the far corner. They wore an extreme version of beat make-up and looked like actresses or dancers. In that drugstore there was too much service, Katherine thought, and here there isn't any.

Carrying a pile of clothes, she crossed the room towards the dancers. 'Excuse me; but do you know where the salesclerk is?'

'You want to try some things on?' The girl who said this had a dark tan and long shiny black hair hanging to below her shoulders. 'You can take 'em in there, behind the curtain.'

In the dim dressing-room Katherine struggled out of her dress and pumps and into navy-blue slacks and a sailor shirt. She put her shoes back on, which looked terrible, so she took them off—the carpet seemed fairly clean—and went out to find a mirror. The salesgirls, if they were salesgirls, glanced up.

'Uh-uh,' the blackhaired one said, shaking her head. 'That's no good for you. It looks draggy.'

'The colour's all wrong,' said the other, who was small, pale,

and extremely thin, with a cloud of frizzy hair and immense eyes.
'You should have some light, bright colour, like maybe pink or
yellow.'

'She could wear that set of yours with the pink leaves.' The girl
got up. 'What's your size? About a ten?'

Katherine nodded slightly. She would have liked to be sure that
these girls really worked here and were not merely making fun
of her.

'Here. Try this on.'

Katherine considered refusing politely, but after all, what did
it matter? She retreated to the dressing room and put on pale
yellow pants, very tight, and a matching top appliqued with
baroque designs in pink.

'Yeah! I like that. It really swings,' the dark girl exclaimed as
she came out again. 'What do you think, Dominique?'

'It's right,' Dominique said approvingly.

'She designed that,' the other girl explained. 'She makes a lot
of our clothes. . . . See if you dig it yourself. The mirror's over
there.'

As Katherine crossed the room, the shop door opened and a
group of other customers entered. Suddenly embarrassed by her
bare feet and the costume she was wearing, she averted her eyes
and took a detour between two racks of bathing suits and around
behind the central pillar. But one of the customers seemed to be
moving in that direction too, she noticed, walking directly
towards her across the carpet with a determined expression. She
was a sophisticated-looking girl in her twenties, a very Hollywood
type, in dark glasses and yellow slacks, with shiny pale brown hair
pulled tight back—Suddenly Katherine knew who she was. She
raised her hand, half waving and half warding off; her reflection
did the same.

Dr Einsam's was the first psychiatrist's waiting-room Katherine
had ever been in. She looked at it curiously for signs that this was
an antechamber to the treatment of the soul. But it was like any
doctor's office. The furniture was somewhat Danish and somewhat
modern, Philodendron sprouted from brackets under the diffused
light, and the panelled walls were bare of any image. It was all
innocuous to the point of blandness—perhaps deliberately so.

[195

The waiting-rooms in Purgatory probably looked like this.

Katherine sat down. She did not pick up *Life*, *Time*, or *The New Yorker* from the neat piles on the walnut veneer, but continued to stare round the room, as if after all it might contain some clue to the strangeness of this city, or of Dr Einsam. Because they were related somehow. In his own terms, Iz was perfectly consistent. He had a way of looking at this world, and a system for dealing with it. He even had his own language—in a way, the language *was* the system.

She had tried to translate some of his more striking statements back into ordinary English, but when she did so explicitly she usually got into trouble. *I don't have any insecurities in that area* meant 'I'm not worried about that'. But *I have no serious emotional commitments now* might mean 'I'm not involved with anybody else', or it might mean 'I'm not in love with you or anybody'. 'Love?' Iz had said, when after a silence she tried to settle this point. 'I don't know what that word means to you. What I feel for you is completely unique. It doesn't relate to anything else in my life. . . . Can you understand that?' 'I don't think so,' she had said, turning her head away on the sheet. Gently, Iz turned it back towards him. 'Try to,' he said. 'Listen, Katherine,' he continued, as she did not respond. 'The kind of relationship you call 'love' is something that's been very bad for you. It's all fucked up with ideas like duty, and morality, and giving up everything for some other person in a very grudging, painful way. I don't want to take part in this self-destructive fantasy.'

'Katherine. Come in.' Dr Einsam held open the door to his office. 'Sorry to keep you waiting.' As he stood there in his heavy glasses, neat dark silk suit and tie, well-trimmed black beard, and expression of sympathetic welcome, he looked like an advertisement for a psychiatrist. Even his faint European accent seemed more pronounced. The door itself, Katherine noticed as she entered, was heavily padded with sound-proofing material in a somewhat sinister way.

The office was another small ordinary room, anonymously well-furnished. A group of jungle plants, like those in Iz's apartment, sprouted before the window, putting out red feelers and large, spotted leaves.

'Sorry I was late,' Dr Einsam repeated. 'I just had a rather hard hour.' He pushed up his glasses and rubbed his closed eyes.

'I've been in the waiting room about fifteen minutes,' Katherine said. 'I didn't see anyone come out.'

'By the other door.' Rapidly, Iz opened and shut a door giving on to an empty hallway.

'Oh.'

'You don't think I bother to invent social lies for you. Uh.' He stretched his arms up and out, yawning. 'This patient really has a problem. Twenty-three years old and still sleeping in the mother's bedroom.'

'Oh, really?' Katherine had expected something more unusual.

'Naturally, that's not all. There's also educational failure and an intense terror of elevators. Those were the main presenting symptoms; they didn't see anything wrong in the family set-up.'

'But there aren't any elevators in Los Angeles,' Katherine said, 'at least, not very many.'

'Ya; that is why they moved out here.'

Iz smiled only slightly; Katherine felt ashamed of the laugh she gave. 'Poor girl,' she apologized. 'I'm sorry. You really shouldn't tell me things like that about your patients though, should you?'

'I don't tell you anything identifying.' The temperature of Iz's voice dropped at this criticism. 'I didn't even say it was a woman; you only assumed that.' He looked at Katherine coolly and intently; she looked down. 'Well. How are you today?'

'Oh, I'm all right.'

'Good. Sit down, why don't you?'

Katherine glanced at the couch by the wall, an innocuous rectangle covered in brown tweed. But in her mind's eye she saw the sobs and howls of souls in pain rising out of it like thin smoke, and felt the bolster at the far end damp with demented tears. She veered away and sat on a straight chair facing the desk.

'So.' Iz leaned on the corner of the desk and loosened his tie. 'And how is everything? How's Paul?'

'All right, I guess. He hasn't talked to me much lately. How's Glory?'

'Oh, she's just fine,' Iz spoke bitterly. 'She's been going out with Rory Gunn, seen around with him all over town, haven't you noticed?' Katherine shook her head. 'But I suppose you don't follow the gossip columns. I don't either, but someone called it to my attention. Some friend.' Katherine could not think of anything pleasant or intelligent to say; all that occurred to her was the Department of Social Studies criticism: A movie star? What on earth does he want to marry a movie star for? 'So,' Iz went on. 'Hey. You bought some clothes.'

'Yes; I found something. I don't know whether it'll do.'

'Show me.'

Katherine unwrapped the box from Jax, rustling tissue paper. 'That's not bad. . . . Put it on; let's see it.'

'You mean now?'

'Why not?' Iz smiled. 'You didn't really expect to come up here this afternoon and not take off your clothes, did you?'

'I didn't really know.' Katherine felt herself beginning to blush under Iz's look; to hide it she stood up and started changing her clothes as quickly as possible, not looking at him.

'Hm. Turn round. . . . Ya, I like that.'

'It feels so strange. I never wore anything like it before.' She held out her arms at an awkward angle, as if she were learning to fly. 'I had an awful shock in that store; I went to look in a mirror, and I didn't recognize myself. I mean, I thought I was somebody else.'

'Ah?'

'You see, I had on sunglasses, so I couldn't see my face very well, and my body—Well, anyone might not recognize my body, if they were to meet it in a crowd in strange clothes.'

'No: I think I would recognize it,' Iz said, sliding off the desk. 'But probably I have looked at it more closely than you ever have.' He put his hands up under the loose top of Katherine's new costume. 'For example: your breasts point outwards, but the right one does so more than the left.' He forced his fingers beneath the tight band of her bra. 'Did you ever happen to observe that?' Gently, Iz pushed Katherine's breasts up out of the bra, and stroked them in demonstration.

'No, I don't think so.' A tremour of heat and motion rippled downwards through her. At the same time, she was embarrassed to think that this was happening in a professional office.

'You see, you're not very narcissistic, for a woman. You're

unusually attractive, yet you don't seem to know it. I think you actually don't have too much consciousness of your own body image.'

'Is that bad?' She answered in a daze.

'Not necessarily. In your case, possibly it's a good thing, since you've been pushed around so much by other people's preconceptions. It might be easier for you to change. Come on; I want you.' Iz half led, half dragged Katherine towards the daybed. 'Take those clothes off.'

She found herself doing so, almost automatically, laying each garment on the sofa separately, but Iz scooped them up and threw them across the room in the direction of a chair. The tweed cover was rough and itchy against her bare skin. She felt somebody should say something, and ventured, as he lay down beside her, 'It seems so strange, making love right on your office couch. Have you ever done it here before?'

Iz did not answer, except with one of those steady silences she had learned to understand as a refusal to comment. With an impatient movement, he pulled the bolster out from under her head, and put his open mouth to hers.

'When I remember that you thought you weren't very interested in sex, I have to laugh, Katherine,' he said presently, laughing. 'How many times did you just come? Three?' His chest shook. 'Am I too heavy on you?'

'No; I like it.' Katherine laid her hand on his shoulder. Even here there was a light growth of curly hair, now damp with sweat, like grass after a storm. 'Iz. What I want to know is—Why does it work for me with you, and not with Paul?'

'That's an interesting question,' he said, pulling up a tweed cushion so he could rest his arm on it. 'Why do you think?'

'I don't know. Maybe it's partly because you, well, force me. I mean, of course I don't have to come here. And I still do have all kinds of trouble about that; even today I stood in front of your building for about five minutes trying to decide whether to run away. . . . But then, once I'm with you, I know that no matter what I do you'll make me sleep with you. It's completely settled, so I don't have to worry or feel responsible. . . . And I trust you. And then— Katherine stared across the room at the window,

[199

but could see nothing of the city except for scraps of sky between the plants.

'Ya, so then?' he encouraged her. The psychiatrist's phrase and intonation sounded odd in this position; Katherine smiled.

'Well, then, it's as if what I do here doesn't really count. I mean, Los Angeles is so far away from everywhere and everything here is so peculiar; it's as if it weren't real.'

'And I am so peculiar.'

'You know what I mean.' Katherine laughed. 'By Cambridge standards, you are.'

'And reality is judged always by Cambridge standards?' Iz propped his head on his hands and looked down into Katherine's face.

'I don't know.' She smiled. 'Maybe if I were with you long enough, I'd begin to see everything your way.' It would be like when she used to lie upside down to drain her sinuses, she thought, when after a while she would begin to imagine that the furniture was fastened to the ceiling, and she could walk along underneath it over a white plaster floor from which lighting fixtures grew like strange plants. Only she didn't have sinus attacks now.

'I hope not; I don't want you to exchange one tyranny for another simply. That's no solution. Uh.' Iz raised himself off Katherine, sighing, and lay down beside her, next to the wall, fitting himself to the curve of her hip.

'But I thought you *wanted* me to be influenced by your ideas. I thought that was the whole point,' Katherine said half-seriously. 'Isn't that what's supposed to happen in —' she hesitated, and chose one of Iz's neutral terms— 'a relationship like this? Almost like when people get married.'

'I don't know what you mean by "supposed to happen".' He laughed. 'I'm against institutionalized love affairs. I'm against all institutions, you know that — including the institution of marriage.' He swung up his arm to within a few inches of his face, squinted at his wristwatch, smiled, and let it fall again. 'You understand, it's the job of an anarchist to break up all authoritarian systems. With us, adultery is a matter of principle.'

'But you have been married,' Katherine reminded him.

'Yes,' Iz admitted. 'Occasionally I've made that mistake. . . . I've let myself become involved, and been hurt, and all of that.

So, we all make mistakes, even us anarchists.' He grinned.

Katherine laughed too, wondering how seriously he meant it. One could never be sure, with Iz. Meanwhile, silently, he began to trace the outline of her back with his finger.

'And how is your husband these days?' he asked.

'Oh, all right. I don't know. He's been talking about going back into teaching. I think he must be tired of his job.'

'Ya?' Iz's hand moved further down, drawing the line of Katherine's white hip and thigh against the dark tweed of the analytic couch. 'A question occurs to me,' he said. 'Why has Paul, apparently so healthy, so extroverted, etcetera, why has this man chosen the academic life?' Used now to Iz's rhetorical questions, Katherine simply waited. 'Answer, because he is basically unfree and dependent on existing patterns. He has to feel part of some benign system that will smile on his little adventures. Or frown, perhaps.'

'But Paul's not the scholarly type at all,' Katherine objected rather stupidly. The truth was, no matter how angry she felt at her husband, and discouraged about her marriage, it annoyed her obscurely that Iz should sum him up this way.

'Not externally.' Iz did not press his point; he moved his fingers along Katherine, thinking.

'I brought my shorthand notebook,' she said, smiling as she noticed it sticking out of her bag across the room. 'I thought you really wanted to dictate something.'

'Ya, I ought to. But let's forget it.' Iz continued the outline.

'Mm. . . . You know, I never do any work for you any more. It's really awful, considering I'm being paid so much an hour by the grant. We're exploiting them dreadfully.'

'Foundations exist to be exploited.' Gently, Iz drew a series of fine parallel lines across Katherine with his nails.

'And it's not only you. I'm not really working very much for Charlie or Bert either. Even when you're not there now, I just sit up in the office sometimes in a kind of daze. I guess—' She stopped; Iz said nothing. 'I guess maybe I'm getting too involved to work,' she concluded, almost in a whisper.

'You're not as involved as you think you are,' Iz replied after a short pause. 'Or let's put it this way; you're deeply involved in the experience, that's true; but your commitment to me as an individual is not so very great. Do you really want to know what I think?' He raised his head to look at her. 'Are you comfortable?'

'Yes. Go on.'

'All right. I think it's easier for you to let yourself go with me because I'm not a man of your own class and background. I'm a foreigner . . . a—what shall I say?— Wandering Jew, with a beard and an accent. In one sense, what you have with me is the kind of thing well-to-do women look for, perhaps not quite consciously, when they go abroad on a tour. Under those circumstances they can have what they call a 'romantic interlude', even a very intense one, without feeling they're really deceiving their husbands. . . . I don't mean to imply this is only a phenomenon of the middle class. It's the same thing with the little housewife who figures it doesn't really count when she lets the plumber push her up against the basement wall some afternoon.'

'No. That's just not true!' Katherine exclaimed. 'I don't think of you as a foreigner or a plumber. I know you're a very intelligent, highly-educated professional man.'

Iz laughed. 'The way you say that proves it. Don't be simpleminded, Katherine. You know what I'm talking about. You were saying almost the same thing yourself earlier.'

In silence, Katherine admitted to herself that she did, although of course Iz had put it much, much too crudely. 'All right,' she said. 'And you know what I was talking about too. About working for you and that. Because it does worry me, really. You know.' She looked at him. He smiled; slightly nodded.

'All right. I will give my serious consideration to your problem,' he replied in his professional manner. 'Ahh.' He yawned and, raising himself, leaned across Katherine's body and felt about on the floor with wide, half-blind gestures. Then he found his glasses, sat up, and put them on—changing at once from a naked and bearded satyr to a small, middle-European man at a nudist camp. This man looked at his watch.

'I hate to end this pleasant experience,' he said; 'but I've got a patient coming at four, and it's quarter of now.' Automatically, Katherine checked her own watch. It had stopped. 'Ah,' Iz added. 'If you don't mind, let's write that letter after all, since you're here? It won't take long. Get your book, hm? . . . This goes to Dr Philip Lambert, Department of Educational Psychology,

University of Wisconsin, Madison, Wisconsin,' he said rapidly. 'Hm. Dear Phil, work on the social adjustment learning project is progressing well. . . .' He walked away and then back across the carpet, in a naked parody of a boss dictating to his secretary, while Katherine, after a scramble in her bag for pencil and note-book, sat on the edge of a chair, also naked, taking notes.

'. . . . yours ever. You can type that up for me when you get back to the campus? Okay, that's it. Thank you, Katherine.'

Iz picked up off the floor and put on his white cotton under-shorts. The serious nudist turned into the comic butt of a silent film comedy, one of those respectable bearded gentlemen whose clothes are always being stolen by Chaplin or Keaton.

'Umm, about your current problem,' he said. 'I have to give it more thought, but I have an interim suggestion right now.'

'Oh?' Katherine was putting her arms into her dress. 'Tell me.'

'Very well.' Almost dressed now, he had again become Dr Isidore Einsam, Beverly Hills. 'I thought, if you really feel you're getting too involved here, why don't you consider testing your newly-discovered abilities on some other man?'

Within her tight, hot dress, Katherine felt a moment of panic. 'And you mean you think this should stop,' she said in a thin voice.

'Shit, no,' Iz exclaimed. 'I'm not going to give you up yet.'

Katherine pulled her dress down; she saw that he was smiling.

'But I don't know any other men in Los Angeles,' she said. 'I certainly don't know any that I'm attracted to at all.'

Iz pulled up the knot in his striped tie. 'Ah no?' he said. 'How about Paul?'

19

A SWATH of desolate jungle two blocks wide curved across Los Angeles towards the sea, and Paul wandered in it, among torn streets, overgrown gardens, broken walls, derelict houses, and shallow holes full of white rubble where buildings had once stood. The lawns and most of the gardens had withered from lack of water, but some deep-rooted rank bushes and weeds still grew greedily; devil-grass cracked the sidewalks, and vines, some flowering profusely, poured over the ruins. Overhead the avocado, lemon, and olive trees rustled their hard leaves in the hot breeze.

It was late in the day, but still very warm. Katherine was in the kitchen doing the supper dishes, and Paul had gone out to think, or brood, in this waste land across the street, where the freeway was to be built. Plaster cracked under his feet as he walked, and far above a jet plane hummed in the fading sky; otherwise it was unnaturally quiet. Only fifty feet away from his front door, but completely out of sight of civilization, Paul sat down on a crumbling block of cement, and thought how much his surroundings resembled his state of mind.

The fact was that he could not forget Ceci O'Connor. This affair had started so simply and passionately, like a sudden plunge into a clear, bubbling spring. Now the waters were turgid and muddy; everything had gone wrong. It was really all over, but still he could not stop thinking about it. He could consider Ceci rationally, dispassionately, historically even, and realize that she was a confused, half-educated, stubborn social rebel with no background or traditions (a victim of social change and disorganization, not her own fault, of course); but physically he was still, to use her term, very hung up.

Movements she had made, things she had said, kept repeating themselves inside his head, taking on different, darker significances. Like the time once he had suggested that when summer came he would arrange to get off from work for a few days so that they could go together to Catalina Island where, he had heard, there was white sand and wild peacocks. But Ceci wouldn't agree to make plans. Parting the long streaky hair over her face so that she looked out at him as through a bead curtain, she said, 'Sure, that'd be great. But I don't believe in figuring out things that far ahead. You start fixing all these plans and rules for something, it gets wrecked. I mean like as long as you want to do this and I want to do it, it'll happen; and when one of us or both of us don't want it any more — it'll stop. That's the way it really is anyhow, huh?' Bemused by her great eyes looking into his, her freedom from the laws of time, her trust in a continuing impulse, he had enthusiastically agreed.

A few weeks, even a few days ago, houses had still stood on this block of Mar Vista, deserted, with wooden signs nailed to them: 'This House For Sale. To Be Moved.' Though vacant only a short time, the little stucco villas and castles had already begun to come apart. Long cracks had appeared in the flimsy pink and green plaster walls, tiles had fallen from the roofs, and panes in the variegated windows had been broken by children or tramps.

Then, one by one, the houses had been taken away. Gangs of workmen came to cut the electric, gas, water, and telephone connections; then they would slowly jack the house up, forcing heavy beams under the floor. By evening it would sit several feet above its foundations, looking more than ever like a great awkward toy.

The actual moving was always done just before dawn, when traffic on the streets was lightest; the noise of truck motors and heavy machinery first woke Paul one morning at about four a.m. He thought it was, first, a nightmare; then, an atomic war. Climbing out of bed groggily, he went into the living-room, pushed aside the slats of the blind, and looked out. By the light of flares and headlamps, men and machines were working around an undermined house, easing it slowly on to the bed of a huge tractor-trailer.

After this, the process was repeated almost every few days, or rather nights. Katherine managed to sleep through the racket more or less, but it always kept him up. He would lie awake in bed, drowsily listening to the coughing of the bulldozer engines, the shouts and silences, and the straining of wood against metal.

The one that had taken the longest to move was the little French château. They got it out into the street, and then it turned out that the turrets in front were too tall to pass under the telephone lines at the end of the block. Heavy engines churned and sputtered in front of Paul's house while they consulted about what to do (wondering what had happened to break the sequence of sounds, he had got out of bed to look). Lights swung and flashed in the dark; presently a workman armed with bristling tools climbed the roof of the house, apparently to test the possibility of knocking off the pointed, pistachio ice cream towers. Standing at the window, Paul held his breath.

The man climbed down. There was a long delay now, but Paul could not bring himself to go back to bed. He wouldn't sleep anyhow, and he wanted to see what happened. Finally a telephone company truck pulled up; two men got out, shinnied up the pole, and tied back the wires. The colourless unsteady light of dawn was spreading across Mar Vista by the time the château slowly turned the corner on to Sepulveda Boulevard — propped up with boards and chained on to the bed of the truck, but listing a little to the left — and disappeared forever.

By an ironic, destructive coincidence, it was later that same morning that he saw Ceci at the Aloha Coffee Shop, for the first time in several days after their outdoor quarrel. She asked him immediately, 'Are you still living in Mar Vista? Or have you moved out?' No, he couldn't resist saying, *he* was still there, but everything else was moving out. It had been the wrong answer, because Ceci had thought he meant that Katherine was going. A big lovely smile appeared on her face, but by the time the joke had been explained to her she was furious with him and refusing to listen to anything he said.

An oleander shrub next to the broken steps where Paul sat was thick with fleshy purple flowers. They were poisonous, he had heard somewhere. Beside it scarlet weeds covered the ground; the flowers were gay and profuse, but the two colours clashed badly. Paul pointed out to himself that Ceci too was only crudely pretty; her hands were too broad and stubby, her teeth were uneven, she dressed badly, and did not wash her streaky gold hair enough — often it smelt and tasted of the beach. She was morally loose, too. Everything he had ever jealously suspected was true: his Ceci had lain not only under the scrawny body of her weird Chinese husband, but under all those other men, and rubbed herself against them, and cried out with pleasure. Half Venice West had probably been into her, so why should he give a damn?

Paul picked up a chunk of broken cement from the ground and threw it at an avocado tree across what had been somebody's back yard. Crunch.

Obviously Ceci didn't give a damn herself. She didn't care if she ever saw him again. With the girls he had known in the East, Paul had always remained more or less good friends. Even when they had married someone, or made up with their husbands, or had a baby or a new lover, there was still a special warmth in the way they looked at him across a room. They still belonged to the 'underground' in spirit, even if they had retired. Often there would be a discreet lunch now and then at which Paul and his friend would reminisce, discuss topics of mutual interest, and confide in one another, over imported beer or iced coffee. The Oxford Grill was pleasant for such lunches.

Only Ceci didn't believe in Paul's underground. 'You mean like there's a club of people who cheat on the cats and chicks they're supposed to be making it with?' she asked. But she had her own underground, cruder and sloppier than his, not discreet and careful of other people's feelings, but rebelliously noisy.

She wouldn't meet for lunch; she wouldn't meet anywhere. 'Don't you know when something is over?' she had said that afternoon, when Paul, swallowing his pride again, telephoned her at the place in Santa Monica where she was now working. (He knew, or suspected but did not want to ask, that she had quit the Aloha Coffee Shop last week in order not to have to see him any more.) There was a long wait while Ceci was called to the phone. In the background he could hear restaurant noises, the ring of the cash register, the rattle of plates. 'Listen, don't call me at the gig any more, okay?' she said almost as soon as she got on the line. 'They don't like that here.' 'But I have to,' Paul objected. 'You haven't got a telephone. . . . Listen, if today is out, how about tomorrow? Shall I come down to your place tomorrow morning? I want to talk to you.' Glasses clinking. 'No,' Ceci said. Her voice was faint among the clatter of plastic dishware, as if she were standing some feet from the receiver. 'Well, how about——' he began again. 'Aw, Paul,' she interrupted. 'I mean, what's the point, huh? What could we talk about? ... Don't you know when something is over?'

All right, the hell with it; he knew when something was over. He would change gigs himself. Already he had written back East asking about teaching and fellowship prospects for the fall. He should have done it sooner; the trouble was, out here it was so easy to lose track of time, especially around Ceci and her friends. So far, there had been no replies.

The sun above the trees was turning into a flat vermilion circle as it sank into the layer of smog over Mar Vista. He'd better get home, or Katherine would ask: where had he *been*; what had he been *doing*? She would probably ask anyhow; it was nearly eight o'clock.

But Katherine made no such remark when he walked back into the house. The dishes were done, and she sat in her usual corner of the new wicker sofa, sewing something under the lamp. On evenings when Paul didn't go out, which meant every evening now, the convention was that he worked on his thesis. He had done so when he first arrived in Los Angeles, and in the last few days he had tried to do so again. It gave him the feeling that he was struggling uphill with a tremendous grey rock. Who the hell gave a damn about early Elizabethan trade policy and its social influences? It was so much easier to throw some records on the phonograph or look at a magazine, and a much better distraction from the thought of Ceci. Nevertheless he had written in letters to New England recently that he was finishing his thesis.

The metal desk-lamp hummed fluorescently as it shed its cold light on the stacks of index cards. Each one of them had been covered with scratches of ink by his own hand: words and numbers and bibliographical abbreviations. He stared at them through a mist of obsession.

'Paul,' Katherine's voice said. 'Paul. Paul?'

'Hm?'

'I'd like to ask you something, if you have a minute.'

'Hm.'

'I — I wondered if you wanted to go swimming this Sunday afternoon. The Skinners are organizing a beach party. Everyone's going to bring supper and beer. Susy says it'll be mobbed in Santa Monica, so they're going down to Venice.'

'Sunday?' Paul stalled. 'I d'know.' He didn't want to go anywhere with the Skinners. Once he had found out that the Nutting Research and Development Company had hired him to do practically nothing while looking like a Harvard historian, he had also realized that Fred Skinner had suspected this from the beginning, but had refrained from putting him wise. And Susy Skinner bored him. But above all, he did not want to go to Venice Beach with these people. Besides, he had to work on his thesis. 'Let's not make it this weekend,' he said. 'I have to work on my thesis.'

Katherine did not protest; she opened and shut her mouth, but said nothing.

'You don't really mind,' Paul told her. 'You hate the beach anyhow.'

'Oh, I don't know.' Katherine pulled her thread through something yellow. 'I'm really getting to like it rather, now that the water's warmer. I'm even getting a tan; have you noticed? And I think my hair's lighter.'

Paul had not noticed; he did not notice now. He was thinking of Venice Beach, with illustrations. One foggy night Ceci and he had gone down with a blanket to lie on the damp, salty sand, and listen to the waves licking the shore; and Ceci's breasts tasted of salt. Goddamn it, he wasn't going to let her get away like that; he would go down there, tomorrow afternoon—

Katherine was still speaking. '. . . you see, what it is about Los Angeles; what happens here doesn't *count*. That's how you have to think about it. I remember you said something like that when we first got here, but I didn't understand then. I think the way you put it, you said it was all an amusing joke.'

'An amusing joke?' Paul repeated. He felt a peculiar impulse to laugh wildly, as if he were in a Frankenstein movie. No, he would go there tomorrow morning.

'Yes. But you see I wanted to take it all *seriously*, or at least I didn't want to, but I thought I had to. I couldn't think of how else to take it, because I'd been so serious all my life. That's what Dr Einsam says; he says—'

Katherine paused. Paul recognized that it was his turn to say something, so he said, 'Oh. Who's Dr Einsam?'

'Dr Isidore Einsam. You know, he's one of the people I work for. I've told you about him.'

'Oh, mm.' No doubt she had, Paul thought. 'One of those psychology professors.'

'No. He's sort of an international Jewish capitalist anarchist,' Katherine said, smiling; it was a joke she and Iz had recently made up. Paul looked at her suspiciously, or bemusedly. 'He's a psychiatrist. Anyhow,' (she got a grip on herself and shifted the subject) 'he says people with an academic background like mine often think the whole world is a small classroom they can't ever get out of.'

'Hnh.' Had he had more energy to spare, Paul might have registered a stronger reaction, protested against the flip diagnosis of academic life made by this crank psychiatrist his wife was working for. Not that he thought psychiatrists were cranks in general, but in southern California they well might be. This city was full of amateur wisemen, self-made experts on everything. If only Ceci had some education and sense of proportion; if she could only realize— He hadn't meant to deceive her; he had simply assumed that she assumed— 'Ceci, I need to see you,' he had said, laughing somewhat to take the edge off the statement, that last time they met, at the Aloha Coffee Shop. 'I get so bored without you.' 'Yeah,' she had replied, balancing her plastic tray against the hip of the cheap green uniform. 'You get bored easy. You know what Steve Tyler said about you? He said, "Paul's not going to change an inch, and when nothing and nobody you meet can change you, pretty soon everything seems like a drag. . . . And the next thing is you get to be a great big drag yourself." ' Ceci's voice had grown very rough; she turned her face away. Paul almost thought she was crying, but when she looked back her eyes were hard and dry. She pushed back some ends of streaky gold hair under the coarse hairnet all the Aloha waitresses wore, and put Paul's check down on the table beside his empty glass.

'Well,' she said in a flat voice, as she took off for the kitchen. 'See you.' Which had meant, he thought, the opposite, because since then she had not seen him, and would not see him.

Crawling in the mists of these memories, Paul was aroused by a touch on his shoulder. Katherine had come over and was sitting on the arm of his chair, speaking to him; he realized that she must have been speaking to him all along.

'. . . and I know I've been difficult,' she was saying. 'When I first got out here, when I had nothing to do and I was sick with sinus all the time, I was really dreadful.'

Some answer was called for. 'Oh, that's all right,' he replied with about one-third of his conscious mind. 'I know it was hard on you to come out here where you don't know anybody.'

'Yes, but all the same; I was *awful*.' Katherine smiled. 'But I'm going to make it up to you now.' She leaned against Paul; then she put her arms around his neck and kissed his forehead in an unusual way. It was not unprecedented for Katherine to kiss him affectionately, and when she did so she usually favoured the upper parts of his head—his eyes, his ears, his forehead (as now), the section of hair under which he had been told that the super-ego was located—as if, he had sometimes thought, these were the only parts of him she really approved of or felt comfortable with. But in this embrace now there was a kind of deliberate physicality which was completely uncharacteristic of his wife; which she must, therefore, be straining at in order to gratify him. A sad mistake. Quite automatically, Paul turned and put his arms loosely around Katherine, patting her back in a calming way.

'There, there,' he murmured.

'You know, you've got attractive eyebrows,' Katherine said. Placing one delicate hand on his thigh, almost in his groin, as if to steady herself, she bent over and licked his near eyebrow with her tongue. Paul's eyes twitched. He found it very unsettling, in fact disagreeable, to have his wife suddenly start acting like a loose woman.

But there was more to it than that. He felt wrong about touching Katherine at all now, guilty, even—unfaithful. That was what Ceci had made him feel; for her, that was how it really was. While Katherine bent farther over him and started on his other eyebrow, the idea came to him that if he refused her now, he could tell Ceci that he had done so, that he had stopped making love to his wife (well, it had been, let's see, nearly two weeks now). Then Ceci would see him again; he was sure of it.

'Hey, Katherine,' he mumbled, freeing his head. 'You don't have to make up to me like that, hon.'

'But I want to,' Katherine said. She lifted her face and looked at him, but rather at the surface of his features than into his eyes. 'You're really a very good-looking man,' she announced.

'Well, thanks,' Paul said, still more disconcerted. He was sure that Katherine had never spoken to anyone in her life in this tone. The whole situation felt profoundly false to him; his impulse was to start up and hurry away. Of course that would look awkward and terrible, and it would hurt Katherine's feelings. It wasn't her fault he was so preoccupied tonight that she, reversing their usual parts, took this awkward initiative, after two weeks. He should find it touching, really. Besides, there was a part of him that did not recognize tone, that only grew warm when a woman's hand was pressed against it; and now it was very warm. What guaranteed that Ceci would see him tomorrow, anyhow? That she was not already shacked up, in some shack on Venice Beach, with somebody else? Right now, very likely, some 'cat' was lying on her bed under the painted forest of flowers. Who was Ceci O'Connor that he should do for her what he had never done for anyone else, not even his wife? Katherine might be clumsy at imitating love, but she did love him, and only him.

'You're pretty attractive yourself,' he told her, without looking to see whether this were true. Moving Katherine's embarrassing hand off his leg, he pulled her down into a more comfortable, familiar position in his lap. But even now she would not settle down; she twisted round and rubbed her mouth across his, using her tongue as Ceci might have done, holding him like Ceci—

No: it was all wrong, disordered, Paul thought, as he half-reciprocated—as if his craving for Ceci was so great that now it had got out of his head and into Katherine, so that she was deliberately imitating, or rather was possessed by, Ceci. As if he were going crazy or something, even, because of course Katherine didn't know Ceci, didn't even know she existed.

With some effort, he pulled his head back. 'Hey, listen,' he whispered, afraid to voice his hallucination aloud. 'What's happening?'

'Nothing,' she whispered back. If it were all in his mind, he thought, he must take a firm hold on himself now, behave normally. And Katherine had stopped moving about now. She seemed to melt in his arms; her eyes were almost shut.

'Do you want to go into the other room?'

'Mm, yes.'

Never in the course of their marriage, he thought, had they got into bed so quickly. (Or did it only seem so?) Katherine, who usually was so slow about taking off her clothes, methodically hanging each garment up or folding it on to a chair, lay spread out on the sheet before Paul even had his socks off. She was smiling up at him suggestively—or was it just affectionately? Was it all in his mind? What the hell was going on? Though physically excited, Paul frowned and hesitated, standing by the bed.

'Paul?' she said finally. He knelt over her, but still hesitated, stroking her arm absently. 'Mm, Paul,' she added. 'Maybe you'd like to try something different tonight? Would you like to do it this way?'

Coming from Katherine, this suggestion, and the gesture that went with it, was as shocking as a physical blow; Paul flinched as if he had in fact been struck.

'Where did you hear about that?' he exclaimed; but simultaneously there was a flash of cognition. 'I get it now,' he said, standing up. 'You've been reading some book; some marriage manual or something like that, haven't you?' For the first time that evening he looked directly at Katherine, but she avoided his eyes and did not answer him.

'Come on now,' he said, more gently, touching her shoulder. 'It's true, isn't it? I know you couldn't think of something like that yourself.'

An anxious pause; then, almost imperceptibly, Katherine nodded yes.

'I thought so. Oh, Kathy.' Paul lay down next to his wife. All his passion had drained off; he felt only affection and pity, as well as tremendous relief (after all, he was not suffering from delusions). 'You don't want to read that kind of thing,' he told her. 'I mean, I'm not angry, I know you meant it well. But those books are just cheap. They're all wrong, anyway.'

He stroked his wife's face and hair; but she turned on her side away from him, drawing up her knees as if she could hide inside her own body.

'Besides, hon,' he went on. 'I like you the way you are. I don't want you to learn any techniques.' Since it was presented to him, he caressed his wife's back. 'That kind of thing is all wrong for you, because you're not really like that.' Now Paul stroked his wife's hips, pale and smooth. As he did so, desire began to rise in him slowly again; not the burning greed he had felt earlier for Ceci in Katherine's body, but a gentler lust, mixed with compassion.

'Come on back, silly,' he said. He turned her face towards him. It was set in a sullen inward expression. He shut his eyes, and kissed the pretty prim mouth. It remained resistant, even under warm and continued pressure, and when he drew back the expression had not changed.

'Ah, Kathy. Don't be hurt. I'm sorry. Come on. I want to make love to you.'

'Not now,' Katherine said distantly. 'I don't feel like it now.' Pulling away from his arms, she sat up. 'Excuse me,' she said in the voice she might have used in a hospital corridor. 'I have to go to the washroom.'

Paul blinked, left alone in the room; then he sat up on the edge of the bed, feeling depressed and baffled. Bending down with what felt like a great effort, he picked his crumpled shirt off the floor. Ah, damn them all to hell. He smiled wryly.

But then a real smile, though not much of a one, appeared on his face. Everything mended itself in time; Katherine would get over this, though not at once (such an exposure could not help but be very mortifying for a girl of her delicacy and inexperience); and, above all, he had just succeeded in completely forgetting about Ceci for nearly half an hour.

20

KATHERINE gripped the steering-wheel with both hands as the car swept along Sunset Boulevard towards Hollywood, past the mansions of the stars. The road banked and curved like an amusement-park track; what must it be like in the winter!—but of course that didn't matter: no time was winter here. Expensive, shiny cars gunned their engines behind her, and blew their horns to make her go faster; so recklessly she went faster, spinning past castles and palms, fountains, banks of roses, and gateposts with plaster lions or urns.

It was her afternoon to work for Dr Einsam, but instead she was going to Hollywood to answer Glory Green's fan mail. It was Iz's idea, of course. Katherine did not know exactly what it meant, or what she thought of it. Was she being sent as a spy, or an emissary? Or was she merely bearing coals of fire, as Iz had suggested when he said: 'She needs a secretary; I've got a secretary. So, I can help her out; it's as simple as that.' When Katherine began to inquire further, he interrupted her, saying that she didn't have to go if she didn't want to: it made absolutely no difference to him. Meaning, for she knew his language by now, that it made some absolute difference to him. It would have been very uncomfortable in the office and everywhere else, if she had refused. Besides, she was curious.

Following Iz's directions, she turned up towards the Hollywood hills, driving more slowly. Now that she was nearly there, she felt not only curious but uneasy, even frightened. Thinking to prepare herself somehow for this job, or this meeting, she had gone to a musical film in which Glory had a part. It was the sort of movie she would never have seen, otherwise. Sitting alone in the dark theatre, she saw projected before her the image of a bright, noisy, completely artificial world in which everyone was handsome and physically vital, ageless and brand new, like their clothes and furniture. At every opportunity they broke into loud song and dance. Presently Glory's first scene came on. A group of chorus girls with identical costumes and differently coloured hair (chestnut, orange, yellow, black) flashed across the screen, strenuously smiling and kicking and winking. Was that Iz's *wife*? she thought, astonished, as a face five feet high, framed in pink curls, came by; she turned round to look at the rest of the audience, as if they too might be surprised. But the three hundred faces behind her, lit by the reflections of Technicolor, all wore the same expression of passive enchantment.

Katherine drove more slowly still. If Glory were really like that, why had Iz married her? Maybe that was what he—what all men—wanted, or thought they wanted. If she weren't like that, after all, why had she become a movie starlet? Katherine could imagine no profession more horrible. The idea of exposing oneself, almost naked, to all those people, prancing about in front of them to be stared at invisibly and intimately by hundreds and thousands, was revolting to her. She wondered how any normal human being could bear it, no matter for what reward.

But Glory Green was obviously not a normal human being. She had pink hair and a thirty-eight-inch bust at least, and no education; she had been on the stage since she was five and had been married three times, starting at fifteen, when Katherine hadn't even been kissed. That was what the secretaries in the Social Sciences office said. She had lived all her life in a violent, vulgar world, and even Iz hadn't been able to change her. The girls in the office said that she had just been in a public brawl, where she screamed at policemen and reporters, and slapped a girl in the face who hadn't even spoken to her. Katherine hadn't seen the papers, so she didn't know how much of this to believe. Iz had never mentioned it, and she wasn't going to ask him. It was bad enough for him that he had to be married to, and obsessed with, a girl like that (because he was still obsessed with her, she knew).

Oh lord, here was the house already, or rather its number on a rustic mail-box, at the bottom of a steep bank topped with a red-wood fence. Katherine began to wish she had not come, but she pulled her car to the side of the road and, setting her mouth, got out. She climbed some steps to a gate in the fence, and rang the bell.

There was a long wait. Katherine wondered if she should go away; she wanted to go away; but Iz had promised that she would come. Finally she could hear someone approaching. Movement was visible through the slits in the gate; then it was flung open. A figure completely enveloped in a long pink beach-robe, sunglasses, and a huge conical straw hat, stood looking at her. It was Glory, but Katherine, not unnaturally, did not recognize her.

'Does Glory Green live here?' she asked.

'Maybe,' Glory said in a hoarse whisper, looking Katherine over from head to toe. 'What d'you want her for?'

Katherine reminded herself that whatever happened in Los Angeles did not count and was in fact amusing. 'I'm her new secretary,' she explained. 'Dr Einsam sent me.'

'Yeah, I thought so.' Glory paused only a moment, but long enough for Katherine to think: suppose this weird person is Glory. Because if it is, and she knows, or suspects, about me and Iz, what kind of noise, violence, or even crime, is going to happen? 'Only there's so many cranks wandering around this town, you never know. Hi.' Glory suddenly extended a hand and a cold, brief, dazzling smile from the shadows of her disguise.

'How do you do,' Katherine said nervously. Glory's handshake was firm and warm, with long silver-pink finger-nails.

'Come on in. I guess I should say come on out; we're sitting on the patio.'

Partly but not completely reassured, Katherine followed Glory across a landscaped yard, through a dark interior-decorated room, and outside again. Wicker and wire furniture, beach umbrellas, bright cushions, and orange trees in tubs surrounded a swimming-pool. A beautiful girl in a bikini lay on the diving-board. It was like an advertisement for success, or pleasure, or Los Angeles—except that the pool was completely dry.

'Mona,' Glory said. The girl in the bikini lifted her head. 'This is Ramona Moon.'

'Hiya.' Mona propped her face on her hands in order to observe Katherine more comfortably.

'Hi,' Katherine echoed. She was relieved to see a third person, any third person. She ran over in her mind what Iz had told her about Ramona Moon. She was Glory's best friend, a TV actress from the Italian section of Los Angeles. Iz had described her as a simple, good-natured, practical girl, which was not what she looked like.

'Well, siddown,' Glory invited. 'Take a chair over there in the sun if you want to; I just got to stay out of it so's I won't tan.' She sat down under a large umbrella, and for further protection wrapped her robe tightly round herself. 'Mona has to get brown; but I hafta stay white, so they can paint me green.'

'Oh?' Katherine did not understand, but she was too nervous of Glory's great dark sunglass eyes, so she looked inquiringly towards Mona. 'How is that?'

'It's account of my type,' Mona explained. 'I always do the passionate-Latin parts, see, so I've got to be very dark. What a drag, huh?'

Aware that Mona was trying to be friendly, or at least polite, Katherine tried to reciprocate. 'Yes, that must be an awful bore,' she began, and paused. She had never thought of herself as having an accent—her speech was simply that of any educated New England person. But now, in contrast to Glory and (especially) Mona, she sounded prissy and affected. She made a conscious effort to moderate her tone, and went on: 'But do you really have to do that? I mean, I don't know, but couldn't you just wear dark make-up?'

'Yeah, sure I could, for the cameras. On TV everybody's got a ton of gunk plastered over them, anyhow. Only the trouble is, you have to look right when you go for a part. That's when it counts.' She shook back a mass of black Latin curls.

'Sun is bad for you,' Glory announced, speaking from the shadows of the umbrella like some strange idol. 'It ages your skin, and gives you freckles.'

'Maybe.' Mona frowned. 'But geez, you know, being out of a job is worse for me. That *really* makes me sick.' She laughed; Glory joined her briefly, and so, tentatively, did Katherine. But when this laugh died away there was an awkward silence. Out of the corner of her eye Katherine saw Glory's sunglasses apparently fixed upon her, and felt guiltily conscious.

'Well,' Glory said finally. 'So how's Iz making out these days?' For the first time she really spoke aloud, projecting her theatrical voice with force. This, as well as the question itself, made Katherine start.

'Uh, oh, he's just fine.' Obviously this was an inadequate answer —inaccurate, too, and even insulting, since it implied that Dr

Einsam was doing just fine without Glory. 'He's as well as you could expect.'

Now she had said too much. Glory was still staring at her; she wanted her to betray Iz somehow, Katherine felt. But she must defend him, she must give nothing away, not even neutral information, because there was no neutral information. This was an impossible situation; she wished she had never come, and even blamed Iz for sending her. But since she was there, she had to make an effort. 'I mean, really, how can I possibly tell you how he is now, when I don't know what he was like before?'

'Well, okay.' Glory smiled a little, paused, and went on. 'You like working there at the university? It's a pretty easy job, huh?'

'No. I mean, I like it; but there's usually plenty to do,' Katherine lied, sensing a criticism (there can't be much work at U.C.L.A., or you wouldn't be here now—or, I work harder than you do).

'Mm. And how's Iz getting on with the other professors up there? Are they still speaking to him?'

'Why, yes,' Katherine said, stiffening against this continuing inquisition. 'They all seem to get on very well.'

'What d'you know,' Glory remarked sceptically to Mona. 'You think he's reformed? Maybe he's turned into a nice guy.' Mona giggled. 'Or maybe they're just finally seeing it his way. . . . Of course, the fact is he's a fantastically brilliant person,' she added, now to both of them. 'He knows he's got it all over the other professors in brains, and he doesn't bother to keep it a secret, so naturally the rest of them are screaming jealous. I mean he may be a complete shit personally, but in his own scientific work he's practically a genius. Isn't that so?'

As Glory looked at Katherine now, her voice vibrated not only with theatrical tone but with genuine nervous emotion. Why, she's more upset about him than I am, Katherine thought with surprise—much more. She's really in a state. She tried to think of something calming to say, and to get out of the line of fire, as it were. She had never heard anyone at U.C.L.A. suggest that Dr Einsam was a scientific genius. The idea had not occurred to her nor, as far as she knew, to Iz himself. But rather than contradict Glory and sacrifice Iz's prestige, she chose to sacrifice her own.

'Heavens, I don't know,' she said. 'I mean, I just wouldn't know. I'm no psychologist: I'm only the secretary for the project.

They dictate their ideas, and I just take them down, I don't have to understand them.'

She seemed to have said the right thing; both girls laughed this time.

'Yeah,' Glory said. She pushed back her hat and removed her dark glasses. Blinking and squinting at the light, she felt her hair, which was rolled up on about two dozen large metal curlers. Her face was round, shiny, and completely bare of make-up. Why look, she's not beautiful at all, Katherine thought; she's just an ordinary pretty girl.

'Hey.' Glory smiled more openly. 'Would anybody like some iced tea, or a beer or something?'

'Have you got any coke, hon?' Mona asked. 'I could really use a coke.'

'Yeah, I think so. If you want to ruin your teeth. You want a coke?' This was to Katherine.

'No, thank you, I'd rather have iced tea.'

'Okay.' Trailing her robe behind across the dust and grass, Glory went into the house. Katherine looked after her, frowning. She was beginning to feel, of all things, sorry for this vulgar, nervous girl who had a hateful job, had lost Iz, and wasn't even beautiful.

'Aww.' On the diving-board, Mona set up and stretched voluptuously. 'Holy gee, I wish there was some water in this goddamned pool,' she complained, looking down into the empty cement hole, in the corners of which dead leaves and trash had collected.

'What happened to it?'

'Ah, it's all a big mess. The pool is sliding downhill, see, 'cause they put it in wrong. You can see the cracks in the ground over there at the other end. It's really something.'

Curious, Katherine walked down the length of the empty pool. She looked into a deep, branching fissure with walls of dried mud. 'Heavens. That's awful,' she said, returning.

'Yeah. The way it looks to me, that whole side of the hill is falling off. I told Glory she oughta sue them, but she's so down now she won't do anything. . . .' Mona lowered her voice as Glory came out of the house, carrying a tray. 'Say, that looks great! Thanks a lot.'

'I brought out the stuff Maxie got from the studio, so you can look it over,' Glory said, setting a cardboard carton on the table beside Katherine's iced tea. 'And here's some stationery.' It was pink, embossed with silver initials. 'I got a lot more back in the house when you need it; I practically never use the stuff. I mean if the phone's working, why write a letter? . . . Here's some stamps; I guess you better get some more, though. . . . And these are the photos.' She put down a stack of postcard-sized pictures of a stupid chorus girl grinning in costume and showing fantastic cleavage. Katherine looked from them to Glory in her beach robe and curlers—there was no resemblance whatsoever. 'And all the rest of the crap is letters. Here.' Glory tossed a handful of mail back into the box and shoved it across the table to Katherine. 'Have fun.'

'But what am I supposed to do?'

'Answer them.' Glory shrugged, and poured beer into a glass, tilting it to keep down the foam.

'But I don't know what to say,' Katherine protested, feeling embarrassed and incompetent. 'I never did exactly this kind of work before.'

'Just give them what they want. . . . Didn't Iz clue you in what this is all about?' Katherine shook her head. 'Ah, for shit's sake.' Glory set her beer down and wiped foam off her mouth. 'Well, it's like this, a kid socked me at a première last month, a fan, and so I socked her back and got myself some bad publicity, you probably read about it.' (Katherine shook her head again.) 'So Maxie Weiss, that's my agent, had the idea to put out a release, a story for the papers, see, I'm really crazy about fans, I just love 'em so much I answer all their creepy letters personally, instead of letting the studio do it; get the picture?'

'I think so,' Katherine said, taken aback by the insouciant directness of this statement, rather than by the assumption that she was going to be composing lies for Glory. Dealing in lies, or at least polite half-truths, was something one took for granted on any job. 'You want me to write to them and say how much you appreciate their interest and that kind of thing.'

'Yeah. Just keep it short and sweet. For instance—' Glory reached into the box, took a letter at random, and tore it open. She squinted close at the awkward handwriting, done in pencil on cheap lined notebook paper, and read as rapidly as possible:

' "Dear Glory Green I saw *Three Dumb Mice* four times I enjoyed it very very much especially your scenes I am 15 years old besides you my favourite stars are Doris Day and Sandra Dee I am enclosing 25 cents could you please send me an autograph picture for my album yours truly Florrie Ridley." Here. Just write her thanks very much and send the photo.'

'But she said she wants it autographed.'

'So autograph it. She's not going to know the difference. . . . Lessee. Here's a longer one. "My dearest Miss Green since I first saw your extremely lovely face and form in *Restless* I have been Restless about you I have 23 pix of you already My favourite one is in the bikini with the octopus that was in *Screen Lives* I just want to let you know that You are my new Secret Movie Love Dream and I am sleeping with this photo every night next to my pillow not under it as I do not want to tear or crush your very lovely form please send all your most recent pix I enclose one dollar to cover mailing costs your not-so-secret admirer Earl G. Jorgensen." How d'you like that!' Glory giggled and held out the letter to Katherine, who took it by the corner as if the paper were smeared with invisible slime.

'Boy,' Mona said. 'What a creep.'

'You don't want me to answer this one.'

'Naw, I guess you better just mail him a couple of photos.'

'You send that nut a picture, you know what he'll do with it,' Mona remarked.

'So what? He's paid for it.' Glory felt her curlers again, unconcerned. 'I've got plenty a lot worse than that. . . . The poor jerk, after all. He probably can't get his kicks any other way.'

'Yeah, all right. But all the same it's kind of disgusting to think of that creep sitting in his room somewhere playing with your photo and pulling himself off, 'cause he can't find himself a girl.'

'Aw, how do you know? Maybe he's even married. There's a lot of people can't feel physical about what they've got around at home.' Glory shrugged. Katherine, still holding the letter, looked from one to the other. She had never heard women speak so bluntly, and wondered if they were doing it on purpose to embarrass her, though they seemed not to be paying her the least attention.

'Oh hey, that reminds me. I knew I had something to tell you!'

Mona exclaimed. 'You know that kid Lucille that was in the Johnny Espy Show with me, she was going to the doctor for these awful cramps she had every month? Well, she got to talking to him about her private life and she finally let on her and her husband just weren't getting any bang out of doing it any more. Well, so this doc told her it wasn't psychological like she was scared of; the trouble was she didn't have any muscle tone down there at all, since she had her baby.'

'Yeah?' Glory considered. 'It could be. That was how Brandy said it was with her after she had Joe Junior. They sewed her up wrong or something and her clutch was all flabby for months, she couldn't feel a thing. She said she coulda driven Joe's motor-bike through there without getting a charge. You know she went on one of those dumb health plans.'

'Lucille's really sold on this doctor,' Mona went on, sliding down the diving-board towards them. 'He taught her these crazy exercises you do in the bathtub, to strengthen your muscles. She said it took her a couple months to really get into condition, but now her and her guy are having a ball. So now she's trying to turn everyone on; she wants me to go to her doc and learn the routine. What d'you think? I mean, it's scientific. You could come too.'

'No, thanks,' Glory said, laughing. 'Not me. There's only one kind of exercise I ever want to do with that part of me.'

Nearly positive now that Glory, at least, was trying to shock her, Katherine was equally determined not to react. So she laughed too, as well as she could, and said: 'I agree. I certainly wouldn't go. . . . Well, after all,' she went on as they looked at her expectantly. 'What kind of a doctor would it be that would want to be doing that sort of work all day long, instead of taking care of people who are really sick?'

'You mean he might be some kind of weirdo,' Mona said. 'Sort of a mad scientist.'

'No.' Katherine recognized a stereotype which, in her experience, had no basis in reality. 'Just rather unprincipled.'

'She means he might jump you when he had you on the table, or something kinky,' Glory interpreted.

'Aw, they can't do that,' said Mona. 'They get thrown out of the union if they try to get funny with a patient.'

'Yeah?' Glory said. 'What about that guy over on Crenshaw

that was making out with all the girls in the Blue Dog? . . . Hey.' She lifted her head to listen.

'Your phone's ringing.'

'Goddamn it.'

Glory got out of her chair and slouched across the patio. Inside the house, they could hear her answer the phone in a completely different voice, full of sex and sleepy enthusiasm: 'Hel-lo . . . Oh hi, baby . . . Yeah, swinging . . .' fading out as she crossed the room and flung herself on a sofa. 'She's talking to someone she's intimate with; she's having an affair,' Katherine thought. Or was she only superbly pretending? 'Glory and I have the opposite problem professionally,' Iz had explained the other day. 'See, the actor has to express what he in fact doesn't feel. That's their job, and sometimes there's a carry-over. Well, that's her problem. On the other hand, a psychiatrist often has *not* to express what he does genuinely feel. Which is even harder on him.' (Had he meant her to take that personally? Was it a kind of excuse he was offering?)

'I'm sorry,' Katherine apologized, realizing Mona had spoken. 'What did you say?'

'I just asked what's your birth-date.' Katherine told her. 'Uh huh. You have an adventurous temperament,' (Katherine smiled at this miscalculation) 'balanced by strong practical capabilities, same as my mother.'

'Thank you.'

'Hey, about this pool foulup,' Mona continued. 'Now you're working for Glory, you oughta convince her she should get after those bastards that built it. I mean you could write a letter or something, tell them they don't fix it up right she'll get a lawyer. I bet they could fix it if they wanted to. And it would really do a lot for her morale.'

'Um,' Katherine said. It was a new idea to her that by agreeing to answer Glory's fan mail she had somehow become responsible for her welfare in general. But perhaps a good secretary was, in a way, responsible. . . . 'All right. I'll try to mention it.'

'Great. You do that; and I tell you what, if you don't get any results, I'll ask this friend of mine to go see them. He could give them a real scare if he wants to.'

Iz had told her, Katherine recalled, that Mona was the girl

friend of one Piero Pasanetti, a restaurant owner with underworld connections.

'I mean, gee, we gotta do *something*,' Mona continued, looking at Katherine earnestly out of her great dark eyes. 'You see the way she is. Sh.'

Glory dragged her robe (grimy at the hem, Katherine noticed) across the patio and sat down wearily.

'What was that?' Mona asked.

'My date from last night.' She felt her hair again. Katherine became extra attentive. If she had been sent here to spy, Glory was certainly playing into her hands.

'Oh, R—'

'Uh huh.' Glory shook her head at Mona not to mention the name. 'The poor guy, that little creep Brian walked out on him again about five a.m. this morning and didn't come back yet. He's practically flipping.'

'He oughta be glad. You think maybe the kid's gone for good?'

'Nah, he'll be back soon as he runs out of loot.' Glory began to take her curlers off, releasing one by one what looked like coils of pink embroidery floss. 'The only thing going to get Brian out of that set-up, is if he ever makes it on his own, which that no-talent little fag isn't going to in a thousand years, or else he crawls on to somebody he thinks will do his big nowhere career more good.' The door-bell rang. 'Ah, for shit's sake. This is getting to be like a vaudeville routine. . . . Mona, honey. Could you go? I've about had it for this afternoon.' Mona yawned and rose. Thanks, hon.'

Glory continued taking down her hair. Her face was now surrounded by silvery-pink serpentine curls. In her matching pink terry-cloth robe, she resembled a Walt Disney Medusa.

'Ah, screw it all,' she murmured, making a Disney grimace.

'What's the matter?'

'Aw, nothing. . . . It just gets me down, that's all, a decent guy like, like my friend I was just talking to on the phone, has to be hooked on other guys and go through all that crap. If you ever want to see a fucked-up relationship you got to take a look at the queers. I mean when you get two guys living together, then you really have a dumb scene.'

Katherine had come to this house as to the camp of a heartless and soulless enemy. Now, finally, she realized that Glory was not trying to embarrass her or frighten her, but speaking sincerely in her own terms.

'I suppose most homosexuals are pretty unbalanced emotionally,' she suggested, trying to reciprocate. 'I mean I really haven't known many, but—'

'It's not just them. It's *men*. All men.' Glory stared ahead stonily, as if over a landscape of exposed and petrified heroes. But then her face softened, and she murmured: 'Well, that's the way they are, they can't help it, I guess. . . . Men are all children. In the end, you just take the child whose personality you go for most.'

'You might be right.' Katherine thought, nodding. Yes, that's how it is—and then had to remind herself that the man Glory's conclusions were based on was not someone like Paul, but Dr Einsam.

'Hey, there's a kid wants to see you,' Mona said, coming out of the house. 'Some teenager. . . . Listen,' (she lowered her voice to a whisper of crisis) 'I think it might be that one that made all the trouble. She looks kinda like the picture that was in the *Mirror*.'

'For Christ's sake. Did you let her in?'

'No. I didn't know what to tell her, so I said I didn't know if you were here.'

'So what does she want?'

'I d'know, she wants to see you. She's all charged up and talking kind of kooky.'

'Well, I don't want to see her. She's got no business coming up here. Tell her I'm not home, and you don't know when I'll be back. . . . Huh?'

'Uh, okay.' With obviously reluctance, Mona re-entered the house. Presently Katherine and Glory, sitting in silence, heard the door slam.

'She said she'll try later,' Mona reported. 'Maybe you oughta call up Maxie, huh?'

'Yeah.' Glory half rose from her chair, then fell back. 'You know I go on bugging Maxie all the time about this business, he's really going to get sick and tired of it. He was kidding me yesterday, if I wanta keep on this kick I should better find myself another agent with no ulcers.' Glory mimicked Maxie's voice. 'You know, kidding.'

'You better call him,' Mona said. 'You don't know what flippy thing that girl has in mind, coming up here.

Glory frowned and ran her hands through her pink silk hair. 'What do you think I should do?' she asked Katherine.

'I don't know.' Both flattered and frightened to be consulted, Katherine thought a moment. 'I guess I would telephone your agent.'

'Okay.' Again Glory rose, and again subsided. 'Ah, hell, I can't do it now, he's already left the office. It's after five. . . . Well, I could ring his house and leave him a message.'

After five? Katherine had completely forgotten the time. She should have started home an hour ago. She said so, and stood up; taking Glory's cardboard box under her arm, she promised to answer the fan letters and return for more next week.

Why, I really quite like her, Katherine thought, as she crossed the yard and let herself out of the gate. She's not at all what I thought. She has a hard life, really.

Ee! She jumped, and nearly screamed, as a figure burst out from behind an oleander bush, rushed headlong towards her, and then stopped suddenly, breathing hard. It was a girl dressed in the extremest Hollywood manner, with a tangle of teased yellow hair, frantic heavily-made-up eyes, and a blurred violet mouth. 'You're not *her*,' she gasped, staring through Katherine rather than at her. 'Listen, is Miss Green in there? I hafta see her.'

'She's not home.' Katherine told her first lie for Glory, to lend it verisimilitude looking straight at the girl—at the child, she realized, for under that heavy paint she was very young. 'What's the trouble?' she added in a more maternal or at least aunt-like tone.

The intruder did not answer, but her wild eyes focused on Katherine, and seemed to register her existence.

'Who're you?' she asked. 'Are you in films?'

'No,' Katherine said. 'I'm Miss Green's secretary. What did you want with her?'

Plunging forward again, the girl clutched Katherine's arm with a small plump hand that ended in violet-enamelled claws. 'I want a screen test,' she breathed, staring into her eyes with what seemed intended for hypnotic intensity. 'I'm terribly photogenic —look at my profile; no, the other's better. You can fix it for me. You're *her* secretary, you can tell her—Bobi Brentwood, B-O-B-I, not Y. Do you like it? My name—I made it up myself. I know tap soft shoe and ballet and I'm starting voice. All I want is a chance, just a chance; my coach says I have a very sexual voice quality— Madame Carmelita Woodruff, you can ask her; ask anybody about *Bobi Brentwood*. I just know I have star potential.'

'I'm afraid I can't help you,' Katherine said, as Bobi paused for breath. She tried to disengage her arm. 'Miss . . . Green . . . isn't . . . here,' she repeated, speaking each word slowly and distinctly. 'She probably won't be back until quite late. I'm sure she won't be able to see you today.'

'She hasta see me today.' Bobi Brentwood's face, under the chalk-pink make-up, trembled between tears and determination. 'She owes it to me. This is my big chance.'

'But it's already late,' Katherine said, getting her arm free. 'Nearly supper time. Miss Green may not be home for a long while. You might be waiting here all night. Now why don't you go on home?' She would catch cold, too, Katherine thought, in those flimsy clothes, as soon as it got dark.

'Why don't you mind your own business?' Bobi retorted, clumsily sarcastic. Turning her back on Katherine, she sat down deliberately on the top step and rested her chin on her fists, as if prepared to wait for ever.

Katherine wondered if she ought to go back in and tell Glory that her house was still besieged. But that would look awfully suspicious to Bobi, and it would only upset Glory—if she answered the door at all, now. She would do better to hurry home and call from there.

So she made her way around the potential star, who sat gazing out in front of her—as oblivious now of Katherine as if she had dropped into a hole in the hillside—and down the steps to her car. She put the box of fan mail on the front seat (what if all these people, too, were suddenly to appear at Glory's gate?) and turned to get in. As she did so, she noticed the star's feet and legs, now on a level with her head. Bobi Brentwood wore cheap white patent-leather sandals smudged with dirt, and her feet (the toenails thickly painted violet) were badly soiled and bruised; one knee was scraped raw as if she had fallen. Katherine realized that in this huge diffuse city where no one went anywhere on foot, Bobi must have walked at least three steep miles uphill from Sunset Strip, possibly all the way from wherever she lived, to Glory's house. And that would have been a long way, for Los Angeles is stratified socially as well as geographically, from the slums in the centre of the valley where the smog is thickest to the pools and palaces on the hill-tops.

'Say, let me give you a lift home,' she called up. 'Where do you live?'

No response. Then draggingly: 'Huh?'

'I said, I'll give you a ride home, if you like.'

'No, thanks.' Bobi gave her a cold, miserable look, completely void of trust. 'I'm staying here.'

'Well, all right.' Katherine started to get into the car, then stopped. Though surprised at the way in which she was becoming involved in Glory's world, she tried once more. 'Oh, come on,' she said. 'You can see Miss Green some other time.'

Bobi looked down from the top step, and tossed back her bird's-nest of hair with a movie heroine's gesture of scorn.

'Ah, why don't you beat it?' she said. 'I wouldn't ride in a cheap heap like that if it was the last car in California.'

21

PAUL drove across Los Angeles under a sky for once swept clear of smog by the desert winds that occasionally, at this time of the year, blow over the mountains towards the sea. The city shimmered in the dry, warm air, every detail sharp, but all colours bleached out by the intensity of the light, like a mirage.

But if it were a mirage, he thought, it wasn't the harmless decorative sort, but one of those false visions that hover just above the horizon of the desert, luring travellers on to exhaustion and despair. Only now he knew what was behind the mirage. Yesterday at Nutting he had made a final effort to get back one of the copies of his history of the company. Even if it were never published, the MS. would be something to show when he got back East; besides, he had written the book, and he wanted it. At the end of the afternoon, greatly exasperated, he went into Fred Skinner's office to complain that whenever he asked for a copy of his own work, everyone in the place became vague and obstructive.

'Yeah,' Skinner replied. 'I heard something about it. You sure did some goddamn fancy research for that book, didn't you? You got everything into it.'

The implication was false. In fact, as Paul told Skinner, he had handled the classified material with extreme care, taking precautions not to give away any trade or government secrets. Most of what he had found out with such difficulty had to do with the early history of the company, anyhow, not with current military research.

'Boy, you found out too much.' Skinner gave his sardonic ape's grin. 'I heard you even got the name Pike from somewhere.'

'Pike? Oh, Nelson Pike. He was in on the first incorporation. I think he was the assistant treasurer.'

'Yeah, well, he was also one of the defence witnesses for Dave Hume, along with his glamourpuss wife. The papers were talking about a perjury charge before he left the state. They don't mention that name around here now. And I heard that's not the only thing. All that stuff about financing, union problems, what happened to the Kinsman Corporation back in '56 when it tried to muscle in—I mean, shit, you should of known better, expecting them to print that.'

Stunned, Paul had only been able to say that Nutting itself had done nothing illegal, and that, after all, everything in the history had in fact happened. Skinner sighed, then frowned. He stood up, leant against his desk, and spoke slowly, as if explaining something to a dull child.

'Look at it this way; what good can it do them to put out that kind of info? And it can sure do a hell of a lot of harm, to publicize the fact one of the guys started this company had those kind of associations, for example. They'd be out of their mind to publish a thing like that. Hell, anyhow, what does it matter? It's all in the past.'

Olympic Boulevard, along which Paul was now driving, rose up between the two sections of the Twentieth Century Fox lot, where oil derricks and the plaster-and-lath towers of disused movie sets showed fleetingly above the trees. Ahead, Los Angeles was visible from Beverly Hills all the way to the pale violet mountains, looking like a set itself, or even a painted backdrop, in the flat light.

It was a beautiful landscape, in its way, but inhuman, like some artist's vision of the future for the cover of *Galaxy Science Fiction*. People looked out of place here: they seemed much too small for the roads and buildings, and by contrast rather scrappily constructed, all small awkward limbs and shreds of cloth. However, very few people were visible. The automobiles outnumbered them ten to one. Paul imagined a tale in which it would be gradually revealed that these automobiles were the real inhabitants of the city, a secret master race, which only kept human beings for its own greater convenience, or as pets. . . . Of course, if one of the humans were to realize the true state of things, it would give him limitless freedom and opportunity.

Freedom and opportunity; he smiled ironically. It was his old dream about Los Angeles, which he had given up, but still half believed. It wasn't even his own; it had come to him straight out of American history: 'Go West, Young Man.' Some time after he got here he had lost sight of his original stated intention, of visiting southern California as a detached historian. He had begun to play childishly with the fantasy of becoming a corporation executive here, or an intellectual beatnik, or—most naïve and stupid of all—both at the same time.

So Mar Vista (that is, N.R.D.C.) had let him down; and Venice had let him down—though of course, from their points of view, he had let them down. Anyhow, he was disgusted with both places.

Still, Paul thought now, with Los Angeles spread out before him in the sun, that was no reason to condemn a whole city. Maybe it had been his own mistake, starting at the wrong end down in the shabby seaside towns and industrial waste areas—as if one were to go to Boston and visit only Revere Beach and Somerville.

Well, he was making up for that now. He was on his way, this Saturday afternoon, to swim in a movie executive's private pool in the plushest part of Beverly Hills. He wouldn't see the owner, who was away, but (even better) he was going to meet the movie actress to whom he had lent the pool—and for whom Katherine, of all people, was now working. That was Los Angeles for you— a place where you find a shy New England girl like his wife and a Hollywood starlet in the same pool.

Paul had turned off the freeway now, and as he drew nearer to his goal the houses grew larger, the lawns wider and greener, and the underground sprinklers rose into higher fountains, as if heralding his coming. In Los Angeles, water equalled money. He had noticed this before, driving past the dry, barren yards of the slums near the Nutting Corporation—and down in Venice Beach, where the taps in Ceci's kitchen often gave only a brownish, brackish trickle, and no one could afford to water anything larger than a potted plant.

Across Wilshire Boulevard, and through the Beverly Hills shopping district. Now Paul drove along wide streets lined with palms and flowers, richly bathed in artificial rain, and the houses had swelled to castles—but castles reminiscent of the cottages on his street, in that each one was built in a different style. Here the grounds, too, had been made to conform to the owners' whims, so that the Louisiana plantation house was hung with limp wisteria and climbing roses, while the Oriental temple next door had a Japanese garden and a monkey-puzzle tree.

The movie executive's castle, when he located it, was glaringly Colonial—white, with gables, shutters, wrought iron, and a comic weathervane, behind an expanse of lush green lawn. A pink Thunderbird convertible stood in the driveway. Paul parked around the next corner, ashamed to leave his soiled, shabby Ford next to that vulgar beauty. It was the colour that made it vulgar, mainly, he thought as he walked back; the lines were good, and everyone said the engineering was superb. With a car like that, you could count on getting service anywhere, too, not like with one of these foreign jobs. The idea occurred to Paul that he might buy a T-Bird. He would have to look into that.

Following Katherine's directions, he went down a path at one side of the house, and pushed open a gate in the wall. He saw an expanse of sunlit white tile, a profusion of tropical flowers: purple Bougainvillaea, camellias, orange trees, tall lilies. The pool was all he could have wished: immense, oyster-shaped, deeply blue, and surrounded by white iron-and-glass furniture.

'Hello?' he called.

A girl in a pink fringed rubber bathing-cap, swimming at the far end of the pool, waved, swam towards him, and climbed out by the ladder.

'Hi . . . Paul? I'm Glory. Happy to meet you. Your wife isn't here: she asked me to tell you she had to go up to the university. She said she has a lot of scientific work to do for my husband.' Glory smiled, and spoke, sourly. Paul, taking this as an expression of scorn for science on Saturday afternoon, smiled back. 'Yeah,' she went on. 'So she said she'll be here around five, if you could wait for her, okay?'

'Sure, okay,' Paul said, somewhat bemused. He had expected Glory to be good-looking, for Katherine had shown him some publicity photos, but had not expected to be much stirred by her. He did not like the chorus-girl type, as a rule. But Glory's low, breathy voice, and the intense, melting way she had of look-ing up into his eyes as she spoke (automatic for her with all men, but he did not know this) took him by surprise. Then there was her incredible figure, and above all, the fantastic bathing-suit she was wearing. Made of tight pink jersey, with a high neck and long sleeves, it was full of coin-shaped holes, ranging in size from ten to fifty cents. Not only were parts of her arms and back exposed, but random samples of her stomach, and a good deal of one breast. Particularly disturbing were some holes in the lower rear section of the bathing-suit, through which that area of Glory gently bulged.

'You want to go in?'

'Oh yeah, sure.' Paul jerked himself into intellectual alertness, and became aware that Glory was smiling at him almost ironic-ally, if chorus girls were capable of irony.

'Okay, you can change in the pool house; it's open. Over here. . . . The, uh, washroom's in there.' Glory led Paul around the far end of the pool and opened a screen door. Then, turning her attention off as completely as if she had flicked a light switch (the silent kind), she walked away to the diving-board and did a neat jack-knife dive into the water.

Paul looked after her, blinked, and went in. The interior of the pool house was expensively disguised as the deck of a yacht. A wooden railing trimmed with brass and life-pre-servers ran round the room, and above it the walls were painted in a lush Technicolor style to imitate ocean views, with fluffy white clouds, soaring gulls, and tropical islands on the horizon.

It was to be expected, he thought, beginning to change his clothes. Among the thousands of pretty girls in California who wanted to be in the movies, one would have to have something pretty special to succeed. But even if Glory were, as was likely, completely insensitive, stupid, and vulgar-minded, he now felt he had to make an impression on her, make her notice him. After all, he was more than just Katherine's husband, another New England mouse.

The bathroom, in the cabin of the imaginary yacht, was nautically decorated. A glance at himself in one of the mirrors trimmed with rope and flags was somewhat reassuring: he didn't look so bad, though pale for southern California. The blue plaid cotton bathing-suit was pretty depressing, though. On an impulse, he took down one of two fancy yachting caps that hung on the pegs of a steering wheel, and placed it jauntily on his head. Then, carrying his towel, and whistling to show unconcern, he went out.

Glory was floating on her back at the far end of the pool; her eyes seemed to be shut.

234]

'Is it cold?' Paul called. She did not reply. Perhaps she had not heard him; he repeated the question.

'Huh?' Glory opened her eyes, rolled over, and swam a few strokes nearer.

'I said, is it cold,' he repeated, now feeling stupid.

'So-so.' Glory raised her eyes to the hat, but made no comment.

Paul's impulse was to test the water with his foot, but that would seem sissy. Trying to regain ground, he threw his towel towards a deck-chair and leapt on to the diving-board, testing its spring. But the hat. He snatched it off and sailed it towards the chair; what a fool he would really have looked, diving in with it on.

He was, luckily, an excellent diver, and his jacknife was as good as or better than Glory's. Bubbles blew past him as he plunged down into an element much warmer than he had expected, clear and soft. He surfaced, feeling better, and shook the water out of his face.

'Great!' he exclaimed, and struck out for the other end of the pool in a fast splashing crawl. After nearly a year of struggling with the steep, treacherously churning ocean surf, he had forgotten what it was like to swim in a block of tamed fresh water, in which all the movement was one's own—where one could float, dive, skim on one's back under the sun or shoot down through blue-green depths as clear as jello. He did all these things; he played with the passive water, sweeping it aside as he swam into shallow waves and kicking it up in fans of white spray; so delighted with the game that for a few moments he forgot where he was and in what company. Then, rising after a surface dive, he noticed Glory watching him from where she floated at the pool's edge.

'Great,' he said again, but less spontaneously. 'It's just fine.' Glory smiled faintly.

It was certainly funny, he thought, that he should find himself alone in a pool in Beverly Hills with a movie starlet. From what Katherine had said, he had assumed there would be a crowd, or at least a large group, present. 'Hey,' he said, swimming over. 'Listen. Where is everybody?'

'They're out of town. Baby, I mean Mr Petersen, he's the fellow that owns this joint, uh—home. He and his wife flew to Europe;

[235

he's looking for some Scandinavian types for a new film.'

'Oh.' Paul hung on to the edge of the pool near Glory. The warm, soft water lapped between them like a live element.

'Yeah, he's in Finland now, testing the Finland girls.'

'That must be hard work.'

Glory smiled, but only briefly, saying nothing. She rested her elbows behind her on the white-tiled gutter, throwing her breasts into even greater prominence. Her lovely white, bare legs floated up through the chlorine-green water, only a few feet from Paul's. He swallowed, and sought a topic of conversation.

'Katherine's been telling me about this crazy kid that's been giving you so much trouble. . . . This teenager that's been persecuting you,' he elaborated.

'Yeah.' A dark look came over Glory's face. 'Persecuting is right.'

'That's too bad.' So angry was her expression that he wondered if she were angry with him for mentioning the topic.

'You want to hear the latest? Now I've got the kid's *mother* after me.'

'Her mother? What does she want?'

'I d'know, the same thing I guess: wants me to get the kid a movie contract. What an ass-hole idea! I couldn't get my best friend a movie contract, but that's what they all think.' As Glory spoke her voice altered: the hesitation and over-refined accent was wiped off its surface, leaving only an angry, throaty whisper. 'I didn't see her; she only got me on the phone this one time; she started screaming and carrying on crazy, so I hung up. . . . I mean it was too damn much. Christ knows how she got my private number: some dumb bastard at the studio must of given it out. Anyhow, the way it is now, I don't dare pick up my own goddam phone when it rings.'

'Hell, that's tough.'

'You're telling me.'

'Being practically driven out of your own house that way.' Paul appreciated Glory's misfortunes; they made her seem more human, more approachable. He swam slightly nearer.

'Aw well, if it had to happen, it could've happened at a worse time.' She shrugged and splashed water on her shoulders to prevent sunburn, though this part of the pool was mostly in shadow.

'How's that?'

Glory explained that there wasn't much percentage in her staying home weekends when she couldn't use her pool. Though Katherine had already mentioned this, Paul listened with expressions of surprise and concern. That was very interesting, he said. It reminded him of a piece on the geology of Los Angeles he had read, which maintained that due to a fault in the rock structure, one section of the Santa Monica mountain range was gradually disintegrating. As he spoke, Glory's deep brown eyes, ringed with waterproof lashes, widened in concern.

'Jee-zus,' she said. 'Listen, what's the name of that book? I want to get it.'

The article had appeared in a technical volume which had been pretty heavy going for Paul himself. Since Glory had left school at thirteen, she would probably find it quite unintelligible. But Harvard had taught him never to discourage anyone by suggesting that they would be unable to learn.

'Gosh, I don't remember exactly. But I could look it up for you, if you like.' (He promised himself that he would find her something easier on the subject at the same time.)

'Yeah; that'd be really swell, if you would.' Glory's serious, breathless enthusiasm could not be wholly put on, Paul thought. She really wanted to know, to learn. It was an overtone that Paul enjoyed in his relations with women—one reason, perhaps, that he was often drawn to students.

'I'll bring you some other books too. I came across a pretty good one on the structure of this whole region. With pictures.'

'Yeah? That's swell. But what I really want to see is the thing you told me about first.' Glory splashed her face. 'I mean if that whole part of town is going to fall apart, I better put my house on the market pretty quick, huh? before everybody finds out.'

'It's not going to fall apart now,' Paul said, smiling. 'Even if this guy's right, the whole process will take a long time.'

Glory's expression remained troubled. In his mind he saw what she probably imagined: a great slow semi-comic landslide and explosion above Sunset Boulevard, scattering trees and cars and houses and fragments of earth. Of course such landslides did take place in Los Angeles, he recalled, on a smaller scale. He became more definite. 'Thousands of years, maybe more.'

[237

'You mean it's not going to happen for thousands of *years?*'

'Well, probably not.' Paul noticed the scornful way in which Glory turned from him, as from a self-confessed false prophet. 'Of course we can't be sure.' She turned partially back. 'That range of mountains is relatively unstable geologically.'

'You've really read up a lot on this place.'

'Well, I've had to. It's part of my job. You see, I was writing a kind of history of the company I work for, back to when there was nothing around here but the dinosaurs.' Glory frowned, as if puzzled or bored. 'You know, right where we are now there used to be a prehistoric jungle, full of ferns twenty feet tall and giant carnivorous reptiles.'

'Oh, yeah? Really?'

'Really,' Paul assured her. He watched a circle of white, wet flesh rise and fall with Glory's breathing, and contrasted her interest in history favourably with that of Katherine, Ceci, and N.R.D.C. 'You can see their bones down in the Los Angeles County Museum. . . . The climate was very different from what it is now. It was terribly hot, and it probably rained most of the time.'

'Jesus. What a scene, huh?'

'Of course there weren't any men around then. There were no animals, not any of the ones we know anyhow. There weren't even any birds, except for a kind of flying dinosaur, sort of a cross between a lizard and a bat.'

'Ugh.' Glory shuddered. 'Yeah; you know I saw one like that in a film once, but I thought it was something they made up.'

'No; they've found fossils of it, prints in the rocks. It was called a pterodactyl.'

'This crazy thing was about ten feet long, though.'

'They were that big. Some of the ones that couldn't fly were about sixty feet long and thirty feet high, as high as, well, about as high as the house there.' Both of them looked at Baby Petersen's house, an expanse of white shingles and glass glittering in the sun. Glory frowned, and shaded her eyes with her hand, as if she saw a procession of dinosaurs, or Colonial houses, passing.

'That's funny,' she said.

'What's funny?'

'Lookit that water coming off of the roof. I don't get it. I mean where's it coming from?'

238]

Now that she had pointed it out, Paul observed a thin trickle of water falling from the gutter above the back porch. 'It looks like it was raining,' he said.

'Yeah.'

'But it's not raining.' Paul tilted his head back and gazed into a flat blue sky, blurred with sun.

'Nah, it hasn't rained here in months.'

The dripping off the porch continued.

'It could be from somebody's sprinkler system,' Paul suggested.

'Yeah. Somebody next door watering their garden, or kids playing with the hose. . . . I guess I better go tell them to quit it.' She pulled her body up out of the water on strong, round, dancer's arms, scrambled on to the tiled edge of the pool, and stood up.

'You want me to come with you?' Paul asked. Glory ought not to go out on the street alone, he felt, with those big holes in her bathing-suit.

'No thanks.'

But the truth was that her nakedness was not vulnerable, he thought, as the gate swung shut behind her; on the contrary, it was a kind of armour. It also had nothing to do with intimacy. This situation, which was charged for him, meant nothing to her.

'Hey, I couldn't find anything. Nobody's got their water running now, anyhow. What d'you think?'

'I don't know.' Paul left off looking at Glory's legs, and climbed out. 'If it was from some hose that was on earlier, it would be stopping now. . . . Do you think it's stopping?'

'It looks to me like it's getting worse.'

In fact, the descent of water had increased from a scattered dripping to a more or less continual drizzle, splashing into silver puddles on the tiles.

'It must be coming from inside the house,' he said.

'Yeah. Something must be leaking in there.'

'We'd better go in and look.'

'We can't,' Glory objected. 'I don't have the key.'

'Let's try, anyhow.' Paul crossed the patio and tried the back door. Then, ducking under the water, he rattled the handles of French doors that opened onto the porch, while Glory tried to look inside, but unsuccessfully, since all the curtains were drawn.

'So what do we do now?'

The sun, striking through the falling drops, dappled Glory with gold light and shade as if she were standing under a waterfall. Dazzled by her appearance, and flattered by the way in which she referred the problem to him, he volunteered:

'I'll climb up on to the porch roof. Maybe I can get into one of those windows.'

Luckily, the supports of the roof were made of iron wrought to resemble leaves and flowers, offering Paul some foothold. There was a bad moment while he negotiated the gutter, thinking not so much of the pain of a possible fall, as of the ensuing inconvenience and humiliation.

'It's all wet up here,' he called, as he reached the sundeck, which was slippery with flowing water. 'Wait a sec, I'll see where it's coming from . . . Christ!'

Through a glazed door, Paul looked into what appeared to be a small dressing-room in ruffled Colonial style, now awash in three or four inches of water, which was seeping out over the door-sill and on to the deck—although the door itself, he discovered, was locked.

'We have to get in there,' Glory said when he had got down, with some difficulty, and described the scene. "They must've left the water on: that'd be just like Marianne, she's so dim anyhow. . . . We can try around the front, but if nothing's open we'll have to break a window.'

'Okay.' Now that he had managed the porch, Paul was ready for anything. As they circled the house, unsuccessfully shoving at the doors and windows, he began to recognize this as the kind of comic and surprising adventure he most enjoyed, one which would make an excellent story later; he felt partly repaid for Glory's evident disinterest in him.

From boyhood reading of detective stories he recalled that glass could be broken neatly and safely if it were first covered with a piece of cloth and then hit with a blunt instrument. The back door was conveniently divided into small panes, and his towel would do; but there was nothing to strike it with, so carefully pruned and raked was the yard. Feeling impatient, and recklessly heroic in a minor way, he struck the glass with his fist, at first tentatively, and then harder. There was a loud, sharp crack—and at the next blow, a satisfying crash. Still shielding his arm with the towel, Paul reached in and unlatched the door. He got scratched, but not badly.

'Wow!.... Aw, that's great.' For the first time, Glory gave him a smile of straightforward warmth. 'Come on.'

Following her into the house, Paul passed rapidly through a large Early American kitchen, all hanging copperware and pine panelling, through a pantry, and into a dark dining-room hung with candelabra.

'Jesus. Look at that!'

Glory stood on the edge of a long, luxurious sunken living-room, done in Beverly Hills Chinese Chippendale. It was now sunken indeed, under two feet of water, which lapped softly at the green plush carpeting of the steps as at a mossy shore. The skirts of the brocade slipcovers stirred in the current, and brightly-coloured silk pillows floated here and there. The wallpaper, a Chinesy design on a gold background, was bulging and peeling away from the walls. A small rain mixed with flakes of plaster dripped steadily from the ceiling in several places.

'It must be coming from upstairs,' Paul said, he felt rather inanely.

'Yeah.'

'How do we get up there?'

She shrugged. 'I guess we have to wade.'

With a sense of unreality, Paul followed Glory Green, in her pink Swiss-cheese bathing-suit and fringed rubber hair, across the flooded living-room. The water was quite lukewarm. In a drowned magazine rack, copies of *Variety*, sodden with damp, had begun to disintegrate; all this must have been going on for quite a long time. They climbed the mossy steps into the front hall, where the carpeting was also wet; more water, he saw, was running quietly down the carpeted stairs.

'Geez.' Glory giggled suddenly; her voice was strangely loud, as in an underground cave. 'C'mon.'

They splashed upstairs. Here too the rugs and floors were wet. Glory hurried from room to room, flinging doors open and shut so fast that Paul had only an impression of expanses of tinted mirror, polished maple and mahogany, and immense silk-shaded lamps held aloft by the glazed figures of Chinamen. Then, in the largest bedroom, she pulled open a bathroom door which seemed to stick more than the others. A tidal wave of water rushed out at them, with such force that it knocked Glory down. Paul, a few feet behind, had to grasp at a chair to keep upright.

'Hey! Are you all right?' Wading across the rug to Glory, he helped her up, damp, dripping, and half-stunned. The warm wet flesh of her body pressed against his arm.

'I guess so,' she said, blinking and still leaning on him. Her bathing-suit had been pulled round somehow so that the wet pink tip of one full breast pointed out through a small neat hole, as if it had been designed that way. Without stopping to think, Paul put his free hand over it, whether out of modesty or lust he could not have said. Instead of jerking away, Glory swayed towards him. He pulled her nearer; for an instant she looked into his eyes from a distance of about four inches; then they were involved in a sudden, dripping kiss. The circular samples of Glory were pressed against him in a juxtaposition so openly sensual that he was giddy for a moment; she spoke, but he had to ask her to repeat it.

'I said, better turn off the water.'

'Oh yeah, okay.' Through the bathroom door Paul could see a gilt faucet running into the marbled basin in a thin, steady trickle —much too small, it seemed, to have caused all this.

He shut it off and turned round; Glory was sitting on the bed, a huge vulgar expanse of shiny pale-blue satin, now streaked dark with water.

'I— You're really—' he began as he moved towards her, not knowing what he was going to say, but determined to say, and do, something.

'C'mere.' If Glory's ordinary speaking voice had a taste of sexuality, that she now used was like dark jam. Paul felt as if he had got into a dream, or more likely one of those surrealist movies that imitate dreams, but he was too aroused now to care. In a moment, with Glory's help, he was peeling off her wet, very tight bathing-suit, which left faint red circles on pale skin. He released first breasts of a size and pneumatic roundness that he had seen only in *Playboy* magazine, then a sculptured, almost concave stomach, and finally a patch of curly hair coloured a vivid silver pink, which completed the unreal perfection of the whole. He knelt back from it, dazed.

'Jesus— You're—'

'Don't tell me, huh.' Glory pulled Paul hard towards her; her breath warmed him. As they kissed and clung, he began to notice little imperfections, visible only close up, that reassured him with their proof of her humanity: a freckled roughness in her skin, a smudge of mascara by one eye, the pucker of an appendicitis scar on her belly.

'Come on.' With strong, pink-nailed fingers, Glory dragged Paul's wet bathing-suit down off his hips, down his legs, and flung it, like a damp rag, into a corner.

'Ah,' she began to murmur. 'Aw, that's it. . . . Come on. . . . Do it do it do it. Do it to me.' In the flooded room, like an actor in a surrealist—no, a pornographic—film, he dug his toes into the satin bedspread and drove into her again and again.

'Aw.' Glory sighed, and pulled one of the satin pillows towards her, propping it under her head—which, as she had never taken off her bathing cap, was still covered with fringed rubber hair. 'Don't get up. . . . Hey, that was good.'

'You liked it?' Paul felt as if he had received some film award. 'So did I.'

'Yeah. That'll show them, huh?' She laughed.

'Mm.' Show whom? Paul wondered; probably the whole world.

'Hey, y'know, this room.' She laughed again.

'It's pretty weird, isn't it?' he agreed, surprised however that Glory's taste would condemn this luxurious set.

'Weird? Yeah: all that water.' She gestured towards the soaked carpet. Somewhere below, Paul could still hear a residual dripping. 'No, what I meant was, I was thinking, how many times Baby Petersen's tried to get me on to this bed, and he never made it.'

'Poor guy,' Paul said, smiling, so pleased at this evidence of his competitive success that he could be magnanimous. He had gone to bed with a movie starlet; he, Paul Cattleman, had actually done and was doing this.

'Ah, don't feel sorry for him. Baby's a shit from the word go. His whole life is dedicated to the proposition the way to get ahead at Superb is by putting out for Baby Petersen. Which is a big lie because he just doesn't pull that much weight around the studio. He's a nothing, but by the time you find that out, it's too late.'

Glory noticed Paul looking at her. 'Not me. I'm too old to fall for that kind of line.'

'How old are you?' Paul realized he did not know the first thing about this beautiful girl with whom he had just been intimate: not even her real name or the true colour of her hair, though she lay there naked beside him, one leg thrown over his.

Glory was silent. Paul thought she was angry at the question. But the truth was that she had trouble herself remembering her age, so many lies had been told about it. Before Glory was out of diapers her mother, who had been divorced rather too long before the birth, had begun to add months to Glory's age to forestall suspicions of illegitimacy. She had never officially corrected this error; but a little later, when Glory became a child actor, she had subtracted a year or two, or three — nobody really knew how many. Later, professional exigencies had dictated a change in the opposite direction, for you had to be sixteen to get a working permit for a job as a night-club dancer. As time went on, Glory took matters into her own hands, and often became older or younger in order to flatter a man or sign a contract; she had come to feel that her age, like the colour of her hair, was a matter of choice.

'I'm twenty-six,' she said now, adding two years to her studio age.

'I'm thirty-one.' This produced no comment. To re-establish communication, Paul went back to the last topic. 'You said this guy who lives here is married, though. What's his wife like?'

'Oh, she's okay. Only she's been kicked around so much she's kind of slap-happy, you know. She cries all the time. Well, she's actually kind of a lush, but you can't hold it against her, what she has to live with.'

'Why doesn't she divorce him?'

'I d'know; I guess she doesn't want to. She's still kind of sweet on him. I think she keeps hoping he'll stop screwing around and come back to her. And he plays up to it, see. He uses her as a front with his other girls, if they get too serious or they starting wanting to marry him, then he always has an out: he tells them how basically he really loves his wife, only she has serious problems. I think in a way he believes his own line, cause he's just as screwed up as everybody else in the business.'

An uncomfortable feeling, which he did not analyse, passed through Paul. 'Are they all screwed up in your business?'

'Christ, yeah. They really are, you know.' Glory turned on her side towards Paul. 'Maybe it's the dumb climate. A friend of mine says that once you get out here, and get into the sun, you kind of gradually go soft, if you're not used to it. . . . I don't like the sun. I always try to stay out of it myself. . . . How long since you moved to California?'

'About nine months. But we haven't come for good. We're just here temporarily.'

'Oh yeah, really?' Her voice was intimate, as usual, but somehow casual. Paul realized that no words of love or even liking had been spoken between him and Glory; there had been no explanation of what had happened. Physical desire had simply been turned on and flooded them, like the house. Was this going to be an affair, or was it only an incident? He didn't know what she thought, and that was perhaps one reason the whole thing seemed so unreal.

'When're you leaving?' Glory asked.

'I don't know exactly. Probably sometime this year.' A week ago Paul had had a very promising letter from his thesis director telling him about a job at Convers College; he was waiting now to hear from them directly. 'I'm kind of sorry, now.' He accompanied this avowal with a warm but gentle kiss, intended to convey gratitude and affection. Glory met it at a higher temperature.

'Mmm. And where're you going to?' She stroked his leg with her knee.

'Well, probably to Convers. It's sort of north of Boston.'

'That's in New England. Y'know, I've never been in New England.' Glory rubbed his leg higher up, expertly.

'I wish I could take you with me.'

'Yeah? I'd like to go. I've always had a kind of kooky dream to see that part of the country. All those old-fashioned towns and historical places: I really think I would go for them. There's a New England set out on the back lot at the studio, with these neat little white wooden houses and big barns and fences and tall trees, y'know. When I was first working at Superb I used to walk through it on the way to where we were shooting *Mexican Mamba* —what a bomb that turned out to be—and I d'know, it sort of picked me up.'

'You ought to see the real thing.' The educational impulse stirred in Paul again, along with other impulses. The idea of Glory walking alone through an imaginary village had something pathetic about it, too. 'Seriously. Why don't you take a trip and visit New England?'

'Maybe I will. I'm so goddamned fed up with all the creeps and phonies in this town. . . . Hey! You know what I'll do?' Taken with her idea, Glory left off rubbing against Paul. 'Soon's we finish making this picture, that's probably only a couple months, I'll go East. . . . I'd love to walk out on this screwy dump right now, only I couldn't let Rory and the kids down.'

'New England is good in the summer,' Paul said. 'Not too hot. Cape Cod—'

'Yeah. That's what I'll really do. I'll take a couple months off, Maxie can fix it—'

'That's a fine idea.'

'—and I'll come and stay with you. Maybe in September, huh? What did you say that place was called?'

A new image appeared in Paul's head: a New England college town. Mr Cattleman, the junior instructor in history, has scarcely arrived, when he is visited by his mistress, a Hollywood starlet with pink hair.

'Uh—Convers. But it's a fairly small town, you know. There wouldn't be much for you to see there.'

'Aw, I don't care about that. As long as there's a lot of nature and scenery. Y'know I really go for the country. I love to get out in the open spaces and run around and look at all the trees growing and grass and flowers. That's one reason this town makes me so sick.'

'Yeah, but what I meant was, I'm afraid the people won't interest you much. Convers is pretty much a college town, mostly students and professors.'

'But that's what I'd like most.' In her enthusiasm, Glory sat up. 'Shit, you don't know how much I want to meet some real, serious, intellectual people, professors and thinkers, that you can learn something from. People that don't spend all their time getting loaded or screwing somebody or pulling a deal over the next guy. I want to go to the kind of parties where everybody is talking about serious things, like art and philosophy and history and those kind of things.' Visions of some academic gatherings he had attended passed across Paul's mind. In imagination, he added Glory to them, dressed in her pink bathing-suit.

'Uh, well,' he said.

'Maybe you think I wouldn't know how to act right with people like that. Listen, I wouldn't say anything or do anything funny; I wouldn't want to. All I'd want to do is just sit quietly in a corner and listen to their conversations, and nobody would even notice me.'

'That's what you think,' Paul said. Glory turned her face towards his, frowning.

'I get it,' she said. 'You mean you don't want me to come. You think I would embarrass you or something, because I'm so un-educated and dumb.' Glory's voice was hostile and hurt; she turned her face away.

'No; I mean you're a very beautiful girl, and people are going to notice you wherever you go.' No response. Paul sat up and put his arms round Glory, like a child with an expensive new toy, which he suddenly fears will be taken away from him again. He stroked her neck, her shoulders. 'You're really incredibly beautiful.' No response. 'I think it'd be just great to have you visit me in New England.'

'Is that straight?' Sulkily, Glory turned towards him.

'Yes.' Calling up the resources of his experience, he pulled her nipples towards him, twisting and squeezing them gently.

'Ah. . . . Yeah, do that. . . . Really?'

'Really.'

'Listen, though,' Paul said a moment later. 'I mean, what time is it? Shouldn't we do something about the house, telephone some-body or something?' He raised his head from her lap; Glory pushed it down again.

'Sure,' she agreed. 'Later.'

22

SATURDAY noon. An anonymous crowd of sightseers loitered and drifted along Hollywood Boulevard west of Vine Street. They stopped to gawk at the photos in front of second-storey night clubs and dance halls, at the windows of discount dress and hat and shoe stores, at stand-up lunch counters where red, rubbery hot dogs fried and orange drink bubbled perpetually. They entered souvenir shops and bought accordion strings of coloured postcards, dummy books titled *Los Angeles Confidential* (which opened to reveal a toy privy or a naughty plastic doll), pink china vases, and rayon panties with 'Hollywood, California' printed on them.

They were of every age, or no age. The little girls had permanents and nailpolish, sometimes even lipstick and high-heeled sandals, while the mothers or grandmothers who dragged them whining along the sidewalk wore ruffled baby dresses and curled, tinted hair—as if they had changed into each other's clothes for a joke. Elderly men and women, some at the far edge of their lives, shuffled by, muttering to themselves and fingering their handbags or the parcels they carried. There were plenty of young people too: watchful delinquent boys slouching by in leather jackets, and clusters of teenage girls giggling stupidly and clinging to each other as they swept up the sidewalk. There were family groups of tourists, noisily crude, or silent, because they had known one another too long; and pickup couples blinking as they emerged from five-dollar hotels, noisily crude or silent.

All these people had something in common: a look of being cheaply made—put together, like the clothes they wore, out of shoddy materials, and coloured with harsh chemical dyes. Their faces wore a common expression—that of people anxiously searching for something: for success, for adventure, for love. Or if they had given up these ends, they were at least searching for some excitement; for a scene, a spectacle, a hero to watch. Above all, they were looking, with the intensity of castaways on a desert island, for the beautiful and the famous—looking for stars. Whom, of course, they never found—except for their footsteps in cement in front of Grauman's Chinese Theatre.

So they wandered under the merciless sun, and Katherine wandered with them.

What was she doing there? She had come to Hollywood that morning to pick up a new lot of fan letters at the rehearsal studio where Glory was practising for a charity show (another of Maxie's gimmicks). Once she had the letters, Katherine could have stayed to watch rehearsal, or she could have gone home on the bus. There was no reason to hang around Hollywood Boulevard, except that it seemed a good place to be miserable in.

And it was all her own stupid fault; she had done it to herself. She had told Iz that Glory was still in love with him.

It had taken a while, first to know it and then to tell it. Originally she had believed what Iz said: that Glory had no interest in him any more, that she was glad to be rid of him so that she could go out with Rory Gunn, the handsome song-and-dance star, and get her picture into the papers. After Katherine had met Glory, she realized that that could not be completely true, for Glory grew upset over even the mention of Dr Einsam's name. But she said to herself that that was simply something Glory would have to get over. The truth was, they just weren't suited to each other; it was an impossible marriage. As the Social Sciences professors said, it was unhealthy, unbalanced of Iz to have chosen such a wife. And the same thing could be (and was) said on the other side: Mona had confided to Katherine that a lot of Glory's real friends were glad she had got rid of that intellectual creep, who had no appreciation for her career.

Katherine herself felt sympathy for Glory. Women, she thought, always have something in common. However different their backgrounds or occupations; they can always meet upon the basic general topics: food, clothes, houses, people. When she, Glory, and Mona discussed men, for instance, it did not seem to matter any more that they were speaking respectively of a Harvard graduate student in history, a European-born psychiatrist, and a small-time Italian gangster. Katherine felt a purely altruistic regret when she first learned that Rory Gunn, the handsome star who had been taking Glory out twice a week in the most public and expensive way, was the same person as the sad homosexual who telephoned her almost every day to report the crises of his hopeless affairs.

Aimlessly, stopping and starting slowly, Katherine drifted along the sidewalk from one ugly window display to another, her eyes fixed on, but not seeing, trays of glazed chocolate doughnuts, or painted and varnished plaster images of flowers and fruit. Occasionally other tourists bumped into her, but she was usually too late to apologize or acknowledge their apologies, for depression had slowed her reaction time.

She had known all along, too well, that Iz was still 'emotionally involved' with Glory. He admitted it himself, though as a psychological fault. If she were to tell him that Glory was in the same state, she had realized, that Rory was nothing but a publicity stunt, it might send him back to her. At any rate, he should have the choice. But Katherine had kept putting it off, saying to herself: not yet, just a little later. She had repeated to herself, in excuse, Iz's own statement that his relationship to his wife was 'a neurotic attachment to a highly original but basically immature personality'.

Until the day last week when, arriving at Glory's house, she found her hunched over a portable FM set, screwing the knobs round and bending the aerial this way and that so as to catch the weak signal of the U.C.L.A. student radio station and hear a symposium in which Dr Einsam was taking part. 'Ssh, just a sec.' She twisted the dial back and forth, and fragments of Iz's professional voice leaked out into the room, roughened with static. When the programme was over, Glory sat up, patted her hair into place, and said to Katherine, 'I thought it'd be kind of a gas to hear him shooting his mouth off again, telling the whole world what to think, but you can't get a thing on this ass-hole set.' Katherine was not fooled. Throughout the programme some analogy had kept eluding her, but now she had it: Glory was Iz's fan. She treasured these half-audible, irrelevant phrases ('. . . ya, I would say that . . . in this case the existence of a control sample . . . essential') as a fan might the scribbled autograph of her chosen star, or the bent paper cup from which he had drunk.

Katherine thought that she would not have gone to such lengths to hear Iz's voice, no matter how long they had been separated; she just did not care for him that much. She didn't, she realized, want any more of Iz than she had, however much she wanted that. Certainly she didn't wish she were married to him. Not only that there was (perhaps) something in his suggestion that this affair was a vacation trip for her, something outside of real life. It was also that he was too much the guide of the tour. There was something too preceptorial, even too analytic, in his manner .owards her, for what he would have called 'a permanent relationship'. After all, to stay with your doctor too long is to confess your illness chronic. If cured, you.paid the bill and went away.

So there had been nothing to look forward to. Iz would never like her any better than he did, while she was in danger every day that passed of becoming more and more — well, the word he would have used was 'dependent'. And meanwhile, there was the persistent consciousness that she knew something Iz ought to know, and was keeping it from him.

It was hard bringing up the subject, since after her first visit to Glory's house Katherine had stopped telling him what she saw and heard there. She had trained herself, long ago, to be secretive about her employers' lives. But beyond this, she had wanted to avoid mentioning or thinking about Glory when she was with Iz, because it felt too awful and uncomfortable. The truth was, probably, she should never have got into the situation of working for Glory, and Iz should never have put her there.

Yesterday at the office she had told him. Iz listened silently, attentively, while she spoke, asking only one question: 'Gunn is definitely a fag? Ya, I heard that rumour, but I thought he could be AC–DC.' When she had finished, Iz looked at her. Then, breaking a rigid rule of his about behaviour on campus, he put his hand over hers, and said, 'Thank you for telling me this.' 'Oh, that's all right,' Katherine replied in a thin, formal voice. 'I should have done it sooner.' 'No.' Iz still gripped the back of her hand. 'Don't feel that; there was no need. Unless you wanted to.' She did not answer, or return his look. We can't say anything more, she had thought, because maybe I'm wrong. Maybe Glory doesn't want him, but what does that matter, if he wants her? Students passed in the hall; Iz took his hand away, and work continued. Only at the end of the afternoon he had remarked, throwing it off with painful casualness, 'So they're rehearsing for the benefit tomorrow. Hm. They'll be there all day?' That was all; except that for the first time in many weeks he left the office without making arrangements for her to come to the apartment. All the same, Katherine knew that Iz was at Glory's rehearsal now. Or more probably, because he seldom got up before noon, on his way there.

She had miscalculated, she thought; she hadn't known she would feel like this. If she had known that, she still should have told Iz, but would she have done so? He might have found out anyhow, eventually. But not right now, not today.

'It's over. I did it to myself,' she said aloud. 'It's finished.' Talking to herself right out on the street, like a crazy person. She must be in a state to act like that. She was in a state. She must get hold of herself, and do something constructive. She didn't want to go home: somehow she felt that in the empty house (Paul had gone to work, though it was Saturday) it would all·be even worse.

Ahead of Katherine on the street corner was a news stand, displaying 'Home-Town Papers from 50 States' and glossy magazines dealing with every possible hobby and interest, from auto-racing to Zoroastrianism, from birth (*Your New Baby*) to death (*Casket and Sunnyside*). The Boston *Globe* and *Herald* were there, of course, but she felt no impulse towards them either. They were irrelevant to the people she knew here, the things she had done with them, the vacant pain inside her. Still, the news stand gave her an idea: she would look for some interesting book to read over the weekend, to take her mind off everything.

There was a large bookstore, the Pickwick Bookshop, almost directly across the street. Katherine stopped briefly at the bargain tables outside, where for fifty-nine or seventy-nine cents you could buy books whose glossy paper jackets were beginning to be rubbed dull and torn around the edges. Inside, the latest successes were piled into bright pyramids. What did she want to read: biography, sociology, history, travel? Katherine disliked most current fiction, but she had a wide range of general interests, and the various jobs she had held had left her with some special ones. But nothing seemed what she wanted. What was it Iz had said, when she complained that she couldn't find any good new biographies at the library? 'Once you've tried reality, imaginary lives seem flat.'

Still, there must be something— She wandered about the crowded store, turning covers over listlessly to read blurbs, lifting books and setting them back, and then simply standing, frowning at the flat coloured faces, pictures, and letters.

'Hello, there.'

Katherine looked up. Across a table of books, a strange man was smiling at her. Automatically, she began to make her face stiff and blank.

'I know you. Don't you work in the H-building?' he continued. 'Over at U.C.L.A.?'

'Oh; yes.' Tentatively, Katherine relaxed her face.

'You're working for Smith and Haraki—isn't that right?'

'Yes, that's right.' And Einsam and Einsam, she thought dully.

'I thought so. I'm Jim McKay.' He came around the counter towards her; a small, pale Irishman with sharp features and black cropped hair. 'I'm in Anthropology,' he said, and held out his hand. After a fractional hesitation, due to her preoccupied depression, Katherine took it. The firm, warm touch of another live being acted like a slight electric shock. She focussed more clearly on Mr McKay, who seemed to be about thirty-five and was wearing a blue work shirt, a striped tie, chino pants, and sneakers. She moved the features of her face into a smile.

'And what's your name?' he went on.

'I'm sorry. . . . Kath-er-ine-Cat-tle-man.' Katherine felt it incongruous that these, or any similar series of nonsense noises, should belong to her.

'Katherine Cattleman.' He repeated the syllables as if, at least for the moment, they meant something to him. 'And what's that project? Perception and something. Perception and what?'

'Delinquency.'

'Mhhm. Well.' He glanced round the store, as if deciding what to look for next. The insignificant interruption to Katherine's state of mind was over, and misery began to rise round her again. She stared at the display of travel literature in a fixed way.

'If you've finished your shopping,' Mr McKay said, 'how about having a cup of coffee with me? You look as if you need one.'

A cup of coffee? There was no reason why she should. On the other hand, there was no reason why she should not. There was no reason now why she should do, or not do, anything. 'All right.' Even in her present state, that sounded ungracious. 'Yes; that would be nice.'

They left the bookstore. 'This way,' Mr McKay said, and took her bare arm above the elbow, pressing it. At the same time he gave her a quick glance of sensual interest and pleasure which, as she turned her head, he altered into a friendly smile. He doesn't know how miserable I am; he thinks I'm just an ordinary girl he's succeeded in picking up, Katherine realized. He thinks I might like him. Well, if anyone saw her now, that was what they would think too. Katherine gave a slight jerk, or twitch, as if to get away.

'Come on.' Jim McKay took a better grip on Katherine's arm; she felt through his fingers the firm intention to have at least a cup of coffee with her. And after all, what difference did it make if she went with him? Nobody she knew would see her, and it was a better idea than going home to her empty house with a book on meteorology, south-western humour, or intelligence testing— or the biography of some romantic, exciting, successful dead person.

'This way.' They had crossed Hollywood Boulevard; now they turned down a side street. Suddenly, between the low, shabby buildings and the stunted palms a great view opened out down-hill in the distance — all of Los Angeles, or so it seemed: an immense white city sparkling in the smoggy sunlight.

'Awright awright, let's take it again from "maybe it'll rain".'

The pianist broke off playing, and on the bare stage of the rehearsal studio the four other girls and Glory stopped their routine, dropping their arms awkwardly. One pulled up her blouse; another scratched her thigh.

'Roxy, baby, you're crowding Glory too close; you gotta keep farther back on the turn. Okay, Eddie.' The pianist resumed.

> Maybe it'll rain tomorrow,
> But it's not tomorrow today-ay-ay,
> Let's play!

'Okay, okay, that was better, but you still don't all get the gesture. "*Rain* . . ." Ginevra, you got to wiggle your fingers on that, when you bring them down, darling—like so. Let's see it now. . . . Terrific! No, not you, Roxy, you got to wiggle yours

254]

less, *much less*. Now this time let's take it back to "If you wanna know the way". Okay, Eddie.'

In the rear of the bare hall, Paul tilted his folding chair back and sighed deeply with boredom. For Christ's sake, when were they going to 'break for lunch'? At twelve, Glory had said, but it was already nearer to one. He had heard the fragmented lyrics of *Let's Play* sung about a thousand times; these trivial, hedonist lines, he felt, would be incised on his mind as long as he lived, scars of the trivial, hedonistic relationship he had got himself into.

Not that he held it against Glory. It wasn't her fault; it was part of her nature and training to grab what you wanted when you wanted it. He was grateful for Glory's sensuality, and deeply delighted with it; he was also pleased with himself because he had been able to respond to this in her, and to satisfy it. On the other hand, he definitely missed something in this affair (if it was an affair—he had only seen her twice), something that he had always taken for granted before.

That sudden embrace in the flooded house had deprived him, Paul thought, of almost as much as it had given. He had missed the intellectual pleasure of the chase—all the suspense and excitement from the first sighting of the quarry through dodge and feint and flight and pursuit, until that climactic moment when he held the warm body, and also its soul, down quivering in his arms.

In his worse moments, he said to himself that this was a relationship merely of two warm bodies, not of two people. He and Glory didn't really know each other, and as far as he could tell they never would.

But Paul had another, more definite, reason for concern, and that was Glory's proposed trip to New England and to Convers College, in the fall. (He had heard from Convers now, asking him to come East for an interview next month, and offering to pay his way—which looked like a good sign.) Was Glory serious? He didn't know, but the more she described her plans, the more clearly he saw that she mustn't come, at least not then. Driving from Mar Vista to Hollywood that morning he had spent much of his time trying to invent persuasive arguments to this effect.

She wasn't going to be allowed to visit his life, though he was, at that moment, visiting hers. Did that seem unfair? But in Hollywood anyone passed; he wasn't obvious and incongruous the way she would be in New England.

The piano stopped, then started again. Only four girls were on stage now, and Glory was walking towards him. She wore a scoop-necked leotard, shabby dance slippers, hair shrouded in a scarf, and dark glasses. He jumped up with relief.

'Hi! Can you come out to lunch now?'

'Aw, no.' Glory sighed. 'I got to stay. Jackie's just running the girls through the new introduction. Come on back with me while I put on my make-up: there's some big shots coming.'

'All right, but I'm starving.'

'Why don't you go get yourself something? There's a couple places round the corner.'

'No, I'll wait for you.'

The dressing-room at one side of the stage was bare boards too, not very clean, and glaringly lit. Glory sat down in front of a mirror and took off her sun-glasses. Paul was surprised at how young, and how undistinguished, even nondescript, she looked without make-up. Her skin in the electric light was freckled and flawed. He felt compassion, and was glad that he had thought of the kindest way to make his point.

'Say. I've been thinking about your trip East,' he began, drawing a wooden chair towards him and sitting down on it backwards, the way the good guys do in Western films. 'Seems to me the best time for you to come would be in the spring.' Always make positive suggestions, as a friend of Katherine's, a nursery-school-teacher, had once said. He paused. Glory was not obviously listening to him, but opening her bag, and beginning to lay out tubes, brushes, bottles, etc., on the dressing-table. 'You said you'd never seen a real spring. You know, that's pretty bad. The flowers. . . . Why don't you plan to come say about next April, maybe in spring vacation?' Paul ended awkwardly, but on an up note.

'Yeah,' Glory said, not in assent, rubbing brownish-pink paint over her face and neck. 'Maybe.'

'You'd like it then. It's really beautiful. All the leaves coming out on the trees, the spring flowers. . . .' He realized he had mentioned the flowers before. Glory said nothing; she was applying glue from a small bottle to something that looked like a dead, hairy centipede. She screwed the top back on the bottle, lifted the

256]

centipede carefully, and stuck it on to her left eyelid, where it turned into a strip of curly artificial lashes an inch long.

'And by that time,' Paul went on, 'I'd be settled in and know some people you could meet.' Among any faculty, he reasoned, there would be a proportion that would not only not disapprove of Glory, but would admire him for knowing her.

'Aw, Paul. I d'know.' Glory held one eyelid down while she filled in above it with purple eye-shadow, then with silver. 'I mean, sure, I'd like to see the flowers and all. But all those old professors.' Dipping a brush in dark brown liquid, she drew a wide curve above the lashes and out towards the temple. 'Y'know, I could never really make that scene.' Glory powdered her lid to set the colours, opened both eyes, and glanced over the shoulder of her reflection at Paul, smiling apologetically. With one eye un-painted, the other metallic purple, she looked grotesque. 'Aw, baby,' she added. 'You know it was a kooky idea anyhow, 'cause by that time Kay'll have found out and she won't want me in the same state with her, forget the same town.'

She means Katherine, Paul thought. 'Found out? How's she going to find out? *I'm* not going to tell her.'

'You're not? How come?'

'Huh?'

'I mean, you never tell her we made it together' (Glory began on the other eyelid), 'how the hell's she going to know we paid them back?'

'Paid them back?'

'Yeah. Like we said, your turn my turn; fun for mama; fun for daddy. Boy, are you slow today!' As Glory looked at Paul's puzzled expression in the mirror, hers also grew puzzled.

'You mean you think your husband has been—' Paul broke off.

'Aw, I know he's been making out for a long time, ever since he walked out on me. I was all broken up for a while, then I said to myself: He thinks I'm just going to sit around on my ass bawling about it; well, I've got better things to do with that piece of equip-ment.' Glory laughed.

'But you mean you think he's been making out with—'

'With your wife,' Glory finished. 'Yeah.' She began pencilling in an eyebrow, then stopped and turned round so as to look

[257

at Paul directly. 'You mean you didn't know that? Shit.'

'It's not true. Who told you?'

'Nobody. I just know, that's all.'

Paul began to feel better. 'Oh, that's impossible,' he said. In Glory's world, no doubt such promiscuity was the rule, but not in Katherine's. 'I know Katherine,' he asserted. 'She wouldn't do anything like that. She's just not the kind of girl that——' He stopped; he had been about to draw a definition insulting to Glory. 'How do you just know?'

'From watching her.' Glory began on her eyebrows again, thickening them and extending them up and out like antennae. 'The way she says his name, kind of tense, or the way she turns on when somebody else mentions it. Hell, everything.'

'It couldn't be,' Paul said. He felt much better now. 'I mean, she might have a kind of intellectual crush on him, sure. Kind of a hero-worship.'

'Hmh.' Picking up a brush, Glory began to outline her lips, which expressed scepticism. She did not believe him. The cool charm, the modesty of Katherine's temperament, love without sensual passion, was probably something she had never come across in her life, or even conceived of.

'See, Katherine does get that way sometimes when she's working for somebody. She really gets to think they're the greatest living expert in whatever it is they do,' he explained, trying to put it into terms that Glory would understand. 'I guess that's one reason she's such a good secretary.'

Stretching her lips, Glory filled in the outlines of a sensuous mauve-pink mouth, blotted it on a tissue, threw the tissue on to the floor, and dipped into a box of pink powder.

'Baby,' she said. 'You're living in a little dream world.' For a few seconds she disappeared from Paul in a smog-thick cloud of powder. Then, turning her head, she unknotted the kerchief, pulled it off, and shook out her hair. When she turned back, Paul almost gasped; the nondescript freckled face had turned into a hard mask of unearthly, if vulgar, beauty.

'Yeah,' she said, smiling not so much at him as into the mirror, testing her reflexes. 'So listen, I got to get back on stage now; but just hang on, we hafta eat some time.' She stood up and smiled again, more genuinely. Paul understood that she was sorry for having, as she thought, undeceived him. But it was really she who was deceived, living in a dream world—but a vulgar, empty one.

Opening the door to backstage, Glory waved to him; he raised his hand in a half-hearted return. A jangle of trivial dream-music poured in, dimming as the door shut. He looked at the mess of theatrical paint spread out on the dressing-table along with soiled tissues, smudges of powder, and a bottle of tablets—tranquillizers, he realized, picking it up—marked 'for nervousness, restlessness, nervous irritability and excitability'. He thought that he ought not to be angry at Glory for her opinion of his wife's chastity. He should be sorry for her instead, because she was sunk so deep in her shoddy, neurotic world. Paul walked back and forth in the dressing-room. It wasn't her fault if she figured everyone else was the same—if she thought that every man was on the make, every girl a cheap whore like her—Paul realized that he *was* angry, very angry. He was suffering from nervousness, restlessness, nervous irritability and excitability.

He went out into the rehearsal hall. Again, the girls were grinning and rotating and high-kicking on stage, their breasts bouncing in unison.

If you want to know the way—

How had he got into this place? He turned, and began to walk towards the exit.

Outside in the hall, an altercation was going on. A middle-aged woman in an unattractive hat was arguing with the doorman.

'Hey, listen,' the man said, stopping Paul. 'Maybe you can help this lady; she wants to see Miss Green. I told her already a hundred times she can't go in.'

'But it's very important.' The woman turned the screwed-up intensity of her expression on Paul. 'I have to speak to Miss Green about my daughter's screen test. My daughter, Dawn Nefflinger, only she calls herself Bobi Brentwood.' She gave a nervous laugh; her voice trembled with maternal hysteria and anxiety. Paul realized that this must be the mother of the teenager who was bothering Glory.

'I'm sorry, I can't help you.' He pushed through the swinging doors on to the sidewalk.

The rehearsal hall was at the end of a blind alley. As Paul got to the corner, a sports car drove in: a black Jaguar. He watched it park with a loud squeak of brakes. A bearded man in dark glasses got out. Paul wondered if he hadn't seen him somewhere; he frowned, trying to remember. No, he hadn't *seen* him, he thought, as the man entered the building. He knew him instead from the blurred picture that Glory carried, and from Katherine's description: it was Dr Isidore Einsam.

'Have lunch with me,' Iz told Glory, rather than asked her, as the groups of dancers, singers, producers, agents, musicians, and other people connected with the charity show began to break up and move towards the exit. Whether it was the lack of a question in his voice, or just the months of separation, Glory answered flatly.

'I'm not eating lunch today; I hafta take the car to the car wash.' In the state of nervousness into which Iz's appearance had thrown her, it was the first excuse she could think of. As for Paul, she had completely forgotten about him.

'All right, I'll come with you.'

Iz took her arm; she let him do so stiffly. Why should I say a nice word to this conceited bastard? her whole attitude seemed to announce as they walked out into the blinding sunlight (god-damn it, she'd forgotten her glasses). What does he think? he turns up out of nowhere after all this time, I'm supposed to throw myself into his arms? She saw Iz's Jag in the alley, practically underneath a No Parking—No Standing sign, and thought, Hope he gets a ticket.

Glory's own car was parked round the corner. She refused Iz's offer to drive, and kept up her silence on the way, interspersed with short, discouraging answers to his questions and comments about the show. She was not going to get excited, she resolved; she was going to be very polite and distant. However, as they sat in the line of automobiles waiting to enter the automatic car-wash, she remembered an obligation and said coolly to Iz:

'Hey, I oughta thank you for talking to that crazy kid's mother for me. It must've been a drag.'

'Ah, it wasn't so hard. All she wanted was for somebody to listen to her for a while.'

Glory let her foot off the brake, moved up in line, and stopped again. 'The last time *I* listened to her, she started right in screaming about money, and how she didn't have much loot, but she was an American citizen. I figured she was trying to put the grab on me. I mean, how was I to know she wanted to keep the kid out of the studio? I thought they were playing it together.' Glory laughed shortly, then sighed. 'You figure it'll work out all right, that phoney screen-test business?'

'I think so.' Consulting hastily together in a corner of the rehearsal hall (while Bobi's mother waited in the lobby), Iz and Maxie Weiss, Glory's agent, had agreed that an imitation screen test was to be arranged for Bobi Brentwood on the Superb lot. She was to be informed afterwards that though she looked pretty good, she needed some professional training. She would then be encouraged to enroll in an acting class which was also a kind of group therapy. 'The trouble is,' Iz said, 'the mother definitely needs help too; but what can you do—you have to start somewhere.'

'She's not in such bad shape,' Glory said, moving up in line again. 'She's not near as flippy as my mother was.'

'That's a great recommendation,' Iz began. He was going to go on, but luckily for his marriage an employee of the automatic car-wash opened the door of the T-Bird and began to vacuum the interior around them. 'You want to get out?' Glory shook her head. 'Okay.' Iz shrugged. The man finished, wound up the windows, shut the door, and motioned for Glory to drive forward.

At the entrance, another employee hooked the car on to the rotary chain that would pull it through the building. Glory shifted into neutral and sat back. Up till now she had been unnoticed, but the man with the vacuum tank had recognized her and was alerting the others. The word passed round quickly, so that when her car was jerked forward into the tunnel it was met by eight or ten men of varying ages and races, all damp with soap and steam, and many stripped to the waist because of the heat. They stared avidly at Glory in her stage make-up and tight, low-cut dance costume. Undisconcerted, she sat coolly back in the far corner of the seat away from Iz, who self-consciously stroked his beard and frowned.

The car lurched forward again, tripping the switch of the first rinse. A torrent of water poured down over them, streaking the glass and blurring the faces and bodies outside. Within the car the light of a wet dusk softened Glory's face. Iz reached over and stroked the line of her neck, and then down towards her breast. Glory stiffened. The bastard, he thinks he can just walk right back in without saying a goddamn word, she thought. She tried to give Iz a cold stare, but lisped with emotion as she said:

'Tho what's that for?'

The automobile jerked forward again, out of the water, and two men, one on each side, began to wipe it with soapy rags. They swept the pink metal in wide, mockingly sensual gestures, grinning at Glory through the dripping windows, as if it were her own body. As before, she paid absolutely no attention, as unconscious of her audience as an actress on a movie screen; Iz frowned nervously.

'Because I wanted to,' he said. 'You're very attractive, even with all that greasy stuff on your face. I want to touch you. I want to sleep with you.'

It was a tactical error. The tremor went out of Glory's voice. 'I'm a very beautiful girl,' she said flatly. 'Lots of men want to sleep with me.' She turned and gazed out of the window through whorls of soap.

'Aw, babydoll!' the man on that side called to her. 'Don't give me that dirty look.' There was a burst of appreciation around him, followed by more shouted remarks.

Another jerk. The car moved forward under the second rinse, which fell with a blinding crash, drowning the faces and voices outside.

'Listen, pie-face,' Iz began again, putting his hand on hers where it lay on the shiny upholstery. 'It's not only your physical attractiveness.' No response. Her hand lay limp under his. 'I miss the whole relationship. I really like you. And you like me.'

No response. Her head was still twisted away; floods of water passed behind it. 'Ah, shit,' Iz said. 'I love you.'

Glory turned and looked at him. Under the sugar-candy hair her face was in ruins, the perfect mask streaked and wet with clotted powder, dripping mascara, and tears.

'Oh, go fuck yourthelf,' she said, and burst into sobs.

'So it's all set up,' Maxie told Iz and Glory. They were standing together in the rehearsal hall after the lunch break, waiting for the show to get going again. 'Judd says the kid can come over Tuesday p.m. about four-thirty: he'll wait for her. Her mother can bring her over; she should just go to the main gate and ask for Judd Hubert, tell her that's the cameraman, and he'll fix it up. You want I should call the mother, I got her number.'

'No, I'll do that. I told her I would.' Iz took out a notebook and pen.

'Aw, Maxie, that's great,' Glory said. 'That's real quick work.'

'I shoulda had a glass milk,' Maxie complained. 'I didn't eat since breakfast; now my stomach is acting up again.'

'Send out for it.'

'Yeah.' Maxie sighed deeply, and looked round. At the piano a well-known popular composer and the dance director were quarrelling over the second chorus of a song; the effeminate voice of the latter rising at intervals into a petulant shriek. Two beautiful girls were leaning against the stage nearby drinking soda out of cans and complaining in persistently whiny voices about their costumes; and a famous comic sat facing the wall, reading *Billboard*, sulking, and picking his nose. The floor of the rehearsal hall was gradually becoming covered with cigarette butts, coffee-cups, newspapers, candy wrappers, and chewed chewing-gum.

'Will somebody please tell me why I ever went into this business,' Maxie asked. 'Why I didn't just stay with my father. He had a fine movie house in Westchester, a good business. He wanted me to walk into his shoes, but I turned it down and broke his heart. How do you explain that?'

It was a rhetorical question, addressed to the ceiling, but Iz answered it.

'Possibly you wanted to defy him: it's natural.' He shrugged. 'Also you were probably attracted by the glamour of the entertainment world that, as a child, you saw second-hand. You wanted to meet stars, get to know them personally.'

'Yeah,' Maxie groaned. 'Do I know them personally.'

Iz put his notebook and pen up. 'Well, I've got a two o'clock kleptomania,' he said, 'I've got to go. You'll be home about seven?' Glory nodded. 'Okay. I'll call you.'

Alone with Maxie, Glory noticed his fat, sour face. 'Aw, Maxie honey,' she said. 'Don't look so down. It's going to swing all right.

[263

Everything's okay now.' She gave him a warm, natural smile, one of those that had made her famous, full of sensual love for the whole world.

Years of intimacy with actors and actresses had made Maxie impervious to every sort of smile. 'You think everything is okay, baby, you've got a limited view of my situation,' he complained. 'If I live through this I've also got to get Paul Demeray out of his recording contract; on top of that his wife is expecting again in the middle of her picture, Smith doesn't want to work with Foss this year, and a million more.'

'Phoebe Demeray's having another kid? I didn't hear that yet. That's marvy.' Glory smiled. 'I wish I was having one.'

'She's not telling it around yet, keep it——' Maxie broke off, looking at Glory. 'Aw, no you don't, honey.' Glory said nothing. A dreamy expression had appeared on her face. 'Don't be a kook. Think of your career: you know you got two big pictures lined up ahead of you. You don't want to get yourself knocked up now.'

'Uh-uh.' Over the heads of everyone in the hall, Glory stared into the bright, smoggy distance out the window. 'I think I'd really like to be knocked up.'

Part V:
INTERNATIONAL AIRPORT

FOREVERNESS.

—Billboard poster for Forest Lawn

23

High in the air, the jet hummed across the country, carrying Paul back towards California. Mountains and rivers and western cities rolled beneath it, dimmed to a uniform bluish-tan blur, though when he had left New England everything had glowed with the intense live green of early summer.

The greenness of New England! He couldn't get over it. The hills and meadows of new grass near Convers College, with mist white on them in the evening and dew shining in the morning. The air was clear, its distances softened by a blue haze of moisture, instead of the dirty yellowish mixture of gasoline fumes, soot particles, and irritants he had been used to. The rain falling seemed miraculous too; he exclaimed over it naïvely to his friends, explaining that in Los Angeles it had not rained for a year and a half.

Paul's friend had smiled when he told them this, thinking he exaggerated. They were glad to see him, though: they greeted him almost as if he had come back from the dead. The truth is that when you go West you do vanish as far as most Easterners are concerned; he could remember feeling this about others. It was worse than death really—there wasn't even any mourning.

Paul was also delighted to see his friends. He had forgotten how many people he knew in Cambridge, most of whom also knew each other. That was another thing about the East: the interlocking nature of society there, wrapped about itself like a grapevine. Whereas life in Los Angeles had the infinitely branching pattern of exploding fireworks—lines moving on a dark field, which never crossed, or crossed only by accident. In the East you had to go three thousand miles to disappear, but in L.A. you could do it by changing jobs and moving a few blocks. The way people treated each other there seemed to imply this: there was something anonymous, after all, about it.

Seeing the people he knew in Cambridge again, Paul realized that most of his relationships in Los Angeles, for instance with Fred Skinner, were comparatively shallow, acquaintances of convenience. These were his real friends: they spoke his language, shared his past; they wished him well. He remembered how Skinner had reacted when he heard that Paul was going East for the interview. 'Letting the side down, huh?' he had said, his mock anger covering real anger. 'Selling yourself back to those academic bastards for pennies.' On the other hand, Howard Leon, the head of the Publications Department, had surprised Paul by congratulating him. 'I've always felt this wasn't the place for you,' he had remarked. 'After all, this isn't a serious operation from an historian's point of view.'

'An historian's point of view.' Recollected on his way East, the words had made Paul uneasy. He wondered whether, after so many months in Los Angeles, he were still an historian. He thought of the heaps of index cards spread out on the desk in Mar Vista, with dust particles collecting on them. In imagination he saw the smog gathering inside his mind, too, month after month, until——

But thank God, that had turned out to be an illusion. Even the first evening, sitting in a friend's apartment in Cambridge, he could feel the internal smog lifting, and something like an historical sense waking; he heard himself beginning to think again in terms of political, cultural, economic movements and meanings. The next day in Convers, as he talked to the history staff about his thesis, their interest lit his, which had perhaps only been covered with ashes and not put out. He remembered, as it were, that he had (from an historian's point of view) an exciting subject. He began to borrow books and write down titles of articles.

Another surprise was that, in talking to his friends and answering their questions about Los Angeles, he had begun to see it as an historian. Theories and connections that he had never worked out consciously flared up as he spoke. The basic thing about L.A., he explained, was that it lacked the dimension of time. As Katherine had first pointed out to him, there were no seasons there, no days of the week, no night and day; beyond that, there was (or was supposed to be) no youth and age. But worst, and most frightening, there was no past or future—only an eternal dizzying present. In effect, the city had banished historians as Plato had poets from his Republic. The Nutting Research and

Development Corporation cared nothing for history, he said, and even feared their own. They had hired Paul to work in their office because they wished *to have him working in their office*, in the present tense, and to demonstrate him to visitors.

Paul's friends smiled and laughed as he talked, astonished that such things should be. 'Barbaric!' they exclaimed, and looked upon him with mild awe, as upon an anthropologist returned from a year with some native culture. They did not, of course, see the dark side of it: they didn't know what it was like for someone to be born and brought up in a world where history does not exist. Ceci O'Connor, for instance. For Ceci (as for Nutting) life was not the sum of all she had ever been, seen, and done—but a small area illuminated in a vast landscape of dimness, as if by the moving beam of a flashlight in a darkened room.

That was why morality in the dimension of time meant so little to her, and morality in other dimensions so much. A black feeling came over Paul as, rushing through the stratosphere towards Los Angeles, he thought of Ceci. On her own terms he had treated her badly and selfishly; which was no excuse, because not to treat someone on their own terms was in itself selfish. In Ceci's book he was, in fact, a cheap shit.

But he wasn't really like that, Paul pleaded to the slowly-darkening upper air outside the window. They were crossing the San Bernardino mountains now, bare rocks, glowing red in the setting sun, looking like the mountains of hell. At least, he hadn't used to be like that. For the girls he knew in the East he was 'honest', 'serious', 'so great', and they had told him so, several within the last few days. Embracing him with whirlwind warmth, or pressing his hand in quiet significance, according to their natures, they exclaimed how much they had missed him, how glad they were he was coming back—suggesting long, long talks, perhaps more, to come. He had managed to have lunch with one of them, a girl named Amy, and after she had brought him up to date on the intimate side of her life ('Oh, Paul, you always understand everything so well, you make me feel much better') he had tried to tell her about Ceci. 'I had a love affair in Los Angeles with a waitress,' he began badly. 'Really?' Amy smiled, and he heard a fake pastoral note in his voice, as if he were some eighteenth-century European bourgeois confessing his amours with a charming dairy-maid. He tried again. 'She wasn't a waitress really: she was a painter. She just worked as a waitress. She was a sort of beatnik actually.' Amy was still smiling fondly at the traveller's tale. It was at this point, he thought, that he had begun to see how he had behaved to Ceci. 'The thing was,' he said loudly, 'I really loved her. I was in love with her.' This was more than he had ever told Amy, but she took no notice. 'Oh, Paul,' she said, laying her hand on his arm. 'It's so wonderful to see you again. Nobody else I know has the same kind of—I don't know—enthusiasm that you have. They don't really *live*, none of them.'

Paul saw that it was no use. To the next old friend who asked what he had been doing with himself in southern California (this one a man) he replied, as if making a joke, that he had 'got somewhat involved' with a pink-haired movie starlet and the wife of a Chinese exterminator.

He hadn't been so great with Glory either, Paul thought. From her point of view they had been friendly conspirators, taking a well-deserved and enjoyable revenge together. If she had known her suspicions were false, she probably wouldn't have gone to bed with him. Whereas for him the incident had been a matter of opportunism. He had no right really to complain that the relationship was shallow, because he had made it so himself out of incuriosity and greed. The truth was that, having come to Los Angeles in the spirit of an explorer, he had lost track of his own standards and finally almost gone native; doing so, like most anthropologists, with a conspicuous lack of decency and grace.

There was one more thing, worst of all: the way he had treated Katherine. He had insisted that they come to Los Angeles—well, that was all right: even now he didn't regret going there, and once he got safe back he would probably come to appreciate what he had learned there more and more. He didn't think he should have left Katherine alone in Cambridge, but once he had got her out there he should have been much more patient with her fears, her loneliness, even with her sinus trouble, he should have tried harder to make her life tolerable. (For instance, he should have tried to find some friends for them that she could have talked to, other transplanted New Englanders. There were people like that around, but he had avoided them deliberately, just as he avoided Americans abroad.)

Never mind; he would make it up to her. He was taking her back now, and she would never have to see southern California again. How happy she would be in Convers! The picturesque old houses, the green forests and fields that he had promised to Glory, who had no use for them, were all there for Katherine. The faculty apartment he had been shown backed on to a wide mowed lawn ending in open woods; he saw Katherine running across the grass towards him there, smiling, her arms full of leaves and wild flowers.

It was Katherine that he really loved, Paul thought, and he felt in his wallet again for her picture, which he had, so to speak, rediscovered within the last few days. Hers was a real, a classic beauty, subtle, fine, and private—not blatant and public like the Hollywood sort. Glory, for instance, was most beautiful at a distance. When you got really close to her you could see that her bright hair was coarse and dyed; she had freckled, flawed skin. Katherine, on the other hand, was invisible at fifteen feet; but her skin and hair were fair and fine, and every detail delicately perfect.

It was almost dark out now. The whining of the jet's engines had changed key; they were over Los Angeles. Paul looked down at the city, a black plain streaked with smoke and coloured lights. He felt a faint anxiety at having left Katherine alone in such a place, even for a few days; he was glad to be getting back to her.

Paul had not asked his wife to meet him at the airport. It was a long way, and the telling of his news and her reaction to it would be more delightful staged in their own living-room. Too impatient after the delays of landing to wait for the bus, he got into a taxi, gave his address, and settled back to pleasant anticipation.

'Here y'are.' The taxi had stopped on the wrong street, next to a great ugly hill of bare earth. Then Paul looked out the other window, and saw his house. He got out of the cab, realizing what had happened. When he left Mar Vista four days ago, the bulldozers had been at work levelling the lots across the street, while trucks brought in fill dirt. This process had simply continued; the ground was being raised so that the new freeway, like all the others, would cross Los Angeles above the house-tops.

Still, there was something horrible about that long heap of dirt lying there in the street light with machines squatting on it. Even though he knew that the people and even the houses had been moved away, he had the fantasy that everything that had once been across the street was there still, buried beneath the dirt: the flowering bushes, the stucco walls and tiled roofs, the kitchen tables, the lemon trees, the children on their tricycles.

The lights were on in his house, and his car was in the driveway; the same old Ford that he had brought out from Boston. After all, he had never got round to trading it in for a Buick, a hot rod, a Jaguar, or a Thunderbird. But Katherine was out; she had left him a note on the mantelpiece:

> Welcome home—I've gone to Iz
> and Glory Einsam's reunion party—
> meet me there.

Irritated by the delay of the scene he had planned, and the change in the set against which it would have to be played, Paul washed perfunctorily, changed his shirt, found his car keys, and set out for Hollywood.

It was only about nine o'clock Los Angeles time, but in Cambridge it was midnight. No wonder he felt unsettled in his stomach and a little tired. As he drove along the freeway, though, Paul smiled and began to feel better. He was amused and pleased, he found, that Glory was reconciled with her husband; he was glad that she should be happy, and it relieved him of any obligation. Moreover, it was a final proof that there was nothing to Glory's suspicions, for if Katherine really had been involved with Dr Einsam she would certainly not be going to this party. Not that he had ever thought she was, of course.

Paul located Glory's house easily by the number of cars parked along the street and the noise and music coming over the fence. It was a very large party, he saw, as the maid showed him in (after checking his name against a list). The long pink living-room was full of people, mostly movie types, and they were standing in the hall and crowded around the bar in the dining-room. Opposite him, doors stood open on to a terrace, and he could see more people out there.

None of them was Katherine. After he had looked into all the rooms at least twice, and walked round the pool, he had to admit, with considerable irritation, that he couldn't find her. Nor, for that matter, could he find Glory or Glory's husband. He knew absolutely no one here; it was as if he had got into the wrong house.

Probably what had happened, he concluded, was that Katherine hadn't arrived yet, but (having thoughtfully left the car for him) was still on her way to Glory's by some slower means of transport. He must simply wait for her. Holding a drink, he wandered out towards the pool. It must have been fixed recently, for it was full, spotlighted both above and below the water, and slowly filling with the debris of the party. Paper napkins, cigarette butts, and a few potato chips floated· on the surface; their shadows skimmed over the white tiles below like pale fish.

Without making much effort, Paul fell into several curiously meaningless conversations. At one point, for example, he found himself talking to Glory's press agent about airplane fares, at another to an odd pair of women: a pretty plump little Japanese in a cotton shirtwaist named Mrs Haraki, and a handsome bony American named Mrs Smith who wore a silk kimono and had chopsticks skewered through her hair. They were trying to identify the movie stars present, most of whom Paul had never heard of.

It was now after ten o'clock; Katherine should have come. Unless, of course, she had already left, feeling too nervous and shy to bear a party like this any longer alone. But in that case, surely she would have left a message?

Paul went back into the house, where he got another drink and spoke to a couple named Dodge who said they were college teachers, though Paul had taken them both for actors. He asked Mr and Mrs Dodge if they had seen his wife.

'Your wife? Have you lost your wife?' Mr Dodge held out his glass to the bar for more whisky.

'No,' Paul explained. 'I was supposed to meet her here, and now I can't find her.'

'Gee, that's too bad,' Mrs Dodge said, eating salted nuts. 'I don't know, maybe we saw her. What does she look like?'

'Well, she has long kind of light brown hair, done in a knot at the back. She's very pretty. Beautiful, but not, you know, striking. Quite pale. She's rather shy.'

'No,' said Mrs Dodge, shaking her head. 'I'm sorry.'

'No,' said Mr Dodge. 'Marge and I haven't seen anyone like that. But there's lots of pretty girls here,' he added helpfully.

What was he supposed to do now, Paul wondered. It was getting on for eleven, two a.m. by Boston time. Maybe he should go home, or at least call.

The party was growing louder and louder. He drifted into the hall, looking for a telephone, where a dark, striking girl came up to him. 'Hey, I know you,' she said woozily. 'You're the college-boy type was talking to Glory at the rehearsal last week.' She told him, giggling, that Glory and Iz Einsam were celebrating their party in bed. 'Come on in an' say hello to them,' she urged Paul, pulling his arm. "They won't mind. Ev'body's going in. Wait, first we gotta get you 'nother drink. . . . There. C'mon now.'

Against his better judgement, Paul allowed himself to be pulled down the hall and into a huge white room. There were two walls of mirrors, a lot of tropical plants, and a large white bed covered with fur and pillows. The man he had recognized before as Dr Einsam was lying in bed, smoking.

'Brought you 'nother friend,' said the dark girl. 'This is whatsis-name.'

'Paul Cattleman.'

'Well! How do you do.' Iz sat up, naked at least to the waist, and held out his hand. He gave Paul a penetrating look, but not a hostile one; so Glory hasn't told him anything, thank Christ, Paul thought. He crossed the room and shook hands. 'We're going to get up pretty soon,' Iz said. 'You're having a good time?'

'Yes, thanks.' Embarrassed to be shaking hands with the man he had so recently cuckolded, Paul turned to go, and then turned back halfway across the room. 'Only I want to ask you something. What's happened to my wife?'

'Ya.' Iz paused, and narrowed his eyes. 'Let's talk about it later,' he said finally. 'I would like to answer you, but I don't think this is the time and place for a metaphysical discussion.'

Paul stared, then laughed nervously. 'I didn't mean it that way,' he said. 'I mean I don't know where my wife *is*. She left me a note to come here and meet her, but now I can't find her.'

[273

'Ah. I see. Well, I know she was here earlier. I'll ask Glory. Hey, baby.' Instead of raising his voice, Iz lowered it, and laid his hand on the pillow beside him. 'Do you know where Katherine went?'

'Huh?' From under the sheet, Glory lifted a tumble of pink curls, a blurred face. 'Uh-uh. Somewhere round.' Her head fell again.

'Aw, I know where *Kay* is,' the girl who had brought him in said suddenly. 'You wanna find Kay? She's in the living-room. C'mon.'

Closing the bedroom door behind him, Paul followed her into the hall. 'Hey, you're Kay's *husband*,' she said. 'I wasn't so loaded I woulda caught on sooner. I'm Ramona Moon, pleased to meet-cha.'

'How do you do.' Paul and Mona shook hands. He realized that he had finished his third drink. Probably that was why everything seemed so odd.

'C'mon. . . . This way. See, there she is, over by the piano.'

Mona pointed across the living-room to where a girl sat on the piano bench, talking to two men: a pretty girl in tight yellow pants, with a smooth California tan and ash-blonde hair piled up on to her head like a mound of whipped cream; an obvious Los Angeles type; he remembered vaguely seeing her over there earlier in the evening.

'Oh, that's not her,' Paul started to say, when the girl, laughing at some joke that had been made, turned her face full in his direction. He realized that it was Katherine.

He should have known then, of course. But the untangling of any long-standing illusion is a difficult matter, and over three weeks of miserable scenes, baffling explanations, and inconclusive arguments had intervened between Glory's party and the smoggy morning when Paul climbed into the plane for Boston again.

Of it all he remembered now only a few things: for instance, the moment when Katherine, sorting clothes for the cleaners, had finally said that she didn't *want* to go back to New England. Once the words were out, she repeated them many times, each time more clearly. Even her voice had changed: it was louder, with almost a California twang — not Katherine's voice at all. Some-how his wife had disappeared; still, if he could only get her away from Los Angeles, if she would only come back East with him, he was sure, he said, that she would turn into herself again. 'Yes, I know,' Katherine replied. 'That's what I'm afraid of. . . .'

Eating, dressing, undressing, carrying the groceries in and the cans and trash out, through all the small routines of domesticity, their argument discontinuously continued. 'But you know you can't stay here,' Paul remembered saying as he wiped a plate with a damp towel (not since the first months of marriage had they washed up so conjugally). 'Why, the house is going to come down in a couple of months. You won't have anywhere to live.' Katherine, her hands moving beneath the suds, sourly smiled. 'You think I can't even find an apartment by myself,' she stated. 'No,' Paul replied, inaccurately. 'I didn't mean that. But for instance, suppose you did get an apartment; what'd you do with all your parents' furniture, out in the garage?' Briefly, Katherine's face altered: a shadow of her old, pale, complex inward look crossed it. Her wrists were still under the trickle of rinse water. 'After all,' (Paul pushed his advantage), 'those are pretty valuable antiques. You can't just leave them in a garage.' 'Well, if you feel that way,' Katherine said slowly. Sweeping her arm across the sink, she pulled out of the soapy water a handful of knives, forks, and spoons; she splashed them under the faucet and set them bristling on end in the rack. 'If you want them, I could ship them back East to you,' she offered. And he—who of course had nothing to put in the new apartment at Convers, and hoped that Katherine's ancestral furniture would, eventually, draw her back across the country—agreed.

At night, in bed, they had long, vaguely intense conversations —lying far apart, in pyjamas; Paul knew Katherine better than to try and change her mind by appealing to her body—he appealed instead to her emotions. At times, he thought, with some success; at others not. Once, across the chilly landscape of sheet, he asked what she thought would *become* of her, if she stayed in Los Angeles. Instead of answering, Katherine said to him calmly, pushing back her ash-blonde hair (it wasn't dyed, she had insisted, only bleached by the sun), 'You know what's the matter with you, Paul. You're always thinking of what happened before now or what might possibly happen some time later. You're squeezed up between the past and the future; you're not living.'

[275

Finally there was the time, perhaps worst of all, and late at night, when he had come out of the bathroom in a towel and exclaimed to Katherine, 'I suppose what this all means is that you hate me; you can't forgive me. Well,' he added bitterly, thinking of Ceci, of Glory, of all the others whose existence, it had turned out, she had suspected all along, so that finally she had—but he didn't want to think of that— 'Well, I guess maybe you have a good reason.'

'No,' Katherine, or Kay, had said, sitting up in bed, brown now against the sheets except for the pattern of a bathing-suit burnt on to her body in negative. 'I don't hate you. It's funny, but you just don't seem real to me any more, somehow. I just *don't care.*'

The airplane taxied down the field to the end of the runway, wheeled round, and hesitated a moment, its engines blasting harder. Then it started forward, lifting heavily into the air. Out of the cabin window Paul saw Los Angeles tilt and sink away from him. As the plane made a circle he saw, in rapid panorama, the bleached green of the Pacific Ocean wrinkled with white waves against the beach; billboards, factories, and palms; block after block of houses; cars speeding like insects along the glittering freeways; the towers of oil wells on the barren hills.

Straightening out of its turn, the jet began to climb. The outlines of the sun grew harder and brighter as they ascended, the sky more brilliant and blue. Looking down, though, Paul saw that the light, bright colours of the city had begun to blur. Layers of yellowish-grey haze thickened under them. Soon he could hardly make out the shapes of buildings and roads.

The plane rose higher into the clear, hard air. Now everything below, between the mountains and the sea, was gone. Los Angeles had disappeared into a bowl of smog.

Alison Lurie

IMAGINARY FRIENDS

'Dazzling...a comedy of ideas that stands
near the top of its class'
Life

Roger and his all-time hero, Tom McMann, are about to
infiltrate the Truth Seekers – a unique small-town cult
whose credo involves sex, spiritualism and science fiction.
Their flying saucer messiah is Ro, resident of the distant
planet Varna, who sends his daily cosmic messages through
Verena, a nubile teenage psychic who lives with her Aunt
Elsie in upstate New York.

For Roger and McMann the experience is all a bit much.
Held spellbound by Verena's considerable charms and Ro's
imminent trip to Earth, all sense of logic falls apart; and
before they know it, the sanity of rational thought is enough
to drive both of them out of their minds.

'Alison Lurie's most accomplished comedy...a beautiful,
expanding metaphor for the innumerable complexities of
human relationships'
Times Literary Supplement

'Barbed and richly entertaining'
Wall Street Journal

V

VINTAGE

Alison Lurie

ONLY CHILDREN

'A writer of extraordinary talent and promise'
Christopher Isherwood

Two married couples and their children go on a long hot summer weekend to a country house owned by Anna who runs a small progressive school. But – as Mary Ann, aged eight, says – 'Anna likes kids' parties better than grownup parties, because she likes kids better than grownups.' And somehow it not long before these grownups seem to be getting younger and younger; at first hesitantly, then with enthusiasm abandoning the conventions of adult behaviour; sliding ever deeper into a world of childish stories and games and secrets, of sudden passions and violent quarrels. Mary Ann and her best friend Lolly watch this change and are at first excited and pleased, then puzzled and finally frightened and angry. By the time the house-party is over, even Anna finds it hard to return to the adult world. As for the real children, they have become – each in her own way – suddenly rather older.

'A very distinct advance in the work of
an important novelist'
Financial Times

V

VINTAGE

A SELECTED LIST OF CONTEMPORARY FICTION
AVAILABLE IN VINTAGE

☐ BIRDSONG	Sebastian Faulks	£6.99
☐ CHARLOTTE GRAY	Sebastian Faulks	£6.99
☐ MEMOIRS OF A GEISHA	Arthur Golden	£6.99
☐ HERE ON EARTH	Alice Hoffman	£6.99
☐ IMAGINARY FRIENDS	Alison Lurie	£6.99
☐ THE LAST RESORT	Alison Lurie	£6.99
☐ ONLY CHILDREN	Alison Lurie	£6.99
☐ WOMEN AND GHOSTS	Alison Lurie	£6.99
☐ FALL ON YOUR KNEES	Ann-Marie MacDonald	£6.99
☐ PARADISE	Toni Morrison	£6.99
☐ BELOVED	Toni Morrison	£6.99
☐ THE PATCHWORK PLANET	Anne Tyler	£6.99
☐ LADDER OF YEARS	Anne Tyler	£5.99

- All Vintage books are available through mail order or from your local bookshop.

- Please send cheque/eurocheque/postal order (sterling only), Access, Visa, Mastercard, Diners Card, Switch or Amex:

☐☐☐☐☐☐☐☐☐☐☐☐☐☐☐☐

Expiry Date:_____Signature:_____

Please allow 75 pence per book for post and packing U.K.
Overseas customers please allow £1.00 per copy for post and packing.

ALL ORDERS TO:

Vintage Books, Books by Post, TBS Limited, The Book Service,
Colchester Road, Frating Green, Colchester, Essex CO7 7DW

NAME:_____

ADDRESS:_____

_____

_____

Please allow 28 days for delivery. Please tick box if you do not
wish to receive any additional information   ☐

Prices and availability subject to change without notice.